the uniq

"A GRAND MELODRAMA OF EARLY
AMERICA."
—*The Denver Post*

"Fans of historical mysteries should relish this."
—*The Sun*, Baltimore

"IMPRESSIVE AND DELIGHTFUL reading."
—*San Diego Magazine*

"The story is strong, the milieu is exciting. . . . We
highly recommend."
—*Book Page*

"AT ONCE CENTURIES REMOVED AND
IMMEDIATELY FAMILIAR."
—*Publishers Weekly*

"A MUST READ FOR EVERY HISTORY BUFF IN
AMERICA."
—*Deadly Pleasures*

The
High Constable

An Historical Mystery

Maan Meyers

BANTAM BOOKS

New York London Toronto Sydney Auckland

This edition contains the complete text
of the original hardcover edition.
NOT ONE WORD HAS BEEN OMITTED.

THE HIGH CONSTABLE

A Bantam Book / published by arrangement with Doubleday

PUBLISHING HISTORY
Doubleday hardcover edition September 1994
Bantam paperback edition / June 1995

ISBN 0-553-56889-2

Published simultaneously in the United States and Canada

Bantam Books are published by Bantam Books, a division of Bantam Doubleday
Dell Publishing Group, Inc. Its trademark, consisting of the words "Bantam
Books" and the portrayal of a rooster, is Registered in U.S. Patent and
Trademark Office and in other countries. Marca Registrada. Bantam Books,
1540 Broadway, New York, New York 10036.

PRINTED IN THE UNITED STATES OF AMERICA

OPM 0 9 8 7 6 5 4 3 2 1

For Rita and Lenny,
more than family.

Thanks to Linda Ray, Ann Bushnell, Chris Tomasino, Dr. William Gottfried, Dr. Ira Golditch, Dr. Ludwig Leibsohn, and the library staff at the New-York Historical Society.

Special thanks to our editor, Kate Burke Miciak, whose huzzahs we cherish.

NORTH OR HUDSON RIVER

THIRD WARD

FIRST WARD

St. Paul's Chapel

Park Theatre

Abigail Willard's House

Old City Hall

Goldsmith's House

Bowling Green

The Battery

BROADWAY

WHITE HALL

WALL ST.

MAIDEN LANE

PEARL ST.

WATER ST.

FRONT ST.

Jews' Synagogue

The Tontine Coffee-House

Fly Market

Rutgers Hill (Tonneman Home)

FIRST WARD

SECOND WARD

FOURTH WARD

North

EAST RIVER

FIFTH WARD

Simone
Aubergine's
House

New
City Hall

City Alms
House

Jacob Hays's
Home

Road to the
Village of Greenwich

Richmond Hill
(Maurice Jamison's
Home)

New Scots
Presbyterian
Church

GREENWICH ST.

CHAPEL ST.

CHURCH ST.

BURR ST.

EIGHTH WARD

BROADWAY

The
Collect

The Bull Ring
at Bunker Hill

CHATHAM ST.

SIXTH WARD

Butcher
Ned's
Tavern

GRAND ST.

Lipenard
Meadows

To Friends Cemetery and
David Hosack's Elgin Gardens

SEVENTH
WARD

Jewish
Cemetery

PLAN of the
CITY of NEW YORK
1808

THE TONNEMAN FAMILY

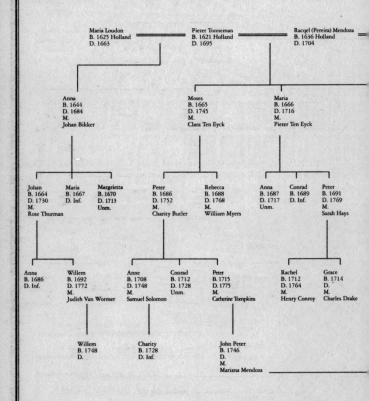

Maria Loudon
B. 1625 Holland
D. 1663

Pieter Tonneman
B. 1621 Holland
D. 1695

Racqel (Pereira) Mendoza
B. 1636 Holland
D. 1704

Anna
B. 1644
D. 1684
M.
Johan Bikker

Moses
B. 1665
D. 1745
M.
Clara Ten Eyck

Maria
B. 1666
D. 1716
M.
Pieter Ten Eyck

Johan
B. 1664
D. 1730
M.
Rose Thurman

Maria
B. 1667
D. Inf.

Margrietta
B. 1670
D. 1713
Unm.

Peter
B. 1686
D. 1752
M.
Charity Butler

Rebecca
B. 1688
D. 1768
M.
William Myers

Anna
B. 1687
D. 1717
Unm.

Conrad
B. 1689
D. Inf.

Peter
B. 1691
D. 1769
M.
Sarah Hays

Anna
B. 1686
D. Inf.

Willem
B. 1692
D. 1772
M.
Judith Van Wormer

Anne
B. 1708
D. 1748
M.
Samuel Solomon

Conrad
B. 1712
D. 1728
Unm.

Peter
B. 1715
D. 1775
M.
Catherine Tompkins

Rachel
B. 1712
D. 1764
M.
Henry Conroy

Grace
B. 1714
D.
M.
Charles Drake

Willem
B. 1748
D.

Charity
B. 1728
D. Inf.

John Peter
B. 1746
D.
M.
Mariana Mendoza

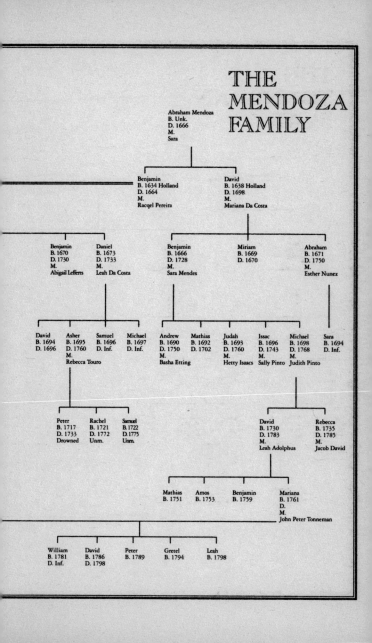

THE
MENDOZA
FAMILY

Abraham Mendoza
B. Unk.
D. 1666
M.
Sara

Benjamin
B. 1634 Holland
D. 1664
M.
Racqel Pereira

David
B. 1638 Holland
D. 1698.
M.
Mariana Da Costa

Benjamin
B. 1670
D. 1730
M.
Abigail Lefferts

Daniel
B. 1673
D. 1733
M.
Leah Da Costa

Benjamin
B. 1666
D. 1728
M.
Sara Mendes

Miriam
B. 1669
D. 1670

Abraham
B. 1671
D. 1750
M.
Esther Nunez

David
B. 1694
D. 1696

Asher
B. 1695
D. 1760
M.
Rebecca Touro

Samuel
B. 1696
D. Inf.

Michael
B. 1697
D. Inf.

Andrew
B. 1690
D. 1750
M.
Basha Etting

Mathias
B. 1692
D. 1702

Judah
B. 1693
D. 1760
M.
Hetty Isaacs

Issac
B. 1696
D. 1743
M.
Sally Pinto

Michael
B. 1698
D. 1768
M.
Judith Pinto

Sara
B. 1694
D. Inf.

Peter
B. 1717
D. 1733
Drowned

Rachel
B. 1721
D. 1772
Unm.

Samuel
B. 1722
D.1775
Unm.

David
B. 1730
D. 1783
M.
Leah Adolphus

Rebecca
B. 1735
D. 1785
M.
Jacob David

Mathias
B. 1751

Amos
B. 1753

Benjamin
B. 1759

Mariana
B. 1761
D.
M.
John Peter Tonneman

William
B. 1781
D. Inf.

David
B. 1786
D. 1798

Peter
B. 1789

Gretel
B. 1794

Leah
B. 1798

Our situation is not only distressing, but truly alarming. The Embargo lately leveled upon our shipping has not only destroyed all employment by Sea, but rendered it impossible to gain a subsistence by our labor on shore. Our humble petition to you Sir, is to know how we are to act in this case, and to beg of you to provide some means for our subsistence during the winter, should not the Embargo be immediately taken off. What has America to boast of but her Agriculture and Commerce? The destruction of one, will be the ruin of the other.

The greatest part of the wages due us from our last voyages is already expended, and more, we are indebted for our boarding. By what means shall we discharge these debts? Should we plunder, thieve or rob, the State prison will be our certain doom.

In a handbill, this morning, You tried to dissuade us from our purpose, mentioning that provision was made for objects of pity. We are not objects of pity yet, but shall soon be, if there is not some method taken for our support. We are the most part hale, robust, hearty men, and would choose some kind of employment rather than the poor house for a livelihood. We humbly beg therefore, you will provide some means for our subsistence, or the consequences may not only prove fatal to ourselves, but ruinous to the flourishing Commerce of America, as we shall be necessitated to go on board foreign vessels.

PRESENTED TO THE MAYOR OF NEW-YORK BY SEAMEN ASSEMBLED IN THE (CITY HALL) PARK ON SATURDAY MORNING, 8 JANUARY, 1808.

Prologue

22 JANUARY. FRIDAY.

The falcon lit atop the broken ridge of mud and debris which encircled the pond, cocked her head, and watched the activity below. She was hungry; in her nest there were four mouths. Her sharp eyes never wavered from the little pig scampering around the feet of the car-men and laborers fifteen feet below, stopping only to nibble a morsel of root on the frozen ground. Above the falcon, slate gray clouds scudded across the sky before the force of the strong north wind.

All day the falcon, a dusky brown shadow, had stalked her prey, rising high, swooping down. The men had shouted at her, had thrown stones. This was *their* dinner; no scrannel bird would have it. They drove her from one part of the ridge only to have her fly in high circles, and return to another part of the ridge, once more digging her yellow claws into the hard earth. After a time they wearied of the effort of chasing her. The falcon had only to wait. She knew darkness would end their activity. Without their fire they couldn't see in the dark. The night belonged to her.

The falcon extended her wings and folded them back against her sides, ruffling the cream feathers at her throat. Patience was her strong suit. She shifted her weight, sending chunks of frosty earth downward.

Back and forth the laborers went, shoveling mud from

the freezing water, loading it on carts, carrying it away. The carts would return brimming with earth, which would be shoveled into what remained of the pond where the falcon had once dined so well.

The darkness fell. As the car-men began shouldering their shovels, the falcon on her promontory perch readied herself, gripping the uncertain mound with her talons, stretching her neck. Her bluish hook of a bill merged with the deepening blue of the sky. She spread her wings and rose. As she did, an eagle plummeted past her and scooped up the little pig in his sharp claws. The terrified creature squealed; outraged at this arrogant piracy, the angry falcon screamed a long, shrill cry.

The little pig's lifeblood rained down on the shouting men, staining and speckling, adding insult to injury, as they shook ineffectual fists at the sky.

The eagle would sup well tonight, but not the falcon. And not the men who worked on the Collect.

1

22 JANUARY. FRIDAY. LATE AFTERNOON.

He stamped the snow from his boots and sneaked into the kitchen, determined to avoid his father, for there was certain to be yet another row. He could hear his father's chiding voice: "The sun won't be down for another hour. Why have you abandoned your work in the middle of the

day? Why do you not take serious things seriously? What
kind of son are you?" The vein in his father's forehead
would pulse. "My father was a physician. I am a physician.
What sin have I committed that my son is not a physician?"

Then his mother would come to his defense and the
war would rage over and around him.

Micah, the hired girl, was bent over, sweeping up the
soot from the hearth, the bottom of her checked ging-
ham apron in her mouth so as not to get it dirty. She was
humming softly and hadn't heard him come in. He crept
up behind her, made a wind with his arms, and said,
"Hoooooh."

"Aaah." Micah collapsed in a heap. Her muslin cap slid
over one eye. When she saw him standing over her, laughing, she giggled. "You'll be the death of me, Peter Tonneman. And then won't your mama and papa be mad."

"I'm sorry, Micah." Peter, still laughing, helped the girl
up and handed her the straw broom which had fallen to the
floor. "I couldn't help myself."

Still giggling, Micah righted her cap and shook her
finger at him. "You better behave or I'll tell them when
they come home from services."

Oh, God, he had forgotten again. Something else to
anger his father. "Why didn't you go?" he asked the hired
girl.

"Because I'm the same sort of Jew you are, Peter. If I can
sweep the floor and serve the food on Friday, I don't attend
services."

He had meant to go this time. It was as if he was living
separate from everyone else. Why was he the only one who
didn't know his place in the world?

He left the kitchen, having forgotten Micah, thinking
only of how he was an outcast and a bitter disappointment
in the Tonneman family. If his brother David had lived
. . . things might have been different.

His foot was on the first riser when he heard the crash.

Then a muffled cry. Someone was in the surgery. He hurried through his father's study.

A tiny figure stood over the old black case of surgical tools, which had spilled its contents on the floor.

"What are you doing here, child?" Peter said in his best imitation of his father. He was good at this. Maybe he should be an actor? That would give them pause.

His sister, Leah, who turned a frightened face to him before dissolving into tears, was only ten. She was fascinated by the surgery. God moved in mysterious ways, their mother always said. How true.

"Lee." Peter knelt beside the child, speaking gently. He loved her best. They were a study in contrasts. Leah, dark-eyed, dark-haired like the Mendozas, Spanish Jews, and barely four feet, and he with the blond hair and deep blue eyes of their Dutch ancestors, and six feet tall.

"Peter." She sobbed into his green velvet coat. "I just wanted to touch them. Why can't I touch them?"

"It's all right with me, but you know Papa." He dried her tears with his linen handkerchief, then began picking up scalpels and other surgical instruments. "Why aren't you at services?"

"I had a bellyache. Papa gave me red raspberry tea. He said I could stay home."

"Was it an ache in your belly or an ache to fondle these things?"

"He would let *you* touch them." It was almost an accusation.

"I know. He would be happier if you were me."

As Leah watched, sniffling, he finished putting the instruments back in the bag, then lifted her to the counter. She wore a blue taffeta dress that had belonged to her older sister Gretel, when Gretel was her age. Peter straightened the rosette in her wide pink sash.

Leah threw her arms around him and hugged him. "You are the best brother a girl could have!"

• • •

BEST BROTHER, PERHAPS, Peter thought, after leaving Leah quite recovered in the kitchen with Micah, but best son, not at all.

His parents and his sister Gretel would soon be home from Sabbath services, and he did not want to be around to hear again how disappointed they were in him.

He went outside not knowing where he was going. Then it came to him. George might be at the White Horse Tavern, lifting a tankard or two.

Peter headed for the White Horse.

Humerous—*A wit observed a day or two since, that by
reading the word Embargo backwards, it would make
O-grab-me! It is thought that a great number will feel the
influence of its* Grab!!!

NEW-YORK HERALD
JANUARY 1808

2

22 JANUARY. FRIDAY. NIGHT.

Angry words penetrated the deep fog. Peter could barely
lift his throbbing head to hear from where the words came,
though, for all that, he knew full well who was talking.
Joseph Thaddeus—dubbed Tedious by Peter, who thought
himself clever for it—Brown, Commissioner of Streets, and
Controller of the Collect Company, had a booming voice.
The better to hear himself. Who in hell was Tedious yelling
at?

"I'll have none of it," Tedious Brown bellowed.

There was a murmured response, something about
choice and matter.

"No choice?" Brown shouted. "We'll see about—"

Peter covered his ears with his hands and rolled over,
sweeping papers, pens, and standish to the floor. Only then
did he realize that he was lying on his desk. An outside

door slammed but Tedious still raged. One could barely hear the hooves of passing horses over the furious stamping in the next room.

Peter opened his eyes a crack. Darkness. If his candle had burned to the end, he must have slept a long time. Where was it? He fumbled in the gloom. Perhaps he'd knocked it over. "Could have burned my silly arse," he muttered. Chuckling, he struggled into a sitting position, scattering more papers and the paraphernalia of his fiddle-faddle position as Tedious's secretary.

The room was spinning. The young man's gorge rose to his throat. He swallowed the offensive taste, groaned softly, and closed his eyes. Groping to steady himself, his hand found the brandy bottle. Ah, God was good. He brought it to his lips, tilting bottle and head, waiting for the divine liquid that would relieve his pounding pate. Blast, there was no sustenance in an empty bottle. He flung the bottle aside. It smashed on the floor.

Now he'd done it. Tedious would know he was here. And Peter would receive anew the ranting tirade about the perils of drink.

Barely a moment later, the door flew open. Tedious appeared, a grim Quaker skeleton in his dreary black cassimere coat, shapeless trousers, and that damnable wide-brimmed, low-crowned black hat, which he never took off. A lamp held before him, the Broadbrim bastard looked in the light like one of those Hebrew prophets from the Bible Peter's mother was always going on about. The youth squinted, putting up his hands to ward off the sharp glare.

Tedious plunged into the tirade with his usual vituperation. "I might have known, thou contemptible sot. I lament the day they foisted thee on me."

"O grab me," the boy mumbled. If the room would only stop its mad swirl. The sermon rolled on; the young man stopped listening. His foot touched shards of broken glass. Reaching down, he grasped the neck of the bottle.

"Consider yourself finished, boy," Tedious declaimed. "I'll explain to your father tomorrow."

Peter's blood boiled. "What happened to your *thee*'s and *thou*'s, you pompous little fraud? The world should know you're not as devout a Friend as you pretend."

Joseph Thaddeus Brown didn't reply. He stamped out of the room, taking his holy light with him.

Now the import of Tedious's words sank in; Peter felt the flood of humiliation as a sobering bath. Tedious was going to tell his father. The youth moved with a swiftness that surprised him. Leaving the disarray around him, he opened the door of the adjoining chamber where Brown kept his office. Tedious stood with his back turned, sorting material on his desk. A miserly fire flared on the hearth.

"Please, sir." When there was no answer, he raised his voice. "Please, sir."

Brown turned, sneering, a packet of paper money in his hand; Peter saw the Collect Company's strongbox was on the desk and opened. "Don't please, sir, me." He turned the contents of the box away from Peter's eyes. "Thou hast had every chance to make good here. Now I wash my hands of thee."

The young man was of a sudden so weary. His eyes stung. His shoulders felt weighted. What was the use? He made to leave.

"Not so fast, thou thieving cull. I want the money thou hast been filching," Tedious cried.

The youth turned back. He stood silent, swaying, too drunk, too stunned, to speak.

"There's nothing for it, then," Tedious roared. "Thy father will hear from me."

"No!" He was bewildered. He had taken nothing. Still, his situation was desperate. His father had threatened to cast him out for his drinking, for his sloth, to disown him. He was a great many willful things but he was not a thief. Yet once Tedious suggested as much to his father . . . "Listen, Thaddeus, old boy, I never stole a cent. . . . I swear."

"Oh, yes," came the thundering response. Tedious slammed the strongbox closed.

The young man staggered closer to his tormentor and shot out his arm, just grazing Tedious's jaw. His inebriated shout matched Brown's. "Hear me well, Broadbrim, *I've stolen nothing.*"

The angular little man stood his ground. He brayed, "Thou art a liar and a cheat. And a drunk—"

Rap-a-tap-tap. The sound came from the large shrouded window behind Brown's desk. Peter ignored it. With one hand he grabbed hold of Tedious Brown's collar, lifting him off his feet. In his other hand Peter still held the neckpiece of the broken bottle. Brown, squirming like an earthworm, clawed the air.

Reason mercifully invaded Peter's sodden brain. He set Tedious on his feet and cast the shard aside. Like a beaver's tail the force of Peter's open hand felled the sneering Quaker, knocking off his hat. Brown made nary a sound as blood gouted from his blade of a nose.

Horrified, Peter came around, seeking to aid the fallen man, but lost his balance. He crashed into Brown's desk, knocking it over, sending the strongbox and a flurry of papers to the floor. There'd be hell for it in the morning. The realization of what he'd done quickly sobered Peter. "My God, I've killed him." He collapsed across Brown's motionless body. "Forgive me, Tedious."

Brown groaned. Perhaps hearing his wretched sobriquet brought him back to life. "Fool." With great effort, the Quaker shoved the youth from him. He wiped his bleeding nose with his coat sleeve. "Leave me be and get out of here."

Unsteadily, the young man climbed to his feet, stumbling over Brown's wide shoes. He slipped on some papers and went crashing down again, this time taking a glazed blue jar with him, smashing it and the sweetmeats inside to sugary fragments. He heard a noise behind him. Turned. A flash of light pierced his eyes. His head thumped unremittingly. Covering his eyes with his arm, he staggered to his feet. The room tipped and tumbled.

"What goes here?"

The youth pushed at the light. It retreated, but only a bit. The Watch Man, a broad expanse of flesh sheathed in a large brown cloak, swept his light, surveying the disorder.

"Nothing," Peter responded in deceptively steadfast tones.

"A great deal." Brown pressed his handkerchief to his nose to stop the bloody flow.

"Here," offered Peter. "Let me. . . ."

The broken bottle, the strongbox, the scattered papers did not escape the Watch Man. "O grab me," he said. "How may I assist you, Commissioner Brown? William Tice, at your service."

"What?" Brown said, snatching the strongbox from the floor.

"Sir, how may I assist you?"

"I'll tell thee how," Brown shouted, the box jammed securely under his right arm. He dabbed his nose, rubbed his little mouse eyes, and, sitting, groped for his broad hat, setting it back on his head. "You can take this piece of cow dung—"

"O grab me, Tedious," Peter joked, hoping to lessen the little man's rage. "That's no way for a Friend to talk. And thou said 'you' instead of 'thee' again."

"The Lord forgive me. I want this little vermin locked up for a hundred years."

"If that's what you want, Mr. Brown," the Watch Man said, thinking only that these rich folks never knew when they had it good.

"No!" Pain surged in the young man's head. This would destroy his parents.

"Get out, thief!" With Tice's help, Brown got to his feet gingerly.

Peter's indignation was a match for Brown's. Were it a fight, man to man, he could deal with it, and prevail. But this? There was nothing he could do. "I am not a thief, sir. I have stolen naught from you nor anyone."

The Watch Man's mouth lolled open; his eyes and lantern light traveled back and forth between the two hostile men.

Brown laughed, his blood-streaked face contorted as much by his fury as by the lantern light. "And don't look to thy mother to save thee," he blustered. "Tomorrow the High Constable will be notified."

That did it. Smoothing back his flaxen hair, the drunken Peter Simon Tonneman straightened himself and said evenly, "Do that, Tedious, and I promise that you will not live to see tomorrow."

3

23 JANUARY. SATURDAY. EARLY MORNING.

Ludwig Meisel's fears had been justified. The storm came upon them quickly, buffeting the oval Concord coach-and-four and its passengers. The merciless wind sliced through Meisel's clothes and thin body like an icy knife.

The *coach-and-four* of the eighteenth-century British squire had become a public conveyance in America. With an added seat to permit nine passengers to squeeze into the wooden box, these coaches contained no springs because crude, rugged roads snapped the coils. They were light, making it easier for them to ford streams. In this country, bridges were as rare as roc's eggs.

"*Scheise——Ratte——fuck*," Meisel grumbled at the weary team of horses. He'd driven the four animals hard in an attempt to outrun the storm. First from Philadelphia the day before, then today from Princeton. Usually he was provided with fresh horses in Princeton, but there had been a problem with the second team, with one having gone lame.

Now Meisel was forced to go at a slower pace and work harder to keep the beasts on a road which was rapidly disappearing under wind-shifting snowdrifts. Behind him, clinging to the baggage rack for dear life, the boy Tom wrestled with the various straps, striving to keep the luggage from flying off into the snow. Coachman, apprentice, and portmanteaux were already coated in a layer of frosty white.

The sky had been ominous, a deep gray overcast when they'd left Princeton at dawn. Meisel could taste the coming snow on his tongue, and said as much, but that Longworth was a stingy fat-arse *Teufel*.

"I'm not paying you to sit by the fire," Longworth said, dismissing Meisel's concern.

Muttering about the bloody English, Meisel had the boy secure the bags and hitch the horses, while he examined the wheel axles to see that they were greased and in balance, with no wobbles, and that the bag of sand he kept at his feet in the driver's seat was full.

Longworth was as insulting to the passengers as he was to his driver. "Get a move on," he jabbered at them. "Snow is coming. If we leave now we can beat it to New-York."

Like sheep, the three adults and the two brats, all bound for New-York, climbed into the coach and pulled their blankets tight about them.

Meisel had a final comment. He pointed to eastward. "Can't see the sun. That's a witch's omen."

Longworth wasn't having any. "Go, go, go," he commanded, slapping the off-horse on the rump.

"If it's as bad as it feels," Meisel shouted in the heightening wind, "I'll wait for it to pass in Hoboken." Had Longworth heard? Meisel didn't know and he didn't give a whore's piss. Ach, yes, he did. Longworth paid extra for these winter runs, and Ludwig Meisel had a wife and six young ones to feed.

Now, with the storm fully on them, the snow stabbed his eyes. He could see nothing of the road and was, God help him, depending on the horses, certainly the Lord's stupidest creatures. He wished he could merely pull off the road and wait this calamity out. But that would mean slow death. They could be buried alive with perhaps no hope of rescue even after the storm subsided. Running headlong like this, if the horses dragged them into a tree or a hole, they would at least die swiftly.

The coach rocked and pitched, rolling precariously from side to side. Any minute they could *über Arsch gehen*.

"Hoy, coachman!"

The cry was a faint sound from where? In this swirling wind who could tell? If it came from anyone afoot, he was ten feet back already. Now a rapping from behind and below, from the coach. "Coachman." Ludwig Meisel could barely make it out. Applegate? "Find an inn, something, somewhere. We're freezing and being battered to death."

"Stupid *loch*, if I could see to find an inn, don't you think I would?"

Inside the coach, the merchant Carl Applegate's normally florid face was pasty. His plump wife, their two children, Edward and Margaret, and the frail young woman from Philadelphia, attired in her black widow's weeds, grew more and more apprehensive with each mad reel of the vehicle.

The outside lead horse stumbled, dragging its mate down. The horses behind, sliding blindly, slammed into the lead pair. Meisel, his work cut out for him, pulled at the reins for all he was worth.

The frightened passengers held their breaths as, in a

heartbeat, the coach quieted. Then came the howl of the
wind and the terrified screams of the horses as they skidded
helplessly. The coach took to the air. Hurtling, splintering,
it tossed its passengers like so many rag dolls into the snow-
shrouded ravine.

*Just received from Washington, and for sale by Matthias
Ward, No. 149, Pearl-street, price $1.50 cents
Vol.I of the Trial of*
Colonel Aaron Burr
*On an Indictment for Treason, before the Circuit Court of
the United States, held in Richmond, Virginia,
May Term, 1807, including the*
ARGUMENTS and DECISIONS

NEW-YORK HERALD
JANUARY 1808

4

25 JANUARY. MONDAY. LATE MORNING.

Maurice Jamison opened his sleep-crusted eyes. The
doxy was gone. Only her musky odor remained. His manservant Stevens had set his hot chocolate and French
brandy, shaving water and gear in their proper places. He
had built up the fire, too.

After a profitable day on Friday, Jamie—as he was
known to his friends—had dedicated himself solely to pleasure on Saturday and Sunday. Of course, he had made his
appearance at St. Paul's Chapel, but not with the doxy.

Profit and pleasure was what made Jamie content. He
tossed off the brandy and sipped some chocolate which he

swirled in his mouth with some delicacy before he swallowed. "Good chocolate."

The gray cat sleeping at the foot of his bed slitted his eyes, glanced lazily at Jamie, and closed them again.

Jamie poured hot water from the pitcher into his basin, stropped his razor on the strip of leather attached to the table, and had another taste of chocolate before he began to shave.

The shaving mirror gave him back the reflection of a mature man. His grin revealed yellow teeth, but they were all there, of which few men many years his junior could boast. As in his youth Jamie had the intense nature and the rounded shoulders of a dedicated scholar. His Scots nose retained its aquiline strength. He still had the exceedingwhite skin that made him appear fragile, but regardless of his sixty-nine years the man was decidedly robust. His once healthy mane of copper hair was now sparse and dyed a bright carrot orange.

And, he was pleased to note, his virility was that of a man half his age. Suddenly he remembered all those years ago when he and John Tonneman had come to New-York on . . . What was that ship? Aha. The *Earl Of Halifax*, out of Falmouth.

The City of New-York had had a raw charm then, and a spirit of freshness, even among the community of prostitutes near King's—now Columbia—College. Jamie had even brought a whore to Tonneman's house in Rutgers Hill, flaunting her presence in the face of old Gretel, Tonneman's pious prune of a housekeeper.

Whatever had made him think of Gretel and her fierce disapproval? He was in his own house in Richmond Hill and he could fuck as many tarts as he pleased. And sometimes he almost did.

Jamie loved this house, from its stately columns and gracious balconies to its Turkey carpets and velvet-covered sofas and the statue of Venus in his bedroom. Only the glue factory, which manufactured its product from pigs' feet, marred the perfection of his existence. Such establishments, because they emitted noxious odors, were compelled by law to be beyond the City limits. The stench was strong at Richmond Hill, but since the glue factory was one of Jamie's many profitable enterprises, he chose not to notice.

He had bought his splendid estate in Richmond Hill at a bargain price from Colonel Aaron Burr, who had served during the War with distinction. Burr was one of the founders of the Tammany Society, an organization of the leaders of the City of New-York, established for the purpose of doing good works. Jamie too had been one of Tammany's founding members.

Although Burr had tied with Thomas Jefferson in electoral votes in the 1800 election, he lost by the House vote and had to settle for being Jefferson's vice president. His long-time feud with Alexander Hamilton led to a duel four years later, in Weehawken, New Jersey. Both Hamilton and Burr's political career died that day.

Last year, after being acquitted of treason for conspiring to secede the Louisiana Territory from the United States and become its president, the former vice president went into exile in France.

Jamie had come to America a loyal and vocal Tory, and he took enormous pleasure that this particular house was now his. He had practically stolen it from that fool Burr, who had been in such a rush to live in *Paree*.

Jamie laughed with the joy of himself, a sixty-nine-year-old man tupping like a bull. And living in America and owning this house while its scheming former owner was denied the pleasures of this great country. He laughed so hard he had to finish his chocolate in one quick draught in order to stop.

This time the cat didn't even open his eyes.

Gretel. Jamie smirked. He'd not thought of the old busybody in over thirty years. Why should he think of her now? He shrugged and continued shaving. Lately his memories of the past had begun surfacing with more clarity than what he had done the previous week.

A more recent memory was his bargain struck with Burr. Jamie's Collect Company was an offshoot company of Burr's Manhattan Company. This had been the dream of a lifetime for Jamie.

In 1798, Aaron Burr, with strong support from Alexander Hamilton, the man he would later shoot to death, convinced the state legislature to aid in the establishment of the Manhattan Company, a private municipal waterworks.

Under all the legal verbiage in this bill was a special clause. The *bank clause*.

> *And be it further enacted, that it shall and may be lawful for the said Company to employ such surplus capital as may belong or accrue to this said Company in the purchase of public or other stock or in any other monied transaction or operations not inconsistant with the constitution and laws of the state or of the United States, for the sole benefit of the Company.*

Because of this clause the Manhattan Company was allowed to use its profits to run a bank, an insurance firm, a trading company, and a real estate office. Or any one of the above.

This had been Burr's goal from the beginning. A bank controlled by him and his followers, the Anti-Federalists. On 2 April, 1799, Governor John Jay signed the Manhattan Bill, and Aaron Burr had his bank. It would form the financial basis of his new empire.

None of Burr's dreams of power through his bank had come to fruition. But Jamie was sure he wouldn't make any of Burr's mistakes. First he would finish building the canal that drained the Collect Pond. Then with his profits he would open *his* bank. In the meantime he would continue to buy land. And one day . . . Who knew what one day would bring? Jamie knew. One day he would own a large chunk of New-York, and the rest of America awaited him.

Jamie rubbed his face to find the rough places and shaved them again. His face pleased him. He took pride in the fact that, except for a slight thickening betwixt waist and groin, he was the same man physically that he'd been three decades before when he first arrived in New-York.

When he finished shaving, and had generously doused his face, body, and handkerchief with cologne that he ordered from Newport, he stood in front of the fire and donned the fresh smallclothes Stevens had laid out for him, the white shirt and dark blue trousers. Only then did he ring the silver bell.

Stevens appeared almost immediately, bearing another brandy and a fresh pot of steaming chocolate. "Good morning, sir." The manservant said not another word as he opened the venetian blinds and let the winter sunshine in. Quickly he cleared away the shaving equipment and the soiled brandy and chocolate utensils, for he knew his master was a meticulous man who rewarded disorder with the back of his hand.

Jamie finished his second brandy of the morning, then drank the newly poured chocolate. Stevens returned, this time without being summoned.

Stevens, a thin young man who had the air and manners of someone trained to attend a royal heir, quickly dressed Jamie's hair. He helped him on with his gray snake-skin boots, embroidered yellow vest, and the single-breasted scarlet jacket with a stand-up collar. The last item was the scented yellow handkerchief for his left sleeve.

With satisfaction, Jamie admired himself in the tall French boudoir mirror. Yes, he could still be taken for a much younger man.

The doxy, Joan, had performed well. He would have her again. Sixty-nine or not, he had strong carnal appetites. But enough dwelling on pleasure of the flesh. Urgent business demanded his attention. It was time to attend to it.

5

25 JANUARY. MONDAY. EARLY AFTERNOON.

Among sailors, oystermen, laborers, and low-paid clerks, butchers were the elite. They were the sporting men, the drinkers with coins in their purses, who liked to have fun.

What butchers loved was bullbaiting.

The rise of land between Mott and Broadway, at Grand, was called Bunker Hill, so named because of the fort erected on that spot during the War for Independence to defend against General Howe and his British troops.

After the war the Hill became the favored location for duels and for mass meetings. Early in the new century Big Ned Winship, the Fly Market Butcher, bought the land, tore down what was left of the fort, and put up a fence. He then created an arena that could hold up to two thousand people. Even in the winter the people came out. Not as many as during the warmer weather, but if you gave them a good contest and let them smell the blood, they came.

This was Butcher Ned's bullring and his boast and delight. And it mattered not at all to him that the Scots Presbyterian Church was but three blocks away. Let them tend to their business; he would tend to his.

Of late, however, the gangs had taken to using the ring for their own man-to-man fights. They'd broken the gate down so many times that Big Ned finally decided to leave the damn portal open for them. If he had the ring for his bull-and-dog shows, he didn't care cow flop for what the gangs did. So long as they carted off their dead when they were done.

As to the matter of Butcher Ned's show: In the center of the ring, for the entertainment of an assembly of his brother butchers and their multitude of friends, half a dozen or more dogs, hungry crossbreed mongrel terriers, fifteen to eighteen inches high at the shoulder, with thin mean snouts and torn floppy ears, would be set upon a staked-out prime bull chained to a swivel ring, which gave the bull limited movement and no escape.

Butcher Ned thought that was a lot of fun. But life was not all fun. Life was business. Ned controlled the betting precisely. Six of his apprentices, rough-and-ready young boys, would circle the area, collecting bets on which and how many dogs would be gored before the bull was done, or on how long the pack would take to put the bull down and dead.

It was to this place that Maurice Jamison made his way of a morning when he was in a gambling frame of mind.

The moment Jamie appeared, Butcher Ned cleared away the raff who liked to congregate at the bullring, so that his gentleman could watch and place his bets without soiling his elbows.

As tall as Jamie was, Ned, at six and a half feet, was taller, but they were well-matched, Ned knew, when it came to brains and cunning. Jamie accepted the taste from

Ned's rum bottle, then followed the butcher to the third tier where a bench and a pillow awaited him. The bull had already been pegged to the ground and the crazed terriers had just been released. Jamie nodded appreciatively when all five dogs attacked at once. He hugged himself against a sudden wind and settled in to watch the bloody encounter. Ned smiled and bowed and continued his tour of the ring.

At the first twitch of his nostrils, Jamie flipped the pale yellow handkerchief from his sleeve to his nose. This place was odious, vile with the high, rancid odor of rotting dead animals. The dead were little worse than the living for their stink, man and animal alike. He sniffed in a deep whiff of his special scent. Even its elegance could only mask the stench about him for a short time.

The bull snorted steam, stamping and pawing the frozen earth. His fury at being tied enraged him. With lowing howls he quickly dispatched his snarling adversaries into blood-soaked corpses.

This go-to between the bull and five dogs left but one dog standing by the time the sand had run through the glass, and that made Jamie a winner. He looked about for Ned. The bull and dogs were fine entertainment, but he'd come to this place with business in mind. When he finally saw Ned in an alcove just off the stands, where the lottery tickets were sold, Jamie's nostrils twitched again. But not at the foul reek. His young nephew by marriage, George Willard, stood huddled in conversation with Big Ned. Now, what would his protégé, young George, have to say so earnestly and angrily to the Fly Market Butcher? Jamie knew the answer as well as he knew his nephew. The boy was addicted to gambling. And to Jamie's chagrin, George's interest in women was less than his interest in wine and wagering.

Jamie saw only the tight slant of George's jaw between the tilt of his top hat and his spotless white shirt collar and wine tailcoat. His fists were clenched. Big Ned rubbed his bulbous nose, which sat like a gnarled potato in the butcher's suet pudding face. The expression he wore as he listened to George Willard was full of contempt.

Jamie pushed as close to the two men as he could without being seen. But by that time Butcher Ned had raised his right hand high and snapped his fingers. Immediately a squat man with arms like tree trunks appeared behind George. That would be Charlie Wright (who-could-do-no-wrong), one of Ned's Bruiser Boys. Seizing George by seat of his fawn-colored trousers and his black velvet collar, Charlie lifted the struggling young man high and headed for the gate at Broadway.

"Don't mess his fine duds, Charlie," Butcher Ned hollered. "He's a good customer."

6

25 JANUARY. MONDAY. AFTERNOON TO EVENING.

A late January thaw had melted much of the snow. Chunks of ice floated in the river. Peter Tonneman had resolved not to go home. Now, instead, he rode to Richmond Hill; he needed the counsel of his godfather. Only Jamie could straighten out this predicament with Tedious and mediate the constant bickering with his father.

It was Jamie who'd convinced John Tonneman that Peter, his son, did not have a vocation for physick and surgery. And it was Jamie who'd gotten Peter the position at the Collect Company as Thaddeus Brown's secretary. Now, it was patently obvious that he had no inclination for business either. What was he to do to earn a living, to support a wife and family?

Jamie had always stood by him; Jamie would know what to do.

Broadway was dense with carriages and drays. Since it had been paved, the road gave off little mud but for the light variety that came from the mixture of dirt and melted snow. Sidewalk vendors called out their wares. A young boy in dirty pantaloons, his face blackened by ash, rested his pail of fire on the cover of a City well. Peter reined in Ophelia and bought a half-cent potato, roasted dark and crisp in a pail of hot cinders.

"Want some water to wash it down?"

"Pump must be frozen," Peter said through a mouthful of potato.

"Not if you put hot coals on it," the boy answered, cunning in his eyes. He was wearing a tattered, oversized gray velvet coat whose tails brushed the ground.

Peter took a drink from the clay mug just as an excuse to give the boy another half-cent, even though it was nigh to the last he owned. "You have some to spare for my horse?"

"Yes, sir." The boy emptied a wooden bucket filled with twigs and lifted the cover to the well.

The water was icy cold. Peter welcomed the heat of the potato through his glove as he chewed through the charred skin and savored the white meal. He offered the last bit to Ophelia, but she, drinking from the bucket and holding out for oats, disdained it with an upward roll of her eye. "Suit yourself, old girl," said Peter. He ate the rest as he took to the road again.

On the approach to Lispenard Meadows, the cobble-stones ended; here Broadway was a virtual quagmire, slowing Ophelia's progress. Snow lay in flaps like white cow dung on the swampy meadow. Peter could see the workmen around the Collect, their breaths puffing white in the chilly air. He turned Ophelia onto Lispenard-street, then north on Varick. The slight thaw had put Varick awash with mud, but already Peter could feel the chill as the sun descended. If he didn't miss his guess there would be fog, and soon.

Beyond Lispenard Meadows, Maurice Arthur Jamison's Richmond Hill house rose, four grand stories of white clapboard, a large frame house with wings, complete with columns and balconies, commanding a view of the Hudson River, which is what the North River was called up here.

Richmond Hill, bounded by Varick and Charlton-streets, was one of New-York's finest private estates. Beautifully kept grounds ran down to the pristine river. Richmond Hill had a history tied to the young country, having served as home to John Adams when New-York was the capital of the United States. Before that, during the War, George Washington had used it as his headquarters.

Peter handed Ophelia over to Bill, Jamie's groom. "Give her an apple after her oats."

The boy saluted from his forelock. "The Master ain't here." Then stiffly, reciting, "I'll inform Stevens of your presence, sir."

"No need, Bill. I'll see myself in."

Stevens was waiting at the door. He seemed to have a sixth sense that informed him of a visitor before the knocker ever hit the door. "Master Jamison has gone out," he said. The manservant relieved Peter of his muddy boots, greatcoat, and leather gloves, then settled him in the parlor on an elegant cabriole sofa covered in rich teal velvet. A fire, perfectly made, kept the room comfortable. Steven brought him chocolate and biscuits. Settling in to wait, Peter found himself nodding off. Once when he opened his eyes he saw that his boots were standing by the door, all clean and polished. A short time, it seemed, afterward, as Stevens was putting another log on the fire, the door was flung open and a disheveled and infuriated George Willard burst into the chamber, followed by two agitated underservants.

George's boots were caked with mud, his collar torn.

Two gold buttons were missing from his double-breasted jacket. His top hat was badly dented, giving him a clownish look.

Stevens waved the servants away and waited.

"What the devil are you doing here?" George demanded of Peter. When he went to the fire, Stevens was there to assist him out of his mud-splattered coat.

Not quite three years Peter's senior, George Willard had always treated Peter Tonneman with disdain. He was Jamie's blood—his nephew *and* godson—while Peter was merely his godson. George, too, worked for the Collect Company.

Peter knew that George thought him a yap for being a fiddling secretary. George Willard was a surveyor. But for all of George's airs Peter had heard Tedious complain to Jamie often enough that the bulk of his nephew's surveying was done from one end of Butcher Ned's bullring to the other.

George fell into a blue brocade wing chair and thrust his boots at Stevens, who promptly had them off.

"Bring me a buttered rum and the bottle. Where's my uncle?"

"Master Jamison intends to return before sundown." Stevens left the room with George's coat and boots.

Peter glanced at George, careful to keep the enmity from his eyes. The man was a head shorter than he and of stocky build. He had a weak chin and, as Peter had learned over the years, the petulant temperament of a bully.

George's mother, Abigail Willard, had grown up on a neighboring Rutgers Hill estate, and Peter knew his own father and Abigail had been friends before John Tonneman had ever met Peter's mother. His mother, on the other hand, had been known to turn waspish at the very mention of the name Willard. This behavior made Peter think that there might have been some link between his father and Abigail Willard that went beyond friendship. Why that should ever be confounded Peter. Abigail Willard might have been all right when she was young, but she couldn't ever hold a candle to his mother, who was truly beautiful.

Stevens returned with George's hot buttered rum and the bottle. When he withdrew from the parlor, he left Peter wondering. Had Stevens shaken his head? And if so, was it a tremor or a comment on George? What was this all about?

George had quickly gulped down his steamy rum drink. He was now replenishing his cup from the bottle. "Where is old Tedious hiding?"

"Hiding?"

George favored Peter with a wily grin. "You're a sly one, you are. I didn't think you had it in you." He took another immense swallow. The liquid dribbled down his chin.

"What are you talking about?" Peter asked impatiently. He rose and crossed to the hearth. What was keeping Jamie? He had half a mind to go home, but that wouldn't do. He couldn't. He had to get his position back and Jamie was the only one who could arrange that. He gave the fire an impatient poke.

George laughed. "Where's the money?"

"What money?"

"I'm waiting. The money."

George had to be drunk. Still, Peter was perplexed. To cover his confusion he finished his chocolate.

"The money?" George fairly sang the words.

"The money?"

George shook his head violently. "Can you do nothing but echo me, you stupid sod?" He stood and staggered several steps toward Peter. "Shit, everyone in New-York knows you and Tedious *stole* the money."

At Auction

BY C. McEVERS, JUN.
*On Monday, in front of the Tontine Coffee-House, at
11 o'clock—100 boxes fresh Raisins.*

NEW-YORK EVENING POST
JANUARY 1808

7

30 JANUARY. SATURDAY. EARLY MORNING.

The man in black was of modest height, but robust of frame. Recoiling at the gloom around him and the gloom of his own thoughts, he drained the coffee from his cup. His hands were so huge the pewter cup seemed made for a child. A fire flickered uneasily on the hearth, adding to the sombre mood of the Tontine.

Today the Tontine Coffee-House had only a spare ten patrons. True, it was seven o'clock and the morning was just showing its face, but last year at this time the Tontine had been overflowing with its usual horde of underwriters, brokers, merchants, traders, and politicians, buttonholing prospects, eager to know the news in order to buy, sell, or insure, all intent on their mission: to make money.

This year, thanks to Mr. Jefferson, God bless him, and

his Embargo, the mission was thwarted. Money was scarce as hen's teeth and there were painfully few prospects to go around. This City of nearly seventy thousand souls suffered audibly, but then New-Yorkers were never shy about complaining.

The burly man's complexion was tawny. His eyes gleamed a pale blue under bushy brows, and his great nose had what was known as a Hebraic curve. A tall beaver hat sat squarely atop his large head. In his right hand he held a thick oakwood stick. As he stepped out on the balcony of the Tontine, he removed the hat with his left hand, revealing a bald pate, fringed with softly curling light brown hair. He rubbed the sweat from his brow with his wrist and restored the hat to its place. In spite of the nip in the winter air, he rarely wore a greatcoat. Beneath his vest he wore a plain white linen shirt. Around his neck, holding the high shirt collar closed, was tied his emblem, a sparkling white silk handkerchief.

From his vantage point overlooking Coffee-House Slip, he could see the entire waterfront, now shrouded in eerie silence and given over to squalor, particularly the area around Coenties Slip.

"It's a terrible thing, Mr. Jefferson's Embargo." The innkeeper, Lemual Wilson, stepped out on the balcony. "This keeps up and I'm moving to Philadelphia."

"What makes you think they fare any better in Philadelphia?" the man in black asked in his rich molasses voice.

"They do not. And I know it."

The two men stood silent, watching as snowflakes began to fill the air. At last Wilson said, "I need a favor."

"Ask."

"Young Tonneman is passed out in one of my back chambers."

The man in black thumped his staff, but that was all the emotion he showed. He'd heard that young Tonneman had gone missing again. But the dissolute youngster had done that before and, sad to say, would without doubt do it again.

"I'll see to it. My driver can cart him home."

"Thank you. Well, appears as if our town is on the path again."

"O grab me," the man in black said, knowing how comical it was for a man of his temperament to be using such a silly expression. But the phrase—"Embargo" spelled backward—had taken hold in the City, capturing everyone's imagination, tickling one and all, the young, the old, the rich, and the poor. "If the Embargo doesn't kill us, the good Lord in His impatience at our sins will. I'm a good Anti-Federalist Republican-Democrat, but where is Aaron Burr when we need him most?"

The landlord nodded. "I haven't been happy since De Witt Clinton was removed and that toad Willett appointed mayor."

"As one Clintonian to another, I agree. With the election over and Clinton reelected, he can take his proper place back and get on with the task of getting the City some work."

"That's thanks to the fact that we carried the First, Second, and Ninth Wards," the landlord, also a staunch Democrat, bragged. "Not till the twenty-second next, though."

"The mills of God grind slow, but sometimes the mills of men are like a turtle in mud by comparison. At any rate the Embargo should bring us Federal money to build up our fortifications. This trouble with the English could lead us into war."

The proprietor of the Tontine nodded agreement and went back inside.

His mood notwithstanding, the man in black stepped jauntily down the steps of the Tontine, beating each step with his oakwood staff of office, holding its golden head in his great right hand. He rested his other hand in the pocket of his white waistcoat as his sharp eyes searched for faces which might seem more at home in quod, and therefore up to no good. Criminals were afraid of him. That was his power. His weapon, fear.

They called him Old Hays. In May he would be thirty-six. This, then, was Jacob Hays, the first High Constable of the City of New-York, head of the Constabulary force.

All about him were the ghostly sights and echoes of the once bustling city. The lightly falling snow contained phantoms: auctioneers mounted on a hogshead of sugar here or a puncheon of rum there, exhorting customers to bid on rich cargos that the busy port received daily, displayed on the balcony or on the stairs of the Tontine or other coffee-houses.

It troubled Jake greatly that the swarms of folk bidding or paying attention to the divers auctioneers the previous year were not here now. It had been a busy, worthwhile time for him, too, seizing many of the brazen pick-purses who were always on hand to fleece the woolly crowd.

No more.

What was this? Actually missing the pick-purses?

He spoke a few words to Noah, his driver, about young Tonneman. "Best haul him home to Rutgers Hill," he told Noah.

"Yes, sir."

"Don't bother coming back out for me."

"First snow this year." Noah pulled off his red wool hat and rubbed his head. The man's skin was brown, his hair, a deeper brown, flecked with gray.

"I know."

"Going to be deep. I can feel it in my bones. So can Copper." Noah indicated the reddish-brown gelding pulling the carriage.

"Are you afraid I'm going to get buried under a drift?"

"No. But it's time for the sleigh."

"So? Tomorrow we use the sleigh. Anything else?"

"No, sir."

Jake Hays saluted his driver with his staff. Then he

started on his foot patrol, the iron tip of the staff tapping on the uneven cobblestones.

The waterfront, Water-street, and Wall-street, where the Tontine was situated, and Coffee-House Slip, which had the year before been a barricade of carts, drays and wheelbarrows, horses and men with barely room for people to pass, was now deserted. His rounds took Hays along Wall-street, past Front to South-street, and to the water. Only a hundred and fifty years earlier, barely a holler past Pearl-street, the river ran here. The new streets, east of Pearl—Water, Front, and South—were man-made: earth, stones, pilings, and whatnot taken from one place and dropped in another, very much like the work being done now at the Collect. Once, the Collect had been the source of sweet, pure water in the City. Sweet nectar. No longer. New-York was changing, and not always for the better.

The few men who were about today wore hungry faces of woeful dismay. Gone were the vitality and optimistic good cheer that was so much a part of Hays's New-York.

Here and there a ragged beggar hopped out of the shadows at the sight of good Old Hays and cadged a small coin.

Ships were lined up in the harbor, all right, as far as the eye could see. But there was no profit in dismantled vessels, in dry dock for the long winter. All decks were cleared and hatches battened down. Hardly a seaman in sight on board. In the streets, they were, all seeking landlubber work, or worse, a landlubber to rob.

Quite a few of the countinghouses, once the lifeblood of this busy town, were battened down, too. And nary a cask, barrel, box, or bale did the High Constable see cluttering the empty piers along South-street, which, deprived of their previous flurry and tumult, made this area more dangerous than it had ever been before. A hungry man was a dangerous man. A hungry criminal was worse.

Public Notices

EMBARGO spelled backwards O Grab Me appears,
A scarey sound even for big children's ears?
The syllables transpose, Go Bar Em comes next,
A mandate to keep ye from harm says my text.

Analyze miss Embargo—her letters I'll wage,
If not remove'd shortly will make a Mob Rage:
Poor Mag dalen's number she chose, d___ take her,
And they tell you "GO BE A ROBBER OR
BEGGAR!"

NEW-YORK HERALD
JANUARY 1808

8

30 JANUARY. SATURDAY. MORNING.

Duffy hated his landlubber job, but truth to say, he was luckier than most and it was a darn sight better than starving. Although five cents a day was hardly living the life of a prince, it was also a darn sight better than the last job that had Duffy standing hip-deep in the bloody cold water digging that stinking mud out of the frigging Fresh Water

Pond, what they called the Collect. It was naught but a dense stagnant mass of sludge lapping the shore.

Hard to believe people once swam and fished in this muck. They say there was trees all along here. Gone now. Cut down for firewood. Duffy had also heard that one of the Royals had played here before the War. And that he learned to skate on it, and made sport by scattering gold coins on the ice, laughing as skaters chased the sliding money. Fresh Water Pond. Fresh water, indeed. The stink was worse than Maggie's drawers.

Three years earlier, a bloody committee appointed to look into the state of the Collect reported that the Pond was filled with the bodies of dead animals and God knows what else. It was, the committee said, dangerous to public health. What a surprise.

Those what favored digging a canal to drain the Pond into the North River were happy as pigs in mud when the report was made public. This gaggle of landowners and other bigwigs also said that the Pond was mosquito-ridden and bred disease.

Those against protested that the Pond provided good fishing and good skating.

The canal people won.

As far as Duffy was concerned, the mosquito fearfuls were daft. Anyone with half a brain knew that the blood-suckers favored still water and would find a new home in the canal.

Landlubbers! They gave him a pain in the prick. He spit and pulled his pea coat close against the wind. At least the snow had stopped. Someone, certainly not him, was going to get rich out of this. That was a winning bet if ever there was one. He rubbed his hands, wriggling his freezing fingers, and wished for gloves.

He'd spent this week cleaning up around the filled-in part of the bloody Pond, where they'd dumped piles of that stinking fishy peat mud and covered it with the dirt they'd

gotten from the hills which used to surround the Pond. The
hills were gone now, flattened to the ground.

He was directed to throw branches and such into the
filled-in part, and to heap large refuse in a pile to be taken
away by the next wagon. Always he kept his eyes open for
something he could sell. Like yesterday, when he'd found
an old English shilling. Thank the good Lord, the mud was
frozen or he'd be sicker for it than he already was.

The plan was to dig a forty-foot-wide canal to drain the
stinking Pond. The canal would go from the North—the
Hudson River some called it—to the East River, passing
through the Collect Pond. The canal would run a bit over a
mile.

A pledge had been given that on either side of the
canal there would be a tree-lined promenade. A bridge
would cross the canal at Broadway. Ha! Duffy was certain
the beetle heads would never get it done, and he didn't
much care if they did. It was work, which meant money,
which meant food.

Come thaw, he was promised the job of carting the
earth away, instead of breaking his back digging all God's
frigging day long. He would get five cents per load for earth
delivered and dumped into the Pond.

Perhaps, with the Blessed Virgin's help, come thaw he'd
be away from these Sodomites and breathing the sweet sea
air once more, living the sailor's life as God meant him to.

He paused and looked out across Lispenard Meadows,
which lay from Broadway west to the North River. The
Meadows was really marshland that now, near-frozen, was
spongy underfoot and littered with branches, leaves, rags,
busted carts and rusted shovels. What a mess of swine landlubbers were.

No sense fretting it though. As soon as this was done he
could go inside for some warm. He rubbed his hands again,
flexed them, and righted an overturned cart.

Duffy leaned on his rake and sniffed the air. Above the
stench of the Pond and the pervasive malt odor from Coul-

ter's Brewery on the banks of the Collect, near Orange-street, he could smell more snow coming.

His stomach growled; all he'd put in it this day was thin barley soup at noon. Well, none of that. He had to keep moving or the blood would freeze in his veins. Some two hundred feet away he could see Fred Smithers just standing there, staring up at the winter sun, as if that could warm him.

Duffy snagged his rake on a branch protruding from the snow-crusted ground. Cursing, he reached down to wrest it from the frigid earth.

"Sweet Jesus." Duffy crossed himself three times quickly. It wasn't a branch. It was a human hand.

SORE EYES, Yellow Fever, and Dysentery, in Old and Young, and all Bilious Complaints are relieved and cured with Indian Medicines, prepared and sold by Mrs. Charity Shaw, corner of Hester-street and Bowery-lane.

NEW-YORK SPECTATOR
JANUARY 1808

9

30 JANUARY. SATURDAY. MORNING.

The room was icy cold. Under the heavy counterpane Mariana Tonneman knew she was dying. As she lay stiffly beside her sleeping husband, her heart fluttered and leaped like a frightened fawn.

All of a moment she was hot. A tremendous blaze seemed to be coming from deep inside her. She became frantic; sweat, under her chin, the back of her neck, across her midsection, poured from her body, soaking her and everything she touched.

The first time she'd been visited with the heat Mariana thought she was pregnant, but her monthly bleeding hadn't stopped.

To make matters worse, of late she had become a shrew, losing her temper for little reason, snapping at her girls, at John, and now at poor Peter.

Her darling boy had been gone for a week this time. When he'd been brought home in such a terrible condition early this morning, she thanked God that her husband was still with da Ponte. Mariana had put her son to bed and returned to her own. John had returned while she slept fitfully.

She shivered. As always, the aftermath of the heat was the chill which tortured her bones. The wind clawed at the shutters, forcing biting cold through the walls of the old house, making her back ache more than ever. The shingles needed replacing, and the roof leaked whenever it rained. Her husband always seemed to have something more important to do than to see to the house. Yet he had cut back on his surgery hours, only seeing a very few old patients. As Commissioner of Health, John was always busy elsewhere.

The High Constable's man, Noah, had half-carried her poor besotted Peter home from the Tontine. That had been the final straw. She'd lost her mind. First screaming, then crying, hysterical, blaming John for again not being there when she needed him.

Signore da Ponte, who was unnerved of late over the launching of his opera company, had sent a boy last night for her husband and John had gone out to tend him. The Signore was not really sick, but since '05 when the writer and sometime grocer had arrived in New-York from Italy, he'd been one of John's best clients and friends, and he would have no other physician.

Indeed, if John hadn't known da Ponte, the girls would never have had the chance to learn Italian. Once a week Gretel and Leah attended the class that Bishop Moore had organized in the parish house of St. Paul's for da Ponte to teach the fashionable, well-born young ladies and gentlemen of New-York. This was the new cachet. To study Italian with Signore da Ponte.

Mariana was so impressed. And because da Ponte was teaching the children of the Livingstons, Hamiltons,

Schulers, Duers, Duanes, and Beekmans, her daughters were meeting them, rubbing elbows with them, so to speak.

John had come home and fallen into bed without so much as a kind word to her. Now Mariana looked at her husband of three decades and hated him with all her heart. As if in response, her heart trembled violently again.

She turned back the bedclothes, reached for her shawl, and slippered her cold, swollen feet. If she were struck blind, she would know her way around this bedroom. She opened the curtains, hoping the streaks of winter light coming through the closed, worn-thin shutters would wake John. It did not help. Old. Everything was old and worn out, including her. She stirred the fire, but John would not stir. He groaned and rolled over, spreading himself liberally across her place on the bed.

The flare of the fire started her sweating again. She rushed to the chest of drawers where the Delft pitcher and basin stood and plunged one hand, then the other, into the pitcher for the icy water to cool and wash her feverish face and neck. She should have known this was a mistake. Now she was shivering from the sudden chill. Disgusted with her condition and her spouse, Mariana opened the bedchamber door with a small thump.

Her household slept. Peter, in John's boyhood room; the girls, Gretel and Leah, upstairs. She could hear Micah, the hired girl, moving around in the kitchen.

The old house in Rutgers Hill had been the home of John's father and grandfather before him, but the City was moving steadily northward, and she wondered if, after she and John were gone, their children would stay on or abandon the house.

The stairs creaked and the wind rattled through the old place. Sighing, she pulled the shawl tighter around her woolly nightdress, and proceeded to John's study.

She would read through his medical books again, as she had often done in the past, when they worked side by side.

. . . With John still sound asleep, she could do so uninterrupted.

Rheumatic Fever. Was that her malady? It had been her mother's.

When she opened the door to John's study, she found Micah, her brown-striped cotton dress and unbleached muslin apron hiked above her knees as she knelt, exposing her worn white dimity pettiskirt with all its patching. Mariana recognized it as one of Gretel's castoffs, too threadbare for Leah to wear.

The girl was mopping up the snow that had seeped through the window frame. The fire was already stoked. The skinny fourteen-year-old sprang to her feet. She straightened her clothes. "Uh, Missis, I didn't know you were up and about."

Distracted, Mariana nodded. She plucked a brown leather-bound book from the shelf and sat in John's armchair, opening the tome to the description of Rheumatic Fever. The disease supposedly was strongest against children. Like the Yellow Fever that had taken her David in the Epidemic of '98. High fever, ever-painful sore throat. But David had not had swelling and pain in the joints. Nor did she now.

So absorbed was she that she hardly noticed that Micah had quit the room and returned with a pot of tea and a mug.

Mariana probed her joints. No pain, no tenderness. But what of the quick fevers? What, then, was wrong with her?

She closed the book and poured black tea into her mug, inhaling the fumes, wrapping her fingers around the hot surface. Mr. Ellis, her grocer, had warned her that tea would be in short supply because of Mr. Jefferson's O Grab Me, so she had stocked up. Even though his worries had been unfounded and he had a plentiful supply from Canada, Ellis's prices did go higher. She was quite content that she'd bought early and cheap. She shook her head. It would be terrible if they had to relive the deprivations of '75 and the war years again. Unaccountably, another flash of heat transfused her. Or was it from the tea?

She would be forty-seven this summer, an old woman. An errant thought strolled through her mind. John had a birthday coming in March. He would be sixty-two.

They'd been together thirty-two years. She'd seen her first child, a beautiful boy, stillborn, and her second, David, dead these ten years, may he rest in peace. He had been named for her father. Tears slid down her cheeks. David was such a loving boy, and John had taken him everywhere. David would have been the doctor-son his father wanted.

John had blamed himself for David's death. Fifteen hundred had died that awful year. One of the dead had been her joy, her David. Many New-Yorkers had rushed to the countryside, desperate to escape the wrath of the Fever. But the Tonnemans had stayed, John working through long days and nights to save the lives of friends and strangers, and when he did sleep, fighting the furies who told him he had let his young son die.

After that, for a short time, John wanted to flee the cursed City of New-York and its tainted water, for he was certain the Fever came from the pollution of the Collect. Mariana would have left gladly. Her brother Ben had begged them to join him in Princeton, New Jersey, where he published a journal, but John had changed his mind. He vowed to do something about finding untainted drinking water for the City. That was why he sought the position of Commissioner of Health and why he became involved with the Collect Company.

He showed so much zeal and goodness that even when the Federalists regained their ascendency in New-York after the Charter election of 1806, John Tonneman stayed on as Commissioner of Health. He remained so even after De Witt Clinton was removed from office by the Council of Appointments at Albany and Marinus Willett replaced Mr. Clinton as mayor.

Mariana wasn't so charitable. She, too, blamed John for

David's death. She knew in her heart she had never forgiven him. They had not been the same since then.

Her one solace was that Leah had been born ten months after young David was buried in the old Jewish cemetery in St. James-street. New life to cherish. But not for John. Leah was only a girl.

Peter was nine that terrible year, and Gretel four. Two sons lost. She still had Peter, but Peter, alas, was not David.

David had always warmed his father's heart simply by being David. John Tonneman's pleasures increased a thousandfold every time the solemn little boy told him gravely that he was going to be a physician, too. Peter, the carefree one, on the other hand, was revolted by the sight of blood and because of his father's insistence that he go into medicine, turned to drink instead. The boy was the crushing disappointment of John Tonneman's life.

Mariana had never liked John's friend, the physician Maurice Jamison. Jamie had been a despicable Royalist and he'd married Grace Greenaway, a widow with Royalist sympathies, for her considerable fortune.

Grace and Jamie had thrilled to be one of the singular circle that knew the King. They had divided their time between New-York and London. Unfortunately for Grace, one of her times in New-York had been in '98. And so she became a member of another singular group: one of the fifteen hundred dead from Yellow Fever.

After Grace's death, Jamie had settled in New-York, living the life of a wealthy landowner. Grace's money allowed him to give up practicing physick and surgery and turn instead to land speculation. More than that, Jamie was an officer of the Collect Company.

To be fair, he'd come forward to rescue Peter from John's ire and had gotten him the position as secretary to Thaddeus Brown, the Commissioner of Streets, who was in charge of the Collect project for the City. "Come now, John," Jamie had cajoled, "not everyone has the vocation for medicine."

True, thought Mariana. Not everyone has. But she saw it burn in the eyes of her younger daughter, Leah, as it had in her own when she was not much older. Some day, Mariana was certain, girls would be allowed to attend classes at Columbia. Some day. She dried her tears and rose to return the book to its place. She paused. Women. Mariana felt a moment of panic, and the nausea and fever started again. She dropped her shawl and fanned herself with her hand. She sat and opened the book again, leafing through it for references to women, female. Ah. Female reproduction. Cessation of female . . . She began to read.

Climacteric. A period of decrease of reproductive capacity. *Hystericus*—hysteria. Uncontrollable outburst of emotion or fear, laughter, weeping, being peculiar to women and caused by disturbances in the uterus.

Her malady, then, was being a woman.

10

30 JANUARY. SATURDAY. MORNING.

Did it make any difference? Mariana asked herself. She had returned to their bedroom and was dressing while John slept on. She stared resentfully at her husband. He lay on his back, emitting short grumpy snores.

She cinched the straps of her corset, wondering what had happened to the girl she'd been. Whither Mariana, young patriot, giddy with a lad's freedom in her brother's clothes, ready to take on the entire British army and the world?

This being the Sabbath, she put on her newest dress of rich purple cotton with woven stripes. The bodice was demurely cut, high and narrow, with white muslin shirring around the neckline, its sleeves puffed at the shoulder, long and narrow to the wrists. The skirt, soft and sleek, was tied with a tassled cord at her back and covered her ankles.

Although her dark hair hadn't lost its luster, it showed white strands here and there along the center part and in the chignon at her nape, but not in the curls around her face.

Muffled squeals and footsteps outside her door told her that the girls were about. Mariana smiled. They had no doubt discovered that their brother had returned.

She stepped into the hall. From behind Peter's door, high-pitched giggling and an unhappy grunt.

Mariana opened the door. Leah and Gretel were trouncing their brother, who lay on his stomach with a pillow resolutely over his head. While Peter was blond, almost pure Tonneman, looking like a Christian, the girls were her family, with the dark skin and hair of the Mendozas of Judea and Spain.

"Oh, look, Lee," Gretel cried. "The prodigal has returned and is sleeping. He must have drunk the magic potion again."

Another muffled grunt from Peter.

"Girls, this won't do. Your father was out late. He is still asleep."

They didn't even pause.

"Girls, if you don't stop torturing your brother and making all this racket I'll get Old Hays after you." That was the signal: *Mama has had enough.*

"Yes, Mama."

"Yes, Mama."

Mariana shook a cautionary finger at her daughters, then turned back to her son.

"Go away. Leave me be." Peter's head felt as big as the two-mile stone, and twice as heavy.

"Girls, downstairs. Micah has your porridge."

Gretel put her hands on her hips. Her dark eyes, so like Mariana's, sparkled. "Mama? May we go to the Circus?"

"Ask your father."

"But if you—"

"Go. Do as I say."

Compliant, but hardly repressing further giggles, the girls danced out of their brother's chamber in a taffeta flurry of bright colors, and thundered down the stairs.

Peter rolled over and lifted the pillow from his bloodshot eyes. He groaned. "Are they gone?" His day clothes, which he still wore, were creased and crumpled.

Not responding, Mariana brushed back her errant son's blond forelock. "Where have you been? All week, your mother's been yearning for her little hero."

"Villain's more like it!"

John Tonneman, the patriarch in his dressing gown, stood in Peter's doorway, his white hair still half wild from the pillow, his brow furrowed, his eyes hard and angry.

"Sir." Agitated, Peter attempted to sit up. He groaned, lost his balance, and fell back on his pillow.

Mariana caressed her son's cheek and gently tucked the covers back around him. "Rest."

Exhausted, the youth fell straightaway to sleep.

The elder Tonneman snorted. He held a segar in his hand.

"Must you?" Mariana asked.

John Tonneman's answer was to cram the unlit segar into his mouth.

Mariana looked down at Peter's wan face. "He's still so young. . . ."

Tonneman glared at his sleeping son. "He's a grown man of nineteen. You baby him. He should cast away childish things and act his age."

"Oh, John."

"Don't oh, John me. You've spoiled him all his life and whenever I've tried to straighten him out, you've said, 'Oh, John.'"

"Oh, John."

Peter moaned and put the pillow over his head.

Tonneman wanted to kick something. His son would do nicely. Instead, he settled for the fire fender, which he then had to set right again when it fell over with a crash. Peter didn't even stir. "He's been gone for over a week this time. Don't you think that a little amiss?"

"Oh, John."

John Tonneman ran a forefinger along the jagged scar that dented his left eyebrow, then looked over his spectacles at his wife. After thirty-two years she was still dear to him, but she had a blind spot about Peter. The boy was her darling whom she coddled almost to death. He became the center of her world after David died, and remained so to this day. Well, Peter wasn't a boy any longer. He had a name to live up to. His father was a respected physician, the City Commissioner of Health, and responsible for the Collect Project, along with Thaddeus Brown, the Commissioner of Streets.

After Jamie had found Peter employment as Brown's secretary, John Tonneman hoped that it wouldn't be long before his son would be an officer of the company and on his way in life. But if he kept up this dissipation, acting like a sailor and disappearing to God knew where, Peter would end up drinking his life away.

At this time John Tonneman was equally concerned regarding the whereabouts of Thaddeus Brown, whose disappearance with the cashbox of the Collect Company had coincided with Peter's. Now Peter had returned. Where the hell was Brown?

Tonneman stamped to the bed and shook his son's shoulder. "Peter!"

Pain exploded in Peter's head. "Leave me be," he moaned.

Old Tonneman persisted.

His son snarled, "You do that again, Tedious, and I'll kill you."

"Oh." Mariana's hand flew to her mouth.

Disgusted, John snatched the pillow away and pinched the end of his son's nose.

"Ow!" Peter cried, coming full awake. "What did you do that for?"

"Where in tarnation have you been?" John's hands were shaking. Was it anger or that damn tremor come back to afflict him?

"Language, John," Mariana whispered.

Now John Tonneman felt like shaking his wife. Instead, he shook his son. "Explain yourself, young man."

The boy, his color quite green, leaned over the bed. His mother quickly pulled the chamber pot from under the bed. The boy retched into the pot.

"Now look what you've done," Mariana chided.

John Tonneman, disgusted, left his son's bedchamber.

Over the years he'd continued his practice of maintaining an open surgery. When he'd married Mariana Mendoza, he'd studied and learned the basics of Judaism. He admired the philosophy but he wasn't much of an observant Jew. After his father-in-law, David Mendoza, died, he continued attending services on Friday night at the synagogue in Millstreet, but put his foot down about Saturday services. Still, even though they no longer attended Synagogue on Saturday, the surgery was open on the Sabbath only for emergencies.

Of late, as he aged and his old patients had begun to die off, so had his practice.

His toilette complete, Old Tonneman went downstairs. He could still hear the murmur of voices from his son's room. In the kitchen Micah was peeling potatoes and his daughters were jabbering as they dawdled over their porridge. When he entered the room the girls brightened.

Micah put down her knife and went to the stove for the pot of coffee. They had installed Ben Franklin's stove in the kitchen three years earlier; otherwise, it remained the same spacious, broad-beamed kitchen it had been in John's father's time. Miraculously, the house had survived the fire of '76 with only scorching, and in '78, the conflagration had not touched it.

They had put in a new brick floor fifteen years ago, but the hearth and the bake oven were the same. John Tonneman had teethed his first incisor on the legs of the large oak table. Two more tables had been added, and additional storage space. The family tended to gather in these pleasant surroundings.

"Good morning, daughters."

"Good morning, Papa."

"Good morning, Micah."

"Will you be wanting breakfast, Doctor Tonneman?"

"Just the coffee." As he went into the sitting room, he could hear his daughters squabbling about who was going to bring him his coffee.

"I'll take it."

"No, it's my turn."

This pleased him. He turned as Leah presented him with the sturdy blue Delft cup which had been in his family as far back as he could remember. "Thank you, Leah."

His youngest child curtsied and grinned. "You're very welcome, Papa."

Behind her, Gretel pouted.

Tonneman set his cup down on the breakfast table and held out his arms. "Come. Both my beautiful girls."

After the hug Tonneman patted Gretel's face. "Would you like to do something for me?"

"Yes, Papa. Papa, will you let us go to the Circus?"

"Don't try to bargain with me. You must do as I ask you unconditionally."

"Yes, Papa."

"I'm near out of iron water. Do you know how to make more?"

"I'll show her," Leah said.

"I know how," Gretel insisted, glaring at her younger sister.

"It's easy," Leah said. Then very rapidly, "All you have to do is put the nails in the water—"

Then the two were saying it, loud and fast, in a contest. "The nails get rusty, the rust goes into the water, and—" Gretel stepped on her younger sister's toe. While Leah screamed Gretel concluded, "And Papa has a styptic to stem the flow of blood."

"That will be all, girls." John had little patience for any of his children today. He was concerned about the future of the Collect Project. Streets Commissioner Brown was missing. Peter had disappeared at the same time. The cash box was missing. Anyone could logically conclude that Brown and Peter, or either of them, stole the cash box and the money it contained. And there was the state of the books and that damn note. Peter had a great deal of explaining to do. If Jake Hays ever got his terrier teeth into this sorry affair, there would be hell to pay. Peter would be disgraced and the Collect Project itself might suffer.

The sisters retreated, but only to the door of the kitchen. They stared with moon eyes as their father approached the mantel.

On the mantel sat a wooden box with the legend *Instantaneous Light Box,* carved in script and colored scarlet. John Tonneman took a small wooden splint from the several in another box on the mantel. He dipped the splint, a match treated with a composition of potassium chlorate, sugar, and gum arabic, into the box in which a bottle of sulphuric acid was set, then withdrew it. The match burst into flame. "Ooh," his daughters crooned appreciatively. Smiling at them and his accomplishment, John Tonneman lit his segar.

The girls watched agog. Even though the Light Box had been in the house for over a year, they never got over how it made fire. After all, everyone else used an ordinary tinder box, which was flint and steel. Because the Instantaneous Light Box was dangerous in inexperienced hands, their father was the only one in the household who ever used it.

Tonneman waved the segar so that the pungent smell of the burning leaves would perfume the air in the house and thwart the stink of his son's sour stomach.

He heard Mariana's light footstep on the stairs, then the sound of crockery smashing overhead.

"Oh, dear." Mariana's steps faltered.

"Leave it," Tonneman ordered. "He probably broke the basin." It was what John Tonneman himself had done as a young man, when he was in London and living the life of a rakehell, drinking and whoring all night and studying surgery in the day. Tonneman took a thoughtful drag of smoke from his segar. Jamie had pulled him out of his hellish ways, which was why he now trusted Jamie with his son's life.

"Micah," Mariana called. "Inquire if my son needs assistance." She turned to her daughters. "Come, girls, help me make breakfast for your father and brother."

Moments later, a sheepish Peter appeared in the sitting room. "I broke the chamber pot."

"O grab me," the Tonneman girls said as one.

"Sickening," said Gretel.

"Dignity," said Mariana, going into the kitchen.

Micah nodded stoically and went off to get her bucket and rags.

John Tonneman glared at his son. "Where in hell have you been, boy?"

"That's none of your affair."

"I'm your father and you're still under my roof." Tonneman was exasperated. "And where is Brown?"

Peter, in shirtsleeves, wiped his brow with his arm. He was sweating. "What do you mean?"

"No one has seen the man since Friday last. The two of you went missing at the same time. At first, I thought you might have gone off together."

Peter snickered. "Not bloody likely."

"Language, Peter," Mariana cautioned as she emerged from the kitchen.

"Yes, Mother." The young man grinned.

But John Tonneman's expression remained grim. "Then I rejected that thought."

Peter saluted his father. "Thank you for that."

In Mariana's hands were a vial of essence of peppermint and an earthenware dish. She set the dish on the mantel, poured some peppermint into it, and placed the open vial next to it. The chamber was now pungent with peppermint and Virginia tobacco.

Tonneman snorted and gestured at the dish. "Is that for your husband's segar or your son's vomit?"

"O grab me," the girls chorused.

Mariana and Tonneman exchanged bitter glances.

Tonneman turned back to his son. "This is serious, boy. I stopped by Brown's office, and when I saw the way it looked I didn't know what had happened. I've gotten used to you going off, but this is too much."

"Yes." Peter held his head high, daring further comment. "It is something I do."

"But Brown is a different story. In his position he's responsible for the Collect Company money."

"A position which should have been mine." Peter's mouth went through a series of mops and mows. "I really need a drink, Papa." He clenched his hands to his sides to conceal their shaking.

"Couldn't he have just one, John?"

Offended by his son and his wife, but beyond argument, Tonneman shrugged.

Mariana poured her son a half tumbler of brandy. The boy watched anxiously. But before she gave it to him, she slowly and methodically chose the proper walnut from the dish on the cherrywood sideboard. Just as slowly and methodically, she picked up the red-white-and-blue George Washington nutcracker, placed the walnut between General Washington's oversized jaws, and cracked the nut open. When the meat was in her hands, she held it out to her son. "First food, then drink."

"Oh, Ma," Peter said, but he obeyed. He chewed a bit

of nut quickly, then took the thick glass from her and greedily drained its contents. His father's undisguised contempt galled him, made him long to strike back.

Old Tonneman was just as irked with his feelings about his son. The day was too young for him to drink, but in light of what the boy was putting him through he thought he deserved one. He poured himself a hearty taste of brandy. "I've been going through the books."

Grinning, Peter peered at his father over the rim of his bulky glass. "What's wrong, Father? Don't you trust Tedious anymore?"

"They've been cooked to a turn."

Young Tonneman's arrogant grin spread wider. "There. I told you so. I've always said I was the man for that job."

John Tonneman reached into his waistcoat pocket. He brought out a folded paper. He unfolded it slowly and thrust it at his son. "Unfortunately, he's also left a note saying that it is you who's been stealing money and falsifying the accounts."

Peter's grin vanished. "Oh, no, Papa. Damn him to hell."

"Peter, language."

The two Tonneman men looked at Mariana. Neither knew how to explain to her how serious this matter was. Peter was close to tears. "What am I going to do, Papa? What am I going to do?"

Mariana rushed to her son and cradled him in her arms. "Dignity, Peter," she said, because she could think of nothing else to say. "Always dignity."

11

30 JANUARY. SATURDAY. MORNING.

John Tonneman glared at his son. "Where in hell *have* you
been, boy?"

Peter shook his head. His mind reeled, his thoughts
churned. Where indeed?

EXACTLY ONE WEEK before, in the midst of a sudden
snowstorm, while riding the almost obliterated road south
to Princeton, Peter Tonneman thought he heard the hoot
of an owl above the whining wind. "In this weather?" he
mumbled drunkenly into his muffler. "Good day, snowy
owl. I can't see you. Can you see me? How can I see you?

With your white plumage and brown markings you look like a leaf. Hoo. Hoo, hoo, hoo." In a moment the youth's intoxicated hoot became a fearful cry.

His mount slipped and lurched. "What on—" Only dimwitted luck saved Peter from falling into the ravine just at the mare's feet. That and the animal's brute strength. The mare neighed wildly and dug in her hooves. Snow had drifted as high as the young man's stirrups. He leaned forward, patted the animal's neck, and groped in his saddlebag for his flask.

The snow danced and whirled about him. Sharp, frosty fragments stabbed his face. Peter, holding tight to his beaver hat, drank long from the small leather flask. Too long a drink, too small a flask. Empty. That was happening to him a great deal lately.

A sign. His mother had taught him that the world was a mystical place. Surely, just missing death like this was an omen. He had made a mess of his life, yet Providence had saved him. To what avail? For what purpose?

After the to-do with Tedious and the threats that were tantamount to his ruination, Peter had known immediately there was nothing for him in New-York. His Uncle Ben in Princeton might be able to help. Perhaps a place on his newspaper. The only thing Peter knew for certain was that he had once again disgraced himself and his family.

Again the cry. Not an owl, not a bird. An animal. Peter thrust the flask back in the bag. Ophelia nickered, snorting white steam, which married with the snow. Her ears flattened: she pawed the drifts till a space cleared in front of her.

From somewhere below came another cry. This was no owl. Young Tonneman set his right hand over his eyes and peered into the ravine. The cry came yet again. Perhaps thirty feet down, he thought he saw movement. Was that a flutter of darkness against the white? Cupping his hands about his mouth he called, "Hallo, down there!" The wind howled. His snow-deadened words fell flat. Perhaps he'd been mistaken.

"Help . . ." A faint voice. Movement again. In the same place. He could make out a small figure in black, almost obscured by the swirling snow. A woman, he thought. She struggled, trying to get some purchase on the slippery slope of the ravine. Frantically, she thrust her hands into the drifts, searching desperately for a handhold. At last she found a tree limb and clung to it.

Peter dismounted and immediately stubbed his foot on a boulder hidden by the snow. Cursing, he tied Ophelia's reins to a nearby scraggy fir. His desire for drink was almost overwhelming, but he had work to do. And the flask was empty. Painstakingly, he stomped a treacherous path toward the figure in black below. The woman watched his descent, her face at one with the snow.

"Give me your hand," he called, as he edged closer. Her face was small and pinched, her lips blue-tinged. Her head was bare. Her dark hair flew about her face in icy strands. He found a branch of his own to hold. "Your hand," he repeated, extending his own.

Their hands touched. Briefly. Parted. Touched again. This time he held on, seizing so tightly the woman cried out with pain. Her tiny gloved hand seemed sculpted of ice. He pulled her toward him.

"The coach," she gasped. "The snow—slipped—fell— falling . . . falling . . ." Her slight body trembled. ". . . the children."

Good God, Peter thought. The coach from Philadelphia. "Don't talk. Don't waste your strength," he told her. She was but a child herself.

Hands clasped, he led. They made laborious progress up the steep grade, slipping frequently, stopping to catch breaths. The fury of the storm made the air a shroud of snow. All at once Ophelia's noble head, white patches on her blackness, came into view, peering into the ravine. Peter Tonneman clutched at mane and reins and pulled himself and the girl the last precious inches out of the ravine.

Ophelia neighed and flicked her tail at the snow.

Only now was Peter able to get a good look at the woman. She was petite, with ghostly skin, blue eyes and dark hair. Her clothes—black, mourning clothes—were frozen stiff. Shivering, she clung to him. He held her in his arms, feeling at once strong, proud, and moved by her plight. Was this what Providence had saved him for?

"My baby—" She swooned in his arms.

He was baffled. Was the child lost in the snow? He looked about. It was madness to stop now. He would find nothing in all this white emptiness.

Although he had paid little heed to his father and his surgery, Peter recognized that the girl was in shock. In addition to her dreadful pallor, her face glistened with new moisture; the acrid-sweet scent of her cut through the cold air. She was sweating profusely. The beat of her heart next to his was weak.

Peter wrapped his blue cloak about her and gathered her closer into his arms. Ophelia was calm as he mounted with his burden.

Though every moment was crucial, he forced himself to circle the ravine in the hopes he would find another sign of life. The missing child, perhaps. There was none. Ophelia, impatient for shelter from the storm, pulled at her reins. Finally, chilled and snowblind, Tonneman reluctantly yielded to the mare's good sense and turned her back the way he'd come, toward Hoboken. He brushed the snow and freezing sweat from the girl's face, then with a sudden thought he removed his beaver hat from his head and placed it on hers. Rawls's Inn was closest. He would take her there.

Peter Tonneman had quite forgotten that he was running away.

An hour later, Tonneman left the girl in the care of Mrs. Rawls, a bustling goosedown pillow in a dress, and joined the search party, led by Fred Rawls, the innkeeper. The north wind had not lessened; snow continued to fall. The fir tree where he had tied Ophelia was all but hidden from view. He thought he knew the spot where he'd pulled the girl out, but he couldn't be certain. There was no sign of the Philadelphia coach. The ravine was an unbroken valley of white. It would be courting death to attempt any descent until the storm passed. The search party returned to the inn.

Mrs. Rawls was full to bursting with the story she had prised from the girl, whose name, Mrs. Rawls informed them, was Charity Boenning. A family of four, the coach driver, and his apprentice had undoubtedly perished in the storm. By God's grace, Charity Boenning had been thrown clear of the coach; her skirts had caught the branch which saved her life. The snow had broken her fall. It was a miracle the poor lass hadn't lost the unborn child she carried.

Exhausted, young Tonneman sank into a chair by the blazing hearth, and took several sips of the hot toddy Mrs. Rawls kindly presented him. The strong odor of cloves floated up from the mug. He inhaled the pungent aroma in the steam, but the memory of Charity Boenning's scent was his last thought before he floated into a deep sleep.

Mr. Rawls woke him with a light hand on his shoulder. "She's asking for you."

Tonneman ran his hands through his hair and neatened his waistcoat and collar as he climbed the stairs behind Mrs. Rawls. The cheerful woman talked with her hands in motion, her candle making flickering shadows on the staircase.

"We've made up a room for you, Mr. Tonneman. Only the Devil himself would be out in this storm." The landlady led him down a dark, narrow corridor. His head came near to the low ceiling. She stopped and tapped on a door.

A servant girl in worn green calico, clenching a rough knitted brown shawl about her thin shoulders, led them into the chamber. The small fire gave the chamber only a modicum of heat. "Oh, sir. She's been waiting to see you."

"Thank you, Flora. She needs her rest, Mr. Tonneman, so don't you stay long." Giving the fire a determined poke with an iron, Mrs. Rawls added, "And so do you from the look of you. I've put you down the hall. We'll send up a tray."

He nodded, distracted by the girl propped up in the bed, her small body making hardly a swell in the bedclothes. It was difficult to believe she was with child. Only now, as he approached, did he notice the gold band on her finger. In spite of the bruises on her face she was very beautiful. Her eyes were huge and of the darkest blue. Her thick red-brown hair had been plaited. Her scent, which he likened to frankincense, was sweeter than before. The scent, combined with her blue eyes so intent on him, made it difficult for him to swallow.

"Please sit," she said, patting the bed. "Mr. . . . ?"

Mrs. Rawls cleared her throat and shoved a pine armchair in place behind him.

Peter remained standing. "Tonneman. Peter Tonneman."

"Charity Boenning." She held out a small hand, her skin almost transparent with fine blue veins. Touching it for a moment, he sat stiffly in the pine chair. He felt ill at ease and awkward. His tongue was tied up in knots.

"You are one of the bravest men I've ever met. I want to thank you for my life." Tears welled in her eyes. "Those poor people . . ."

"I only did what anyone would do, ma'am," he answered, his words foundering over his poor, tied tongue.

"I understand you are from New-York, Mr. Tonneman." Mrs. Boenning's cheeks were slightly flushed but her exquisite eyes continued to hold him.

"Yes, ma'am."

"I am on my way there to stay with my kinsman. I trust you will call on us so that we can thank you properly."

Peter Tonneman nodded, rising, unsteady on his feet. What was he to do? "If you'll excuse me." He backed away toward the door shaken to his core. He was running from a scandal that would shame his parents and destroy his life. Now, of all times, he had met the girl who had taken his heart. And she was married and with child.

At the door he paused. "Was your husband in the carriage with you?"

Her eyes glistened but did not overflow. "No, Mr. Tonneman," she replied. "My husband was spared that ordeal. He died in Philadelphia two months ago."

•———————•

Wet Nurse

A WET NURSE *with a fresh Breast of Milk and good*
recommendations, may hear of a place by inquiring at
54 Fair-street.

NEW-YORK HERALD
JANUARY 1808

•———————•

12

30 JANUARY. SATURDAY. MORNING.

His rescue of the Widow Boenning would change Peter's
life. Where he had been was not the most important thing.
Who he had been with, that was the thing.

The Rawlses invited their guests to Sunday services the
following day in the parlor of the inn. Peter chose to remain in his chamber. The day's passage was long and hum-
drum, for the snow had continued well into the night. It
would be impossible, even dangerous, to travel. Peter,
though bored, was content to stay in bed and keep warm.

He was hardly a scholar; still, he tried to amuse himself
with the two books on the nightstand next to the narrow
bed. One was a Christian Bible with both Testaments.

He flipped the pages of the Bible wishing he had a drink
instead. A word caught his eye. He stopped but his fingers

were already past the place. Try as he might, even searching for almost an hour he couldn't find the section again. Still, that was surely another sign. The word had been *widow*.

The other book was by Thomas More, and it was in Latin. Peter had never been a good student of the classics. He set the volume aside. Since there was nothing else in the room to occupy him, certainly no spirits, he went back to the Bible, first searching for the widow again, then looking through the Old Testament for stories his mother had told him. By that time all the begats did for him was make him drowsy. The New Testament with its various versions of the same story were equally monotonous and more bewildering. Peter was not of a religious bent, and scholarship, well . . .

He returned to the second book, *Utopia*. Peter had been tutored in Latin but he didn't know an *amo* from an *amat*. Happily, a previous reader had made notes in the margins, and he was able to crawl through the story. Thus Peter learned that the fictional Utopia was an island with fifty-four cities just off South America. All property in this republic, which had been a kingdom, was held in common and the general good was paramount. The Utopians wondered much to hear that gold, in itself useless, should everywhere be so esteemed. And that even man, for whom gold was made, and who gave it value, was thought of as having less value than the gold itself.

Peter's eyes widened wildly at such a ridiculous belief. He was tempted to hurl the book against the wall but instead placed it back on the nightstand with the Bible.

Snow continued to fall. The wind shifted, raising temperatures. The resulting rain came down in torrents. Wind rattled the shutters, smashed tree branches against and otherwise shook the inn.

In the late afternoon, when the Bible and Mr. More had him almost to distraction, he called for the hired girl, Flora, to fetch him hot water. Shaved and dressed, he went down the stairs. Much to his delight a quite recovered

Charity Boenning was ensconced in the sitting room. Mrs. Rawls was laying out tea and poppy-seed cakes.

And to his further delight Charity invited him to join her. When she smiled at him he was once more unable to speak. Mrs. Rawls fussed with the napkins, as if waiting to hear what he would say. The absence of speech finally confounded Mrs. Rawls, and she withdrew.

The moment of silence extended. When Flora appeared with Peter's cup and saucer, she ogled the couple for a moment, and then reluctantly left, too.

Peter jumped up nervously. "Shall I pour, then?"

Charity, bemused, responded. "Yes, please, forgive me. My hands are still trembling. I keep thinking about those poor people who perished."

"And well you might. It's a true miracle you did not. Do you take milk?"

She nodded. "You are my miracle, Mr. Tonneman." Her eyes settled on the shuttered windows, which hid the view of the torrent outdoors. "Mrs. Rawls informs me that it has stopped snowing."

Peter, careful not to drop the pewter pitcher and not to spill anything, mumbled, "Raining."

"Mr. Rawls has arranged for a coach and driver for me to continue my journey to New-York tomorrow, if the roads are passable."

She seemed so frail. Peter stirred more sugar into his cup than he usually took. He didn't dare look into her eyes, for he would dissolve like the sugar. "Are you well enough to travel, Mrs. Boenning?"

"Oh, yes. I'm eager to complete my journey."

He held a plate out to her. "Cake?"

She shook her head. He couldn't help noticing the way the large dark curls swayed. Very softly she asked, "You told me that New-York was your home. Will you be riding with me, Mr. Tonneman?"

"Oh, no. I'm on my way to Princeton. My Uncle Ben prints a journal there. *The Guardian.*"

"Oh?"

There was another long silence while they sipped their tea.

Out of the blue she asked, "What does 'o grab me' mean?"

He laughed, full and loud. It was the first natural thing he'd done all morning. "Don't they say it in Philadelphia? It's all over New-York. Embargo, backwards. . . ."

Charity mulled this for a few seconds, then set her cup and saucer down.

"For Mr. Jefferson's Embargo . . ." Peter continued.

The blue eyes flashed. "No need to tell me more. I'm not a complete ninny. I do know what the Embargo is."

"A thousand pardons. I didn't mean to offend you, Mrs. Boenning."

"And you didn't, Mr. Tonneman. O grab me. I like it. Will you be traveling back to New-York soon?" She fixed him with her velvety eyes.

Truth to tell, Peter Tonneman had lost his resolution to permanently leave the City from the moment he stumbled upon Charity Boenning and saved her life. At this moment he was near overcome, which wouldn't do at all. "On the contrary, Mrs. Boenning, I will escort you to New-York. Now that I've met you, I could not do otherwise."

"O grab me," Charity Boenning said, blushing prettily.

BY THE NEXT day, the storm had about run its course. Rain came down in great sheets, washing away the snow. And it was agreed that Peter would escort Mrs. Boenning back to New-York, to her kinsman. In the meantime, as he waited for her to make her appearance, he was content to sit in front of the fire in the inn's parlor and dwell on the possibilities before him.

Charity Boenning had enchanted him. She was a widow. After her period of mourning, she would be free to marry again. Her widow's weeds were simple. Did that mean she was modest? Or without money? She was with child. An impoverished widow with a child.

None of this dismayed Peter. He had quite determined to make Charity his wife. He would let her kinsman know his intentions.

But if he were to marry, he would first have to get his position back with the Collect Company. He would become a new Peter Tonneman, a man his father could be proud of, a man who could care for a wife and child.

Only one man could make this all happen for him. His godfather, Jamie.

Peter jumped to his feet as Mrs. Rawls, carrying a large blue greatcoat, led the way down the stairs. Behind her, appearing quite fit in her restored black dress and a borrowed blue bonnet, was Charity Boenning. There was high color in her pale cheeks. Was it her condition? Her adventure? Him? He rushed forward, meeting them at the foot of the stairs, and waited for Mrs. Rawls to pass before offering Charity his arm.

"Now you take care of yourself and that baby," Mrs. Rawls instructed, wrapping Charity in the greatcoat. "You can send my coat back to me when you're settled."

"You have been so kind," Charity said. "But what will you wear?"

"I can wear my Sunday coat. Made it myself." She looked at each of the young people for a moment, awaiting a comment, but they were absorbed in each other. Mrs. Rawls smiled broadly. There was little doubt that the Widow Boenning would not remain a widow for long. Mrs. Rawls drew an umbrella from the stand which stood at the door and handed it to Peter. "We've sent a message to your kinsman in New-York to meet you at the ferry," she told Charity.

Outside, an unhappy Ophelia waited in the chill downpour. The mare was tied to the back of the coach, which was to take them to the ferry at Hoboken and thence to

Manhattan. Peter sheltered both women beneath the umbrella as they hastened to the coach.

Mr. Rawls was seated atop a wagon piled high with ropes and chains. The innkeeper and four mounted men were heading out, too, a search party looking for the bodies of the other travelers on the Philadelphia coach.

"Good trip to New-York," Mr. Rawls bawled out as he and his party rode off over ground steeped with mud. Everyone knew that there was no hope of finding anyone alive. "But at least," in Mrs. Rawls's words, "they will have a Christian burial."

With Charity installed within, Mrs. Rawls placed a cloth-covered, ash-splint basket on her lap. "Just a bit of sustenance for your journey," she said, with a broad smile.

Peter climbed aboard, sat opposite Charity, and they were off. Passage to the New-York-bound ferry was arduous. More than once Peter had to get out and push when the carriage wheels spun uselessly in the oozing mud. He was grateful for Mrs. Rawls's basket, which they shared eagerly just outside Hoboken.

Upon their arrival, they found a shaggy collection of wet souls huddled at the terminal, two fine-looking gentlemen, merchants or bankers, and four fancy-dressed women.

Charity stared at the women, open-mouthed.

Peter smiled. "You'll catch flies."

"Are those . . . ?"

"Yes."

She blushed.

Shortly after noon, all boarded the ferry to New-York. The late January thaw had melted the snow, and massive chunks of ice floated freely in the North River. The rain had finally ceased and the noon sun on the ice dazzled the eye. Peter and Charity enjoyed its thin warmth as they watched the boat's progress between the marshlands of New Jersey and the splendid clutter of Manhattan. After a time, they went inside the cabin, which was fitted with

sturdy maplewood and comfortably cushioned. Peter helped
Charity to a seat and stood beside her.

"Chestnuts," a Negro man sang. "Hot roasted chestnuts." He shook the blackened pan frequently.

Peter bought some, wrapped in newspaper, which they
shared. Through the isinglass windows New-York appeared
magical, the fabled Gotham of Washington Irving.

Peter Tonneman looked down at his companion. "The
City is so beautiful," he said. He was oddly excited about
coming home. She took his offered arm. They went out
onto the narrow deck. The air was cool, with a surprising
hint of balm. In his nervousness he began blathering. "Do
you know about Mr. Fulton's steamboat? Last August, it
was. The *Clermont*. Can you imagine? They say it goes five
miles an hour. In August it went up this very river. *Fulton's
Folly*, they called it. But now it's a fact. We can ride on it
together some day—" He stopped. Had he gone too fast?
Too far?

But Charity nodded, unperturbed. After a time she said,
"You're right. The City is beautiful."

"See." He pointed, expelling a relieved breath. New-
York was coming into view clear as an etching on a copper
plate. Gotham, the fairyland, the land of myths.

"Oh, my," she said softly, shading her eyes. Charity
Boenning looked up at Peter Tonneman. "My husband used
to say—he was well-traveled—he'd even been to China.
He said the Chinese have a saying. If you save someone's
life, you are responsible for it forever after."

He took her hand, then, flustered, dropped it.

She laughed. "Have no fear, Mr. Tonneman. I release
you from the obligation."

"You don't understand," he said quickly. "I don't wish
to be released." Gazing at his City coming toward him,
Peter felt born again. Repaired, body and soul. He was in
love.

Charity took a deep breath. Perhaps, she thought. Perhaps. There were tears flowing down her cheeks when the ferry docked at Peck's-slip. "I am so happy to be here."

Porters came on board to fetch luggage and unload cargo. A stocky man in a brown cap limped over to them. "Mrs. Boenning?" When she nodded, the man said, "I was told to fetch you. Where's your bags?" She handed him the empty lunch basket with a small smile. Her eyes searched the docking area. "There he is," she cried excitedly.

"Where?" asked the young man in love.

"There. The gentleman in black. Do you know him?"

Peter's jaw dropped. It was difficult to be a citizen of New-York and not know the man in black. Charity Boenning's kinsman was the High Constable of New-York, Jacob Hays.

13

30 January. Saturday. Morning to nightfall.

The snow reappeared suddenly. It fell heavily and swiftly. And the winds blew swirls in Duffy's face. The thing at his feet was quickly covered. He cleared the patch with the toe of his boot and saw that it was more than just a hand reaching out to him; the rest was buried in the near-frozen ground.

Duffy could hear the muffled talk of his fellow workers around the Pond. He shouted to them, but the snow swallowed his words. It was like at sea in a storm. So close but so far. He looked again for Fred Smithers. But if Fred was there, Duffy couldn't see him.

Bill Duffy was not a superstitious man, or so he told

himself. But he had no intention of waiting around for all the demons of hell to reach out of the cursed ground to grab him. Duffy was off, half-blinded by the snow, racing down Chapel-street.

He'd heard tell that the High Constable hereabouts could often be found at the Tontine Coffee-House at Pearl and Wall near Coffee-House Slip. A long way.

As suddenly as it started, the snow stopped and Bill Duffy stopped, too. Running like a chick with its head chopped off was not the answer. What was he afraid of? A dead man? When somebody came along, he would show them what he'd found. Meantime he'd do his labor so he could get his paltry pay and feed his growling stomach. He swung around and walked back to the Lispenards and his work.

Nothing had changed. The others were still working their areas, most loading mud from the Collect into waiting carts. But Fred Smithers was gone. And to his right, no one, not even an overseer, was to be seen. Always around when you didn't want them but never around when you did. Duffy snatched up his rake and knocked its frosty covering off against his raggy boot. He avoided the hand.

After a few minutes of raking vigorously, he slowed almost to a stop. What was he doing? There was snow on the ground so thick he couldn't tell the rubbish from the earth. As if to contradict him, his rake found something. He bent to pick it up. A clam. Was it edible? He sniffed the mollusk. Half frozen and a bit high, but all in all, it appeared to be all right. Duffy crossed himself and ate the clam.

What he craved now were a dozen more. And a tall draught of spirits. Rum. And a segar would be oh, so fine. He closed his eyes for a moment.

"Is that what they pay you for? To sleep standing up? Like a horse?"

Before him stood a hog of a man. His face was almost hidden by the long yellow muffler tied around his head, holding an old-fashioned bicorne in place. The top of his green greatcoat was held together by a five-pointed brass star.

"Constable. You're exactly the man I want to see. I found a dead man over there."

"I'm not—" The yellow scarf unfolded one time, revealing three separate chins on a fat face. "—the man you want. This is the Fifth Ward. I'm in the Third. But I'll tell the Copper when I see him."

As green as Duffy was about New-York, he did know that the Copper was the sergeant who wore a copper star. The fat Constable moved away through the snow as quick as bacon through a duck's ass. If he was from the Third, what the bloody hell was the man doing in the Fifth? Probably up to no good. Duffy spat. The freezing wind blew it back in his face. With all the snow he didn't bother to wipe it off. Duffy didn't like the Constables in this town. They were mean and shiftless. Didn't put in a fair day for their wage. Jesus only knew which was worse, them or the criminals, of which he heard tell these were a goodly number.

At that moment the clam turned on him. Duffy gagged and threw up the clam, the barley soup, and whatever was left in his stomach of the dollop of rabbit he'd had the day before. Altogether, today was an evil day.

He wiped his mouth with the sleeve of his pea jacket. There was nothing for it then but to get through this day and pray for a bit of hot food at the end of it. He pulled the collar of the short, double-breasted coat tighter to him, planted a driftwood stake next to the hand, and kept working.

At dusk he hurried to the paymaster in Collect-street, and turned in his rake and barrow. He was thinking to mention the body to the paymaster, but when he looked up the man was gone. Cursing New-York and the Embargo and Mr. Thomas Jefferson, Duffy trudged the nine blocks toward the City limits and the almshouse in Chambers-street. For the edge of town it was a busy place.

Also in Chambers-street was the Manhattan Company's reservoir, a foreign-looking thing, with columns in front and that big statue of Neptune on top, like something he'd seen in one of those eastern countries, he'd forgotten which.

This was where they were building the new City Hall and where, he noted, they had already duplicated the old gallows, whipping posts, and stocks. Duffy hooted. Two sets of gallows was always better than one.

He received his scant ration of oat grits and potato soup in the gray stone building and gulped down the watery gruel. Should he say to the African soup man, "I found a hand today, out at the Collect"? The darky could have cared less.

Duffy sneered and went back on the street where he saw that no work was being done that day on the new hall. Now that his qualmish stomach had eased off he could think a bit. He'd heard that the laborers on the hall made a good wage. Who could he see about getting on that job? He'd come here early Monday morning, that's what he'd do.

The almshouse was a block beyond the City Hall site. West of the new hall was Bridewell, the prison. East of the hall, the City Jail. Across from them all, a big park, which Duffy had used more than once as a bedchamber when he hadn't had a roof. He decided to go into the jail and tell someone about the hand.

The jail was built of the same gray stone as the almshouse. At a high desk an egg-bald man with his head on his arms was sleeping noisily.

Duffy went right up to him and said, carefully, "Pardon me, sir."

The man snapped awake, snorting. At his collar was a five-pointed copper star. "What?" The man was vexed, to say the least. "What? What? Speak up, man."

"Begging your pardon, Sergeant."

"What?"

"I think I've found a body."

"You think? Don't you know?"

"Well, I know I've found a hand."

"Are you some sort of jester, cull?"

"No, sir."

"This is one of Simmons's jokes, ain't it?"

"No, sir."

"You tell him Alsop doesn't think he's funny. Get out."

"But, sir, the hand—"

"You say one more word about a fucking hand and I'll throw you in the quod."

Duffy'd had enough. Outside it was full dark. Well, the dead man wasn't going anywhere. Indeed, it had been a bloody evil day.

He trudged toward his room in Anthony-street and his thin horsehair pallet in the crowded room he shared with eight other stranded seamen.

Most nights in this fiendish winter of '08, the streets of fucking-New-fucking-York were dark as the unused pits of hell. The whale-oil lamps, even when lit, offered pitiful light. Soot collected on the lamp glasses and no one ever bothered to clean them and the wicks were never trimmed. What could you expect from a bloody Protestant country?

Though his near-empty stomach was still biting at him, Duffy allowed himself a grin. The snow clouds had lifted, and in the sky was a bare sliver of a moon floating above the horizon and reflecting a light so luminous off the new snow you could read by it. If a man had something to read. If a man could read. Truth, between the snow and the slender but vivid moonlight, the City was shining with an eerie light.

Ahead he heard laughter, then spied two of the Night Watch. One had to be a captain. The captain was standing by while the second man was lighting a street lamp. A bedraggled white mongrel was chasing its own tail around the lamp post, threatening to upset the ladder and the lamplighter.

It didn't seem to be hard work. Duffy had heard that a Watch Man earned as much as seventy-five cents a night. Duffy could eat for a month on that. And a captain got double the Watch Man's pay. Duffy had petitioned to enlist in the Watch but no such luck. Apparently, you had to know someone. They weren't giving away plum jobs like that to some out-of-work Irish seaman simply because he asked for it. Duffy shivered and approached the two men as the one on the ladder lit the lamp. Saints be praised. The one on the ground was actually smiling. Duffy didn't think these Americans had that sort of manners.

"Nice night." The captain nodded at Duffy.

"For some," Duffy replied. "Not for a man I met today over at the Collect where I work."

"Why not?"

"He's had a bit of trouble. Dead, he is."

The captain stepped back, his lips curled in amusement. "What did he have to say for himself?"

"Not much. His mouth was full of dirt. He's buried in it. All that's showing is his hand."

"And you're telling me? Why didn't you tell a Constable?"

"I did. Said I was in the wrong ward to talk to him. Then when I tried to tell a sergeant at the jail, he threatened to lock me up."

"You hear that, Staub?" the captain called up to the man on the ladder. "Just like those shiftless beaks."

"I heard." Staub climbed down and was welcomed by the dog with small leaps.

"I'm Keller," said the captain to the seaman. "Who are you?"

"Bill Duffy." He pointed at the gray house behind them. "I live here."

"Where is the poor bugger?"

"This side of the Collect. Between Church and Broadway. In Lispenard Meadows. I marked the spot so you can find it."

Keller shook his head. "You don't think I'm going to have a look at him now, do you? You hear that, Staub? He wants me to go picking up dead bodies by the light of the moon."

"I heard."

Duffy didn't respond. He was cold and hungry. His mind was on his aching stomach and the bare comfort of his cold room.

"He ain't going anywhere," said Staub, fending off the dog, who was attacking his ladder. Laughing, Staub and Keller moved on along Anthony-street toward the next lamp post. The dog rolled in the snow.

A clatter of light hooves on the frozen dirt road of Anthony-street caught their attention. Everyone stopped, including the dog. A black goat appeared silhouetted in the light of the crescent moon.

"O grab me," Staub whispered hoarsely.

The mongrel began to bark crazily, its wet back hairs bristling.

Duffy was so excited he could have barked, too. According to law, a free-roaming goat was fair prey. It belonged to whoever caught it.

Forgetting everything else but how good goat's stew tasted, Duffy began stalking the animal. "Here I come, you Beelzebub," he cooed. Approaching slowly, cautiously, not to spook the creature, he opened his pea coat, the better to get at the knife at his waist, almost ready to butcher the animal then and there and eat its raw flesh still on the hoof.

No respecter of Duffy's rights, the mongrel dashed at the goat. The billy pawed the hard ground and glared, hissing steam from its nose. Duffy could swear he saw fire, too. With a yip the canine tucked his tail under and scurried off. The goat bleated angrily, then bounded over the icy marsh toward the river.

So much for his stew, Duffy thought miserably. Aye, altogether an evil day. There was a warm, wet touch on his fingers. He looked down. The dog was licking his hand, as if to beg his forgiveness. Duffy patted the animal's head. At once the mongrel was dancing about again, a pretend victory dance which proclaimed he had got the best of the encounter, chased the ferocious goat away, and won the day.

"Snaring that goat would have been like catching the devil by the hindmost," Keller proclaimed.

Duffy licked his lips. "I would have said a Hail Mary and had a wonderful feast."

"One more lamp to go, Cap, then we can eat."

Keller waved an acknowledgment to Staub. "Thank you, Duffy. I'll leave a message about the cadaver for the Old Man at the station. Good night to you."

"Good night," said Duffy. He had his hand on the door of his lodging house when Keller broke wind with the force and explosion of a cannon.

"Damn, my stomach is my affliction. That sausage and fart-deviling pumpernickel is distressing my insides. You want some? Sausage and bread?"

Duffy's mouth watered. He didn't know how to answer. But his stomach did, making a noise almost as loud as Keller's.

"Hey," shouted Staub. "That's my—"

The dog started barking.

"Shut up, Staub. You, too, dog. What do you say, Duffy? Want to share with us?"

Duffy grinned and nodded his head vigorously. This had turned out to be a good day after all.

Conundrum—

*Why is the Embargo like Molly Brown's under taking to
sleep three nights in wet sheets to get a husband?
Because poor Molly died in the experiment.*

New-York Herald
January 1808

•———————•

14

31 January. Sunday. Morning.

Jake Hays shook Reverend Todd's hand vigorously. "Good
sermon, Reverend."

"Thank you, Mr. Hays."

The High Constable's wife Katherine, with a babe in
arms, and their two young boys were right behind him, as
was the pale young woman in mourning weeds.

"My widowed kinswoman from Philadelphia," Jake said
quietly to Reverend Todd. "She's come to live with us.
Charity Boenning."

"How long have you been widowed, Mrs. Boenning?"
the minister asked.

"Two months."

"His Christian name?"

"Philip."

"Any children?"

"Only the one I carry."

"I shall mention you in my prayers."

"Thank you," Charity said, bobbing her head.

"Lovely service, Reverend."

"Mrs. Hays. Welcome to New-York, Mrs. Boenning."

Katherine Hays nodded at her husband, then gathered her children and Charity for the walk to where Noah and Copper waited with their sleigh to take them home. As was the custom, bulky iron chains barred church streets on the Lord's Day in order to keep traffic away and the thoroughfares quiet and peaceful. Charity Boenning and Katherine Hays and her brood crossed to the other side of the chains on Bowery Road and boarded one of the waiting sleighs and carriages.

Jake Hays looked fondly after his wife and family, then stepped out of the Scots Presbyterian Church onto Grand-street, contemplating God's world.

He had opened his heart and his home to his poor cousin, Charity, an Etting of Philadelphia. First, she shared the name Charity with his younger sister. More important, Jacob Hays's mother, Esther, had been an Etting.

Charity had married outside the Jewish faith. True, Jacob's father had been born a Jew, but he'd taken the Lord to his heart and become a pious Presbyterian. Jake, alone among his siblings, had followed his father into the Presbyterian church.

When Charity married a Christian, the artist Philip Boenning, her family had forsaken her as they had Jake's mother when she had converted to Christianity.

Philip Boenning had died tragically, trampled to death by a runaway horse. And Charity and her unborn child had nearly died in an accident on the road from Princeton only the week before. Jake Hays could not have done otherwise but give her and the coming child a home.

Although it had stopped snowing early that morning, there was no thaw and the forest of evergreens behind the church was coated white and glinted in the sun like thousands of diamonds. There was at least half a foot of fresh snow on the ground. The main part of the City lay south of Grand-street. In all other directions, were woods or open fields and farms.

The City of New-York now extended perhaps a mile north of Wall-street, its first boundary. Wall-street, named for the wall built in Dutch times to keep the redskins out, was the walkway on which the gentry took their daily promenade. The City was in many ways simply a large town with much of the countryside woven through it. Trees lined many of the streets, gardens and empty patches of land abounded; fruit and berries were for the picking at many locations about the City. Broadway, the main thoroughfare, was impressive. Wide and beautiful, paved, and other than in winter, green with trees, it started at the Battery and ran to the two-mile stone. From there, Broadway became an unpaved country road.

Still, it was a worldly town. Its residents took pride in the Park Theatre in Chatham-street with its beautiful crystal chandelier hanging from its lofty ceiling. The theatre drew an elegant, sophisticated audience, at least in the boxes.

On either river—really estuaries which fed from the ocean—fishermen cast their nets for all sorts of fish. The waters were plentiful with shad, mackerel, bluefish, chub, suckers, walleyed pikes, great northern pikes, and pickerel. One could also pull sturgeon or Atlantic salmon from these rivers. And in season, clams and oysters.

To the north, fortunately and unfortunately, was the glue factory where glue was made from pigs' feet. It was compelled by law to be beyond New-York City limits, and by law and God's mercies, it did not spew its stink on Sunday. Further to the north was untrampled land, where rocks and dense woodland filled with oak, hickory, and maple had been in place for hundreds of years.

The preacher's homily was still in Jake's thoughts. Any

man who'd been treated kindly by life, by the Lord, had a Christian duty to extend that kindness to those less fortunate. And in these times there was ample opportunity to do just that.

Every day of the week but one, Jacob Hays wore black. Jake's Sunday suit was dark blue: a frock coat and two waistcoats square cut in the front, the inner waistcoat, gray, the outer one, white. His pantaloons were tucked into black knee-high thick-soled buskins with a large fold-over of gray.

He made a pass at the air with his staff, tugged at the white handkerchief at his throat, and tilted his tall beaver hat to its proper angle. Pleased with the Deity, himself, and the world, the High Constable started across Grand-street's wide snow-packed thoroughfare. When he stopped to let the Anderson family trudge by, he nodded, smiling, but his mind was on a wiry man in a pea coat, somewhat younger than he, standing outside the church door, talking neither to the preacher, nor to anyone else. Jacob Hays had noted the man inside the church. A stranger. Not necessarily an outlaw, but not a familiar face.

Jake breathed the invigorating air. His practice was a brisk walk about town, seeing that the Sabbath was being well kept and peaceful, and finishing with a mug of coffee at the Tontine before going home.

"High Constable? Sir?"

Hays turned and saw that the wiry man was coming toward him. "Yes?"

"No disrespect, sir, breaking into your Sunday. It's about the dead body."

Jake squinted at the man who was just a shade shorter than he. "What dead body?"

"There's a message supposed to be waiting for you at the station, wherever that is, but I couldn't sleep last night, worrying about the poor sod's soul."

Jake frowned.

"Pardon, sir, the language."

Jake waved his right hand. "No matter."

Grand-street was bustling with the Scots Presbyterian Church's parishioners on their way to their sleighs. "We're dining with you this night, Jake," a woman called. "Don't be late."

The High Constable waved. "Walk with me," he said to the man in the pea coat. "Where are we going?"

"Sir?"

"The dead body."

"T'other side of the Collect. In the Lispenard Meadows." The two men headed down the Bowery, Jake in the lead.

Sunday was the one day the High Constable did not have his man Noah trailing in his wake. The change in routine allowed Noah to attend the African Baptist Meeting in Stone-street after he delivered Mrs. Hays and the children home.

Jake enjoyed Sundays. The day let him know all was well with the world. Until the first bit of trouble crossed his path. Unfortunately, trouble seemed to be already here, and Sunday wasn't even half over. Oh, well. "Couple hundred years ago this was all wilderness, till the Dutch started farming it."

The wiry man grunted. It was hard keeping up with the High Constable's pace, especially on the slippery wooden walks.

Jake shook his head. "I like town life. But on Sunday, God's day, give me the country." He took a deep breath. "I'm a bona fide Rustic Reuben. With my trees. Apples, peaches. It amazes me, the way this City is growing. Have you seen where they're building the new City Hall over in Chambers-street?"

"Yes, sir."

"That's the edge of town. Ha. In a few years New-York will be double the distance past here. Mark my words. No place to breathe then. Every day goes by we lose more woods, birds, and animals." He broke off. "Seaman, are you?"

"Yes, sir. How'd you know?"

"The coat's dead testimony. Also you step like a sailor. And look at your hands. There's something about a seaman's calluses that are different from a landsman's."

"Yes, sir."

"What countryman are you? No, don't tell me. Irish, right?"

Simple man that he was, even Duffy knew it was no great feat to discern the country of his birth. He grinned and put on the brogue. "How could you tell?"

"Catholic?"

Duffy bristled. Was there going to be trouble? From the man's face he decided not. Duffy's religion was not a hard guess either. "You've caught me out."

The High Constable wrinkled his brow. "I saw you in our church."

Duffy nodded.

"What did you think of our service?"

"Very nice," the seaman answered politely. "But you let anybody at all sing." He pulled a face. "And some of them as can't."

"Granted," said Jake. "But at least we know what we're saying when we pray. Not that Latin gibberish."

The sailor chose not to answer. There was no profit in arguing religion, especially when *he* was the Catholic. "Yes, sir."

The High Constable thrust out his hand. "Jake Hays."

Flustered, Duffy did the same. "Bill Duffy."

"Don't you have any proper gloves, Duffy?"

"No, sir."

The High Constable shook his head. "What's this about a dead body, then?"

Patiently, Duffy explained. "I was working between Church and Broadway, cleaning up around the Collect. I saw something sticking up out of the earth. God help me—" Duffy crossed himself. "—if it wasn't a man's hand. And there's an arm attached."

"Are you sure?"

"What do you mean, am I sure? I know a man's hand when I see it. I marked the spot with a bit of wood so you can find it."

They heard the savage, feral din even before they turned right off the Bowery to Pump-street. "Jesus, Mary, and Joseph!" cried Duffy.

The spot where Duffy had left his marker was now a mad snarl of fur and teeth, a howling, screeching pack of wild dogs.

15

31 JANUARY. SUNDAY. MORNING TO AFTERNOON.

Without a blink of his eye, Jake Hays waded in, treating the ravenous dogs as if they were just so many unruly citizens, his staff slashing this way and that. "Get out! Get away!"

The dogs backed off. But they did not leave. Snarling, drool dripping from broken yellow teeth, they advanced again.

Jake drew his squat five feet six inches up till he seemed a giant. Holding the staff high over his head, he howled: "By the great Jehovah, *begone!*"

And they left.

Duffy stared at the lawman in abject admiration as the wild animals cowered off, whining, matted tails between their skeletal legs.

"Poor starving beasts," Jake said, clucking his tongue. He lowered his staff.

Duffy was staring at the dead hand, now tattered by the dogs' ravaging. "It's a good thing we arrived when we did. Another minute and they would have chewed that to the bone." Duffy shook his head. "Of all the indignities. To be shoved into unhallowed ground, then this. Terrible thing." He tested the stake he'd left. It was still secure. He stamped the ground. "Too hard to dig."

Jake crouched to examine the hand for a moment. Then he rose. "This can wait till tomorrow."

"But the dogs—"

"I'll put a Watch on it. Be of good cheer, Duffy, this man has gone to his Maker. And unfortunately, he's not the only one. If I had a nickel for every body dumped in Gotham's ground, I'd be Croesus."

"Pardon, sir?"

"No matter. With this freeze there will be little work about the Collect till spring thaw. Do you want a new job?"

"Sir?"

"The City will pay you one dollar for today to watch that the dogs don't get at the body again. First, to the Tontine for a hearty meal to get you through what's going to be a long day. I'll have a Night Watch relieve you at sunset."

Duffy hesitated.

"What is it that's not to your liking, man? The job? The meal?"

"Will the hand be safe from the dogs while I'm gone?"

"I have no way of knowing. Probably not. But nothing's perfect. This is the best we can do. Let's go. Praying gives me an appetite. Fighting off dogs gives me a larger one. Come morning there's another job waiting for you. I want you to dig this wretched fellow up, or what's left of him." The High Constable removed the white kerchief from about his neck and tied it to the stake, watching with satisfaction as it fluttered in the keen wind like a signal of surrender.

Above, a falcon swooped low surveying the scene. Duffy shuddered, remembering the falcon of more than a week before. And the pig. And the eagle. And the rain of blood.

"Get a move on, man," the High Constable called, already well ahead of Duffy.

In front of a deserted warehouse in Pump-street, named for the tea water pump, used there until the water became polluted, they came upon two shivering tatterdemalions roasting chestnuts in battered kettles over a meager fire.

The dark boy, lean as a reed, wore a thin coat but no hat. He seemed scarce nine or ten. The Embargo and the unrelenting cold had given the City more than its share of hungry children, most of them orphans. "One cent for five, Your Honor," the boy called.

Jake pulled out his purse and pressed a coin into the small hand. The inadequate gloves on his red claw hands were more holes than cloth. The boy's ancient companion was even thinner. The old man had no coat, and his hands and feet were wrapped in rags. He was leaning on the staff in his right hand, but Jake, who knew about staffs, recognized it for a suitable weapon, too. Jake didn't take the proffered chestnuts which were wrapped in a tear of newspaper. Instead, he gave the gaffer a cent, as well.

"Thank you, Your Honor." The old man pulled at the forelock of white hair that crept from under his oversized cap.

The boy, keeping his limbs moving against the cold, grinned at Jake. "If you give me your hand, sir, I'll tell your fortune."

Jake shook his head. "But there'll be another cent apiece for you if you go to Lispenards, between Church and Broadway. A stake in the ground with a white handkerchief flying from it marks the spot. I want you to keep the dogs away."

"Good as done, sir." The old man came to attention, the staff, like a musket, pulled to his side. "I have my stick. The boy will get some rocks. And we'll build us a big fire, that'll do it. I served with General Greene during the War so I know something about fighting off dogs as well as Englishmen. I had my share." He cackled. "All sons of bitches, if you know what I mean."

"What do they call you?"

The old man stood as straight as his curved old back would allow. "Corporal James Smith. The lad here is my grandson, Danny."

The boy grinned at the mention of his name, then ran into the warehouse and brought out a barrow. In it was a layer of earth. He and the old man placed coals and kettles into the barrow and were off toward the Collect.

"Wait," cried Jake.

They stopped.

"Duffy here will be back in a bit with your pay. I don't care if you have to beat and burn those dogs to kingdom come. They must be kept away."

The old man and the boy and their barrow trundled off.

Jacob Hays's house was only three blocks south of Lispenard Meadows, on Sugarloaf, but although Jake knew his Katherine wouldn't object if he brought Duffy home, he thought it best that he and the seaman should eat at the Tontine.

Duffy was having visions of roasted chicken and potatoes. He had to run to keep up with the High Constable, who was already on the move with the pace of a trotting horse. There was a stitch in his side and a wolf in his stomach as they reached the corner of Wall and Water streets. Finally, thought Duffy. Hays was not even sweating. The man appeared buoyant from his walk.

Flying from a staff on the upper roof of the Tontine were the fifteen stars and fifteen stripes of the American flag. A tall building of three high floors, the street level area jutted out from the rest of the building. Its roof was a single-railed balcony which surrounded the first floor. The Tontine had changed little in size and dimension since Colonial times, but as ground coffee had come into the marketplace and was readily available, the mystique of the coffee-house had dissipated. What remained was a tavern, a lodging house, and an auction place.

Such establishments were no longer gathering places for political talk and commerce. The changing times had shifted that to City buildings and stock exchanges and country houses. But the coffee-house taverns remained hospitable settings to take food and drink.

Duffy had never been nor ever expected to be inside the Tontine Coffee-House. His stomach rumbled like a rolling keg. Surely he would perish before they ever got inside.

In front of the Tontine a half-dozen gaunt men, seamen by their look, were cadging pennies and hollering.

"You inside, give us a bit or we'll break some windows."

"Or you'll what?" Jake roared, advancing on them like the wrath of God.

"We'll break your windows and we'll break your heads," yelled a little leather-faced individual on bowlegs. He wore an incongruously tall hat. Next to him stood a six-foot monster who looked to weigh three hundred pounds.

"Would you like to start with my head?" Jake's smile was sinister. His renowned staff slashed through the air and off came the little man's tall hat.

"Look out," Duffy called from behind, seeing the monster raising a hammerlike hand. His move to help was too slow.

Jake was fast and clever. Around came that famous gold-headed stick, striking the large man—*whack*—in his ample stomach.

Meanwhile the little fool with the leather face bent over to pick up his hat, as Jake knew he would. Jake grinned at Duffy and kicked the man solid in the arse.

Still grinning, Jake studied the remaining four. Assured there was no fight in them, he said, "All right, lads, you know this is not the thing to do. Hop over to the almshouse in Chambers-street, and get yourself some potato soup."

"They're closed," Leather-face complained as he rubbed his backside. "There's no more soup."

"Closed."

"All gone."

"I'm hungry, mister," grumbled the three-hundred-pounder, getting painfully to his feet.

"You don't look it," said Jake.

"You're Old Hays, ain't you?" Leather-face asked.

"The same."

The monster cuffed the little man. "Arsehole."

"Go around back to the kitchen and tell them to give you some soup. If there's any trouble tell Lem Wilson to come see me."

"Yes, sir."

The six failed desperadoes scurried to the back of the Tontine while Jake Hays and Duffy climbed the stairs in front.

In no time Duffy was mopping up the remnants of rabbit stew with a thick slab of soda bread.

Hays, who ate at the same pace he walked, had already eaten most of what was on his plate. He pulled a hard leather case from his inside coat pocket, produced a cheroot from the case, and lit it from the candle on their table.

Duffy's eyes watered from the thick tobacco smoke. Still, catching the sweet tobacco whiffs in his nostrils, he hoped Old Hays would offer him one. When he did, Duffy grinned, sniffed the open-ended dark segar, and immediately lit up.

Hays stretched contentedly, rose, and crossed to their host. Lemual Wilson was taking his Sunday doze behind the serving counter. "A thousand pardons for disturbing your snooze, Lem, but I need some twine or rope."

Duffy paid little attention. He had one bit of bread left and was about to pop it into his mouth when his eye caught the morsels of potato and turnip nestled lovingly in thick brown gravy on the High Constable's plate. Duffy stole a quick glance at Old Hays, exchanged his wiped clean plate with Hays's more tempting one, and began the mopping all over again.

"Ah," he mumbled, at last sated. He sat back in the big oak chair and picked up his segar again. Across the room two men, in traveling garments, merchants most likely, sat smoking their pipes.

"It's the best I can give you," Wilson said, handing Hays a ball of yellow yarn. "And the wife will not be happy when she sees it's gone."

"It will suffice, and many thanks," Hays said. He clapped Duffy on the back, and gave him the wool, a loaf of bread, an earthenware jar, and a bottle. "There you are. And . . ." He produced a dollar bill and two pennies from his purse. "The bread, stew, water, and coppers are for our less fortunate friends."

"What's the yellow wool for?" Duffy asked. "To knit us all yellow mufflers?"

The High Constable snorted. "You're a funny fellow. I want you to stake the ground around the hand and cordon off the space with it. I want the area contained and untrammeled until I can get a better look. I'll be there at nine tomorrow morning. I don't want a shovel to touch the ground until I show the scene to the Coroner."

"The Coroner?" repeated Duffy, the hot meal in his belly making him brazen enough to ask.

Old Hays nodded. "John Tonneman."

16

1 FEBRUARY. MONDAY. MORNING.

Duffy was up before the sun. He set off with a pick and a shovel, a pot of hot coals, and a wagonload of wood. It was so cold that the snot dripping from his nose froze on his upper lip.

At the site there was no Watch Man. What a stalwart bunch they were. So much for guarding the hand. But there were no dogs either. And the hand looked as good as it had the last time he'd seen it, if you could call that good. The ravaged gray fingers reached up out of the frozen mud. Eastward, over Brooklyn, a brittle sun crept into view.

As instructed, he'd strung the yellow wool the day before, after his sumptuous meal with Old Hays. The yarn was still here. The hand seemed to be beseeching, pleading, begging. Duffy crossed himself. Twice.

The coals he'd brought were nowhere near enough for the task. He'd have to make more.

It took a long time to get a hot fire going near the hand. And it was even longer before he had embers enough to lay about the hand to soften the ground. Then he had to pull the coals away because while they were softening the ground, they were also threatening to roast the frozen fingers. Duffy did not think Old Hays would be too happy with that.

As was his custom the High Constable had walked, with his driver Noah trailing behind, today in a dark red sleigh, copper bells merrily announcing his presence. "Good day to you, Duffy." Hays handed the seaman a pair of worn but serviceable gloves.

Duffy was overcome. Rabbit, they looked. He put them on. Rabbit they felt. "Thank you, sir. . . ."

The High Constable waved his stick. He looked down at the softening ground and the beseeching hand. His eyes scanned the earth inside the yellow line. Then he walked the area in an ever-widening circle.

Jake freed his mind from extraneous thought. There was nothing obvious to see, but he knew from experience to assume nothing.

For his part, Duffy waited patiently, glad for the respite, unhappy with how cold he felt when not working, all the time watching the High Constable's curious behavior.

At last Hays returned to the hand. "Very well, Duffy, you can start digging."

THE DAY WAS cold and dry and crackling crisp as the frozen snow under John Tonneman's boots. He tied his bay gelding to a weathered birch.

The Collect hereabouts had almost disappeared, filled in, blending now into Lispenard Meadows. The familiar landmarks of his City had begun to disappear with an alarming regularity. His grandchildren, should he ever live to see them, would reside in a terrible, splendid metropolis. Gotham, Washington Irving had dubbed it, the village of wise fools.

The land sloped gently downward. As Tonneman approached, the High Constable, who was supervising the digging, came forward to greet him. Tonneman had great respect for Jake Hays, as did most of the honest citizens of New-York. As did many of the dishonest citizens.

"What have we here, High Constable?"

"A dead man, by all appearances," Hays answered, an unlit cheroot clamped between his teeth. "This fellow's digging him up for us."

Beyond Hays, Tonneman saw an area marked off by yellow yarn strung on short posts about a foot high. In the center something protruded from the ground. A hand. Well, now he knew why he was here.

Around the hand the ash-strewn earth was a thick mud which moment by moment was threatening to freeze all over again. The workie had to dig as fast as he could.

The ravaged fingers seemed to reach out from the earth. Over all his years as a surgeon and Coroner and during the War, Tonneman had seen hundreds of bodies and thousands of body parts. But his experience did not prevent the terror that took hold of him at this moment.

More than thirty years ago, not far from this place, on the first day he'd arrived from England, he'd been asked to look at another body. And not long after that Gretel, the woman who had raised him from infancy, had been brutally murdered by a madman.

He and Mariana had named their first daughter Gretel in her memory. It had been the fulfillment of a promise.

"How's your boy?" Jake Hays asked softly.

Tonneman, brought back from his reverie, if that's what

it was, didn't answer. He merely nodded, his eyes on the corrupt earth. "The Negroes sometimes buried their dead around the Collect."

Hays shifted his segar from one side of his mouth to the other. "He's as white as you and me, sir."

Duffy breathed heavily as he worked, grunting, sending snowy plumes into the air. He alternated digging with laying more coals and rebuilding the fire. Mercifully, the dead man was not a big package. By the looks of his clothes—the drab coat, baggy trousers, and wide shoes—he'd been a Quaker. And, rare for a body in the ground, he even had the broad-brimmed, low-crowned hat jammed on his head.

"God's truth," said Hays, "this time the meek has inherited the earth."

Tonneman's horse at the tree whinnied and shied. Amazing, thought Tonneman, even though he'd seen such phenomena before. There was no smell, it was too cold for that. But somehow the animal sensed death, and was not happy to be around the dead. Neither was Duffy. The old wagon nag Duffy had borrowed from the Collect Company placidly nibbled the snow crust.

Glad to have the digging done with, Duffy laid out a canvas sheet. Face to ghastly face with the dead man, he shoved both his hands under the armpits and with one strong heave, he tore the wasted corpse from the ground and dropped it onto the sheet.

Tonneman stepped over the yellow yarn. He looked first into the shallow hole, then at the body that came with the hand. Jake Hays joined him. The cadaver was frozen stiff. Crouching, Tonneman studied the chewed right hand.

"Dogs," Duffy mumbled.

Tonneman touched the other hand. It was a half-closed claw containing a fistful of frozen earth. Fearful of breaking the stiff fingers, Tonneman chose to put off opening the hand till he was in his surgery, but what the damaged hand had hinted the whole one attested to. The handful of earth, and the broken nails crammed with more of the same. "My bag," the doctor instructed. "On the saddle."

"Yes, sir," the digger said, running to fetch it.

"Irish?"

Hays nodded. "Duffy. Good man, though. Seaman."

Duffy was back with the bag and handed it to Tonneman. The Coroner took strips of cloth from the bag. Delicately he cleaned away the mud from the corpse, inspecting the cloth after each wipe.

Duffy tugged his new gloves tighter. "Let me help you, sir," he said, about to straighten the corpse out.

"Wait," Tonneman said. He moved the body slightly.

"Jesus, Mary, Joseph," Duffy breathed, closing his eyes, signing the cross.

Hays leaned over to get a better look.

Adhering to the back of the body, its teeth caught on the dead man's coat, looking for all the world as if it were biting the dead man's arse, was a human skull.

17

1 FEBRUARY. MONDAY. MORNING.

Tonneman was instantly intrigued. He held the skull in
his palm, studying it. Something plagued his mind. It was as
if he should know that ghastly grin. . . . The snagged in-
cisors. He had seen just such a configuration of teeth before. . . .

"Is that the neckbone hanging down?" asked Duffy.
The seaman's face was pasty.

Tonneman nodded. "What's left of it."

"I wonder where the rest of this fellow is," Duffy said,
dourly.

Jake Hays was impatient with the detour the strange skull had brought. Skulls and other old bones turned up all the time as the City moved steadily northward and built over old burial grounds. "He'll come up soon enough, and if he doesn't we won't mind a bit. Now, can we get back to the matter before us?"

"Of course," said Tonneman, giving his attention to the more recent corpse, whose identity he'd known since first setting eyes on him. Tonneman placed the irksome skull aside and removed the crushed, muddy, and blood-caked hat from the corpse, revealing blood-matted, drab brown hair. The face, too, was stained with dry blood. This he gently brushed away.

Tonneman cleared his throat and spoke so Duffy wouldn't hear. "There's something I have to tell you, Jake. I know this man."

"As do I." The High Constable nodded twice as if he were agreeing with an unheard voice. "Joseph Thaddeus Brown, himself. Let's keep this quiet, John, for the time being. I believe Mr. Clinton would like to appoint his own new Commissioner of Streets without Mr. Marinus Willett putting his oar in."

Tonneman shrugged. "I'm not political."

Jake nodded. It was well known that John Tonneman tried to keep above the political fray. Did that make him a better man? Or worse? Jake Hays did not judge him for it. What did bother Jake were the things the physician was not telling him. And for that he couldn't help but judge him. What secret was John Tonneman keeping from him about young Peter Tonneman's involvement in Thaddeus Brown's demise? And what of John Tonneman's own involvement?

Tonneman inspected the hands again, then the rest of the body. He shook his head. "Stubborn Broadbrim. Kept his hat on even in death. The Friends are like that, I'm afraid." He smiled. "As are the Jews. Some Jews."

Jake Hays grunted, acknowledging Tonneman's moment of self-deprecating humor. "How long has he been dead?"

"I would say as much as eight days."

Jake exhaled, spat and stuck his cheroot back between his teeth. "As long as he's been missing."

Tonneman contemplated the High Constable. There were very few things that escaped Jacob Hays's scrutiny. And Commissioner of Streets Brown's disappearance had not been one of them. "If the weather were warm I could be more specific. In my experience the stiffness of death lasts no more than four days. But with the body frozen as it is . . ." He shrugged. "Still, there's something else I can tell you."

"What?"

"Though the dogs chewed away the thumb and damaged the first finger of the right hand, you can see by the other fingers and the left hand that the nails are broken and crammed with dirt, the same peat he was buried in and on which we're standing."

"Which means?"

"The hand didn't just rise to the surface because winds blew the earth hither and yon. It clawed its way up. The only other wound I've discovered thus far is the blow to the forehead. Cracked his skull open. Bled profusely. See the blood? It soaked through his hat and hair and collar and mixed with peat. From that I would venture to say he was still bleeding when he went into this ground."

Jake's stern eyes narrowed. "And continued bleeding until he died."

"Yes. The gray cast of his skin attests to that. This man was buried alive."

18

1 February. Monday. Morning.

Bleak as a cold fire, the sun hung over them.

Much to Duffy's dismay, Jake had ordered him to dig up all the earth to the depth of the body within the yellow boundary. Jake wanted the Coroner to sift through it, to see if the murderer or murderers had left any evidence of themselves.

Duffy took a deep breath of the cold air. "And after that I expect you'll want me to dig some more till I find the body to go with that skull."

Jake's lips stretched into a smile. "Skeleton, not body. Not needed. These grounds are filled with bones from the last 150 years, if not more. No telling how old that skull is. Just dig inside the yellow."

At the sight of Duffy's sour expression, Jake added, "Be

of good cheer, I've got another job for you. How would you like to be a member of the Night Watch?"

Duffy's grin threatened to break his ruddy face. "I don't know how to thank you, High Constable—"

"Just get over to the jail when you're done with this. You go on duty at sundown."

JOHN TONNEMAN WALKED his gelding toward Hays's sleigh in Church-street after arranging for Duffy to take Brown's mortal remains, the snagged tooth skull, and a load of dirt to Tonneman's surgery.

"That Irish fellow's an affable soul," Tonneman said, tightening the gelding's saddle strap.

Jake nodded. "Well, John, Duffy's job and yours are done." The High Constable cast his eyes toward Duffy, who was attacking the frozen ground with a vengeance. His lips twitched; Tonneman took that for a smile. "Well, not quite. But mine has just begun." The stocky man's demeanor became grim. "I take it as a personal affront that an honest citizen is killed in such a horrible manner in my City. Do you have any suspicions as to why and by whom?"

"I don't know who," Tonneman replied. "But I'm sorry to say the why is clear. Since Friend Brown disappeared eight days past, I've discovered that fifty thousand dollars is missing from the Collect Company."

Hays poked a patch of ground with his stick. For a moment, he said nothing. Then he gave the Coroner one of his famous piercing looks. "I always reckoned Brown's disposition rather too snappish for a Friend."

Tonneman found it curious that Hays made no comment about the missing money. "That doesn't make him a thief."

"No, it doesn't. Sounds like '03 all over again."

Tonneman's brow furrowed. "Oh? You mean when Livingston's man stole those funds?" Both men were referring to the time New-York's Mayor Livingston had been ill during yet another Yellow Fever epidemic and his fiscal agent misappropriated nearly $45,000 from the Federal government. Livingston recovered his health but was forced to resign his office. Governor George Clinton then appointed his nephew De Witt Clinton as mayor.

Hays grunted. "That was Federal money. What we're talking about here is New-York money that was meant to make this City a better place." The High Constable took his cheroot from his mouth, examined it, decided he didn't like it anymore, and tossed it in the snow. He lifted his spiked gaze to Tonneman's face. "It would have been cordial, John, if you'd informed me about Brown and the missing money."

"I'd hoped to solve the problem on my own."

"And where was Peter during the time Brother Brown went missing?"

Tonneman pulled himself up tall. The wind whipped his scarf against his face. "What do you mean?"

"Don't try to trick a trickster, John. I have heard that your son and Brown had a violent altercation ending with Brown bloodied on the floor."

To avoid the High Constable's forbidding stare, Tonneman mounted his horse.

The two men nodded curtly to each other and Tonneman, dismayed, rode toward his home on Rutgers Hill. The gelding knew the way. Tonneman let his mind loose. At once without volition he conjured up Thaddeus Brown's odd companion in death, the strange skull. Snagged teeth. He'd seen many a snagged tooth the years in his practice of the dental art. Was the skull that of a man or woman? He hadn't given it that close a look, but his intuition said woman. And over the years his intuition had served him in good stead.

He smiled suddenly. Except. There had been a time years ago when he'd mistaken his own Mariana for a lad. That was when his father had passed and John had returned to New-York, the City of his birth, still nursing the wound Abigail had given him by marrying Richard Willard.

He had fallen in love with Mariana Mendoza, an amazing girl of great passions, who wore boy's clothing and wanted to be a doctor. Through her he had gotten involved in the Revolutionary cause. Those wonderful times. He had never felt so alive.

Oh, Mariana. What a sorrowful path we've taken.

Lost on Sunday last, about 10 *o'clock, A.M. a HAIR BRACELET, mounted with Gold, a gold clasp with the initial E.G. on the outside and M.C.G. on the inside. Whoever has found the same and will return it to No.* 13 *Maiden-lane, shall be suitably rewarded.*

NEW-YORK EVENING POST
FEBRUARY 1808

19

1 FEBRUARY. MONDAY. MORNING TO AFTERNOON.

By the time he reached home, John Tonneman had worked himself into a rage. He stormed into the house, raving. "Peter!"

The chatter of female voices in the kitchen ceased.

Peter was in the sitting room, a bottle of brandy in his hand. "Can't you even wait until the sun sets?" John demanded.

"I'm not drinking."

"What, then?"

"Merely looking at the bottle."

"Bah, another of your childish lies. Stand up when I'm speaking to you."

"Please, Papa—"

"Don't please Papa me. I've had enough of you and your doings for today."

Peter sighed, but obeyed. "What have I done now?"

"How odd that you and Joseph Thaddeus Brown disappeared on the same day. Then you reappear and Brown is found dead."

The boy gasped as if he'd been hit in the stomach. "Oh, no."

"Is that all you have to say? Oh, no? There's also a report from one of Jake Hays's people that you and Brown went at it that Friday night. And that he was bleeding."

"True, but—"

"My God," Tonneman cried. "Did you kill him, Peter?"

At that moment Mariana burst into the chamber. She was on Tonneman like a spitting cat. "How dare you ask that? He's our son."

"But Old Hays—"

Angry tears streamed down her cheeks. "Like that, on a —a *rumor*—you abandon your son? Everyone knows Jake Hays uses a vile group of informers. Drunkards and thieves, they all are. They would tell him *anything* to buy their way out of trouble."

"But why did Peter run away?"

"Peter didn't run away. He simply left. He's a grown man. He has a right to go where he wishes."

"But where's the money?"

"How should I know?" Mariana's eyes blazed. "But why should you think he took it? Most likely Brown took it. Or one of the Watch Men. They're not to be trusted. Or perhaps it was your precious Jamie."

"No, not Jamie. Jamie would never—"

"Oh, how easily you defend Jamie's honor. But not your son's. Would that be too much to ask, for you to stand at your son's side in his time of need?" Her voice rose as he'd never heard in over thirty-two years, as he never imagined he would hear it. "Why aren't you in your proper place? Why aren't you *defending* your son instead of *accusing* him?"

Peter, the subject of the argument but not a participant, went upstairs to his room. They didn't even notice he was gone. He took the brandy bottle with him.

The midday meal of apples and cheese and beef stew with biscuits, which John Tonneman usually savored, today made him bilious. Tonneman was angry, Mariana was sullen, Peter was absent, and the girls were quietly anxious. It was at this point that Duffy delivered his goods. Grateful for the distraction, Tonneman went at once to his surgery, much to Mariana's apparent displeasure. She was not done with the argument.

Two elderly patients awaited his attendance in the surgery. His wife's accusation about his treatment of his son continued to rankle as Tonneman placed a kettle of water to heat atop the Franklin stove and tended to a badly cut finger, lanced a boil, then diagnosed the second patient for a gastritis.

Was Mariana correct? Had he abandoned his son? Thaddeus Brown was a problem that wouldn't go away. His death and the theft of money could destroy Peter's life and the reputation of the Tonneman family, perhaps for generations. It had to be resolved.

He handed the second patient a packet of peppermint tea, and sent him on his way. With that Tonneman expelled his own problems from his mind in favor of his obligation as Coroner. Thus, though the skull continued to intrigue him, he set it aside and stripped the body lying on his examination table. In the pockets of the Quaker's clothing he found a ten-dollar note and two three-dollar notes from the Manhattan Bank, a gold quarter eagle, a silver disme, four copper half-cent pieces, a cotton handkerchief, and a flat leather prayer book.

He looked to the kettle; the water was still not hot. Tonneman set the twelve buckets of earth Duffy had dug up in two lines of six. When he straightened up, he felt a sudden pain. His old back couldn't tolerate that sort of exercise anymore. Nevertheless, he rolled up his sleeves, got down on his knees, and sifted carefully through six of the pails, shaking dirt into his makeshift sieve. He found nothing but ants and one beetle larva.

Once the water had heated he proceeded to clean the soiled corpse with hot soaked rags, starting with the hand holding the knot of earth. When the heated rags allowed the fingers flexibility, he prised open the right hand and removed the tightly packed earth. On it he could still see the indentation of Brown's fingers.

He set the lump atop the earth in bucket number seven and finished washing the corpse, then covered it with a sheet of canvas.

Only a chance, frail glimmer brought his attention back to the seventh pail of earth. The clump of dirt from Brown's hand had crumbled, revealing a bit of metal. Tonneman scooped up the interesting find and fingered the dirt away. Before him, attached to a section of broken gold chain, was a small onyx cameo, engraved with a woman's profile. "Could have saved myself all the bother of searching through the dirt Duffy dug up," he grumbled good-naturedly.

He cleaned the cameo, then put it on his desk in his study to be dealt with later. That done, exhausted, he crawled up to his bedchamber, where Mariana was taking a nap, or pretending to.

Damn. He was certain that when she awoke she would want to continue their argument. And there was still Signore da Ponte's opera to attend.

20

1 FEBRUARY. MONDAY. EARLY EVENING.

Muffled somewhat by the snow, the wheels and runners of carriages, sleighs, carts and drays, and hooves over cobblestones made the air leaden with sound. Above it all, the mongers cried out their wares.

"Chestnuts here, missus."

"Sharp your knives."

"Roast potatoes. Red hot. Half cent."

More snow was in the air.

Tomorrow might be lost. Today was the day to make money.

If there was any to be made.

Because of snowdrifts, they'd gone up to Broadway first. Then they drove past St. Paul's Chapel, whose steeple proudly declared itself above all other buildings, and turned right on Chatham-street.

The hammering hooves and the whining mongers did not help Old Tonneman's headache. He did not want to be at the opera this night.

He would have preferred to be in his surgery, with his son beside him, sharing his life as a physician. John yearned to be free of worry about Peter, and what Peter might or might not have done. God help him, he wanted to be at home with that damnable skull. There was something it was prodding him to remember. What? The past? He clucked his tongue at his own infirmity. Of body? Mind? Soul?

Even in his mood, it was difficult for Tonneman not to notice along the route that the City was filled with hungry people, the homeless, the beggars.

"Give an old tar a cent for a bit of bread."

Fires were lit along the streets for the homeless to keep warm. The Night Watch monitored the fires lest an errant spark burn the entire City to the ground.

Mariana, clothed in her finest gown, apricot taffeta with a silk ribbon border, continued to glare at him with a look of vehement reproach. They had not spoken since Duffy had delivered Brown's body and the skull.

The girls, stiff in their best evening outfits, were silent, too. They knew all was not well with the Tonneman family. Only Peter kept up a nervous chatter. A new subject for him. Marriage. Was he ready for marriage, he kept asking his mother. And what kind of girl should he marry? Mariana, intent on nursing her fury, granted her son only terse answers.

In Chatham-street in front of the Park Theatre, other vehicles disgorged beautifully dressed men, and women in bonnets, shawls and gloves, fur-lined velvet cloaks, and muffs, all wrapped well against the intense cold.

The attraction this evening was the opera *Don Giovanni*. Music by Mozart. But more important to operagoers in New-York, the libretto was by Lorenzo da Ponte, citizen of the City since 1805 and the singular, if dribbling, font of Italian opera in the New World.

Mariana Tonneman had been planning this excursion since she'd seen the notice in the *Evening Post*. Her enthusiasm had grown when Signore da Ponte had presented John with special passes. In spite of Peter's difficulties and her fierce feelings toward her husband, she was determined they would not miss this event.

A path had been cleared of snow on the wooden sidewalk. As they approached the theatre, a gray-haired black man dressed in the latest fashion appeared before them. "Excuse me, Doctor Tonneman. Do you remember me?"

"I'm afraid not," said Old Tonneman, squinting. The man was broad as a house beam, and as tall as Tonneman himself.

"Well, of course," exclaimed Mariana, smiling broadly in a new rebuke to Tonneman. "Quintin."

"Yes, ma'am." The African was wearing a black cape over a green velvet jacket with a shawl collar and a very distinctive green-trimmed, high-collared vest. His tall beaver hat was in his hand. His smooth face was marred by a sizable scab over his right eyebrow. "Quintin Brock. I'm working as a hairdresser now with Pierre Toussaint. Signore da Ponte hired us to help them in the show with their fancy wigs."

"Well, that's all very nice, Quintin," Tonneman mumbled.

Quintin cupped his hand behind his right ear. "Sir? Sorry, didn't get that."

Tonneman nodded. The black man had been half-deaf since Hickey's damnable bomb had gone off all those years ago. "That's nice," he repeated loudly.

"Yes, sir, I don't mean to bother you, but could I come see you tomorrow?"

"Yes, yes," mumbled Tonneman, whose head was pounding. He rubbed his forehead. He craved one last smoke before he had to sit through an interminable opera. "In the morning at my surgery. Nine o'clock. You know where?"

"Yes, sir," Quintin answered, pleased. "How could I forget? The house on Rutgers Hill." He bowed and backed away, disappearing into the night.

Candles glowed from tall candelabra in front of the theatre. In the entry hall the Tonnemans were greeted by a strutting man of some years. His clean-shaven face, on closer inspection, would show broken veins near the surface.

The man's clothes strutted even more, all bespoke for him in London: crisp high-collared shirt, pleated and ruffled cravat and collared waistcoat, topped by a single-breasted azure velvet coat with rolling collar and lapels, fawn-colored trousers, flat black pumps with gaiters.

This was John Tonneman's oldest friend, Maurice Arthur Jamison, known to all of his class as Jamie. Jamie had been a surgeon in London and had traveled to New-York with Tonneman in 1775, to take the position of Chancellor at the new College of Medicine at King's College. But the War intervened. Not one to let grass grow beneath his feet, Jamie had married Colonel Richard Willard's wealthy, and widowed, sister.

A lithe black boy, dressed like a colonial lord, handed each a penny sheet listing the performers. "Ah, a playbill." Jamie tossed the lad his coin.

Theatregoers dressed in every style flowed into the lobby. Some gentlemen still preferred the old-fashioned knee britches, stockings, and wigs to the very modish trousers and silk top hats.

The main hall was a pit with a stage at the far end. At the back of the pit were ranks of benches. Above, at the second landing, were boxes in a semicircle where the gentry of New-York sat.

The Park Theatre, which had opened in 1798 with a performance of *As You Like It,* was quite as beautiful as the best of London's theatres. Costing the grand sum of one hundred and thirty thousand dollars, it accommodated twelve hundred people at one time. Pit seats cost fifty cents; box seats, one dollar. The theatre played a repertoire of Shakespeare, some contemporary English playwrights such as Richard Sheridan, and, like tonight, the occasional visit of an opera troupe.

The attendance in the pit was mostly male, the mechanics of the City, the workies. And in the opinion of those in the boxes, rowdies all.

"I'd like a word with you, John," Jamie said, taking Tonneman aside.

"And I with you." Tonneman motioned to Peter to get the family settled in their box.

"Your son—" Jamie began.

"There's been—" Tonneman began.

Politely, each waited for the other to continue, but the entering crowd buffeted them.

Jamie, while fluttering his scent-laden yellow silk handkerchief, attempted small talk. "Did you see any of da Ponte's season of Italian theatre last year? Manfredi and his company of Rope Dancers." He winked. "There was a Roman tableau in scenes never seen before in New-York, I'll tell you that. Did you see it?" He didn't wait for an answer. "Did you see *The Rivals* last week?"

"No," said Tonneman. Jamie's stinking handkerchief was making his headache worse. His nose wrinkled in distress.

"A divine odor, is it not?" Jamie continued. "Caswell-Massey *Number 6* Cologne. It's the Marquis de Lafayette's favorite, don't you know."

In spite of himself and his pounding head, Tonneman had to smile. "Jamie, you're priceless."

"And a good long time it's taken you to realize." Jamie's canny blue eyes were always moving, always searching for the political opportunity. "Aha," he said, waving his yellow handkerchief like a standard. "Our past and upcoming mayor." Standing not twenty feet away was De Witt Clinton, the once and soon-to-be-again mayor of New-York. He was talking to Washington Irving, Lorenzo da Ponte, and his friend, Professor Clement Moore. Obviously Jamie wanted to see and be seen with these four men of position in New-York.

Tonneman reminded himself that he had to stop after the performance and tell the Italian how fine it had been, even though he didn't understand a word of Italian and hated opera and thought his head was going to split wide open.

Workies brushed past them, finding places for themselves in the pit, calling loudly to one another.

Jamie curled his lip. "The poor they are always with us."

The lobby was narrow but abundantly lit by the many ensconced candles. Aiding the illumination were the mirrors on the walls and well-placed clear bowls of water on tables and ledges.

Jamie and Tonneman, in turn jostled and greeted, finally gave up trying to communicate above the din of voices, meandering feet, and tuning musical instruments. They withdrew to the doubtful peace of their railed boxes, where they discovered behind the plush red velvet curtain Tonneman's old cohort Daniel Goldsmith and his wife Molly, talking to Mariana.

Though only a year older than Tonneman, the stubby man seemed ten years his senior. The round bald spot on the top of Goldsmith's head was a fairly recent addition. The former Constable's face was discolored, the skin drawn by the old, ridged scars, mementos from the night the bomb near the Bayard Camp—the same bomb that had deafened Quintin—exploded, splashing him with hot tar. The years had made the scars even shinier.

The one-time Jew Molly, the whore of Church-street, now Goldsmith's wife, had lost her plumpness. Her youthful breasts had shriveled to pancakes, and the hair which had been likened to black silk was now gray. But Molly Goldsmith's clothes were of the latest mode and she was known for her grand hats, which she made herself and wore proudly. The one she wore tonight, a brilliant scarlet repleat with towering ostrich feathers, was ornate as a wedding cake.

Jamie's lip curled again, but what he muttered was lost in the babble and the new surge of more organized sound from the orchestra. Everyone standing began scrambling for a seat.

"Molly, stay," Mariana called out. "You, too, Daniel. There's room. Peter, girls. Downstairs. You can stand for the first act."

"O grab me," the girls complained, but happily bounced out of the box. Peter followed. He didn't seem displeased either.

A bellow from the pit cut through the noise. In the pit behind the stalls, the groundlings were clamoring. "That's my beer you're drinking, dung face!"

A burp loud as the bellow followed. "All my eye. Too late, all gone."

"How do you make a Yankee into a Dutchman?" the bellower cried.

"Break his jaw and knock his brains out," was the answer, and the fight began.

While men of the Night Watch streamed into the theatre to reluctantly and ineptly aid theatre workers in their attempt to stop the fisticuffs, Tonneman thought to take advantage of the interim.

"Jamie." He stepped outside the box. Jamie followed. Adjacent to the box, also curtained in red plush, was a small gallery that looked into the theatre. Tonneman quickly led Jamie past the curtains and onto the balcony. "Can you come to the surgery tomorrow morning?"

"Ha! At last. You've reconsidered joining my association of real estate investors."

"No, Jamie, not that at all. I haven't changed my mind."

"What then?"

"Thaddeus Brown. He's dead."

"Oh?"

"His remains were uncovered in a shallow grave near the Collect. But that's not all." Tonneman noticed the red velvet curtain moving ever so slightly.

Jamie cleared his throat dramatically. "My friend, I'm afraid I've been keeping something from you. That's what I've been trying to tell you."

Tonneman's brow furrowed. But before he could speak, a shout and another tussle began below; instead of ending the fight, the Night Watch and theatre workers had only extended it.

"How do you make a Dutchman into a Yankee?" someone yelled.

"Can't do it. There ain't stock enough," was the response. Now the fight had spread to the stalls. The brawl reached such a pitch that it rendered a performance impossible.

Suddenly, in the midst of the melee, Jake Hays appeared, knocking off hats with his stick and kicking arses.

"It's Old Hays."

"It's Jake."

Quick as it began, the fight was over.

"It seems," said Jamie, "there was an altercation. And . . ." He paused and cleared his throat again. "And Peter and Thaddeus came to blows."

Tonneman's already throbbing head felt as if it had received the ax-man's cut, although he had heard as much from Hays. Perhaps he had fostered in his heart the hope that it was an exaggeration. "Jamie, how do you know this?"

The orchestra began the overture again. And very somber music it was, much in keeping with Tonneman's humor. The crimson curtain moved again. "I have been informed,"

Jamie began. The curtain parted. Goldsmith stepped from the box. Had he been listening?

"Your surgery," Jamie growled. "Nine." Brusquely he brushed passed Goldsmith and entered the box. Tonneman arched his eyebrow at Goldsmith. "Daniel." He moved to follow Jamie.

Goldsmith placed a trembling hand on his arm. He was no longer robust as he'd been as a young man. His frame had shrunk and harbored no meat on it.

Tonneman patted Goldsmith's hunched shoulder. "The years have taken their toll, haven't they?"

"It's not the years," Goldsmith answered harshly. "It's your old German woman, Gretel. She's come back to haunt my dreams. I can't rest without seeing her wretched bloody head."

From the box, Molly leaned over the rail and hissed at her husband on the gallery. He ignored her reprimand, but then fell quiet. The music changed, becoming lighter and gayer.

The overture ended. There was applause, the conductor bowed, the curtains parted.

"Gretel tortures me," Daniel Goldsmith said finally, in a desperate voice. "She comes in the night and whispers to me until I wake in a cold sweat."

"Good God, man, what does she say?"

But Goldsmith's answer was lost as Don Giovanni's servant, Leporello, began his basso complaint.

21

2 FEBRUARY. TUESDAY. EARLY MORNING.

The spectre dripped blood from the jagged wound that
severed head from body. "Johnny . . ." The hoarse
whisper came at him through swollen lips. Red gout
splashed from the ensanguined head to a form beneath it,
the body of his son, Peter. The spectre wailed. "Johnny
. . . Johnny . . . open your eyes."

"Tell me," Tonneman shouted, soundless as a tomb.
"Tell me—"

He awoke, his head bursting with pain. Damn that
Goldsmith. Now he, too, had dreamed of Gretel. *Johnny*
was what she had always called him and Johnny was what
he'd dreamed. "Open your eyes," he mumbled. A bitter
smile creased his face. They would stay open the rest of this
night, that was certain.

And Peter. He'd dreamed of Peter. Peter lying dead.

John Tonneman eased himself from his warm bed and quickly got into his dressing gown. He left his nightcap in place, for the room was icy. He crossed to the fire, stirred it, and added a log. Mariana groaned and threw off the comforter. "Mariana?" She did not answer. Even before the problem with their son, the woman had been acting very strange of late, not at all herself. What the devil was ailing her?

While he mixed himself a willow bark powder in water at the chest of drawers, his musings returned to Gretel. His mind drifted back three decades. To '76, the year of the Declaration, the year America began. The same year Gretel died, brutally murdered by a madman who had plotted to kill George Washington.

Tonneman lit a candle from the fire and carried it down to his surgery. Further examination of Brown's corpse revealed nothing he didn't already know. The man had bled to death. If he hadn't, he would have suffocated to death beneath the earth.

Covering the remains again, Tonneman picked up the skull. His fingers played over the mastoid bones, the bony prominences on the base of the skull behind the ears, and then in and around the orbits.

Skull in hand, he went into his study and closed the surgery door. He sat, staring at its grinning face, at the snagged teeth.

The skull was human, of that he was sure. From the size of the jaw he would say this human once weighed over one hundred pounds. The teeth seemed to be that of a young adult between the ages of fifteen and twenty years. Because of its size, the small mastoid bones, and the sharply outlined orbits, his analytical mind agreed with his earlier intuition: a woman. A young woman.

Now he examined the cervical vertebrae, all seven of which were still joined to the skull. As he did they came loose. "Ah, me. Together so long and separated by my clumsy hands." He held the vertebrae under his magnifying glass. The cut across the fifth cervical vertebra was fascinating.

The skull grinned at him obscenely, its snagged teeth plaguing him more than his headache. He was not given to nightmares. That was Goldsmith's country. Tonneman remembered that it had been Constable Goldsmith who had found Gretel. Afterward, Goldsmith had claimed that Gretel appeared in his dreams demanding vengeance against her killer. But her murderer had been arrested and hanged long ago. Tonneman sighed and leaned back in his chair. His headache was receding. Soon he nodded off to sleep.

He was awakened at dawn by Micah. She tucked a shawl about his shoulders and poked at the fire until it took, sending off comforting waves of heat. After a cup of hot black tea, Tonneman abandoned the mysteries of the skull and the vertebrae. He returned to his bedchamber, where he found Mariana dressed and fixing her hair.

At that moment, he was seized by a wild longing to run his hands through her thick, dark hair as he used to. To hold it to his face and breathe its heady perfume. But when he touched her, she pulled away from him and left the room without a word.

She was furious with him. About Peter. And, if his guess was right, about other things unknown. The woman seemed to hoard grievances against him. Tonneman sighed. His back ached and the tremor in his hands returned.

He washed, shaved, and dressed with dispirit. The evidence thus far left him little hope for exculpating his son. But Mariana was right. He would talk with him.

Much to Tonneman's surprise his son was not still abed, as was the boy's wont. In fact, as he descended the stairs he heard Peter going over their lessons with his sisters.

"Good morning, Peter. Girls."

His dark-eyed Leah's face brightened for him. She was

her mother in miniature—as Mariana had been when first he knew her.

"Papa." Leah jumped up and her hornbook fell to the floor, spilling papers. Her fingers twitched with excitement. "Are you going to do the autopsy now?"

"O grab me." Gretel's face turned pale. "How horrible you are, Lee."

"Autopsies are not for the likes of proper young ladies," Tonneman said, chucking Leah's chin. "Micah, coffee in my study, please."

"Yes, sir." Micah bobbed her head.

"Perhaps Peter would like to observe," Tonneman said, making a special plea to his son.

But the boy turned away. "No, Papa."

Tonneman felt the band across his chest. He was heart-sick. The painful truth was he would be the last of a long line of physicians.

"Let me, Papa, let me." Leah clasped his arm. "Please let me watch."

"Ah, Lee." The old physician knelt and hugged his slender daughter close. "You are your mother all over again."

"What's this?" Peter asked. He picked up Leah's horn-book along with several pieces of paper.

Leah broke away from her father's embrace. "That's mine," she wailed, attempting to recapture the papers, but Peter, ever the tease, held them high above her head, laughing. "Papa, make him stop."

John Tonneman got to his feet, his knee joints creak-ing. He pushed the ache of Peter's rejection away and smiled. "What have you there, Peter? Give it back to your sister."

Instead Peter stood stock still, staring at the paper in his hand. He said nothing. He did nothing.

Leah burst into tears. Peter, shaken, attempted to re-turn the papers to her, but she pushed him away and ran out of the room. Her tiny feet could be heard thumping up the stairs.

"I'll take that," his father said sternly, hand thrust out like a sword.

Mute, Peter surrendered the dubious prize to his father.

Astonishing. There on the top sheet was a flawless drawing of the corpse of Joseph Thaddeus Brown, every detail clear as if he were viewing the authentic entity himself.

"I'll see to Leah, Papa." Gretel flung a haughty look at her brother and quit the room.

"I didn't mean to hurt her, Papa. . . ."

"I know that, Peter. But women are sensitive creatures, and we must protect them." Even as he spoke, John wondered at his words. The women he had known well: Gretel Huntzinger, who had raised him from infancy; Molly, the whore, now Goldsmith's wife, who had become Tonneman's housekeeper after Gretel's death, and Mariana. All were women of unique merit with a certain strength of will.

Only one, who had been his betrothed and had not waited for his return from London, only Abigail Willard—Abigail Comfort, then—did he consider a frail creature. Yet even Abigail had brought her four children back from London and raised them alone after her husband's death.

When he entered his study, his mug of coffee awaited him. So engrossed in thought was he that he had not even seen Micah pass him.

He set Leah's hornbook on his desk, placed her papers on it, and studied her drawing until his eyelids drooped.

Quintin Brock's knocking at the door between the surgery and the study roused him. The scab over Quintin's right eyebrow had been joined by an ugly gash across his nose and a deeper one on his brow.

"What's happened to your face?"

"Not the first time, Doctor Tonneman. They came after me again on the street in front of the theatre last night after the performance."

"Step back into the surgery," Tonneman ordered. "Were you robbed?" These days the tough gangs of New-York that gathered around Bunker Hill and the Lispenards were inserting themselves more and more into the middle of the City.

"That wasn't it." Quintin removed his gray beaver and his gray greatcoat.

"Why, then?"

Quintin stared as if in a trance at the canvas-shrouded body on the examining table.

Tonneman shook Quintin's shoulder to get his attention. He faced the Negro directly and mouthed his words carefully. "Why did they do it?"

"No reason."

"Don't be daft." Tonneman took Quintin's hat and coat and hung them from the hook adjacent to the door. Next he helped the man off with his wine-red jacket. Quintin's shirt was of choice linen. It appeared to be freshly laundered. The former tar worker had come up in the world. "Why should anyone hurt you for no reason?"

"My skin is black," Quintin said, impatient with Tonneman's naïveté.

"And bruised," Tonneman responded, tugging at the man's shirt. "Take this off."

Quintin did as he was told.

By Tonneman's recollection Quintin was not yet sixty. His physical condition seemed good for a man his age. Not like mine, the physician thought, his bones aching.

"Ribs seem all right. No cuts. Only contusions on your chest. Nasty, though. Put some ice on them tonight. I'll give you willow bark for the pain." Tonneman cleaned Quintin's facial wounds with iron water. He covered the nose and brow lacerations with a bit of cloth and sticking plaster, then stepped back so that Quintin could read his lips. "In this civilized City the colored people have almost as many rights as the whites," he muttered as he worked. "Now, down South—"

"Why almost? Why not all? I'm a free man."

Tonneman looked over his shoulder as if someone could hear him in the privacy of his surgery. "Don't talk that way."

"Why not?"

"It's the way of the world. The way things are."

"Does that make it right?" The black man put his shirt and jacket on and placed his hat firmly on his head.

Tonneman sighed. "God in His infinite wisdom chose to create many races."

"Why is it when the white man wants something his way, he cites God? God's scripture, *Do unto others*, he ignores. I've been worrying this all night long and even as I stand here. Do you really want to know why I'm getting my face smashed once a week or more?"

Tonneman, who was readying a small packet of willow bark powder and a cake of his Splendid Hard Soap for Quintin, gave the African his full attention. "Tell me."

"Because a white man wants my land. Butcher Ned Winship wants my land. Tomorrow I could be dead as him." Quintin pointed to the mound of Brown's body. "Everybody in the City knows what they did to him."

Tonneman placed his hand on Quintin's. "They? Who is they?"

Quintin shot him an odd look and shook off his hand. He placed a silver quarter dollar on the instrument cabinet, grabbed his greatcoat, mumbled something unintelligible and left the surgery.

Columbia College

DOCTOR HOSACK will commence his course of Lectures on BOTANY and MATERIA MEDICA, on Monday, the 8th of February

THE SPECTATOR
FEBRUARY 1808

22

2 FEBRUARY. TUESDAY. EARLY MORNING.

Tonneman shuffled back to his study. His coffee was cold. He entered his care of Quintin in his patient book, then jotted a note to talk to Old Hays about the Negro. Without these memoranda to himself he'd have trouble remembering. As he was closing his book, Jamie arrived.

The room seemed suddenly cooler for Jamie's presence, as if his friend had brought all the cold from the outside world inside with him.

"But this is extraordinary," Jamie exclaimed, accepting the mug of hot coffee from Micah. He was staring at Leah's drawing of Brown's body. "Where did you get this?"

"Leah."

"An amazing talent. For a girl. We must nurture it."

Tonneman nodded; a thin smile graced his lips. Illogically he stated, "She has the call to be a healer. She would be a physician. 'Tis pity that the world won't allow it."

Bored, Jamie dropped the drawing on Tonneman's desk. "That may or may not be, John. But more to the moment, it's all over town that Brown has been discovered."

"He's stretched out on my examination table under canvas. He's the reason I asked you to come."

"I don't give a fiddle about Brown. Somebody took our money. I want it back."

"As do I."

Jamie rubbed the tips of his fingers together. "That is the primary question. Where might our money be? More specifically, who might have it?" He narrowed his eyes. When Tonneman didn't offer any comment, he added, "I told you last night that Peter and Thaddeus came to blows a week ago Friday evening."

Tonneman had agonized over this. He'd already tried to discuss it with Peter after Hays had mentioned it, but as always, he'd lost his temper. He would let Jamie give him the entire story before confronting his son again. "How do you know this?"

"One of the Watch came upon them, but I've greased his palm and he'll not talk."

Tonneman felt nothing but despair. "I thank you, my friend. Your deed was kind but ill advised. Hays already knows of it and spoke of it to me. The Watch must have come forward. . . . It will be harder to exonerate my son now that Hays has a witness. What do you suggest we do?"

Jamie shrugged. "Find the money, of course." His eye chanced on the skull, and the sections of vertebrae which Tonneman had placed on the shelf among his books. Jamie picked up the skull and cradled it in the palm of his hand. " 'Alas, poor Yorick,' " he intoned. Then, seriously, "What have we here?"

"A conundrum. Found in the same shallow grave as Friend Brown."

His friend's mouth twisted into a cynical smile. The

blue eyes lit up. With a delicate motion of his hand, he ran a slender finger over the snagged teeth. "Ahhhh."

"Have a look at the vertebrae," Tonneman suggested. Jamie picked the vertebrae up and rolled them in his hand. "Note the cut across the fifth cervical vertebra."

"I see, I see." Jamie's blue eyes gleamed. "Finally, a problem to tax the brain. I grow weary of the diurnal drudgery."

"As you get richer and richer."

Jamie's smile deepened. "Isn't that why your ilk invented this country?"

"Not at all."

"Well, it's what my ilk is using it for." He set the skull and vertebrae on either side of his coffee on Tonneman's desk. "America is a marvelous place to make money. And you know what the money is for?" He didn't even pause to let Tonneman react. "In the words of George Washington, 'Land, land, land.' "

Now Tonneman had to smile. "That's priceless. An old Royalist like you quoting George Washington."

"That is absurd, isn't it?"

"There's more to life than money and land, Jamie."

Jamie cackled. "According to who? What the hell do you think Tom Jeff was about when he bought all that land from the French? From the Mississippi River to the Rocky Mountains, from Canada to the Gulf of Mexico. The Louisiana Purchase was not about politics—it was about land. With that one transaction, your man Jefferson more than doubled the area of this country. And this Embargo has nothing to do with impressed seamen either. That's about land, too. Of course, there's more to life than money and land. There's wine and women." Jamie cackled again. He fingered Tonneman's brown velvet jacket. "I dare say you're not in the almshouse yourself."

Tonneman fluttered his hand, rejecting the remark. "I can't get this skull out of my mind. I keep thinking there's something I've forgotten. . . ."

Jamie put his forefinger to his lips. "No, that's what's wrong. You're not thinking."

Tonneman peered at him. "I recognize that superior air of yours. You *know*, don't you?"

"So do you. It's merely that you've let your brain go rusty all these years so that you don't know you know. It's clear as the sun in the summer sky, my friend."

"In my brain it's winter."

Jamie's blue eyes narrowed. "How many snagged-tooth people have you known in your life?"

"Enough. Patients. But no one of any import."

"Poor Grace. My dear departed wife. Gone but a few years and so quickly forgotten."

"Don't be ridiculous. How could I forget Grace? But what's Grace got to—? Ah . . ." It came to him full blown. "Emma!" In his mind's eye he saw Grace's daughter clearly. Her red hair, her blotchy pale skin, her nervous laughter. "She had snagged teeth. So snagged, one almost covered the other. But as I remember, Emma Greenaway ran off with some man—to Philadelphia? Or was it Richmond?"

"Philadelphia. We only know she was seen boarding the coach to Princeton."

"What makes you think this skull is Emma? That doesn't make any sense."

There was an amused twinkle in Jamie's eye.

Tonneman's eyes lit up in response. "But what if she never left the City after all?"

"Now, that's much better, my friend. And here are these captivating vertebrae." He rolled them almost lovingly in the curve of his palm. "We both know this head didn't merely fall from its body after many years in the ground. It was chopped off."

"Agreed."

"And if you take that thought one step further?"

Tonneman's brow furrowed as he cast his mind back in time. "Hickey?"

"Exactly. Hickey and his fancy for red-haired women."

"But Hickey's victims put me no closer to the answer. Are you suggesting this is one of Hickey's girls? That Hickey chopped off Emma's head?"

"Exactly."

23

2 FEBRUARY. TUESDAY. AFTERNOON TO EVENING.

The City of New-York's first High Constable, Jacob Hays, was cock of the walk, and he played the role to a fare-thee-well. The doughty bantam had a most singular gait; he was the City's most famous citizen, and he took this designation very seriously.

And he was a remarkably powerful man, touring his City day and night, break of dawn till after sundown. To-day, as usual, Jake Hays had already been at it since sunrise, a few minutes after seven that morning, when he'd left his house on Sugarloaf-street, just off Broadway, in the Fifth Ward. Recreation and sleep were afterthoughts. He had grown an international reputation among law men as a thief-taker and a "terror to evildoers."

Though there was a force of men called the Constabulary, if Jacob Hays didn't do the job it wouldn't get done.

The Constabulary force consisted of two lone Constables for each ward, and there were nine wards from the tip of the island to beyond Chambers-street, where the City ended. The Constables were elected annually, and it was well known all were idlers who wore the badge and did little to uphold the law. Unless soliciting bribes was to be considered doing something.

Come sundown, Watch Captains saw to a special citizen's Night Watch who had their own day trades. The Night Watch were often set upon by gang ruffians if they dared to trespass on what the gangs considered their domain. That domain was the City of New-York at night.

Oak staff in hand, Hays was a formidable opponent, able to vanquish men twice his size. Every day, with Noah following, he walked the length of Broadway to Chambers at least once, making certain stops on Broadway and along the side streets. Other than these specific locales, his route was left to whim and inspiration, wherever his instinct told him trouble might be. And his instinct was rarely wrong.

And on this nippy February afternoon, which was passing quickly into evening, in the year of our Lord 1808, Broadway was, as it always had been, crowded with people and horses, traveling every direction.

A pack of cats stalked through the garbage dumped in the middle of the road. The three street sweepers, who had the distinctive walk of sailors, half-heartedly swept the road of manure. The cats ignored the men, the men ignored the cats. The populace and Walter Dalton, one of the two Fifth Ward Constables, ignored the cats and the men.

"Afternoon, High Constable." The brass-starred Constable Dalton straightened up as he saluted. He showed a more pleasant face to the world at large when Old Hays was about. If it weren't for Jake Hays, the Constables wouldn't even be wearing stars to mark them. It was Hays who organized the police, giving them their five-pointed stars—brass for patrollers, copper for the sergeants, silver for lieutenants

and captains, and gold for Jake himself and the commis-
sioners.

Jake nodded curtly to Dalton.

"Good afternoon, Jake," a citizen called.

"And to you," Hays roared back.

"Good afternoon, High Constable," others called as
they passed. Jake saluted each with his stick to his tall
beaver.

At half four Jake stopped for some beefsteak pie and
coffee at the Pine-street Tavern. By that time of day he'd
drunk so much coffee he was fit to burst, so the stop was as
much to relieve himself as to eat his evening meal. He
never had supper at home except on Sunday, the day he
usually reserved for his family.

After his supper, Hays spied Cyrus the Giant, who daily
laid his tree trunk across the Broadway road insisting on a
one cent toll fee from anything on wheels or runners, or
horseback, and a half cent to those afoot. Some paid to be
charitable, many out of fear. When deep in his cups, Cyrus
was a terror. Jake could take him down, but even for Jake
Hays it was a chore.

Today Cyrus was only passing drunk. "You all right,
Cyrus?"

Cyrus, who enjoyed making snorting noises in his
throat, produced one now. "*Awk* dandy, Jake."

"Get the tree off the road."

The giant ducked his head, on which a filthy cap sporting a turkey feather rested, and complied, scattering coins
as he did. He was wearing a combination of two stitched-
together greatcoats, one brown, the other green. The green
sleeve had been gouged away at the shoulder.

"Put them in your pocket."

"*Awk* holes."

"How much money have you collected?

"This much. *Awk. Awk.*" Cyrus showed him a handful
of copper coins, grinning, revealing an immense mouth of
rotting teeth.

"You use that for food, not booze. You hear me?"

"*Awk.*"

"Does that mean yes?"

The giant nodded vigorously.

"Wait here."

"*Awk*, Jake." Cyrus shuffled his feet inside makeshift boots. His protruding toes were wrapped in rags.

Jake thrust his head into Leonard's Tavern. "Leonard, wake Tom up."

A tall youth bounced up from a bench, knocking his beer over. "I'm up, Jake." This was Constable Thomas Burton of the Second Ward.

"Get out here, Constable Burton. Take Cyrus to jail for a good night's sleep."

"Yes, Jake."

"And tell Sergeant Alsop that Cyrus had better have all his pennies when he leaves in the morning."

"Yes, Jake."

"That goes for you, too."

Burton saluted, and he and a docile Cyrus started their trek to the City Jail in Chambers-street.

Jake Hays squinted up at the near-setting sun. That made it a bit after five. The gentry were on their way to or were already snug in their homes. Perhaps they would reappear later, families and couples to the theatres, lone men seeking the conviviality of coffee houses or taverns. Many of the workie women had already served the gentry their dinner and were trudging homeward with food they had bought or bartered for or gotten by fair means or foul from their mistresses' larders to feed their own families.

Next Jake surveyed the Collect. After making a complete tour around the remains of Fresh Water Pond, he stopped at Coulter's Brewery, in the Sixth Ward. The five-story building sat on what until recently had been the banks of the Collect, at the intersection of Orange, Cross, and Anthony. There, Dirk Heinlein sent an apprentice out with the beer. One for Jake, one for Noah. It was the way they ended the tour, and was always welcome.

Heinlein usually had two or three apprentices who worked by the usual contract, signed before a magistrate. The master had to provide food, clothing, washing, and lodging, and at the end of the contract, a new suit of clothing. By law, the apprentice had to be given lessons in reading and writing. The apprentice, on his part, had to agree that when he later plied his learned trade, it would be at a safe and specific distance from the master's shop.

As Jake sipped his brew, he pondered the hills of New Jersey across the North River. New-York was getting too crowded. Perhaps he should move his family across the river? No. An idle thought. He liked this town.

"You having a good day, Mr. Hays?" Noah asked.

"Bright as sunshine."

"But . . . ?"

Jake Hays's lips twitched in what was meant to be a smile. "This Brown predicament. A tough nut."

"You'll crack it."

"By and by. But it's not just another smashed head. This man was shoveled under while he was still breathing."

"That's nasty."

"Indeed. And there are things connected to the man that need investigating. From what I hear there's cash missing."

"There's folks in this town who'd kill you for ten dollars."

"New-York can be a mean place," Jake agreed. "This time a great deal more than ten dollars is involved. And Brown worked for the City and the Collect Company."

Noah nodded. "That should give you lots of ideas."

Jake rolled his eyes. "How much money is going into the Canal and how much is going into someone's pocket?"

"Don't ask me, Mr. Jake. I just drive the horse."

Jake lifted his beaver and wiped his brow with the back of his wrist. "Want to trade jobs?"

"No, thank you, sir." Noah smiled. It was an exchange the two men indulged in often.

"How about you, Noah? You having a good day?"

"Can't complain." Noah handed his empty tankard to the waiting apprentice; Jake drained his tankard and did the same. Noah returned to his vehicle.

"Good night, Dirk," Jake called.

"See you tomorrow, Jake," came from within the brewery.

Coming toward them down Orange-street was a woman with a dray. She was only twenty but had the look of forty years. Her four children were piled atop the low cart. A mixed-breed terrier kept jumping off and then on and then off again. The same thing over and over. The children gazed at Jake out of deep-set, hollow eyes.

"Evening, Meg."

"Evening, Jake." One of the children, a tyke of perhaps six, climbed down from the dray and began scavenging for food in the garbage which was strewn over the road.

"What do you know?"

"About what?"

"What have you heard about Joseph Thaddeus Brown?"

A second child, maybe seven or eight, jumped from the wagon carrying a pot and headed toward the brewery. Meg Doty watched her progress for a moment. "Commissioner of Streets? Also worked for the Collect Company?"

Jake nodded.

"Dead, you know." She rolled her eyes back to the whites.

Jake grimaced. Meg liked to think she was funny. "Was he stealing from the Collect Company?"

"Some say yes, some say no."

"You're a great comfort, Meg."

"I try, Mr. High Constable, sir."

"We dug him up near the Collect on Monday. I reckon he was put there during the ten days—that would be two Fridays before when he was last seen in the Collect office. I need to know if anyone saw him that first Friday night. Or after. But let's concentrate on that first Friday night."

Meg scratched her faded blond curls under her black woolly bonnet. "That would be twenty-two January. Friday. In the night?"

"Yes. You know anything about him?"

"Afraid not. Is there any other way I can assist the law?"

"Yes, and keep this one under your hat. Do you know Peter Tonneman?"

"Old Tonneman's son? He's partial to the milk of the grain. He and that young Willard, who's nephew to high-and-mighty Jamie Jamison, like to bend an elbow of an evening. What about young Tonneman?"

"I'd like to know where he was after that same Friday."

"Is there a connection between him and Brown dead? I know he worked for the man."

"I don't know. Keep it quiet when you ask about young Peter. I don't want to hurt his reputation if there's nothing to it."

"I'll keep my ears up and ask about."

Jake gave her a half disme.

Meg took the coin, inspected it glumly, and placed it in her cowhide purse, which hung by a strap from her wrist.

Jake waited for her to rub her nose and say the usual.

Meg rubbed her nose. "Now that I think of it, something does come to mind. . . ."

"That is?"

"Brown was taking bribes."

Jake nodded. It was something he'd considered. "And?"

"From contractors and carters and the like. Those who want to get on the Collect money wagon."

Jake dug into his coat pocket. "Yes?"

The two boys remaining on the dray were fighting now over a bit of bread. "I heard tell," Meg said, placidly observing the tussle, "he was sharing money with this partner of his."

"Who would that be?"

Meg stared wide at the High Constable for a moment then hissed at the boys in the dray. The boys stopped and watched their mother cautiously.

"Who, Meg?"

"Now that I wouldn't know."

"How much?"

"God is my judge, High Constable, I don't know. If I did I would ask for the moon and take my kids and do some farming up-country."

"Who killed Brown?"

She sniffed. She wiped her nose on the sleeve of her patched coat. "Don't know. But I hear it was bought and paid for."

"Who paid?"

"This is just chatter picked up here and around, you understand." She smiled, having caught sight of her little girl carrying the pot of brew from Coulter's.

Jake brought out two quarter dollars. "Talk. Who paid to have Brown killed?"

Meg gaped at the silver coins. She reached her half-gloved black-incrusted fingers for them. When the coins were secure in her grasp, she said, "John Tonneman."

*Thirty Dollars Reward—Yesterday afternoon, a sailor,
meeting one of our carrier-boys at the corner of New-Slip
and Water-street, asked him to give him a paper, and
being denied, set a large dog on him, which bit his leg,
through his boot, in a terrible manner. Subscribers living
on this route, from Fly-Market to New-Slip & C. will
have the goodness to excuse emissions for the present.
The above reward will be paid to any person who will give
information so that the villain may be detected.*

NEW-YORK HERALD
FEBRUARY 1808

24

2 FEBRUARY. TUESDAY. NIGHT.

"There's not a rogue in this City I don't know." Jake was
talking to Noah.

Noah nodded; he'd heard it before.

It was coming on to eight o'clock, nearly two hours
since Meg Doty had named John Tonneman. They'd been
following Meg. It was Jake's view that the best way to find
out about crime was to follow the criminal.

And Meg had led them up one road, down another,
into alleys and cul-de-sacs. She had pawed through garbage,
kicking what she found unworthy out into the middle of

the road, stopping in one tavern after the other along the way, leading them a merry chase as if she knew she was being followed.

Finally she left her dray, her children, and the jumping dog at a gray house in Mott-street. From there Jake and Noah trailed her to Mulberry, where they now watched. And waited.

All the street lamps in Mulberry were out. If not neglected by the Watch, then certainly they'd been vandalized by Ned Winship's Bruiser Boys, who considered a working street lamp a challenge. It also shed too much light on what they did. The naked mulberry trees, for which the street had been named, stood silent sentinels, as in an unhallowed graveyard.

Jake couldn't help but wonder how many nameless bodies were buried beneath the mulberries, to make them thrive and grow so tall.

These thoughts led him to Thaddeus Brown. Now why was Brown's body more important than any of the nameless ones? Simple. Because of the money.

Meg had gone into Ned Winship's Tavern. She was taking too long to come back out.

"Wait for me," Jake told Noah.

Noah eyed Winship's Tavern warily. "Don't I always?"

Jake had just crossed the road when the door to the tavern slammed open and a body came flying out. The elegant gentleman should have known better than to be in such a place. But as Jake watched, the misguided fellow crawled back to the door, butted it open with his head, and crawled in. "Where's my hat?" he brayed. Out he came again, soaring, his tall hat behind him. He started back again.

Jake tapped him on the shoulder. "I don't think they want you in there, brother."

Glaze-eyed, the man peered up at Jake. "I presume not," he replied with inflated dignity.

Jake retrieved the man's hat from the muddy ground

and gave it a quick brush with his forearm. He offered the man a hand up. "Can you walk?"

The man shook his head, then stopped abruptly. "Shouldn't do that. Dizzy." He slumped.

"I can let you sleep in the jail."

At that, the drunkard bolted upright. "Heavens, no. No." He straightened stiff as a rod, seized his hat from Jake, clamped it on his pomaded curls, and staggered off into the blackness of Mulberry-street.

Jake gestured to Noah with his staff, then used it to push the tavern door open. The long, narrow room was murky with smoke and the stink of cabbage, tobacco, and sweat. Underfoot, the floors were gritty with sawdust, strewn with broken glass and other refuse. A counter on a slight downward slope was thrust up against the right-hand wall. The rest of the chamber was jammed with ill-standing, rough-hewn pine tables.

The tavern was swarming with depraved humanity. Chief among them was the proprietor. Down the bar, Butcher Ned Winship was scratching the ears of a striped orange tabby cat settled at his elbow on the bar, while he played a game of Patience with a new deck of Black Eagle cards. Each time the tavernkeeper played a card the cat pawed his arm. When Ned scratched, the cat purred deeply. To the left of the door, five men were playing cards.

When Jake appeared, the five cardplayers went still; the others in the place followed suit as bleary eyes watched the High Constable cross to the bar. The corollary to Jake's statement was true, too: there was not a rogue in this City who didn't know him.

Not only were they watching Jake, they were watching his stick. All knew he could be vicious with it when he chose to. And no one wanted to be his target. Not four feet from Jake, at a table for three, sat a man who didn't have the wits of the others. He wasn't watching Jake or his stick.

Nor was he paying attention to Wicked Polly, the brawny prostitute who sat across from him, signaling with lifts of her thick black eyebrows. He was too busy working his sharp knife, slicing away a sleeping mark's pocket.

Nor did the cut-pocket pay any attention when the tabby leaped up on the table and watched the process as intently as Jake watched, as intently as everyone in the tavern now watched.

When the perpetrator had finished his task, folded his clasp knife, and placed it and the victim's pocket-wrapped wallet into his own pocket, Jake marched right to him. "Well, Pockets?"

Pockets didn't bat an eye. "And good evening to you, High Constable. Can I offer you a beer? Wet your whistle? My treat."

"You know I don't drink with scum."

Pockets displayed a crooked grin.

"Put it on the table."

"What? Sir."

Jake thumped the table with his staff. The table responded with a resounding jump. Hissing, the cat leaped to the sawdust-covered floor. The candlestick swayed, shimmering shadow and light, but did not fall. Rum sloshed in the three glasses on the table. Only one glass tipped. It rolled, and fell to the floor with a small crash. The cat darted away but inched back almost immediately to sniff the spreading rum. Waking, the victim blinked and twitched, then immediately returned to his stuporous sleep.

"All right, all right," Pockets whined, slapping the dupe's wallet on the table.

"The knife."

Pockets twisted his lips and set the folded knife next to the wallet. "Can I go now?" As he stood, he scooped up the cat and flung it at Jake. Jake merely raised his left hand and parried the spitting feline, who lit on the bar with all claws extended, ready to take care of Pockets when Jake was through with him.

From the sheath behind Pockets's back, a second knife

appeared. This knife was not folded. It was straight and to the point and on its way to Jake's belly.

Jake's stick went into action. *Whack!* Across the wrist. Another *whack*. This one across the side of Pockets's head. Pockets fell into his chair, his knife clattered to the floor. Jake picked up the knife and stabbed it into the bar.

From the other side of the counter, Charlie Wright (who-could-do-no-wrong) roared with laughter. Ned Winship pounded on the bar with his mug. The tabby, deciding the state of affairs was all too human, licked her fur.

Charlie Wright was new to the City, another gift of Mr. Jefferson's Embargo. The High Constable had heard about him the month before, the day after Wright's ship, the *Lucy Belle*, had beached Charlie, along with most of its crew, and sailed off to Canada.

Charlie had been first mate on the *Lucy Belle*. A seaman who had sailed under Charlie had thought to take his revenge for the first mate's constant bullying. According to Jake's informers, Charlie had beaten the man near to death. Within three days of his beaching Charlie had found employment with Ned Winship, and shortly thereafter, having proven his worth and then some, Charlie became Ned's chief henchman. Like Butcher Ned, he was a thorn in the side of Jacob Hays.

Who-could-do-no-wrong was added to Charlie's name because if you accused him of doing wrong, he would beat you half to death, then announce that he was "Charlie Wright, who could do no wrong," and dare you to deny it.

This was the first time the High Constable had set eyes on Charlie. He hadn't liked what he'd heard; he liked what he saw less.

"Well done, High Constable," Ned said. His voice was thin and gravel-filled.

Jake glared at the Butcher. He tilted Pockets's chair. Pockets fell to the floor with a thud. "Open the door, Polly."

Polly obeyed.

Jake grabbed Pockets by the scruff of his coat and heaved him out into Mulberry-street. "Noah," he yelled. "Hold this cut-pocket for me." He turned back to the sodden victim, who was sleeping peacefully, unknowing, unworried. "Polly, take this poor saphead out to my man and watch over him till I come out."

The whore fingered her black braid. "Yes, Mr. High Constable." With great skill she lifted the unconscious man. As she draped his arm about her shoulder, Ned started to sing, *"Young people who delight in sin, I'll tell you what has lately been. . . ."* Charlie Wright joined in, all the while motioning with his hands for others in the smoky room to do the same.

The tune was *Wicked Polly*, a religious song out of Rhode Island, and whence this Polly had gotten her sobriquet. Now everyone, with the exception of Jake and Polly, was singing it. The blaring voices threatened to bring the roof down. Or Polly. For the song, though it sang about a Rhode Island sinner, was in truth a warning to Polly. A warning about being too cooperative with the Constabulary. As everyone knew, the last words of the song were: *"Lest you in sin, like Polly die."* Polly blanched. She did not stay to hear the end of the ballad, but rushed the dupe outside.

Jake waited patiently for the tune to be over.

"Lest you in sin, like Polly die," thundered through the room. It was followed by laughter. During the song and the laughter, Jake stood steadfast. The laughter faded and the various culls found places to look at other than Jake Hays's sharp eyes.

Ned shouted, "Huzzah! Drinks on Butcher Ned." The mob crowded to the bar. "Beer, High Constable?"

Jake nodded. Dealing with Pockets and listening to that song had given him a thirst. He drank his tankard of beer in one long swallow. Jake leaned to scratch the cat, then he placed two copper pennies on the bar. On a whim he added a half cent. "The halfpenny is for the song."

"Your money's no good here," Ned declared.

Jake ignored him. He peered about the dim chamber. Meg was nowhere to be seen.

"Cold night." Ned's thin lips curled in false good nature.

Jake didn't bother to answer. Stopping only to light his cheroot from one of the candles on the bar, he went outside. Polly and the cut-pocket's dupe were inside the carriage. Leaning on the back of the vehicle, his hands tied securely, was a sheepish Pockets.

The dupe, it turned out, lived nearby in Crosby-street. After delivering him and his wallet safe and sound, they headed for the City Jail, Jake and Polly inside, Noah at the reins, and Pockets tied to the boot, stumbling behind.

"Damn it, Jake, this is not kind," Pockets grumbled.

"In your business I'm certain you know a great deal about kindness, Pockets," Jake replied. To Polly, he said, "Give me one good reason why I don't lock you up along with Pockets."

"Because inside your jail Ned will have me a dead mackerel soon enough, and you wouldn't want my life on your head, now would you? Let me go and I'll leave town tonight."

"Why should I?"

"Because I can tell you about Thaddeus Brown's lady friend."

"Oh?" Jake savored his cheroot. "Go on. I wasn't aware he had one."

"Well, I don't know her name. I only know the Broadbrim enjoyed her companionship this past year. Seems he come into some money. . . ." Polly paused, cocking an eye at Jake, waiting for a response. When none was forthcoming, the whore continued in a rush, "She's a Frenchie, I think. Big girl. Works out of a house in Duane-street and she has a small scar, what do they call it, like part of a moon with points on both ends."

"A crescent."

"That's it, a crescent scar on her left cheek where her man hit her once."

"And who is her man?"

"I don't know. But some people think it was this fellow what killed Brown."

25

3 FEBRUARY. WEDNESDAY. MORNING.

After a night spent in a cold, wet, cramped cell, Pockets was eager to talk. He stepped close to Jake. "I hate rats," he confided.

The man reeked of piss and garlic. "I'm certain the rats feel no love for you," Jake told him.

They were in a room only slightly larger than Pockets's cell. The sole furniture was a low stool. "Except to have me for breakfast, which, by the way . . ." Pockets made a show of sniffing at the scent of cooking from down the hall. "My belly tells me it's well after eating time. Hot bread and tea with a bit of cider in it would go very well, thank you."

"Sit."

"Oh, no, sir. There's only one. You take it."

"Sit."

Pockets sat.

"First we talk, then you eat."

"I reckoned as much."

"Stop wasting my time, Garrit. What do you have for me?"

The cut-pocket's eyes widened. "Garrit? Nobody's called me that since my ma."

"Well, I'm not your ma, Garrit Ellis, that's for sure. What do you have?"

Pockets looked at Jake, sly-eyed. "What do you need?"

"On Friday night, twenty-two January, Joseph Thaddeus Brown, the Commissioner of Streets. Someone or ones bashed him on the head and stuck his body into the marsh ground of the Collect. I want to know who did it."

"Shit, High Constable, if I could tell you that, I would expect a banquet and a bit of gold."

"If you're lucky you'll get stale bread and a kick in the arse to send you on your way. What do you know?"

"Not much," he whined. "Could I have my tea and cider now?"

Jake kicked the stool out from under Garrit Ellis, sending him sprawling to the grimy floor. "Talk."

The thief picked himself up and made much of dusting himself off. "I don't know what one has to do with t'other, but our Ned is now in the digging and building trades. Why do you think it's taking so long to complete your new City Hall out there? You think you or the Mayor, old or new, run this town?" Pockets shook his head vigorously. "It's Big Ned. Ned likes the Canal. And the digging of it. He steals City supplies. Then he sells what he steals right back to you ninnies who run this City. He threatens anyone who dares to cross him. And he gets them to pay him if they want to stay in the game. 'Pay us or you can't work.' Or 'You can't sell food here.' That's Ned. He says jump, lots of people say where to? If someone wants to dig holes, fill them, cart, mason, lay brick, and all that sort of thing—"

Sergeant Albert Alsop came in with a mug of black tea for the High Constable and a folded piece of paper.

At once Pockets became agitated, rubbing his face, scratching his head.

Alsop ignored him. To the High Constable he said, "This note just came for you."

Jake read the paper, nodded. But Alsop didn't leave. Pockets coughed. Alsop looked at him. Jake didn't miss the poison in the sergeant's stare. Was it merely hate for criminals or was it more? Alsop left the room.

Jake wanted to hear more of what Pockets had to say. During the British occupation, much of the City had been destroyed by the fires of '76 and '78, leaving thousands homeless. After the War ended in '83, New-York had been more than half rebuilt. And since then, people like Ned had been engaged in bleeding the City. "Go on," he said to the cut-pocket.

Pockets shrugged. "Digging and carting and all those things. They have to get Butcher Ned's all right, else Charlie Wright will rebuke."

"How?"

"O Grab Me, Jake, you know as well as I. You're not from New Jersey, for Jesus' sake."

Jake raised a cautionary finger.

"Sorry. But you know what I mean." Pockets blew his nose into his hand, shook the effusion to the floor, and wiped his hand on his trousers.

"No. Sum it out for me. What?"

"Depends. Punch in the nose. Kick in the stones. Knife in the gut. All the same to Charlie Wright, who, as we all know, can do no wrong."

JAKE REREAD THE note Alsop had given him, then took a walk down to City Hall. It was only a dozen blocks or so to Number 26 Wall-street, at Nassau, where the City Hall had stood since 1747. This was Old Federal Hall where Washington took his oath as president on 30 April, 1789, when New-York was still the nation's capital.

It would also be Old City Hall as soon as the new City Hall on Chambers was completed. Whenever that would be.

This Hall was an impressive brick building of three stories with a basement. At the top of a brief staircase were columns and three arches. On the roof were two large chimneys, and in the center, an elaborate dome on which a rooster weathervane surveyed its dominion.

One of the large chambers in City Hall was known as the Picture Room because of the portraits on the walls. The large room displayed George Washington and other heroes of the War for Independence, the late Louis XVI of France, his Queen, Marie Antoinette, and Christopher Columbus.

Next door to the Picture Room was the New-York Historical Society which had been founded four years earlier. The room was let rent-free. Both Jake and the man he was going to meet were members. As Jake approached, a heavy man of striking height left the Historical Society and headed into the Picture Room. Jake hurried his steps so as not to keep him waiting.

The man had a well-shaped head, a broad forehead, a Grecian nose, curly chestnut hair, clear hazel eyes, and the smooth complexion of a woman. He stood some seven or eight inches over Jake Hays.

"Good morning, sir."

The man went to the door, opened it, peered up and down the corridor, closed the door, and returned to Jake, who was contemplating President Washington. "It is now three days since you found a body."

Jake nodded. "We find a great many bodies in this town, sad to say."

"But this one was a *political* body. Commissioner of

Streets Brown. Three days is too long for me to wait for that kind of news."

Jake sighed. He was a practical man, but like John Tonneman, he did not care for the game of politics. "Yes, sir."

"This is the sort of thing I have to be informed of immediately. The time between now and the twenty-second is delicate as eggs. I want my own man in that job."

"Yes, sir."

"I would greatly appreciate it if that Federalist arsehole Willett was not informed."

"I won't tell him. But it is about town, sir."

The big man pulled at the lobe of his right ear. "That I know. My concern is most likely wasted. Come the twenty-second, I'll appoint John Hunn to the job and that will be it. But I want to be told of your progress. Thank you for coming to see me, High Constable."

Jake nodded his head and left the Picture Room. De Witt Clinton was a good man, a good Mayor. And some day he'd probably be a good Governor, perhaps, hopefully, even a good President. But today he was just another politician and a pain in the arse.

Suddenly of peevish disposition, the usually cheerful High Constable made today a rare occasion. He went home for his midday meal.

A NEW NOVEL—*this day is published and for sale by M. & W. Ward, No. 149 Pearl-street, price $1.25, in boards,*

CORINNA, OR ITALY

BY MADAME DE STAEL HOLSTEIN

This work, since its translation, has gone through several editions in England, and it is pronounced by the different Reviews to be of first-rate merit.

NEW-YORK HERALD
FEBRUARY 1808

26

3 FEBRUARY. WEDNESDAY. AFTERNOON.

Abigail Willard, plump in her blue damask dress, her small slippered feet on a footstool, was reading Miss Owenson's latest novel, *The Wild Irish Girl.* She put the book aside and rose from the gold silk Sheraton sofa to greet Tonneman, kissing him lightly on the cheek. An infant slept peacefully in a cradle near the hearth. The ample fire and the soft illumination of the many lamps made the room warm and cozy.

"John, a pleasant surprise." Her forefinger grazed her lips.

Tonneman nodded. The baby. He would speak softly. It always amazed him to see Abigail. Her face had filled out but barely aged; it still looked much as it had so long ago. Cheeks dimpled and eyes, still cornflower blue, vivid against her pale skin and silvery hair. Ah, the hair, that was the difference, the only way age had laid claim to her beauty. As Mariana had never taken to the Willards, nor they to her, Tonneman alone had become a frequent visitor since Abigail was widowed twelve years earlier.

She crossed to the door and tugged three times on an embroidered band that hung next to the doorpost.

Tonneman sank into a broad-bottomed wing chair, keenly aware of the sense of calm that swept over him. So different from the strife and chaos in his home. In his marriage.

A timid knock, and the parlor door opened. The maid entered, curtsied. "Yes, ma'am," she whispered.

"I rang three times," Abigail said, a kind reproof. "That means tea."

"Yes, ma'am."

As the maid left, the infant gurgled and hiccoughed.

"Elizabeth's youngest, Mary." Abigail settled herself again on the sofa and rocked the cradle gently with the toe of her velvet slipper. "Here from Albany to visit their granny for a fortnight. Elizabeth's taken the other three to the circus."

"Granny?" John laughed. It was difficult to think of Abigail as *granny*.

"Very much so, John. Twelve times over. And soon to be fourteen. Harold's and Charles's wives, too. . . . You seem tired, John."

"I am. I'm getting old."

"We all are, my dear."

They chatted in this fond vein for a bit until the maid returned with a tray bearing a Wedgwood china pot of tea under a cozy, two cups, embroidered linen napkins, silver spoons, and a plate of shortbread.

"That's fine, Nancy, thank you." Abigail poured the tea and held out a cup to Tonneman, who accepted with a heartfelt sigh.

Since she'd jilted him and married Richard Willard all those many years before, Tonneman never knew exactly how he felt about Abigail. He decided he knew now. Envy. Everything came so easily for Abigail. He said, "Do you know that over the years your home has been a sanctuary for me?"

"I know, John. It's a restful haven for me, too. Sometimes. When only George and I are in residence, which is rare." She smiled. "And George can be wild. But then, he is his father's son. Thank heaven for Jamie."

Tonneman sipped his tea. "Yes, thank heaven for Jamie. Peter is a constant source of worry."

"How are the girls?"

"Gretel is a young lady. And Lee—" He smiled. "If Lee were a lad, she would be a physician and carry on for me. And my father."

"Mariana is well?" Abigail offered Tonneman the plate of shortbread, watched him select a piece and bite into it.

"Delicious." She was waiting for his answer. "Mariana is splendid." He did not meet Abigail's challenging eyes.

"Is something wrong, John? Is Mariana ill?"

"She has never gotten over David's death. She blames me. Hell, I blame me. . . ." He set his cup down on a side table. "She gives Peter his head in all matters. The boy has no discipline. Spared was the rod, spoilt is the child."

"She's a mother, my dear. . . ." Abigail chose a slice of shortbread.

"She paces the house at all hours. She is always furious with me."

Abigail chewed her shortbread thoughtfully, listening intently.

Distressed, Tonneman shook his head. "I'm a man of medicine, Abigail, and I don't know what ails her."

"But John, it's so perfectly clear. Don't you know? It's woman's problems." Abigail's cheeks grew rosy. "She's of an age, and I'm well beyond." There was a green-and-black French fan on the table. Abigail picked it up, snapped it open with a flourish, and fanned herself with deliberate loftiness. To all effects, the words she'd just spoken had never passed her lips.

Tonneman stared at her. He stood and leaned his elbow on the mantel. "How can a man be so stupid? How could I?" He patted his breast pocket for a segar. "May I smoke?"

"Of course."

His face contorted. He was perplexed. His hand had found something. It produced, not the segar, but the cameo. He'd forgotten that that was why he'd come calling in the first place.

"What have you there?"

He placed it in her palm without a word, and was rewarded with a gasp of recognition. "You know it?"

Abigail traced her finger over the etched profile on the onyx, then the broken chain. "It was my niece's, John. Emma Greenaway. Where in God's name did you find it?" She became agitated, recalling her husband's anger at the time her niece disappeared. She set the cameo down near the tea tray and rose from her chair, not too steadily. Her face grew pale. She fanned herself rapidly and licked her lips. "Has Emma returned?"

"In a manner of speaking." Tonneman took Abigail's soft hands in his. "We found that cameo and what we believe are Emma's remains when we dug up Joseph Thaddeus Brown's body at the Collect Monday morning."

Horrified, Abigail dropped her fan. "Oh, no. Are you saying Emma never left New-York?"

He nodded. "It was her red hair, Abigail. She was killed the same way Hickey killed his other victims."

"Dear God, dear God. When I thought Emma was alive I accepted things the way they were. But now that I see she died this horrible death . . . I must know who did this to her."

"I would assume Thomas Hickey."

"But do you know for sure?"

"No."

"Then you must find out. For my sake." Abigail sank back on the sofa, dislodging her novel, which fell to the floor with a thud, rousing baby Mary, who began to cry.

Distracted from Tonneman's terrible news, Abigail rushed to the child and gathered the swaddled form to her breast.

John Tonneman bent, without thinking, to pick up the book. Absently he thumbed through it. "Abigail, do you remember your servant girl, the one who gave her clothing to Emma? Betsie? Bessie . . . Betty?"

"There, there, sweetheart," Abigail crooned to the red-faced infant. "Betty."

"You sent her to your parents after Richard and Grace . . ." He stopped. There was no need to say more. Both remembered all too well how the brother and sister, Richard Willard and Emma's mother Grace Greenaway, had near beaten the maid to death. "We must find Betty. If she's still living."

"Betty is very much alive, John." Abigail kissed her granddaughter, rocking her in her arms, murmuring to the infant, fussing with her tiny lace-trimmed cap. "That's my good little Mary . . ."

He could feel the blood of life pounding in his veins. Excited, he asked, "Where is she?"

"I brought her back directly after Richard died. It was Betty who made this shortbread."

Wanted a good Cook, to whom liberal wages will be given
—Apply at this Office.

NEW-YORK HERALD
FEBRUARY 1808

27

3 FEBRUARY. WEDNESDAY. AFTERNOON.

The Betty who presented herself to Tonneman with a courteous respectful bob bore no resemblance whatever to the slight, horribly beaten girl he had treated so long ago, just as war was breaking out. This Betty was a small round ball with a tiny chin buried in another plumper chin. Her pale hair was streaked with gray and covered by a crisp, white cap. A prominent nose was smudged with flour.

Obviously she'd been wearing a large apron, for within an outline her dark linsey-woolsey dress was spotless. Without the outline, dots of flour and grease stains. She rubbed her hands together as if to soothe them. Tonneman recognized the gnarls of arthritis.

"You remember Doctor Tonneman, Betty?" Abigail asked.

Betty's eyes widened over her fat cheeks. "Of course, ma'am." As she bobbed again she looked at Old Tonneman furtively.

To put the cook at her ease, Tonneman gave her what he hoped was a pleasant smile. "You appear well and happy, Betty."

"That I am, sir. Mrs. Willard is good to me."

"Betty, Doctor Tonneman would like to ask you some questions about—"

"Yes, sir." She bobbed yet again.

"Emma Greenaway," Tonneman said.

Betty stepped back as if he'd struck her. She stared at him, the color of her face matching the flour on her nose.

"John . . ." Abigail's tone was a silky reprimand.

"I've got my cake to see to. The oven. The hired girl is not . . ." Betty backed out of the room, clutching the sides of her dress. She closed the door, leaving Tonneman and Abigail alone, taken by surprise at the abruptness of the cook's departure.

But neither had a chance to speak. For there came a great clamor and all at once the room was filled with children. The infant added her shriek to the din. Tonneman quickly took his leave, but not before asking Abigail's permission to depart via the kitchen.

She nodded with a distracted smile as her grandchildren clustered about her.

The kitchen in the Willard mansion was below the stairs. The old doctor had to hug the wall in order to negotiate his way down the cramped, narrow steps. Once he bumped his head on the low ceiling. Sugar and butter in sweet combination seeped from behind the closed door at the foot of the stairs, teasing his senses.

When he opened the door he came into a spacious room. Various and diverse cauldrons and pots bubbled on the large hearth. Four chickens roasted on a spit. The smell of crisp chicken skin filled the air, making his mouth water. A broad work table was busy with pewter tins, bowls, and measures. Under the table rested a basket of eggs.

Betty was now wearing an enormous, bibbed white apron that covered her torso and was tied twice around.

She was mixing thick yellow batter in a huge yellow-ware bowl.

Beyond the kitchen in the scullery a small girl was standing on a bench over a deep sink, her hands immersed in steaming water.

Tonneman came to a halt across from Betty, watching as she beat the batter, then turned it out on the floured table, tossed it with more flour, and began to knead. The procedure was engrossing, and, he imagined, very restful, something he might enjoy doing. Betty's sob made him raise his eyes. Copious tears slid down the cook's round cheeks and onto her substantial breast, where they were absorbed by her apron.

"Betty." His voice was low.

"Sir? Would you care for a cup of tea . . ." Betty covered the dough with a cloth, then took one of the clean bowls on the table and six eggs from the basket beneath. Breaking the eggs into the bowl, she began to beat them furiously with a wooden spoon, adding sugar as she beat.

"Betty."

She sighed, letting the wooden spoon settle into the batter, then dried her eyes with the hem of her apron. "Miss Emma was such a sweet child. Won't you sit, sir?" Betty pointed to an old chair which stood against the wall. The chair was lopsided and though he wondered if it wouldn't collapse beneath him, he sat, for his bones ached and his arthritic left knee complained.

"Child, Betty? You were the same age. Sixteen? Seventeen?"

"Sixteen." She wiped her floury hands on her stomach and drew a handkerchief from her rolled-up sleeve. The spot of flour on her nose was still there. Larger, perhaps. "That mother of hers was a mean one, sir. She was jealous, if you ask me. Always clothed Miss Emma in the most awful-looking dresses. Forever scolding her, you know."

Tonneman recalled the time soon after he and Jamie had arrived from London when they first dined in this very house. Crown-street then. Thanks to Independence, Liberty-street now.

That was the first time he'd met the widowed Grace Greenaway and her daughter Emma. And Richard, Abigail's husband.

Betty was quite correct. Emma had worn a hideous dress that night. Poor thing. Tall and awkward, she was as plain as a stick, with a large nose in a fleshy face and blotchy skin. Like her mother, she had enormous breasts. But what was attractive in Grace was merely cowlike in her daughter. And, of course, Emma had those snagged teeth.

Grace had demeaned her throughout that evening. The poor girl had been humiliated in front of him and Jamie, two complete strangers. Tonneman had felt sympathy for her; Jamie, too, as he recalled, had been gallant. But then, Jamie had already had his eye on Emma's mother, the wealthy widow.

In the back of his mind Tonneman smiled. He'd suddenly remembered how Richard Willard had tried to make a match between him and Emma. Tonneman cleared his throat. "Betty—the man Emma ran off with. Did you ever see him?"

Betty shook her head. She picked up her spoon again and worked the sugar into the frothy eggs.

"Did she ever say his name?"

Again, the head shake.

Tonneman persisted. "Surely, she told you something about him."

Betty sighed and attacked her batter with a vengeance. "Miss Emma was wearing my clothes the first time she went out alone. That was when they met. By chance. He thought she was a servant girl, in the beginning."

"And later?"

"I don't know if he ever knew." Betty dipped her finger in the batter, tasted it, and added a dollop of milk from a pitcher in which a dark strip of vanilla bean floated.

"Think. What did she tell you about him?"

"Only that he was a gentleman."

"Not a common soldier, then?"

"Oh, no, never."

So much for Thomas Hickey. "An officer, perhaps?"

"I don't think so, sir." Betty frowned. "But it may be. He would have to be a man that would put her mother's nose out of joint. To show her. Miss Emma was that proud of her gentleman."

Slowly, Tonneman got to his feet. "Thank you, Betty."

"Yes, sir."

To test himself he stepped up the stairs apace, then breathless, let himself out the back way. As he walked to his horse, his mind bubbled with too many questions.

Tonneman had learned long ago to apply the Socratic method with himself by posing questions to develop latent ideas and establish a hypothesis.

"What do we have?"

"An old skull."

"Whose . . . ?"

"Emma Greenaway."

"Where found?"

"The Collect."

"How was she killed?"

"Her head was severed from her body."

As Hickey had slain his victims over thirty years before. But Betty described Emma's friend as a gentleman. This didn't necessarily mean that Hickey hadn't killed her, but it did mean that there might be another suspect. Who was this gentleman Emma was to go to Philadelphia with? Who was Emma's lover?

And why Philadelphia? Who had said Philadelphia? He could not recall. No good. He was wandering all over the place, coming to no valid conclusions. Socratic questioning couldn't work with one person. The questions he posed were those he knew he knew the answers to. The point of the drill was to ask questions he didn't know he knew the answers to. It required a partner. Like Jamie. That was the way it had been when they were young. It was, wasn't it, how they had solved the murders of all those red-haired women?

Tonneman took his bay's reins from the rail. He was about to mount when a ragged boy with the dark hair, swarthy skin, and the black-as-coal eyes of an Espanole plucked his coat. "A penny for your fortune, sir." The emaciated boy, ten years old at the most, was covered by a threadbare coat, the gray tails of which dragged on the ground. He wore no hat. This was enough to make Tonneman give him a cent piece.

The lad pounced on the coin. He jammed it into his coat. "Your hand, Your Honor."

Tonneman removed his glove and held out his hand. At last, an entertainment to ease a long day.

The child's voice deepened. "He who escaped the lion has the answer from the past." Releasing Tonneman's hand, the boy scampered off, anxious to find a new client.

"Wait!" Tonneman called.

But the boy paid him no heed.

Vexed, the physician mounted his bay gelding. "All right, Socrates, we'll soon be home. Tell me, my wise Greek, what in tarnation was that lad talking about? Foolishness. Why do I bother with such superstitious twaddle?"

With a toss of his head the gelding whinnied. It picked its way around the refuse strewn along the cobbled road.

But suddenly Tonneman knew. "Thank you, my equine friend. Who escaped the lion? Daniel, of course." His thoughts were still bubbling. But how could he pay attention to the Spanish ragamuffin's words? He was a man of science. Still, he could not ignore this sign.

Daniel Goldsmith lived on Garden-street, just below Wall, only four or five blocks away. He would go there now.

His partner in this Socratic dialogue was not to be Jamie, but Daniel.

Then it occurred to him that it had been Constable Daniel Goldsmith, not Jamie, who had helped him find Hickey. Tonneman rode on with a lighter heart. With Daniel, perhaps he could pick through the bloody past and arrive at some answers.

28

3 FEBRUARY. WEDNESDAY. AFTERNOON.

Sugarloaf was a bucolic tree-lined street of modest homes and gardens running west off Broadway. It lay outside the City limits and well beyond the center of the town, which was why Jacob Hays chose to live here. It reminded him of the farm up in Bedford, in Westchester County, where he'd been born, and where he'd spent his childhood helping out in his father's country store.

The High Constable's homestead was a large white

shingled frame house surrounded by evergreens and oaks. A well-constructed coach house and stable were the primary outbuildings. The coach house was built of a size to hold a pair of carriages and a sleigh; the stable had stalls enough for four horses. The coach house also accommodated an apartment on the second floor, where the fifty-year-old Noah Douglas, a widower these ten years, lived.

Behind the house on the far side of the garden was the fruit orchard, which yielded apples, pears, and peaches in spring, summer and autumn.

In the house now lived three children; a servant girl, Anna, who also cooked; Jake; his wife Katherine; and of late, Jake's second cousin once removed, Charity Etting Boenning. Charity had scandalized the Jewish community in Philadelphia by running off and marrying a Christian widower more than twice her age, an artist whom she'd met when he was painting her parents' portrait.

Jacob Hays was both proud of his Jewish heritage and fervent about his Christianity. But neither explained why he had welcomed his cousin Charity. She was his blood and in need. That was reason enough.

"I'll give Copper some oats, Mr. Jake," Noah said as he walked horse and carriage to the stable.

Jake's attention was elsewhere; he had just glimpsed a patch of blue cloth across the road. The High Constable scowled, rubbed the side of his huge nose, and screwed his eyes to the trunk of a giant oak where most of the woods had been cleared to make room for the new home of Cornelius Philipse and his family.

Was someone behind the tree? Watching him? His house? This displeased Jake no end. Part of Jake's policing tactics was to follow thieves to their lairs, their homes and taverns, in order to get a line on their comrades. He did not relish the idea of some miscreant turning the tables on him.

Noah was already in the stable. He would deal with this himself. Pretending to enter the house, Jake went behind the structure as far as the orchard, then used its cover to go further west. He skimmed across the road and into the woods. There he continued his circle until he came behind the oak tree.

As he suspected, a man in a blue cloak was watching his house. The gall of him. Nobody spied on Jake Hays.

Silent as a cat, the High Constable came within a foot of the offender and seized his arm through the cloak. Jake had a strong grip, and though the man was taller, he could not break free. Jake easily spun him around.

The man's free arm was a confusion of gestures, first pulling at his hat, then covering his face, then dropping resignedly to his side.

"As I live and breathe," Jake said. "Peter Tonneman. Just the man I've been wanting to see. Come with me. We've got a lot to talk about." Jake steered Peter across the road. "Boots," Jake said at the side door, pointing to the boot-scraper on the third of three steps.

Peter scraped and scraped again. The last thing he wanted was to give the High Constable something else about which to reprimand him.

"Enough," Jake finally said. He then carefully scraped his own mud-encrusted boots, and both men stepped into the kitchen where Anna was tending a jumble of pots and kettles. Two apple pies just out of the oven had been set to cool in the pine pie safe, and the kitchen was dense with wonderful smells. A surprised Noah, sitting on a bench by the fire, looked up from his soup.

Peter Tonneman, wretched, cold, and hungry from his morning vigil, was overwhelmed by the warmth and aroma. He sank gratefully into the slat-back chair Jake shoved under him.

Jake motioned to the girl. She stopped her work and poured each a mug of hot cider.

Seating himself opposite Peter at the long maple table, Jake said, "Explain, Mr. Tonneman. What are you doing skulking around my house like a thief?"

Peter sipped the hot cider and let out a long breath. "I

beg your pardon, sir. I was hoping for a glimpse of your kinswoman, Mrs. Boenning."

"A glimpse?"

"A word, actually."

"By the Eternal, what's wrong with coming right up to the front door and presenting yourself?"

"I was afraid you were going to arrest me."

Jake's eyes went soft. These were the eyes he showed his children. "Why? Have you done something wrong?"

"Yes, sir. I got drunk and hit Commissioner Brown."

"Anything else?"

"No, sir, I swear to God."

Jake frowned. "Don't take the Lord's name in vain."

"No, sir. I swear I didn't have anything to do with Mr. Brown's death."

"You tell me."

"If you mean the cash box, last I saw of it was that Friday night. Brown was locking it up. He accused me of stealing from it."

"Had you stolen from it?"

"No, sir. That's why I hit him."

"The cash box is missing."

"I didn't take it."

"And the other money?"

"I'm sorry, sir, I don't know what you're talking about."

"The bribes."

The boy shrugged. "Sorry, sir."

Jake had been fishing and Peter hadn't bitten. Well, it was worth a try. He took a taste of cider before continuing. "I'm glad we had this little talk, boy. Clears the air."

"Thank you, sir."

Suddenly Jake's eyes turned hard. These were the eyes he showed criminals. "However, you are on my list. If you hadn't come to me, I would have come to you. Tell me again what happened that night. The night you had the fight with Brown."

Peter flushed. He drew himself up in his chair. "Sir, I did not kill Thaddeus Brown. We had an argument—"

"And you knocked him down."

"Yes. He accused me of stealing."

"Had you stolen anything?"

"No. I told you. He said he would ruin me. I lost my temper."

"Never a good thing to do."

"No, sir. I hit him. But when I left, he was still alive enough to continue to threaten me and my reputation. You can ask the Watch Man who came to investigate."

"And the money?"

"I told you. It was still in the office when I left. Maybe the Watch Man took it. Or the other man."

Jake's mind sang. At last. New information. "What other man?"

"Before Tedious—Mr. Brown and I had our words."

"And you hit him."

"And I hit him. Before that I heard Commissioner Brown having an argument with another man."

"Who?"

"I don't know. I was in one room, they were in another. I'd had too much to drink. I was sleeping it off. On my desk."

"It's my understanding that you and George Willard have been keeping the taverns open."

"That was before. I've changed, sir." Peter's face was solemn. "Believe me, I have."

"My cousin says you saved her life."

Peter fingered his collar; he was suddenly quite warm. "Charity—er, Mrs. Boenning told you?"

"It's the reason you're not sitting in a jail cell having your poor arse chewed by rats." Jake undid the white kerchief from around his neck and dropped it on the table. "My family and I owe you a debt of gratitude."

At that moment the door leading to the dining room opened. Katherine Hays, babe in arms and with a little boy clinging to her skirts, entered the room. "Ah, husband, you're home. What a lovely surprise. I'll have you fed quick as a wink." Moving to the hearth, she stirred a pot with her free hand and tasted. "Needs salt."

Anna offered the salt dish to her mistress. Mrs. Hays took a handful of salt and strewed it liberally.

"This is Peter Tonneman, Katherine. He'll be eating with us." Jake turned to the little boy. "Aaron, why are you looking so sad?"

Katherine gave her husband a knowing glance over the small boy's head. "Aaron has a stomachache."

Jake picked his son up high above his head.

"Jacob. His stomach," Katherine cautioned.

"How are you feeling now, Master Aaron Burr Hays?"

The boy laughed. "Good, Papa."

"That's my boy. Off with you, now."

"Yes, Papa." He ran happily out of the kitchen.

Peter had to ask. "You named your son for Aaron Burr?"

"Yes. It was Mr. Burr who got me my first job with the Constabulary. All I am, all I ever hope to be, I owe to Aaron Burr. He's a good Democrat. And he was not a traitor. Never a traitor."

"Yes, High Constable."

"Welcome to our home, Mr. Tonneman." Katherine Hays was a comely woman, with an abundance of good humor, all the better to deal with her unorthodox husband. "It's only barley-and-bean soup and apple pie, but will you dine?"

"Yes, ma'am. Thank you."

Katherine nodded to her husband and withdrew, taking the infant with her.

"Brown," Jake said, immediately back to business. "Give me your sense of him."

Peter cocked an eyebrow at the High Constable. No one had ever asked him a question like this. The sense of the man? He fought any exhibition of joy. Old Hays was actually asking his opinion. "Well, for one thing, Brown didn't always behave the way a Broadbrim is supposed to."

"How so?" Jake drummed his fingers on the table.

"Often, after a meeting outside the office, or so he said, he would come back smelling of scent. With rouge on his collar."

"Perhaps he went home to see his wife."

Peter shook his head. "Not Mrs. Brown. She's a true Friend. Plain as a little brown mouse."

"Quite amusing, Peter."

"Sir?"

"Never mind. So you're saying the Quaker had a doxy. Any notion who she was?"

"No, sir. Only, once or twice he had me take a bundle to a woman in a house in Duane-street."

A combination of memory and inspiration led Jake to his next question. "Did this woman have a crescent scar on her left cheek?"

"Yes, sir. How'd you know?"

"Never you mind. What number Duane?"

"Thirty-nine."

"Good boy."

"What else?"

"She's quite large, if that's what you mean."

Jake's eyes were gleaming, his nose twitching. He was the wolf going for the kill. "Tall or wide?"

"Both. And French, I think."

"Yes. Yes. Yes. Better than good. Perfect."

"How did you know about her?"

"People tell me things. Such information, plus the power of observation the good Lord gave me . . . In my work you must keep your eyes and ears open. Then use your brains."

Peter was intrigued. "I never knew constabulary work could be so interesting."

Gut instinct told Jake that the boy had nothing to do with Brown's death. Young Tonneman came from good, solid stock. Still, instinct was not enough. What Jake needed were facts. But until he had those facts he would watch this boy. What better way to watch him than to give him a job? Jake was certain a pretty young woman like Charity would not long remain a widow, and she had talked more than once of young Tonneman's bravery and graciousness. Jake weighed these facts against the fact that Peter was suspect in the Brown murder case. A moment's thought, and Jake Hays resolved that while he wouldn't help, he wouldn't hinder.

"There's got to be a new job for you in a big City like New-York. And if there is I'll ferret it out for you. Stop by the jail later today and you and I will talk further. After you've paid your respects to Mrs. Boenning, of course."

Well, perhaps he would help a little bit.

29

3 FEBRUARY. WEDNESDAY. AFTERNOON.

The Goldsmith house in Garden-street was fewer than
five blocks away from that leaky wreck of a place in Water-
street and King where Goldsmith, as a young Constable,
had lived with his difficult first wife, Deborah. Tonneman
had met him shortly before the War.

Together, Tonneman and Goldsmith had tracked
Hickey, the murderer of red-haired women.

Deborah and her nagging mother, the ever-righteous
Esther, had perished in the same Yellow Fever epidemic of
'98 that had taken Tonneman's son David and Grace
Greenaway. Goldsmith's daughters Ruth and Miriam had
grown and married. Both were now living in Albany, and
Goldsmith had eight grandchildren.

After Deborah's death and the marriage of his daughters, Goldsmith had finally been free to marry Molly, who had established a profitable business after the War as a milliner.

Goldsmith's small domicile was simpler than Tonneman's in Rutgers Hill, and certainly it was dwarfed by Jamie's manse in Richmond Hill. And the house could never compare with the small palaces that the Livingstons, Hamiltons, Schuylers, Duers, Duanes, and Beekmans lived in.

The narrow two-story house wore a fresh coat of white paint. Its shutters were a bright green. A wooden hat and feather hung outside the front door to proclaim Molly's trade as a milliner. Few remembered that before the War she'd been Jew Molly, one of the many prostitutes who lived and plied their trade in the area called the Holy Ground near what was then King's College.

After the Revolution, King's College became Columbia College. And as the City spread and the College attracted more and more students, the Holy Ground was swept away.

Goldsmith, who'd been reinstated as a Constable after the War, retired when he married Molly. He now pottered around the house, for the most part, getting in Molly's way. In reality, Daniel genuinely enjoyed being idle, and reacquainting himself with the Torah, for he had taken to studying Hebrew with his tenant, Joseph Lancaster. Molly and Daniel occupied the first floor and rented out half the second to the widowed schoolmaster.

Tonneman found Molly in the middle of her sitting room, surrounded by pieces of lace, bolts of cloth, and feathers of various colors, sizes, and textures. She was fitting feathers on a hat of burgundy velvet. Other hats in different stages of completion sat on small wooden stands on her work table. Nearby were stubby pencils and sheets of paper alive with sketches.

"How goes it with Peter?" Molly mumbled. Taking two

pins from her mouth, she smoothed the lace on her lap and began pinning it to a hat brim.

"Peter." Tonneman paused. It seemed a burden to even think of a proper answer. Chagrined, he had to admit to himself he was unable to deal with his son's terrible predicament.

"John," Molly prodded. "Peter needs you."

He brushed aside her admonition gruffly, waving his hands at her, grumbling, and wrote a note for Daniel with one of her stubby pencils. Having no doubts that the canny Molly would read the note, and not wanting to get into a discussion with her about Emma Greenaway, he wrote simply:

Goldsmith——Please call on me as soon as possible. I have discovered something of interest from the past.

Tonneman put the pencil down. His hands were trembling.

Molly's sharp eyes and sharper intuition told her that John Tonneman was deeply troubled. He left abruptly, muttering, "Things to be done."

As he rode from Garden-street to Rutgers Hill, Tonneman couldn't keep his mind from wandering, back and forth, past and present. The skull . . . Emma . . . the War . . . Hickey . . . the dead Gretel and the young Mariana.

The surgery was closed today. There would be no patients to interrupt him. He could clear the clutter of his mind by delving into all the medical journals he hadn't yet read, and the pamphlets from London that he'd received in November before the Embargo. By his not dwelling on the problem, he knew from experience, the solution would present itself.

His house in Rutgers Hill—his father's house, his grandfather's house—stood three stories. It was, as it always had been, shingled with white pine. Surrounding the house and the barn were towering oaks and elms that had stood since the land belonged to the Indians. The barn too stood where it had always stood, to the side of the house opposite the surgery. But it wasn't the same barn as his father's. That one had fallen down in a great wind twenty years before, and they had replaced it with this one.

At that time, they had also replaced the roof tiles, but leaks had appeared and Mariana had been after him to have the roof repaired.

He was out in the barn absentmindedly brushing Socrates when Micah appeared, a knitted shawl over her thin shoulders. "I've lit the fire, sir," she said, her voice raised to accommodate the old man's faded hearing.

"What?" He squinted in an attempt to rid his eyes of a slight blur. When that didn't work, he patted his pockets for the spectacles he recently made for himself. He couldn't find them.

"The soap, sir."

"Yes, of course." How could he have forgotten? That morning he had directed Micah to ready twelve gallons of water, five pounds of quicklime, ten pounds of sal soda, seven pounds of pure grease, eight ounces of rosin, and ten ounces of rose water. Once a month, they made soap.

The two left the barn together. When they reached the house, the servant girl opened the door, then helped him out of his coat and hat.

"Would you like something to eat?" She hung his things from the maple knobs on the wall near the front door.

"Yes." He took his canvas apron from another knob and went to his study. He paused at the door.

Mariana, the disagreeable woman who'd been causing him so much misery of late, sat at his desk, Tonneman's new spectacles on her nose, reading one of his medical books. The disagreeable woman was bathed in the soft radiance of what remained of the afternoon sun glow. The sight was an enchantment to his old eyes. She looked like the

girl she'd been when he'd first seen her with her hair down.
A lump formed in his throat. He tried to swallow it but it
wouldn't go away. "Ah, my scholar, do you have a question?"

"Mmm." She continued to read. Or pretended to.

He tried again. "You might ask your husband. I think
he's a surgeon."

Mariana lifted her head. "My husband's too busy seeking answers of his own. To conundrums."

"Life is a conundrum."

She removed his spectacles and laid them on the desk.
"So he says."

He took her hand and pulled her to her feet. "You are
my most difficult conundrum."

"John."

He took her in his arms. The familiar rush of blood
flooded his veins. He kissed her and felt her response. "I
love you, Mariana."

"I know that. And I love you, John Tonneman. On the
days I don't hate you."

"What you don't understand is that I understand."

"What?"

"What you're going through."

"I'm becoming an old woman."

"An exaggeration. I am, alas, an old man."

She pushed him away. "The girls will be home from
school soon." Gretel and Leah attended the public school
in Chatham-street. In fact, one hundred and fifty students
now attended Public School Number 1, which had opened
in April of the previous year. The schoolmaster, Joseph
Lancaster, taught the older students, who in turn taught
the younger students. This made Gretel particularly happy;
as one of the older students she was also a teacher, passing
on Mr. Lancaster's teachings.

Micah knocked tentatively, then set a tray of bread and
cold chicken and a cup of black tea on the desk. Mariana,

taking advantage of the interruption, fled. Micah curtsied and left, too.

Tonneman stroked his chin. Too much stubble. Not a proper shave, not a proper shave at all. He was doing that more and more lately. Not shaving properly. "Mariana . . ." But she was gone. He shrugged. Women. He used to think that, being a physician, he understood them more than other men. He'd been mistaken. Never mind. He had work to do. Neglecting his supper he drank the tea. Then, muttering to himself, he went outside.

Behind the house, Micah had already heated the water to the boil and poured half over the quicklime in the deep iron cauldron.

While they waited for the remainder of the water to cool slightly, Micah told him that a box of herbs had arrived from Doctor David Hosack's Elgin Gardens.

One of Tonneman's father's legacies had been the recipes for herbal medicines handed down through the generations of his family, learned from Europeans and Indians alike. As herbs were far more interesting a subject than soap, John had the sudden urge to stop what he was doing and start pounding and brewing his precious herbs. But, made uneasy by his wandering concentration, he cautioned himself. One step at a time.

Abstracted, surrounded by a steamy fog, Tonneman stirred the contents of the cauldron. Without warning, he suddenly recalled clear as a painting the day Hickey was hanged. The bright sunshine, the throngs of people. The noise. As if he were there again, he saw Mariana shouting at Hickey.

"*But why Gretel?*" *the young Mariana screamed.* "*Why did you kill Gretel?*"

Hickey's brutal mouth twisted into a frown. And he asked, "*Which one was Gretel?*"

Tonneman shuddered. Hickey never knew Gretel. That much was becoming certain. And something else was certain: Hickey had not killed Gretel. This realization stunned him. But wait, if not Hickey, who?

He shook the cobwebs from his mind. He was growing old. Or mad. How he envied Doctor Hosack. He was sure it must be a near perfect existence, living on that stretch of twenty acres five or six miles to the north, where Hosack had founded his gardens in '01. The man was famous for raising a renowned collection of medicinal plants and cultivated foreign and American flora. Tonneman was sure he must be happy, too. Of course he was; he was a man without a wife.

Tonneman sighed. First things first. He dissolved the sal soda in the cooled water. He would unpack the herbs later.

Next, as Micah watched, he combined the two mixtures, the quicklime water and the sal soda water. "Tomorrow," Tonneman instructed the girl, "pour off any clear liquid sitting on top. Take care not to lose any sediment."

"Yes, Doctor Tonneman."

"Take care," Old Tonneman warned. "What you'll have will be lye. It can cause severe burns. Be wary. Use my gloves."

"Yes, Doctor Tonneman."

"Hallo! Where is everyone?" Daniel Goldsmith came around the house, limping.

"Rheumatism acting up?" Tonneman asked.

"What else? I got your note."

"I'll give you something for the rheumatism," Tonneman said, grateful for the distraction. He wiped his hands on a rag. "Come." With Tonneman leading, the two men went into the house by way of the kitchen. "Some Port, Daniel?"

"I don't mind." Goldsmith placed his coat over one of the kitchen chairs. His hat stayed on. His bald spot was also a cold spot during the winter months. A great Jehovah joke, the former Constable thought. Daniel Goldsmith, the irreligious Jew, with his head covered in the house, like his father, and his father's father.

When they were seated in Tonneman's study, heating old bones in front of the fire, nibbling cheese and bread, and sipping their Port, Goldsmith sighed contentedly. He studied his old friend with a shrewd eye. "You seem troubled."

Tonneman nodded. "My world is collapsing all about me. Thaddeus Brown is dead. Collect Company funds are missing. Jake Hays believes Peter may be involved."

"Peter is your son, John. I refuse to believe he would do more than some drunken mischief. Is that why you wanted to see me?"

"No. I called on Mrs. Willard today."

"Oh?" Daniel knew the gossip, that decades before Tonneman and Abigail Willard had been sweethearts. Molly's clients brought word that they were again. Daniel didn't believe it.

"About the skull we found."

"Yes, I've heard about it."

"Who do you think it is?"

Goldsmith's eyes widened. "You're asking me? How would I know?"

"Guess."

"For God's sake, John." He made a humming sound, then said, "Benedict Arnold."

"Be serious."

"This is ridiculous. Who?"

"Emma Greenaway."

Goldsmith gave Tonneman a long look. "You *know* it is Emma Greenaway, or you *think* it is?"

Tonneman considered the wine in his glass before replying. "I know it."

"The little I remember—that girl ran off with . . ." Daniel frowned.

"I don't believe that. I found a cameo in the same dirt the skull was found in. Abigail—Mrs. Willard—identified it as belonging to her niece."

"All right. Wasn't it Richard Willard who reported that

Emma had run off to Philadelphia? What would her skull be doing in New-York?"

"Her head was chopped off."

"Ah . . ." Daniel was beginning to see the light.

"By the same kind of sword that killed Gretel. The serrated one that had been stolen from Sam Fraunces."

"God in heaven, not that again." Goldsmith's face went ashen. During the spate of killings in '75 and '76, Sam Fraunces's serrated sword had been found bloodied near Tonneman's house, with no clue as to whose blood was on it. Constable Hood was supposed to keep it safe, but then it disappeared and was used to kill Gretel. Hood, afraid for his own position, had blamed the loss on Goldsmith, and this had cost Goldsmith his job in the Constabulary. Goldsmith had found the missing sword in the tar hut with Gretel Huntzinger's head impaled on it. The memory put Goldsmith into a cold sweat. He set his wine down; he had no taste for it now. "I dreamed of Gretel again last night."

"At the opera, you told me—"

"Yes, ten days or so ago the dreams started again. She comes to me, says it over and over and over again." His hands began to shake. He grabbed his wine and drank it straight down.

Grimly, Tonneman refilled his friend's glass. "Steady on, Daniel. What does Gretel say?"

Goldsmith held the glass of Port up to his lips and wished for that moment he could remember the blessing for wine. He'd known it once. "What she's always said, off and on these past thirty-two years: 'Avenge me. Avenge me.' "

30

3 FEBRUARY. WEDNESDAY. AFTERNOON.

With more suspects than he needed, Jake Hays took to his challenge like a duck to water. Sorting out who did what took a great deal of dreary work, but Jake was a born ferret.

His method in each case was to ask questions of everyone. What he got were cockeyed observations, lies, and imaginings sprinkled with a few facts. But once the cockeyed and imaginings were eliminated, what was left had to be the truth. This was now his task: to eliminate the cockeyed, the lies, and the imaginings.

First, Meg Doty swore John Tonneman was responsible for Thaddeus Brown's death.

Second, Wicked Polly told Hays that Brown had a lady friend who was French, fat, and had a crescent scar on her left cheek, and that the lady friend's other lover had done the dirty deed.

Third, Young Peter Tonneman not only backed up Polly's story but supplied a house number in Duane-street.

So. His two suspects were John Tonneman and the French whore's unknown lover. Perhaps.

Butcher Ned Winship needed special attention, but that was nothing new; Ned was a corruption and men like him were a certainty of life in the City of New-York.

Fourth, Pockets's reluctant confession had made only a faint connection between Butcher Ned and Brown. Ned and his villainies were connected to Brown only because both were most likely involved in what Jake had begun to suspect were crooked dealings concerning the Collect. Jake had been keeping his eye on Ned for a long time, but if Pockets was right, his eye hadn't been sharp enough. Jake meant to rectify that.

Peter Tonneman also warranted attention. If Young Tonneman had knocked Brown senseless, how had he managed to cart him up to the Collect and bury him without being seen? Did he have help? Jake liked the lad all right, but Peter still had to prove himself.

Jake would begin his investigation by questioning the French woman in Duane-street, especially as it was only four blocks away from his home.

Number 39 Duane-street proved to be a low, paint-shriveled, weatherbeaten gray house. Jake ignored the brass horseshoe knocker and rapped on the door with his stick. He was certain someone was watching from the window to the right, even though there was no movement in the curtain. But there was a shadow, and Jake prided himself that he had the eyes of an eagle. He gave the window a sharp *rat-a-tat*. This time the curtain twitched. Almost immediately the door opened. "Yes?"

The woman's face was one of the most beautiful Jake had ever seen, marred only by the deep, curving scar on her left cheek. She had black hair, so black it might have been rinsed with ink. And she was as big as Peter Tonneman had said, in all directions. The pale blue dress was cut low, but the way she wore it, the way she carried herself spoke of a lady. True, many whores deported themselves in such a manner, but this one Jake almost believed. "May I help you?" The voice was sweet company to her face and its accent was assuredly French.

"I'm Jacob Hays, High Constable of the City of New-York."

"Yes?" She adjusted the fringed red silk stole around her shoulders, but did not trouble to hide the rich expanse of bosom.

"And you are?"

"Simone Aubergine, high woman of the City of New-York." She smiled.

Jake returned the smile. He was charmed. "You are the Simone Aubergine who was the friend of Joseph Thaddeus Brown, now deceased?"

"Yes." She seemed indifferent. Or was it world-weariness?

"What sort of friends were you?"

"He was a Quaker."

"And you?"

"I am not a Quaker."

"Were you lovers?"

"I love no one. Not even myself."

Jake marveled at this woman. She spoke in such artful circles. If she were a man she could make a fortune in the legal trade. As it was, she was the best he'd ever confronted when it came to parrying his queries. "I'd like to ask you a few questions."

"I thought that's what you had been doing."

"A touch," he said. "Quite a good touch." He bowed to her, acknowledging, if not defeat, then stalemate.

She stepped back on daintily slippered feet and waved her hand. "Come in, High Constable. Please."

The floor of the entry hall was covered with an India

rug of vivid reds and blues. There was an ornate looking glass with cupids and naked nymphs carved in gold leaf on both walls of the narrow corridor so that a person looking into one could see his reflection in the other.

She passed him, her ample flesh brushing his. He watched her in one of the mirrors. She was smiling. She led him to a sitting room, crowded with French furniture with spindle legs. Lamps glowed; the glow was reflected and repeated in other mirrors. More India carpets covered the floor. The mantelpiece was dark-veined marble and a welcome fire, aided by heavy blue draperies, contrived to make the room snug.

"May I offer you . . . something?" She raised her eyebrows provocatively.

He raised his eyebrows in response.

"Coffee, chocolate, tea, rum? Some *biscotti*? I have a Sally Lunn. I could heat it up and we could watch the butter melt over it." She ran her tongue around her lips.

"Thank you, no."

"Sit, please." She directed him to a sofa covered in pink satin and hanging with fringe. It abounded in little pillows, each stitched with tiny pearls and more fringe. On the floor at the foot of the sofa was a needlepoint rug, ornate with red and yellow flowers on a field of green.

He sat in the *bergère* opposite. Still smiling, she took the sofa. "How may I help you?"

"I understand you have another gentleman friend."

"I have many gentlemen friends."

"Perhaps the one who gave you that scar."

She touched her left cheek and did not trouble to hide her shudder. "He is no longer in my life. Thank God."

"His name?"

She patted her rolled and curled hair. "I'd rather not say."

Jake shrugged. "Why is this man no longer in your life?"

There was a long pause. Then she said: "Because he frightened me."

"And now?"

"He frightens me still." She stared into the fire as if she'd forgotten anyone else was there. Jake cleared his throat. Slowly, Simone Aubergine turned back to him.

"Is he a jealous man?"

"That's one of the things he is."

"Would you think it possible for him to kill a man over you?"

"I would think it possible for him to kill a man for any reason. Or for no reason."

"Do you think he killed Thaddeus Brown?"

"I would rather not think about him at all. If I did I would not sleep at night. As it is, I do not sleep without laudanum."

Jake clucked his tongue and rephrased his question. "Would you think it possible that this man killed Thaddeus Brown?"

She let her stole slip from her shoulders, revealing soft pink flesh over a low neckline and a gold necklace holding a small ruby globe, which nestled in the hollow of her fleshy throat. "Yes."

Jake was not offended by the age-old whore's trick, merely amused. "I ask you again to tell me this man's name."

"I cannot."

"If you don't I will put you in jail."

"If I do he will kill me."

"It's not a very nice jail."

"*C'est la vie.*" Simone fluttered her fingers and shrugged. Flesh rippled sensually.

Jake sighed. He should not have said what he hadn't meant to do. "That was not a threat. But it is a possibility."

She gathered her fringed stole about her. "Shall we go now?"

He rose. "Another time. Is there anything else you would like to tell me?"

"No." She settled into her satin sofa and picked up a small leather-bound book, opened it, and began to read.

"Then I wish you good day."

"Good day, sir. You can see yourself out, I'm sure." She didn't look up.

LESS THAN A quarter hour had passed when Noah said, "Mr. Jake—"

"I see."

They were in Jake's carriage just around the corner from Number 39 Duane-street. Simone Aubergine, in a deep purple cloak, its hood covering her magnificent hair, went by in a small green cart pulled by a sturdy donkey. Evidently the woman kept the animal and cart around back. They watched as the prostitute quickly passed the abandoned Tea Water Pump and went on to where Duane became Thomas-street.

Then Jake nodded to Noah and they followed her.

THE GREEN CART traveled well beyond the City limits via the Bowery, an unpaved country lane, but still the main road leading out of the City. When it turned west off the Bowery Road, Jake saw they were approaching the Friends Cemetery. He bade Noah pull the carriage over to the side of the road near a thickly wooded area and behind Simone's donkey and cart. From here he had a fair view of the cemetery.

Near a stand of pines stood the figure of an old friend. "Do you see who I see?"

Noah chuckled. "Yes, sir. I've been waiting for you to notice."

Jake climbed down. "It will be dark soon. Better light the carriage lamps."

Noah nodded and mumbled, "Would have done had you told me or not."

Jake didn't hear him because he was halfway to the pine trees. "You old rascal," he said to the man who stood watching the members of the funeral party. "There's got to be a reason for an old beak like you to observe J. Thaddeus Brown being laid to rest."

"Just curiosity, High Constable."

"Yes. Of course."

"Getting late." Daniel Goldsmith made as if to leave. "I don't like the wife to worry."

Jake smiled. "Oh, yes. She's the worrying kind." He knew Molly was no such thing. "Give her my best regards."

"I will, Jake. Good evening."

"Good evening, Daniel." Jake watched Goldsmith take one long last look at the mourners, then move off. Something was on the old man's mind. Well, perhaps he would let the stew simmer for a while before he threw in some extra spices.

A Stated Meeting of the New-York Society for promoting the Manumission of Slaves, and protecting such of them as have been or may be liberated, will be held at the Society & School Room, in Cliff-street, at 6 o'clock, tomorrow evening.
THOS. COLLINS, Assist. Sec.
N.B. The Annual Election of officers will take place.

NEW-YORK EVENING POST
FEBRUARY 1808

●━━━━━●

31

3 FEBRUARY. WEDNESDAY. AFTERNOON.

George Willard cocked his pocket flintlock. He aimed it at the skinny nigger cleaning up between fights at the Bunker Hill bullring.

"Come on, you chicken," Charlie Wright jeered. "Do the deed."

George sucked his lower lip. The weather had warmed enough for the snow to melt, but not so much that he should be sweating as he was. He could smell his own sweat. Could Charlie smell him? Not that it mattered. Charlie stank like a barn himself. A barn George couldn't hit the side of. Get on with it, he told himself. What mattered now was, could he make this shot?

"Do the deed or pay me the two dollars," Charlie bellowed in that deep sea-soaked voice of his.

He could do it. One shot at the nigger's feet, close enough so the nigger danced. But he couldn't hit him. And what if he did hit him? It was only a nigger. But then he'd lose the bet, and he didn't have the two dollars.

And today was the first day Ned and Charlie had allowed him back to the bullring. Finding the hundred and fifty in his uncle's desk had been a boon. George had paid off the hundred he owed, and had drunk and wagered away the other fifty. If he played and couldn't pay, Charlie would be very angry. And nobody in his right mind wanted to have Charlie Wright angry at him.

George laughed from the sheer dread of missing. The pocket pistol exploded.

Whack went the ball into the soft ground, spraying clods of muddy dirt. And the nigger danced. And howled like a crazed dog.

George blew at the smoke curling from the barrel. He had no right to make such a shot. Not in a hundred years. Few could. But he, George Willard, had. He laughed and turned to Charlie, holding out his hand. "Pay me."

Charlie smiled. "I won't and let's say I did."

George shrugged. Nobody argued with Charlie.

"I've had enough. Let's go."

"Where?" George asked.

"Let's go." Charlie was not one to explain himself. He hurried outside and mounted his large gray. "You coming?"

George's fingers fumbled as he untied his bay mare from the rail. It was the first time Charlie had included him in a plan.

They rode hard up Broadway, past Chambers-street and along the road, and then the path. It was only after almost half an hour of hard riding up Broadway, then east over muddy roads where melting snow had turned the land swampy, that Charlie reined up. They were outside a small country graveyard in a clearing surrounded by forest. A dozen carriages and horses stood every which way, a clutter over the country lane. Some were assembled on the cleared land across the way. The burial ground was situated across the road from the entrance to Doctor David Hosack's Elgin Gardens.

Charlie sat high on his horse and peered at the group in the graveyard as if searching for someone. It was a Quaker burial. Most of the people gathered wore the somber colors of the Friends: the women in gray mantles, the men, some in baggy pants, others in drab knee britches and stockings; a sea of black bonnets and broad-brimmed hats.

To George, they looked like a bunch of sheep. "What the Devil is that all about?" he complained, wiping his mouth and looking about for a well or a stream in order to quench his thirst.

"I felt like taking a ride to pay my respects to Friend Brown." Charlie pulled a flask from his saddlebag, drank, and returned it to the bag, without offering any to George. "Good. They're still at it. Look at all them Broadbrims. If I had a shotgun, I could take them all with one blast."

"I guess you could," George answered, eyeing Charlie's saddlebag.

They stood there at the fence watching the ceremony. Charlie did not notice, nor did George, either Daniel Goldsmith or the High Constable, both of whom were finding their presence particularly interesting.

Charlie shook his head. "All that talking, all those Broadbrims talking over the grave. Like they was all preachers or something." Yet he seemed pleased, for a satisfied smirk settled on his face.

Suddenly, from out of the woods behind the mourners, a spot of color appeared among the grays and browns. A woman of sizable proportions, wrapped in a purple cloak, joined the people paying their respects. A hood hid her face.

Charlie's smirk turned to menace. "I knew it. That bitch. She said it was Ned she loved, not that jackstraw. She lied. Else why is she here at his funeral?" Spit drooled out of Charlie's mouth.

When Charlie was in one of his rages, George would just as soon be sitting in the Tontine. But he was curious. He'd never seen Charlie in such a state. "Who is she?"

"Simone Aubergine, the woman who swore she was true to only Ned." His voice turned into a growl. "And look who she's got her unfaithful hands on now."

George followed the direction of Charlie's pointing finger.

Simone Aubergine had proprietarily tucked her hand into the arm of Peter Tonneman.

Conundrum—Why is the Embargo like an old musket?
  Because old muskets so contrive it,
  As quite to miss the mark they aim at,
  And though well aim'd at duck or plover,
  Bear wide, and kick their own over.
        M. *Fingal*

        NEW-YORK HERALD
        FEBRUARY 1808

32

3–4 FEBRUARY. WEDNESDAY TO THURSDAY. NIGHT
TO MORNING.

It was just midnight. There was no moon. South-street lay
quiet like a ghost town, deserted thanks to the time, the
cold, and to Mr. Jefferson's Embargo.

Jamie had come to the waterfront to receive a shipment. The ship, a tub flying the Spanish flag, appropriately
named the *Exile*, considering its special passenger, would
not dock, but rather lay off-shore.

Before the Embargo, ships from every part of the globe
had crowded the many spacious wharves and slips of Manhattan. Their goods had filled to bursting the mostly new
and vast warehouses.

Merchants, shipbrokers, and traders all kept their offices

in the forepart of the ground floor of these warehouses. This collection of buildings and wharves ran from the Grand Battery along the Hudson and East Rivers, up both sides of the town. Ships would land goods, then load up with other goods and embark. The port of New-York was continually surrounded with the masts of hundreds of ships.

Now, a different type of trade went on. Goods still came to America from Europe and the East, although there were fewer of them. And everything was more costly because the goods had to go through Canada and be brought ashore secretly to New-York.

And if the goods were stored in the warehouses, it was done at night, when no one could see. More likely, they were stored in caves and sheds deep in the woods or placed in wagons to be transported elsewhere inland, where even more money could be made when they were sold.

Thus, the Embargo did not thwart enterprising businessmen. Men like Jamie Jamison had been in the smuggling game since December of '07, when Tom Jefferson had declared his damned O Grab Me.

This night, as on many another night, the cargo was rowed ashore by a longboat illuminated only by dim lanterns. Tonight the contraband included wine, oil, dried fruits, and ceramics. It would bring Jamie a pretty penny.

And then there was the human cargo. The passenger was delivered ashore on the last trip of the longboat, a passenger who could unlock infinite riches. Together, he and Jamie could end up owning America.

The man in the boat was perhaps fifty and stood about five feet six inches tall. A slouchy hat obscured his splendid Roman face, projecting chin, aquiline nose, and high forehead. Deep hazel eyes were also hidden in the darkness of the moonless night. Ordinarily a jaunty, fashionable man whom women found highly attractive, tonight he wore brown homespun and a muffler to cover the lower portion of his face.

By the light of the one torch a workie held, Jamie spoke

briefly with his ware master. Most of the shipment would go to warehouse number five opposite Catherine Slip. Before the week was out, these goods would turn to gold for Jamie.

When he stepped on New-York soil, the passenger grunted. Even in the faint light, his wily eyes were able to take in Jamie's finery under the dark velvet cloak: the single-breasted maroon velvet tailcoat, standing collar, buff silk vest, maroon wool trousers, and black silk top hat.

Jamie's fashionable garb vexed the usually elegant visitor, disguised as he was in vulgar homespun. The newcomer didn't object to disguises; they were quite useful. However, he was not fond of those which made him common.

But there was business to do and alliances to be sealed. "Have you arranged for a coach?" the man asked.

"On Front-street." Jamie tossed a clinking purse to the waiting Captain Paul, master of the *Exile*, and watched and waited as the longboat, almost invisible, rowed back to its ship with nary a plash or ripple.

Unhurriedly, Jamie and his visitor moved away from the waterfront. The streets were empty except for the shadow of the coach-and-two awaiting them to the side of Edgar's Tavern, which was dark and shuttered. The coachman dozed on his shelf, snoring.

The man in homespun laughed, a high whinny of a laugh. He climbed into the coach while Jamie prodded the driver.

The *Exile*'s passenger unwound his scarf as Jamie settled opposite him. "Good to see you again, Jamie."

Jamie smiled. "Good to see you, Aaron."

WANTED *in an Attorney's Office, a young man who will be attentive, and writes a good hand. Enquire at No. 13 Beekman-street.*

NEW-YORK EVENING POST
FEBRUARY 1808

33

4 FEBRUARY. THURSDAY. MORNING.

The weather had turned milder, as it often did just before another cold spell. Micah was happy to be left to herself. She didn't even mind that work took her outside on a winter's day. Though the air was still nippy, being alone was a joy.

The cauldron was suspended from a heavy metal bar over the cold fire hole. Micah rolled back the sleeves of Doctor Tonneman's old greatcoat, in which three Micahs might have found the room to nest, and pulled the cauldron toward her. She stopped herself short with a *"Careful, girl, that's lye. Don't want to get you burned."* Nodding, she thrust her small hands into the surgeon's bulky canvas gloves.

Taking care not to lose any sediment, she poured off the clear liquid on top of the soap stew into a large, wide-mouthed clay jar. This fluid contained the dregs of lime and soda. Mixed with two gallons of water, it was just the thing to soak and boil her wash in. But first she would have to let it stand for a couple of days.

In spite of her caution, some of the liquid spilled. It cut through the crusted old snow and seeped into the frozen ground. Like a dog peeing. Or a boy. She smiled.

When the deeper voice echoed what she'd just said— "Careful, girl, that's lye. Don't want to get you burned,"— Micah had all she could do not to burst out laughing. The old man had come from the house and up behind her. "Steady on, girl."

"Yes, Doctor Tonneman." She knew. Hadn't she been helping him make the soap since she'd come to work for them three years before? She'd made it so often she could fair do it blindfolded, but the physician seemed at loose ends lately and kept repeating things.

"I'm waiting on a Slippery Elm poultice for Arnos Fink's arse."

"Doctor Tonneman." The girl shook her head. He was getting worse every day.

He watched Micah for a time as she sparked the fire with her flint and steel. The dry wood blazed almost immediately. She poked at it a bit, enjoying the heat, then swung the bar so the cauldron hung over the flames. Only then did Tonneman return to his surgery.

The girl boiled the grease and rosin in the lye till the grease disappeared. She poured the rose water into the mixture and was stirring it when, wouldn't you know, the mistress arrived.

"I'll do that, Micah. You go inside and get on with the rest of your chores. The evening meal is always late during soap time." Even as she spoke, Mariana was pouring the mixture into the soap box. The next day, after it hardened, the soap would be cut into bars.

Micah went into the house. She'd hung the headless carcass of the chicken by its legs to drain and set two kettles of water over the fire. Now she studied the water. Hot enough. She studied the chicken. It had bled well. Holding it by the legs, she plunged the bird in and out of one of the kettles three times.

Efficiently, expertly, she plucked the scalded feathers and laid them out on some canvas to dry for use later. She eviscerated the hen, washed it, salted it, and laid it on the wood board. Then she went upstairs to make the beds and empty the chamber pots. As she worked, she thought happily of the brief respite she'd had working outside in the sun and the cold air. If they would simply leave her be, she would have this house humming. Micah, who'd been born Jewish, but knew nothing about the religion, had come to the Tonnemans an orphan. She'd lived on the street until the day three years earlier when the old doctor had found her near-frozen in his barn. They had given her her own room in the attic. It was a good exchange for Micah, taking care of two crazy old people and their three young ones who, except for Leah, were older than Micah. But all three were out-and-out spoiled to the bone.

IN THE SURGERY Tonneman had just washed the left side of Arnos Fink's spacious arse with his rose soap. "The poultice softened you up, Arnos, but I'm going to have to lance it."

"This isn't going to hurt, is it?" fat Arnos whined.

"Of course it is, you young muttonhead." Tonneman stabbed the ugly purple boil with his hot needle. *Pop*. The boil drained beautifully. Tonneman coated the wound site with rosemary-dandelion root oil, then covered it with a bit of cloth and plaster. "I'll give you some of this oil, and I want you to put it on and to drink rhubarb root tea every night before you go to bed until Sunday night. The rhubarb root will clean out your bowels and you'll feel better for it."

Later, in his study, puffing on a pipe, Tonneman wrote about Fink's boil, but his poor brain kept returning to what he had taken to calling the Emma Conundrum. How had

Emma Greenaway died? Who had killed her? Not too arduous a riddle. Only as difficult as Zeno's conundrum of
Achilles and the tortoise. In order to pass the tortoise,
Achilles had to first reach the point where the tortoise
began. During the interval, the tortoise moved on to a new
place in the road. Only a bit farther, but still farther. That's
how Tonneman felt. As if he were Achilles trying to catch
an ancient tortoise and stuck with Zeno's paradox: Every
time he drew closer, he still had farther to go.

Tonneman could hear the floorboards creak upstairs under the light weight of either Mariana or Micah. But Micah
was working the soap. At least she should have been. It
wouldn't do to leave it untended on the fire. Vexed, he
hurried outside. The fire was out, the soap safe in its boxes.
No one was around. He went into the house through the
kitchen door. Mariana was putting vegetables in a pot on
the hearth, stirring them. The smell of rendered chicken fat
whirred in his nostrils.

He came and stood behind his wife and placed his
hands first on her arms, then about her waist, remembering
a time when they were young. It was at the beginning of
the War. He had taken Mariana Mendoza home to Maiden-
lane from his surgery. He'd held her, his arms holding the
reins, surrounding her. Now, as then, she leaned her body
against his. She turned to face him. Then, as now, he kissed
her.

Their breathing joined as one with each other, inhaling
the warm safe scent of cooking vegetables.

Micah's footfall on the stairs broke the moment. They
moved away from each other. Mariana remained at the
hearth; Tonneman stepped to the opposite wall and inspected some herbs drying in the wall rack.

The girl passed between them, carrying the waste pail,
on her way to the lime-hole in the woods behind the barn.
She gave them a sidelong glance. They must have been
fighting again . . . or . . . ? No, they were too old for
that.

Wordlessly, Mariana stirred the vegetables.

A chicken lay on the oak table, cleaned and salted. Tonneman took a knife from the rack overhead and proceeded to cut it up. He'd never considered this woman's work, and was pleased to show off his surgical skills even with a chicken. As each was ready, Mariana took the pieces of chicken and placed them in the kettle, then added more boiling water. She and Tonneman worked well together, as they had when they were first married.

Tears streamed down Mariana's face.

"Oh, my dear." Tonneman held her close and felt the sobs shake her body. "What is it?"

She pulled away, angry once more. "How can you ask that? You and Daniel sit and talk about the dead, the skull, the past, and neglect the living. What about your son? You must do something."

She was right, but whenever he thought of Peter and the trouble, he felt confounded.

"Good morning."

Like an actor responding to a cue, their son stood before them, shaved and dressed, very jaunty.

"Peter, aren't you full of vinegar?" Mariana was amazed.

John Tonneman cleared his throat. "A word, Peter."

Mariana poured her son a cup of black tea and handed it to him.

"I'm in rather a rush, sir." Peter drank his tea in gulps, tearing a chunk from one of the loaves of bread still cooling on the window ledge.

The young man's demeanor was so cheerful, his parents were nonplussed. They followed as he went into the front entryway, where he took his hat and cloak from the knobs near the front door and put them on.

"Where are you going in such a hurry?" the senior Tonneman asked.

"I have a new position." An undercurrent of excitement was in Peter's voice, and his face glowed with pride.

"Has Jamie—?"

"Not Uncle Jamie. Old Hays."

Tonneman shook his head in total disbelief. "What sort of work could you possibly do for Jacob Hays?"

Peter laughed. "I'm going to be a Constable."

34

4 FEBRUARY. THURSDAY. AFTERNOON.

Big Ned Winship lived among the mulberry trees in Mulberry-street. One, because his tavern was there; two, because he rather liked the tree-lined street; and three,
because it was convenient-close to Bunker Hill. Often cited
as one of the City's worst neighborhoods, Bunker Hill was a
popular locale for the Hot Corn Girls. Truth was, the girls
sold more than hot corn. And Butcher Ned Winship was
their senior partner.

Big Ned never slept, but then neither did the Hill. If a
man in New-York had a thirst, no matter the time of day or
night, he knew where to get it quenched, or an itch
scratched. Butcher Ned's tavern in Mulberry was the place.
It was also a place where a head could get broken or a
throat cut.

The denizens of Ned's part of town were varied: prostitutes, beggars, and thieves of all varieties. There were filthy
whore cribs, sawdusted taverns, and noxious opium dens.

Ned didn't deal with opium. He'd tried it once. It made him so crazy he killed his best friend. He wanted nothing to do with it after that. His bullring and his whorehouse and tavern were good enough for him. Even in these bad times they brought in the money. Though the workies were crammed into tenements and had little to eat, they wanted their betting and they wanted their booze and they wanted their gash.

But Ned was a man of expanding influence. If workies wanted jobs, Ned was the man to see. More than half the mechanics building the new City Hall or filling in the Collect and digging the canal owed their jobs to Big Ned.

Truth, he was a man of many interests. If somebody trod on your boots in New-York and you wanted him chastised for his bad manners and could pay for it, Butcher Ned was your man.

A punch in the face cost fifty cents. Two and fifty bought a broken nose and jaw. For five dollars an arm or leg was broken. A stab anywhere on the body or a gunshot in the leg would cost a bit, say six dollars and twenty-five cents. Of course, stronger, more permanent violence had a higher price. The fee for murder now stood at twenty-five dollars.

And someone had just paid it.

35

4 FEBRUARY. THURSDAY. NIGHT.

The Night Watch was charged with keeping the peace
after dark in New-York, watching for fires, burglaries, and
violence of any kind. But many a citizen of the City could
testify that all the Watch were good for was huddling in
their guard huts, hiding from the weather or the gangs of
toughs who roamed the streets.

On Butcher Ned's grounds his Bruiser Boys, under the
leadership of Charlie Wright (who-could-do-no-wrong),
kept the peace. Or broke it. As pleased them.

Although there were whale-oil lamps along the streets
of New-York, most were cloudy with smoke and soot, or
worse, unlit. Even when the Watch Men were bold or in-
dustrious enough to do their job and light them, Ned and
Charlie decided which would stay lit and which would not.

Duffy held the ladder while Keller handed up the whale

oil to Staub. Staub filled the reservoir, then attempted to light the lamp while still holding the oil.

Keller rolled his eyes at Duffy. "First get rid of the oil, Staub."

Staub handed down the oil, then lit the wick at first try.

"See how easy?" Keller taunted.

"Very humorous, I'm sure," Staub said, climbing down.

Duffy chuckled. It wasn't a bad job; he had his days free to pick up extra work, and most of the Watch were as good comrades as any he'd ever met at sea, especially Keller and Staub. Duffy had never met an officer like Keller at sea who would act like a mate to the ordinaries.

"Ten o'clock and all's well," Staub called.

They were in Chapel-street, making their way to Murray. There they would warm up a bit in the Watch Hut before moving on.

Fog moved like smoke around them; the cobblestones were slick with the slime of the sudden thaw. When Duffy looked back the one block to where they had just lit the lamp, Warren-street was already but a hazy glow. A mildewed, mossy odor hung over all.

"Your Honors." An old woman materialized out of the fog like a wraith.

Duffy shuddered, crossed himself twice.

"It's black as the pit of the damned with my street lamp out," the woman complained. She coughed and spat. "My husband fell over the Manhattan Company water plug not an hour ago and near broke his leg."

"Where do you live?" Keller asked.

She pointed east. "Church-street."

"Duffy, you go to the hut and see how McIntosh is doing. Staub, you're with me." Keller lifted his hat to the old woman. "Lead on, missis."

"Give McIntosh a hot foot," Staub called back to Duffy. "That'll wake him fast."

"As if *you* never sleep on the job," Keller said.

Duffy could still hear their laughter drifting on the fog

as he continued toward Murray-street. When he looked back, the two Watch Men were gone, swallowed up as if they'd stepped off the plank.

He was humming a bit of a ditty under his breath, when he heard a crash and a shout, followed by high laughter. "Mother of God. Now what?"

A muffled shriek came from the same direction. This set his feet in motion toward the disturbance. When he came to Murray-street, there was no Watch Hut to be seen. Duffy rubbed his eyes and looked around, bewildered. He could see on Church the outlines of what looked like the Watch Hut lying on its side, but it was moving, heading toward Broadway. The shrieking was louder, the din from the unusual conveyance was thunderous. That had to be McIntosh inside the hut, screaming for all he was worth.

Duffy saw now that the source of the laughter was a gang of men who had roped the hut and were now dragging it. Behind shuttered windows on each side of the street, lights began to glimmer, but not a sound from any window, not a body to offer assistance. Much to his own surprise it was Duffy who cried, "Get away from there," as he ran after them. "By order of the Watch!"

The toughs—there were five, perhaps six in all—laughed fit to die. "Maybe you'd like a little ride yourself?" The speaker was about Duffy's age but, Duffy saw, nasty as a hungry bear. He had scruffy dark hair straggling from under his cap.

"Help!" McIntosh hammered on the wall of the hut.

"Shut up." One of the gang kicked the hut, eliciting another terrified scream from poor McIntosh. The laughter grew louder.

"Let's give this one a touch of the same," said a man whose face was covered with ripe boils. He made a move toward Duffy.

Duffy turned to run but they were on him. He kicked and punched as he was hammered to the ground. Knowing he was bound for a licking, he tucked himself into a ball and covered his head with his hands.

"What's going on?"

The sonorous voice cut through the mist. Duffy untucked his head and looked up.

"Who wants to know?"

Out of the fog stepped a familiar figure in a high hat. "The High Constable, you miserable sods," boomed the deep and plummy voice.

· "Scatter, boys! It's Old Hays."

As quick as he'd been in danger, Duffy was safe. All he could hear of the gang were the eerie echoes of their footsteps in the fog. He scrambled to his feet. Duffy could hear McIntosh whimpering in his box, scared half to death. He could smell the acid odor of piss from where he stood. He looked around. Where was the High Constable? "Mr. Hays, sir?"

A man stepped out of an alley. Even in the dark and fog Duffy knew he wasn't Jake Hays. This man was a full head and a half taller. And as he drew closer Duffy could see he was not much more than a lad. The imposter, drawing a clasp knife from his coat pocket, flipped it open, bent over the Watch Hut, and cut the rope. The door fell noisily to the street with McIntosh right behind.

Duffy closed the short distance between them. "Who are you? You sounded just like Himself."

Peter Tonneman grinned. "I thought it a fair performance." In his own voice, the young man was obviously drunk.

"More than."

They helped McIntosh to his feet. In doing so, Peter Tonneman fell. Duffy and McIntosh now helped *him* up. When McIntosh fell again, Duffy threw up his hands and walked a circle, hoping things would sort out by the time he finished. And when he had, they had.

"That's the second time they got me," McIntosh whined. "I'd quit, but I need the money. . . ."

The three dragged the Watch Hut back to the corner of Murray and Church to set it up again, not much the worse for wear. But something was lying on the hut site.

"What's that?" McIntosh asked.

"Looks like a pile of rags," said Peter Tonneman, staggering, coughing, getting drunker by the minute, just breathing the fog.

"Must have dropped off a cart," Duffy said. "Kick it out of the way so we can get this thing up again."

Young Tonneman kicked, slipped on the slick street stones, and fell once more. He heaved himself up on his knees and gaped at the bundle. "Oh, God."

"What?" Duffy asked.

Peter Tonneman shook his head. All of a moment he was sober. He looked again at the pile. Touched it. His hands came away wet and sticky.

"What?" McIntosh whined. "I want to get inside. I'm cold."

Peter Tonneman felt his gorge rise to his throat. "It's a dead man."

36

5 FEBRUARY. FRIDAY. EARLY MORNING.

"Quintin was assaulted at least twice before, Jake." John
Tonneman was upset. He closed the door to the sitting
room as if to shut away the tragedy. "I believe he knew this
would happen." Tonneman stole a glance at his son. Peter
stood beside Hays and the other young man.

"Did he tell you why?" Hays rubbed his nose and
squinted at John Tonneman.

But Tonneman was involved with the Instantaneous
Light Box. The process allowed him to collect his thoughts.

He removed a small splint from one of the boxes on the mantel. He dipped the treated matchstick into the other box and presented it as if he were a conjurer with the Circus. The match burst into flame. Duffy was suitably impressed. Tonneman nodded to Duffy, and used the flame to light a lamp and his segar.

Damn foolishness, thought Jake. There was a healthy fire going the physician could have used to light his segar. One of these days an Instantaneous Light Box contraption was going to set the damn town on fire. "Mark my words."

"What?" John Tonneman asked. He hadn't had his morning tea yet, which made him somewhat groggy.

"Did he tell you why?"

The door to the sitting room opened. It was Mariana, fully dressed, carrying a mug of tea. "John? Peter? What is it?" She looked at Jake. "What is it?"

John took the mug from her shaking hands. "Mariana, Quintin's been beaten to death. His body lies in my surgery."

"Quintin? Quintin Brock? Our Quintin?" Her face crumpled.

Her husband put his arm about her and drew her to him. She wept against his chest. He explained to Jake. "During the War, when we were all young, Quintin lived here as my housekeeper."

Mariana slipped from John Tonneman's grasp. "He was a kind man. Who would kill him? Why?" Her eyes rested on her son. "Peter, you look pale. You've been up all night again, haven't you?"

"Mother, Duffy and I found Quintin."

"May he rest in peace," Mariana murmured. "I think, perhaps, you gentlemen will have some tea."

"Oh, Mother."

"Mr. Hays?"

"A cup of tea would be excellent, Mrs. Tonneman. I would like you and your husband to know that Peter has become one extraordinary temporary Constable . . ."

Mariana and John beamed. Rubbing the tears from her eyes, Mariana slipped from the room.

Jacob Hays could be a diplomat when he had to be. "That is not to overlook the work of one extraordinary Night Watch, one William Duffy, whom I've also promoted to temporary Constable."

It was Duffy's chance to beam. He did some steps of a sailor's jig.

John Tonneman raised his eyebrows. "Can you do that, Jake? I mean, Constables are supposed to be elected and with Peter you've got one over your limit already."

Jake's thin lips curved into his version of a grin. "I'm Jacob Hays. I can do anything I want when it comes to my Constabulary. If I can make Peter a temporary Constable, I can make young Bill Duffy the same. Damn it, John, the two of them handled it better than any other Constable I have. They'll be my personal assistants, not restricted to any ward, able to roam the City at will, the way I do. Perhaps as a team." Jake pondered the idea he'd just presented and liked it.

Mariana returned. "Breakfast in the kitchen. Why would someone kill Quintin?"

Jake pulled on his nose. "That's what we're trying to ascertain, Mrs. Tonneman."

"Look no further," said Tonneman. "Quintin lived right on the Collect. He told me Butcher Ned Winship coveted his land."

"And I know why," Jake interjected. "The Common Council is about to sanction paying higher fees for Collect property, lands the City needs for the Canal-street."

Tonneman nodded. "Not three days ago, in my surgery, Quintin pointed to Brown's body on my examining table and told me, 'Tomorrow I could be dead as him.' He also said they had something to do with killing Thaddeus Brown."

"It would have been kind of you to inform me of this, John."

Sheepishly, John studied his segar.

"Who did he mean by *they?*"

"I asked him that. He didn't say. He claimed it was common knowledge in the City."

"Not my common knowledge."

"I assume he meant Butcher Ned."

"So do I. And Ned's my next stop."

Micah put her head in the door. "Breakfast, ma'am."

"But surely it can wait until after a hot meal?" Mariana asked, almost girlishly.

Jake nodded. He was a practical man. He had been unceremoniously called out in the night. And right now he wanted his breakfast.

"Quintin told me he had some property around the Canal site," John Tonneman said, as they followed Mariana into the kitchen.

"Ah." Jake's great nose quivered. He was making progress. "Now, let's eat."

The men sat around the large oak table and fell to with gusto, eating chicken pie and bread and drinking tea and coffee.

"Did you examine his pockets?" Jake asked.

Peter was trying to avoid his mother, who was smiling and kept patting his hair. Duffy was distracted by Micah. She seemed to be putting every piece of food in the place on his plate.

"Oh, my," Micah cried, clapping her hands together at something Duffy had said.

A look from Mariana subdued the servant girl only slightly.

"Boys!" Jake exploded good naturedly. "His pockets. Did you look?"

Peter and Duffy came to attention. Both nodded. Duffy reached into his jacket and held out his hand, palm up, revealing an exquisite comb of tortoiseshell. "Just this."

"Quintin was a hairdresser with Mr. Toussaint," Mariana offered.

Jake grunted, examined the comb, then slipped it in his waistcoat pocket. "No money? No pocketbook?"

"No, sir," Peter answered.

Duffy nodded agreement.

Jake mopped his plate with a piece of bread, popped it in his mouth, and washed it down with a gulp of tea. "That's it, boys. Let's go." To Mariana he said, "Thank you for a fine breakfast." He turned to John Tonneman. "I'll tell Noah to notify Robert Dillon to get Quintin, so he can have a decent Christian burial."

Outside, the two temporary Constables stood at the ready. Duffy was beginning to look like a sleepwalker, his body aslant, his eyes half closed.

"What now, sir?" Peter was as exhausted as Duffy looked but he had no intention of showing it. And he was annoyed that his mother had sensed his deep fatigue. If he kept his wits about him, he would learn this job from Old Hays. Perhaps he might follow in his footsteps.

"Duffy, you go on home," Hays ordered. "Get some sleep and meet us back at the jail."

Duffy nodded blear-eyed and wobbled off.

Jake turned his attention to Peter. "What are you thinking, boy?"

"What my father said. Quintin told him that the men after him had murdered Brown."

"My thoughts, too. They more than outbalance the question of whether you had anything to do with Thaddeus Brown's untimely death." The High Constable glared at Peter.

"Sir, you can't—"

Jake would have liked to satisfy his curiosity about the whore Simone and Peter's attendance at Brown's funeral, but all in good time. He signaled for Noah. When the carriage rolled up, he said, "Tell Robert Dillon to pick up Quintin Brock's body. Find out which church." Then Jake climbed into the coach, mumbling something to Noah which Peter could not hear. At the High Constable's impatient beckoning, Peter, too, climbed into the coach.

After one brief stop in Division-street at Dillon's undertaking establishment, they headed up Broadway. Hays inspected the terrain and people during the ride, but did not speak. As they neared Mulberry, Peter realized where they were going. To that point Jake had not spoken. He did so now, as the coach halted in front of Big Ned's Tavern in Mulberry-street. "Listen carefully, son. Follow a rat to catch the other rats. Ask questions, then follow your nose."

Of course, Peter thought, if I had a nose like Old Hays that wouldn't be hard to do. The young man hid his smile with a cough.

They found Butcher Ned in his bedchamber above the tavern. The room stank of spirits and heavy perfume, but mostly of sweat. Discarded clothes were strewn over an unmade bed. Other furniture in the room consisted of two rough wooden chairs, a surprisingly attractive Chippendale table, and a seaman's chest. A meager looking glass hung on the wall above the bed. The room was lit by a fire in a small fireplace, a lone candle on the table, and whatever sun could find its way through the dirty, narrow window over the chest. A buxom young girl in a low-cut white blouse and a dimity petticoat that had once been white was shaving Ned. As she drew the razor across his cheek, he grabbed behind at one of her generous breasts.

"You keep that up," she said, without stopping her stroke, "you'll get your throat slit."

Ned grinned. He and the girl had not reacted in the slightest to the entrance of the two Constables.

Peter's eyes flicked at Jake. The High Constable's face was stone.

The girl rinsed the razor in the flecked, soap-scum-filled bowl after each beard scrape. When she finished, she dried and powdered Ned. Then she picked up the bowl of dirty water. "Want to see?" She gestured to the mirror on the wall.

"No. Good morning, Jake. Kind of you to stop by." Ned placed his massive hands on the girl's rump. "Get, Amy." He squeezed with one hand and slapped with the other. The water splashed out of the bowl, soaking the girl.

"See what you've done." She was nettled, and had the poor sense to let it show.

Big Ned made a fist.

The girl cowered, put a finger to her lips, and backed away.

"Good morning to you, Jake," she said, polite as a maid, curtsying.

"Good morning, Mistress Wiggins," Jake answered, going her one better. He'd chased Amy off the streets many times over the years of her young life as a prostitute in New-York.

The girl bobbed her body to Peter. "Good morning, sir." She gathered up her skirts and ran down the stairs.

Winship stood, wiped some errant soap from his ears, and lit a segar from the candle on the table. "What can I do for you, Hays?"

Jake nodded to Peter to stay near the door, then paced about the chamber, poking this and that casually with his staff. "Do you know a Quintin Brock?"

"It might happen." Ned took a shirt from the pile on the bed, sniffed it, and put it on. He tucked the shirt in and hitched up his trousers.

"Think about it."

"An old nigger, was he?"

"Was?"

"Is, was? What the fuck does it matter? Only a nigger." Ned laughed and turned his back on Jake. He began rummaging in the drawer of the table.

"It matters because he was beaten to death last night."

"My, my, what a tragedy. The streets are not safe in our City, High Constable."

"I thought perhaps Quintin Brock owned something

you were interested in. Such as a piece of Collect property on the Canal route."

"Well, now that you mention it . . ." Ned produced a piece of paper from the drawer, smoothing its wrinkles. "Me and that particular nigger did do a piece of business yesterday." He grinned. "Seems he sold me his Collect land for five hundred dollars. Four hundred in Manhattan Bank paper and one hundred in gold. Ten gold Eagles. Someone must have killed the dumb bastard for his money."

"Why dumb?" Peter ventured.

Ned cackled. "The pup can bark." His ugly eyes narrowed. "Because I offered to have Charlie escort him home and he turned up his nigger nose at us."

"So," Peter continued, "the sale took place here?"

"In the tavern. I have five men and two women who'll swear."

"Mr. Brock lived along the Collect."

Butcher Ned sneered. "Mister, my arse."

"His body was found at Murray and Church, well beyond the Collect. Why would he leave here with all that money, go past home, and end up that far south in the City?"

Ned spread his hands. "Like I said, a real dumb nigger."

Peter cleared his throat. "It's a bit of a way from here, but isn't that area considered your grounds and under the protection of your Bruiser Boys?"

Ned shook his head in feigned wonder. "Listen to the lad, Jake. My grounds? My protection? Those streets are all part of the City of New-York. And everyone knows the City of New-York is under the protection of Jacob Hays."

Jake cast an approving eye on young Peter. "You are as smooth as grease, aren't you, Ned?"

"Whatever you say, Jake, but I'll bet you rum to beer you didn't find a penny on the nigger."

"That's true." The High Constable took the piece of paper from Ned's hand. It was a deed of sale signed by Ned Winship. Next to Quintin Brock's name was a large, crooked X. Jake showed it to Peter Tonneman. Then without another word Jake dropped the deed on the table and strode out of Big Ned's room. Peter took a moment to grin at Ned, then chased after his new boss.

"That miserable bastard," Jake muttered, as they descended the stairs. "He killed Quintin Brock."

"That's for sure, sir."

"Now we have to prove it."

"That's also for sure, sir. And we can."

Jake came to an abrupt halt. "Spit it out, boy. How?"

"Quintin was a good friend to my family. I haven't seen him for years. But when I was a child he would come by to visit and sometimes play with me. . . ."

"Get to it, boy."

"He helped me to read Mr. Bunyan's book. Quintin Brock could read and write."

37

5 FEBRUARY. FRIDAY.

The top floor of Daniel Goldsmith's house on Garden-street had been divided. Half was let to Joseph Lancaster, the schoolmaster. The other half was Goldsmith's sanctuary.

Although his "sanctuary" was a fair-sized space, it was near to impossible to walk, sit, or stand, what with all the stacks of correspondence, sundry papers and documents, books and newspapers with which the former Constable had surrounded himself.

"Shit." Exasperated, Daniel threw the batch of Collect Company papers which had come from John Tonneman on his desk, obscuring the account books for Molly's millinery business.

As a retired Constable, he'd been watching Jacob Hays for years, and if he'd learned anything, it was that criminals usually left a trail. What he hadn't learned was the magic spell that guaranteed he could always find the trail.

His nose dripped, and though the thaw held outside, his room remained cold and damp. The fireplace was too small and the fire needed fuel, which, with his current distraction, he kept forgetting to carry up with him. Instead, he wrapped the brown wool scarf Molly had knitted for him tighter about his neck. He blew his nose heartily into a linen handkerchief and drank some cold chocolate.

Another road that led to nowhere. When he'd heard about Brown's death and Peter's possible involvement, it had intrigued Daniel to think that as an old Constable perhaps he could solve the mystery of Thaddeus Brown's murder. In the doing he would clear the name of Peter Tonneman and repay the debt he owed John Tonneman, who'd believed in him so many years before.

Now he was beginning to have his doubts. He was just an old man, and his brain didn't work as fast as it had in his youth. What could he do that Jake Hays couldn't do better? As he sipped his chocolate he reflected on Brown's funeral. Peter had seemed very friendly with that fat whore Simone. No matter what he found out on that score, Daniel would have to tread lightly so as not to upset John. But then again, John was no fool. He'd been young once, too. They both had.

There was a knock at the door. Before Daniel could respond, John Tonneman came barreling in, bumping a waist-high pile of *Evening Posts* and *Heralds*, not to mention *Examiners*, which tilted precariously but didn't fall.

"Good day, John," Daniel said pleasantly. He pushed some papers away from a corner of the room to reveal a rack filled with bottles of dry Jerez. Selecting one dusty bottle, he wiped it on the sleeve of the worn black jacket he always wore when he was in his exclusive chamber. He drained the chocolate in one gulp, and cleaned the mug with a piece of lace that had strayed upstairs. The cork on the sherry bottle came out easily. "Care for a taste?"

Tonneman frowned, then nodded. Without a word, the surgeon took off his gray greatcoat and looked for a place to put it. Finding none, he folded it and placed it on top of a tottering stack of papers. The countless packets of papers in the room were of assorted sizes, some tied with various colored ribbon, some tied with string. Dust laid claim to everything and rose like little clouds when surfaces were disturbed.

Goldsmith found a flint-glass tumbler on his desk, holding pencils and pen holders. He dumped its contents on the desk, and wiped the glass with the bit of lace. He raised the tumbler and the mug. "Which flavor? Chocolate or pencils?"

"Pencils."

Daniel poured. They both made a show of sipping the fortified Spanish wine. Each nodded.

"Surprisingly good," Tonneman admitted. "Considering the way you serve it. Why do you store it up here? Wine should be in the cellar."

"Pish-tosh," said Goldsmith. "Molly keeps all her hat material down there."

Tonneman shook his head. "Cloth should be up here. It could rot in the cellar."

"And where would I keep my papers? I like my arrangement just as it is, thank you. Please keep your scientific thinking to yourself." Goldsmith lit a segar with the flame from the lantern on his desk. He flung out his hand, barely missing the pile of correspondence. "Would you like a smoke?"

"No, thank you. I'd be afraid of starting a conflagration." Tonneman crossed to the grate and stirred the dying embers. "What have you found?"

"About Mr. Brown and his friends? Nothing. About the past? Perhaps." Daniel blew his nose again. "But whether what I've found amounts to anything is another story. The most important question is why was Emma murdered."

"Not the most important question. I judge *who* killed her as having greater priority."

"Hmph. Scientific mind." Goldsmith shook dust from some papers. Tonneman sneezed. "Good health. If we learn why, it could lead us to who. Let's look at two things that were happening back then. The War and Hickey."

"You think Emma's death had something to do with the plot to kill General Washington?"

"I have no idea. But I say it's worth investigating. If Emma Greenaway did not die at Hickey's hands, my feeling is that it had to be someone she knew. More to the point, likely someone you knew. But, of course, we can't rule out people we didn't know."

"What you're saying is you've boiled our suspects down to the twenty or so thousand souls who lived in New-York at that time."

Goldsmith grinned. "I hope we can do better than that." His face went serious. "We are hypothesizing that whoever killed Emma also killed Gretel. Thirty-two years have passed since we found the serrated sword near your house with no idea as to whose blood was on it. Our destiny has been leading us to the killer. We just didn't know it. Another thing we didn't know was that the blood on that sword had to be Emma's."

"We don't know it now," said John Tonneman.

"I am certain it was. Then we lost the damn sword, Hood and I. And it was used to kill Gretel. I've wondered and wondered over the years: If we hadn't lost the sword, would Gretel have died?"

"Stop torturing yourself. The killer would have used a different weapon."

"Was the killer Hickey, or someone else?"

Tonneman felt impatience settling over him. Goldsmith was such a plodder. Tonneman sighed deeply. "Someone else . . ." A memory took form in his mind. The sword had been wrapped in fine white silk. Bloodstained white silk.

Goldsmith, too, was lost in the memory—so vivid still —of the day the serrated sword reappeared. He had found it in Quintin's tar hut. Gretel's head was skewered on it. This was different from any of Hickey's other murders. The severed head had been left in the open, a challenge, not hidden like the others. He shivered, drained the sherry in his mug, and refilled it. "I humbly apologise to the soul of that poor girl Emma Greenaway, but I've needed to find Gretel's murderer for so long it feels an eternity. Perhaps her death had something to do with Emma's." Goldsmith cleared his throat, picked up a bundle of papers from his desk, and undid the string holding it together. He ticked off the names on his list. "First suspect. Maurice Jamison."

"Why on earth Jamie?"

"Why not Jamie? Why not you and me?"

"Why not George Washington?"

"Let's not get fanciful," Goldsmith said, a bit annoyed. "Doctor Jamison married Emma's mother and thus gained considerable wealth." Goldsmith was unhappy that Tonneman didn't appreciate the effort he'd put in compiling this information. "Second. David Matthews. He was jailed in Connecticut and supposed to be hanged for the traitor he was, but he dressed as a woman and escaped. If you remember, he returned when the Royalists held New-York and became Commissioner of Chimneys." Goldsmith consulted his list. "But Matthews died July twenty-sixth, 1800, at Sydney, Cape Breton, Nova Scotia, where he had lived since '85, and where he'd been attorney general."

Tonneman rolled his eyes. "I'll wager my life that Matthews never came in contact with either Emma or Gretel."

Goldsmith ignored him. "Third. James Rivington, poor sod. He ended his days renting musical instruments. He died on, of all days, Sunday, July fourth, 1802, a few days shy of his seventy-eighth birthday. Ironic."

"I repeat myself, Rivington never met either woman. Where is the motive, man?"

"Fourth. Sam Fraunces. The serrated sword was his to

begin with. He died in Philadelphia, October twelfth, 1795."

"Stuff and nonsense, Daniel."

"Five. David Bushnell." Goldsmith rummaged through a batch of papers and pulled out a letter written in tiny crabbed writing. "Changed his name to Bush, became a doctor. Lives in Georgia. I understand he writes a lot of letters to all and sundry complaining that Robert Fulton is trying to take credit for his underwater boat." Goldsmith held the letter to Tonneman.

Tonneman ignored it and stifled a yawn. "Well, I suppose there is some merit in what you're doing. Merely naming those people defines our chore. We must eliminate those who are not pertinent. What is left would perhaps help us solve this thirty-two-year puzzle." He raised his eyebrows and with some irony said, "You have forgotten my cousin. Bear Bikker."

"Bear Bikker, number six," Goldsmith mumbled as he wrote. "Was Bear his true name?"

"William."

"What became of him?"

Tonneman shook his head sadly. "After going through the entire War without a scratch, he died at Yorktown, just two days before Cornwallis surrendered to Washington. Bear's last letter said he wasn't ten feet behind Washington during a charge. Probably wrote it the day he died. Just before the charge, Washington said, 'It's a fine fox chase, my boys.' "

Goldsmith nodded his head. "Nice sentiment. If you believe in war." He returned to his list. "Seventh. Mayor Whitehead Hicks. He went—"

Molly's voice called from below. "Visitor coming up."

"Who?" Goldsmith called back. "I'm not—"

Tonneman laid his hand on his friend's arm. "I took the liberty of sending a note to this man to meet us here. I didn't want to see him at my home. To be honest, I didn't want Mariana getting into it."

Goldsmith nodded sagely. Women were all the same. Heavy footsteps sounded, climbing the stairs, then a knock at the door.

"Come."

A sturdy-looking man of short stature appeared in the doorway. He wore a fashionable brown beaver, and a brown greatcoat over a deep green velvet jacket with shawl collar. The high collar of his white silk shirt was visible, as was the white waistcoat edged with green. In his hand was a yellow leather bag. He appeared to be a fine gentleman. Save his skin was black.

"Pierre Toussaint?" Tonneman asked.

The Negro nodded.

"I am John Tonneman. It was I who asked you to call. This is my friend, Daniel Goldsmith. I haven't had the occasion to tell Mr. Goldsmith."

"Tell me what?"

"Daniel, early this morning some men attacked Quintin. They murdered him."

"God in heaven, protect us!" Daniel cried. Tears sprang to his eyes.

"Amen," said Mr. Toussaint, crossing himself.

Tonneman was dismayed. It had not occurred to him that Daniel would take this so. Unthinking fool that he was, John Tonneman had forgotten what comrades Daniel and Quintin had become after being wounded together when Hickey's bomb went off in the tar pits in the early days of the War. "Mr. Toussaint was Quintin's employer. I thought he could shed some light on why anyone would want to murder Quintin."

Daniel tossed off his sherry and reached for more. "Mr. Toussaint?"

"No," Toussaint said. His rich voice sounded of the islands. "Thank you."

Daniel wiped at his eyes with his finger tips, then cleared sheaves of paper from beside his desk, uncovering a pair of chairs. He gestured to them. Toussaint and Tonneman sat. Toussaint removed neither his hat nor coat. The yellow bag he kept on his lap.

The three men talked for a considerable time. But Toussaint wouldn't, or couldn't, help Tonneman and Goldsmith.

"So," Daniel said finally, bringing their unproductive conversation to a close, "there's nothing you can add, Mr. Toussaint?"

"Not a thing, Mr. Goldsmith," the hairdresser replied in his melodic voice. "Quintin owned the land. Certain people were after him to sell the land to them. If he sold it, it was without my knowledge, but he wouldn't have needed my permission either. It was his house, his land. I tend women's hair for my livelihood. Quintin Brock was my assistant. He was also my friend. His two sons are free men, out in the world. Louise, his widow, shall never lack shelter or be in want so long as I'm alive." He pulled a silver watch from his waistcoat fob pocket. "By your leave, sirs. I have a client waiting."

"No," Goldsmith said absently, "not at all. Thank you for your time."

The black man stopped at the door. "One final thing, Mr. Goldsmith, Mr. Tonneman. I may dress well and I hope I have the manners of a gentleman, albeit a gentleman of color. But I don't think my words will have much weight legally."

"Why is that?" asked Tonneman.

"In case you didn't know, gentlemen, I am the property of Mr. John Berard. I am still a slave." Pierre Toussaint smiled grimly, tipped his handsome brown beaver hat, and left.

Goldsmith shoved his segar in his mouth and shrugged. Another empty road. He rubbed his hands together. "Any other ideas?"

"I'm afraid not." Tonneman rose. Six suspects in Emma's and Gretel's deaths, most of them dead. All of them nonsense. Goldsmith was surely addled, perhaps even senile.

"Well, if we can't solve the present, perhaps we can solve the past." Daniel Goldsmith pulled a new batch of papers from a shelf, raising more dust. "Seventh," he said. He raised his eyes to look at Tonneman.

But Tonneman was already on the stair.

38

7 FEBRUARY. SUNDAY. EARLY AFTERNOON.

The fine rosy contours of an exquisite flower shimmered before Charity Boenning's eyes, appearing and disappearing as she nodded over her embroidery. Linens for her baby.

Almost as if in response came the faint quiver from her swelling belly, like a lost bird fluttering its wings. Then the face of her dead husband floated up before her as if sculpted, a bust in marble. One he might have created himself. No. Philip's work was warm. This image was cold, with hollow, lifeless eyes. His sweeping mane of glossy black hair was frozen by death. The flowing silk scarf at his throat, his signature, seemed carved in icy stone.

He had wooed and won her with drama and poetry, sketches, and loving letters. He called her his woman-child. And though Philip was older than her own father, near fifty, she had run off and married him, trusting to God for His blessing since none came from her horrified parents.

Why could she not conjure up the warm vibrant soul of the man? Charity sighed. With the Lord's grace, perhaps that would appear in her son, for she was certain she was carrying a son.

Her bewilderment was great. Since the stagecoach tragedy, all memory of her husband had turned to stone. Dismayed, she now carried in almost every thought the fair features and hair of the brash young man who had been her rescuer.

Peter Tonneman.

Her cousin Katherine had confirmed that Peter came from a good family, but then Charity had known this; his manners were impeccable. He had come to call several times and he had told her about his sisters and his parents. As he talked, she could see how much he cared for them.

He had confessed to having no interest in being a physician. This had been difficult for his father to accept. When he spoke of this, tiny spider lines of pain appeared about his eyes. She wanted to stroke them away, along with the unruly lock of blond hair across his forehead, and hold him. A tender yearning, like and yet unlike that which she'd felt for her departed husband, surged through her, taking her by surprise.

Peter Tonneman cared for her. Peter Tonneman needed her.

What had Cousin Jacob called him? Undisciplined clay? But she could tell Jake Hays liked Peter by the way his eyes smiled, giving the lie to the gruffness of his words. Of course, he liked Peter. Why else would he offer him a position in the Constabulary?

Her reflection was interrupted by the heavy sound of the knocker at the front door. She could hear Anna delivering her favorite harangue about folks not using the back door, as she shuffled to the front door. Charity smiled and changed her position to ease the ache of her back and the painful swelling in her breasts. She picked up her embroidery once more. After a moment Anna came into the sitting room. Peter Tonneman was at her heels.

He had come to take Mrs. Boenning for a ride. If that would be all right. And he had come bearing a gift. "The first Friday of every month is soap day at our house. So, may I offer you Tonneman's Splendid Hard Soap? As my father likes to say, 'Use daily for cleanliness and health.'" Peter grinned broadly.

She smiled back. She'd liked him from the moment she'd seen him above her, a Godly messenger standing at the mouth of the snow-swept ravine. But now she liked him even more. Since Cousin Jake had put him to work with the Constabulary, Peter seemed bursting with good humor. The unhappiness she had first noticed about him was gone. And he talked endlessly of his family. She liked that. Charity Boenning believed in family and missed her own in Philadelphia very much. Cousin Katherine had also told her that Peter came from a fine old Jewish family, descending from the first Sheriff of New-York. If only . . .

In front of the house was the graceful one-horse shay that Peter had borrowed from his father. Ophelia whinnied at their approach. It was not often the saddle horse was pressed into this kind of duty, but she took it with her usual serenity.

Charity patted the black mare and held her breath while Peter almost lifted her into the shay. Both were embarrassed—she, because she needed the assistance, he, because he had touched her with such familiarity. Had they both forgotten his rescue of her? How he had held her as tenderly as if she were a child on the terrifying ride to Rawls's Inn?

They didn't speak as they drove down Broadway to City Hall. The winter air was mild as spring.

Smartly-dressed women in their hats and muffs strolled along leisurely with their gentlemen escorts. Yet there was an underlying energy, a style of walking, Charity thought, particular to New-York. It seemed even the exceeding cold of recent weeks could not keep these people from their promenade. Today, of course, with false spring, was better.

When they arrived at City Hall on Wall-street, Charity exclaimed, "Oh, I'd dearly love to walk." She was developing a particular fondness for this City and wanted to be part of it. Philadelphia was so very staid and proper. And everyone in Philadelphia minded everyone else's business.

"Are you sure you're up to it?" Peter looked worried.

"I'm not an invalid, Constable Tonneman," Charity responded, eyes flashing. Her skin colored. "You'll have to get used to my temperament. It's difficult to stop me from having my way and getting what I want once I decide I want it."

Thus Charity told Peter Tonneman she accepted his courtship. She slipped one small hand from her rabbit fur muff and tucked it into the crook of his arm. They left the shay and joined the other strollers. With so many out taking advantage of the nice weather, progress on the crowded sidewalks was a bit difficult. Everyone seemed to want to stop and talk with friends.

Other women, without escort, obviously of the lower class, moved in a more determined fashion, carrying filled market baskets and bundles, intent on chores. The gentry's children, respectful of their elders in conversation and demeanor, clearly longed to be imitating their poorer cousins, who were running and shouting, sliding about in the melting snow, throwing slush snow balls more mud than snow.

Constable Gurdon Packer, one of two responsible for the First Ward, walked along Broadway saluting his betters, albeit indifferently. When he spied Peter Tonneman, he winked and continued on his way, whistling as he walked. Dogs barked and chased one another and the wheels of passing carts or carriages, missing by some miracle being run down. Vendors offered fragrant roasted potatoes. A young girl sold hot, spiced gingerbread from a wooden tray.

The two young people walked slowly. Charity's eyes

darted every which way, admiring the beautiful avenue, as Peter pointed out landmarks. There was so much to see. Unlike other, more narrow, often crooked thoroughfares of New-York, Broadway was a wide, straight road, lined with poplars, rising gracefully as it wended northward.

When they neared the City limits they stopped to look at the structure that would some day be the new City Hall. Peter bought hot buns, two a'penny, and they ate the sweet cakes in silence, smiling at each other. Cows lowed, wandering through the open muddy fields searching for bits of grass amid the slush. Hogs, more aggressive than cows, found street garbage far more interesting. One black billy goat followed the hogs for a while and then stotted off when two ragged street dwellers started stalking it.

Two-wheeled delivery carts made a noisy racket as their young, white-smocked drivers raced each other over the cobblestones. There would be what-for if their masters discovered they were out on Sunday. A ragged young woman peddled baked pears from a dilapidated cradle.

The sights, sounds, and smell of this City were exotic. Charity felt as if she'd been transported to a foreign land. The excitement fueled her, and she was not a bit tired when they returned to the shay.

Ahead, on the corner of Wall and Broad, a small crowd had gathered in front of what some people were already calling Old City Hall. On a makeshift platform a band was playing with uneven blasts and whistles. The crowd cheered them on.

"I should get you home," Peter said.

"No, please. I love everything. I want to see. I want to hear."

He smiled at her childlike eagerness. They joined the happy Sunday group.

The conductor leading the musical band had oversized white-gloved hands and exaggerated feet. His name was Kasper and he was known to many in the City for his work in the Circus. Light and silly music came from the band, whose members were also making funny noises and foolish faces. The foolishness was well received. Laughter came almost continuously from the spectators.

Then the band sang raucously of the good old colonial times, under the King. Their words were accompanied by more whistles and drum rumbles and swatting each other with pig bladders. The song told of three roguish chaps, a miller, a weaver, and a tailor, who got into trouble because they couldn't sing. This made the crowd roar with laughter.

As the song approached its end, the miller drowned, and the weaver was hanged. Each man's dreadful end was acted out with still more whistles, bangs, and pig bladder blows.

When the players got to the weaver's hanging, Kasper pointed to the City gallows in the square, opposite the whipping posts and stocks, and mimed a rope about his neck with his left hand and a rope above with his right. He sank lower and lower and appeared to be strangling. Everyone laughed. By this time the band had stopped playing and each man was pointing at Kasper and doubling over with laughter at his plight.

Charity turned pale and clutched Peter's arm. He patted her arm and nodded toward the platform where at the last moment the conductor's imaginary rope had broken, and the man fell to the wooden floor of the stage, his long limbs splayed. More laughter bubbled from the spectators. The children shouted and jumped with glee.

Up leaped the conductor, bowing. The audience laughed and cheered. The clown put his fingers to his lips indicating that the people should be quiet. He then pointed to the band and brought his arm down abruptly. The musicians began to play and sing.

In this final chorus, the Devil clapped his claws on the tailor as the tune came to a resounding conclusion. Everyone applauded.

The conductor turned delicately on his elongated feet to the delighted people gathered in front of City Hall and executed a low, sweeping bow to more applause and laughter.

But the fun was not over. Kasper raised his hand and began tugging at his face. It stretched this way and that as if made of dough. With each new silly face, he would walk to a different corner of his small stage to exhibit it to new arrivals, and he would get there with an odd walk, like a duck or like a horse. With every subsequent foolishness, the assembly would laugh louder and longer, and applaud. The conductor chose this moment to fall on his rear end. The people screamed with laughter.

Then the band played and cymbals crashed, obscuring the clattering sound of a racing two-wheeled cart.

Instinct made Peter turn. A pair of delivery carts raced out of control up Broad-street, toward the unaware crowd. He was frozen in place for a moment. Then he shouted, " 'Ware the carts, 'ware the carts," as he lifted Charity in his arms to hold her out of harm's way.

The crowd, now screaming with fear, scattered, as the riderless carts barreled into the platform.

Peter set Charity down and ran to the stage. But he was not needed. The two runaway horses, a gray and a bay, seemed more dazed than injured. They walked back and forth dragging their leather. And when one started grazing, the other followed suit.

"Maisie!" A white-smocked delivery boy ran toward the horses. When he saw that his animal was unharmed, he smiled and hugged the gray.

The conductor, who'd been twirling like a red top when the unfortunate incident began, never missed a step; he kept twirling until he fell. Then he climbed to his feet wearily, tapped the stage to show its durability and nodded his head yes, then he tapped his head and shook no. Some of the crowd, still dusting themselves off, laughed lightly, getting back into the sport.

Kasper shook his head at life's vicissitudes and once more faced his small group of musicians. They had by this time collected on the stage and calmed themselves as if the crashing of carts was a daily occurrence. With a flourish of his large white-gloved hands, the conductor started them playing again.

The delivery boy began leading his gray away, but he didn't get far. Constable Harry Lannuier, Constable Gurdon Packer's partner in the First Ward, had heard the screaming. He approached on the run. "What's going on here?"

Peter explained, all the time keeping a watchful eye on Charity, who seemed altogether too pale to him. Finally the two men saluted each other and Peter walked back to Charity while Constable Lannuier scratched his head, waved the delivery boy off with his gray, and tried to disentangle the bay from its leather.

"Thank you for a splendid day, Peter," Charity said, when he delivered her to Jacob Hays's door. She gave him her hand, then stood on tiptoe and presented him with a feathery kiss. She was gone before he had a chance to react.

Jake found him sitting in the shay in front of the house, smiling from ear to ear.

"Anything to report, Tonneman?"

"Yes, sir. No, sir."

"Then I suggest you go home."

"Yes, sir."

Young Peter Tonneman fairly floated as he made his way through the melting snow to John-street and the house in Rutgers Hill. He would be twenty in September. He had a vocation. And he would marry Charity Boenning. Yet, at this moment, he had an overwhelming desire for his mother's sugar cookies and a tall glass of buttermilk.

Jacob Hays's thoughts were of a more serious bent. He sincerely hoped his instinct was sound and that Peter Tonneman was not the man who had killed Thaddeus Brown.

39

8 FEBRUARY. MONDAY. MORNING TO AFTERNOON.

"You'll pay your score or we'll have to send your mama a bullet ducks about her little man." As he spoke, Charlie Wright (who-could-do-no-wrong) made as if to shake George Willard's hand, but instead gave George's little finger a firm bend-back. George screamed in agony, and fell on his knees in the dung-laden mud.

"Shut up," Charlie growled.

George stared at his mutilated finger. "But you broke it," he whimpered.

"So I'll fix it." Charlie bent down and gave the finger a sharp pull.

George screamed again.

"Shut up, you worm." Charlie seized him by the throat. The world went a dull gray in front of George's eyes; his arms flailed. Charlie was lifting him off the ground by his throat. Gray became black, then nothing.

When George came to his senses, he was lying facedown, gasping for air, inhaling dung. His little finger ached terribly. He climbed to his feet, cursing, and made a halfhearted attempt to brush the filth away. His efforts only made matters worse.

He looked about. Several yards from where he stood a stagecoach passed, its wheels spraying mud, heading down Broadway.

For reasons of his own, Charlie had let George keep his piebald stallion. Tupper, piqued at being tied up so long, was straining on the reins that secured him to a post. The horse whinnied.

"I feel the same way, Tupper." George moaned and lurched toward the piebald. Damn, he felt bad, really bad. He had no idea how long he'd lain in the mud, but his throat hurt like the devil, his finger, like ten devils. The sun was just overhead. Noon? He'd been unconscious for about an hour. Where would he get that much money now? He'd already squandered his inheritance and then some.

George Willard mounted the black-and-white stallion and rode to Richmond Hill, angry, wretched, and humiliated. And now his way was thwarted by a wide wagon which stank strongly of goat, driven by one of those swarthy foreigners with a beard. The driver would not respond to George's demand that he get off the road (and let his betters by). To further frustrate him, George was downwind of the glue factory. What with the dung-mud that coated him, he could hardly keep from heaving, and did so, spilling his aching guts on a cluster of Jamie's boxwoods.

"The master is in Litchfield," Stevens informed him at

the front door, eyeing with distaste each foul footprint George left on the French carpeting of the entryway.

"I need a change of clothes," George croaked.

"I dare say, sir." Stevens's haughty nose wrinkled. "And more."

"Bring me some brandy." George pushed past the servant. He didn't like being kept in his godfather's entryway as if he were a petitioner. "Hot water. I want a bath."

"Yes, sir."

As he climbed the sweeping staircase, George shed his contaminated outer clothing. For all his bravado, he was mortified by his appearance. He was grateful that his godfather was not there to comment on his ignominy.

The hot water eased his aching body; even his finger felt better. When he emerged from the copper tub behind the needlework screen that showed satyrs chasing naked nymphs through wooded glens, he was furious that Stevens had deigned neither to assist him nor to build up the fire. Ignoring the towel draped over the screen, George dripped over to Jamie's wardrobe and wrapped himself in one of Jamie's silk brocade dressing gowns. He was about to close the wardrobe when he spotted the coin on the wardrobe floor. Stevens wasn't as neat as he pretended. It was a two-and-fifty piece.

Pleased, George dropped the coin in his purse, which lay where he had left it on the bed. It clinked against two lone pennies. He went back behind the screen for the towel. Scrubbing his head vigorously, he padded from behind the screen. A young maid was laying out fresh linen on Jamie's majestic bed, which an agent had bought for him from the plundered estate of a French marquis who had lost his head during the Frog revolution.

George caught a glimpse of a pretty profile and curving bosom. A tasty young thing, he thought, knowing his uncle liked them green and virginal.

George leered. His main ambitions in life were to get Jamie's money and to out-fuck the old rogue. He undid the robe and seized the girl from behind. She reached back with both hands to fondle his stones; he was overjoyed. Joy turned to shock when the bitch squeezed, twisted, and butted him with her arse. For the second time that day George Willard was knocked flat. The girl scooted out of the room.

He lay quiet for a moment, letting his vision clear. As his eyes focused, they rested on a curious item. He reached under the bed and was about to drag out the black metal box when he heard footsteps. He stood quickly. Perhaps the girl had come to her senses.

It was Stevens with a bottle of brandy and a glass. George had his drink, hoping that Stevens would leave. But now the fool insisted on helping George to dress, and George was obliged to leave his uncle's bedchamber without exploring the contents of the metal box beneath the bed.

An hour later, when George left Richmond Hill, there was clean clothing on his back and in his purse were the gold Quarter Eagle and two copper pennies.

The afternoon sun had dipped behind rolling clouds. Wisps of mist that could become thick fog floated up from the marshy land as he reentered the City proper.

At once the clamor of the City fell upon him like a sledgehammer. The bugle blow of a roving scissors-and-knife grinder sounded like Gabriel's horn calling forth a host . . . of devils, damn him. Ragpickers added bells to the cacophony. All the while, clam and oyster pedlars hawked their wares, competing lustily with the purveyors of fried fish, hot gingerbread, and buns.

His stomach rolled one way toward hunger, then another, toward disaster, at the smell of the fried fish.

Chimney sweeps with permanently gritty skins roamed the streets in their ash-and-cinder-dusted funereal clothes, calling out their services. Pigs squealed and dogs barked at the vehicles rolling over cobblestoned streets.

But the aching din of life in New-York was the least of George's problems. Even the pain in his swollen little finger was unimportant. How in God's name was he going to get his hands on the two hundred dollars? The image of that metal box under his uncle's bed flashed through his thoughts. He should have found a way to look inside. Damn.

He had to get that money. He could go to Canada. No, London would be better. There was pleasure in that last thought.

His Uncle Jamie was an old man. How much longer could he live? When Jamie died, George would inherit the Greenaway fortune, which had quadrupled under Jamie's stewardship.

At the door to the Tontine, a runny-nosed newsboy was shouting the praises of the *Evening Post*. He thought it most important that everyone in earshot read the stories on the Navy Yard and the new arsenal and the Common Council having resolved to pay higher fees for lands that were required for Canal-street.

George dismounted, tied the piebald to the rail, and tossed the newsboy a penny. The boy reached out, but the toss was short and the coin landed in a pile of fresh, steaming horse dung. The boy's face screwed up in angry disappointment. George glared at the urchin, daring him to say something, but of course he didn't. The boy merely knelt and groped in the mud for his coin.

With his copy of the *Evening Post* tucked under his arm, George entered the Tontine. Smoke hung thick as a winter fog. Hackers coughed, spit, and smoked. Smoked, coughed, and spit. And smoked. The first whiff of the Coffee-House and its tobacco and spirits brought his appetite thundering back. He had a snarling belly and a thirst for porter.

George settled in at a table and ordered his porter. He opened the *Post* and scanned the advertisements. He knew what he was looking for, and he'd bought the paper for just that reason. Brilliant ideas often came to him out of the blue.

He had no real interest in the printed word or in politics. The local news was brimming with politics. New-York stewed like a bubbling cauldron. For all George Willard cared, they could hang together, Federalists and Democrats alike.

What he had to do was come up with two hundred dollars. Fast. But wait, Providence had always cast her blessings on him. He knew something would come his way.

The tankard of dark brown ale arrived. Through the haze, George saw the familiar figure of Ethan Cameron, a clerk with the Manhattan Bank. Who could miss that shock of red hair? They'd all met in passing when George and Peter Tonneman were at Columbia College and spent more time in taverns together than in classes.

Peter Tonneman. Of late, Peter had found religion. George laughed out loud and thumped the table. Oh, he was a wit, all right. Smack a Quaker and catch his religion. Right out of a bloody hole in his head. Peter was a shrewd one all right. Smack Brown, steal the money. Then get religion and work for Jake Hays as a Constable. And stalk the widow cousin. No doubt about it, Peter had his eye on that one. Pretty as a picture and probably brought a nice purse with her, too. Perhaps not a lot of money, but enough for Peter. Shrewd, the boy was. Shrewd.

"Another porter," George shouted. The Quarter Eagle would be gone before he could blink. Then where would he be? Drunk at the Tontine. And without funds. Hell, he'd been in such straits before. All he needed was Mistress Providence to smile on him.

And possibly she just had. He ambled over to Cameron's table. Let Cameron buy a few rounds. The sod was too drunk to know the difference anyway. "Good to see you, old chap." George clapped the man on the back, practically knocking him from his chair. A fat leather pouch fell from Cameron's lap. Cameron scrambled to catch it.

It was George who snatched the wallet from the air. Had he snatched good fortune, too? That remained to be seen. But George was sanguine about his prospects—and Mistress Providence's largess. George set Cameron's pouch on the table between them.

Cameron peered bleary-eyed at George. "I know you." His mouth was filled with mush. "Peter . . . Tonneman."

"Quite," answered George Willard. When his porter arrived, he ordered another round. He nonchalantly reached into Cameron's wallet and paid with one of a great wad of fifty-dollar Manhattan Bank notes. He immediately ordered another round. Then another. The finger didn't hurt at all now.

And when Cameron passed out, George deftly helped himself to the pouch entire. "Peter Tonneman thanks you," he said with a chuckle. He left the Tontine.

The wooden walk surrounding the Tontine Coffee-House gave George a clear view of the rambling traffic along Wall and Water-streets. An old ragpicker with near to twenty hats on his head staggered past, narrowly missing the kegs being unloaded in front of the Tontine. So much for Tom Jeff's Embargo. George mounted his piebald.

"Stop, thief! Tonneman! Constable! I need a Constable. Never around when you need 'em. *Thief!*"

George had gone dead-still at the first call, one foot in the stirrup, the other on the ground. That fool Cameron had come to his senses too soon. George completed his mount, pulling his hat down over his eyes. But Cameron was on him, his hands clawing at George's left leg and stirrup.

"Give it up, Tonneman! Constable! Help!"

By this time a curious, if not helpful, crowd had gathered to watch.

"Here they come!" someone shouted. The crowd parted and two Constables pushed their way through.

"What goes on?" Duffy demanded.

"I'm Ethan Cameron. He stole my pouch," Cameron wailed. "The bank's money. I'll lose my job."

The second Constable recognized the distinctive black-and-white horse before he recognized the rider. "George?"

George raised his hat and smiled his most charming smile. He shook his head ruefully. "Drunken simpleton. Such a fuss. He asked my assistance because he was too drunk to see to it himself." So saying, George tossed the pouch to the ground as if it offended him. "There, take it, you yap. Serves me right for trying to be a good Samaritan for this drunkard."

"He's a liar," Cameron screamed, snatching up the muddied pouch and holding it to his breast like a rescued babe. He stamped his foot, splashing himself and others with mud. "Liar, liar, liar. His name is Peter Tonneman and he's a liar."

"I'm Peter Tonneman," said the second Constable. "This man is George Willard."

Agape, Cameron ran his fingers through his hair. "No, he's . . ."

The other Constable was Bill Duffy. "Get down, Willard," he ordered. "You have some explaining to do." Duffy stood in front of the piebald horse and grabbed at the bridle.

George kicked Tupper hard in the flanks, and the piebald reared. Duffy staggered back but not fast enough. The stallion's powerful flailing hooves came down on him, knocking the Constable to the ground.

"Pull him off, George, damn it!" Peter Tonneman tried to grab a piece of the piebald's leather to stop the horror, but the panicked Tupper kept stomping, trampling Duffy.

George Willard at last gained control of his animal. He wheeled about and galloped off, leaving Duffy crumpled and bleeding on the muddy street.

Peter knelt beside the writhing Duffy. The top of his head was crushed and oozing. His agonized scream cut through the murmurings of the bystanders.

"Somebody get a surgeon," Peter yelled, for the first time in his life wishing he were one.

All at once Duffy stopped screaming. In a clear voice, thick with Irish, he called, "Ho, to the wind'ard. Free me from this hell-hole!"

40

8 FEBRUARY. MONDAY. AFTERNOON.

The old physician arrived at the Tontine quickly. He'd been attending a meeting of the Canal Company board of directors at City Hall. When he came out on the street, he heard an uproar from the direction of Water-street and mounted Socrates faster than he knew he could. He rode hard toward Water-street. Commotions such as this often meant accidents where he was sure to be needed.

When Tonneman arrived on the scene, only the presence of Jake Hays was enough to make the morbid crowd part and let him pass. "What is it?"

The High Constable was near tears. "I've got a Constable down."

Old Tonneman's heart stopped. He held tight to Socrates' reins. His heart thudded. Pain made a tight band across his chest. "Oh, my God. Peter."

"No, not Peter."

Tonneman grabbed his black leather bag from the hook on his saddle and followed Jake Hays's tall hat to where Peter Tonneman, very much alive, knelt next to the bloodied body of his fallen partner.

"Father, thank God."

"Come away." Tonneman offered his hand to his son, but Peter refused.

Jake Hays put a gentle but firm hand on young Tonneman's shoulder and led him a short distance away.

The physician got on his knees to examine the broken body of Bill Duffy.

"Do something," Peter cried. "You can save him. I know it."

John Tonneman knew the only help for this man was from God. It was obvious he was dead. He shook his head. Noah stepped forward and helped Tonneman to his feet.

"All right, Peter. What happened?" the High Constable asked.

"It was terrible, sir. He set his horse on Duffy intentionally. Everyone saw it."

"He stole my pouch," Cameron said, sobered by the situation.

Peter wiped his hands on his trousers. His face was raw with anguish. "I'm going to go after him."

"Who?" John Tonneman and Jacob Hays had both spoken at once.

"Peter Tonneman," Cameron said emphatically.

"For the last time, you sot, I am Peter Tonneman."

"But, he said—"

"Who was it, son?"

"George Willard, Father."

Jake Hays took charge. "Which leads you to think what, Peter?"

"It's a tenuous trail, sir."

"Follow it."

"If George Willard was so quick to kill one man, he may have also killed another."

Hays nodded vigorously. "Go on."

Peter spoke slowly, with some awe. "Thaddeus Brown."

"And?"

"And stolen the cash box."

WHEN JOHN TONNEMAN returned to Rutgers Hill, he was weary and torn with a mixture of emotions. Love and pride in his son. Envy for Jacob Hays's relationship with Peter. Fear for his safety. He felt sorrow, too, for the dead lad.

He was so involved with his thoughts that he didn't at first notice he had a visitor. Hitched to the rail outside the barn was an unfamiliar gray horse and a shiny black buggy. Socrates and the gray exchanged haughty neighs as Tonneman led his bay gelding into the barn.

Although curious to discover who his visitor could be, Tonneman took the time to remove Socrates' saddle and brush the gelding down. He then ladled water from the barrel into the animal's bucket.

He went into the house through the surgery. His coat was stained with Duffy's blood. He hung the coat in the surgery and scrubbed his hands and face. Tea was in progress when he entered the sitting room. His daughters, very pretty indeed, were plying the visitor with tea cakes while Mariana talked to the gentleman. The girls squealed when their father opened the door. Leah threw herself at him as if he'd been gone for a year. Gretel, all of a sudden, was very much the lady, a silk ribboned shawl around her shoulders.

The stranger stood. Squinting, Tonneman saw it was young Isaac De Groat, old Cornelis's son. After Cornelis died last year Isaac had practiced the law by himself.

"Sir." The tall, broad-shouldered young man retained the light hair and coloring of his Dutch ancestors. He remained standing, but watched Gretel with more than a casual interest as with flushed cheeks she brought her father his pipe.

"What brings you here today, Isaac?" Employing only a minimum of drama, Tonneman lit his pipe with his Instantaneous Light Box. Isaac was appropriately impressed. Tonneman caught Mariana's eye. She, too, had not missed Isaac's interest in Gretel.

"Dirk Onderdonk, sir."

Tonneman frowned. "Dirk Onderdonk? Dirk Onderdonk is dead. I closed his eyes myself, not three weeks ago."

"Yes, sir. He's left you his house and property, Doctor Tonneman."

"What house and property? He had rooms on Hanover Square over Nicholas Milly's print shop."

"True. But he also owned a farm of some fifteen acres in the Village of Greenwich, with a house and a barn. He left this to you in his will. He had no living relatives."

"John." Mariana's face lit up. "A farm in the country." She quite forgot herself and jumped up and down, clapping her hands.

John Tonneman rested his eyes on his wife. He loved her to distraction when she was this way. So like the girl he once knew. "Where exactly is the property, Isaac?"

"I have it marked on the map." The lawyer pulled out a fold of paper from his fashionable pea green waistcoat. "See? Here, near the crossing of Christopher and Hudson. I would ride up with you now, if you like."

"No, no, that's quite all right. I'll go myself. Tomorrow, in fact, if the weather holds."

Mariana clucked her tongue.

John Tonneman paid her no heed. He was pleased with the news and even more pleased by what his eyes told him: that Isaac De Groat was quite taken with his daughter, and she with him. Tonneman hid a smile. So it goes, he thought. "Yes, I'll look at the property tomorrow."

"And I'll go with you," said Mariana.

41

8 February. Monday. Morning to afternoon.

George galloped north along West-street on the Hudson
River waterfront, spattering all who happened to be in his
way, dodging delivery carts speeding along at the urging of
their harassed white-smocked drivers. First anger, then fear,
fed his outrage.

He had to get someplace safe. His mother would protect
him, but she would ask too many questions. Of course, the
house in Liberty-street would be the first place Hays would
look.

Money. He needed a stake to get him away from New-
York. Start over. Canada? New Orleans, perhaps. First, a

place to gather his strength. Think. He would go to
Richmond Hill. But Uncle Jamie was in Litchfield. There
was always that box under the bed. He hadn't even tested
its weight. It could be filled with gold or stuffed with bank
notes.

Charlie Wright (who-could-do-no-wrong)? Charlie
would be certain to know what to do in a situation such as
this. Butcher Ned had a lot of power in this town, and
Charlie worked for Ned. Charlie was even his friend, if
anyone could be Ned's friend. Much as George wished for
other choices, he chose Charlie. He pushed on toward the
bullring at Bunker Hill.

The warmer spell had brought people out to the bullring, both paying customers and those who liked to stand
about and talk, wanting their entertainment but not willing
or able to pay for it.

Today, the muddy field would make the terriers even
more vulnerable. It would be a shame to miss the inevitable
slaughter, not share in the fun. But George had no time
now for fun. In haste, he tied Tupper to the rail and rushed
inside the arena. He saw Charlie head to head with Ned,
talking, watching spectators enter. George waited, favoring
one leg, then the other, sweating like an animal.

Ned barely glanced at George as he walked away.

"You got what you owe?" Charlie demanded, peering
through the front gate, shrewdly evaluating each customer
arriving by carriage, cart, horseback, or foot, tallying up the
eventual proceeds.

"No. I need your—"

"Get away."

"But, Charlie—"

"Get away or die." Charlie turned his back and started
toward the bullring.

George pursued, pleading. "I killed a man. A Constable. I need money and a place to hide."

Charlie paused, turned. A strange, slow grin distorted
his face. "You need money? You need help? Look no fur-

ther. We'll tear up your paper. Even give you twenty-five."
He slapped George on the cheek. It was meant to appear
friendly, but George sensed the menace that was always
with Charlie. The light blow had rocked him, but he was
careful not to show it. "What else are friends for?" Charlie
went on, scorning George for the coward and dupe that he
was. "Except . . ." He cocked his head.

"Except what?"

"You have to do us a little favor."

"Anything. Tell me."

"Not much." Charlie's grin grew broader. "Just kill
someone."

IN THE TUMULT after Duffy's death, Peter had begged all
around until Lemual Wilson of the Tontine had finally lent
him his chestnut mare. With the High Constable's blessing,
Peter was now hard on George Willard's trail. Assuming
George would know better than to go home to his mother's
house in Liberty-street, Peter felt it was a good guess that
George was racing to Richmond Hill and his Uncle Jamie.

Peter was all the way to the canal ditch, where Canal-
street was to start, when good sense replaced zeal. He
slowed down. What would Jake Hays do? At once he knew.
He started asking people on the street if they had seen the
piebald.

The fifth no to his query about the piebald, which came
from a gnarled Negro woman carrying buckets of water on a
yoke, was enough for him.

Peter began doubling back and christ-crossing the City.
Although frustrated and tired, he was determined to keep
searching till he found George.

At Chambers, he stopped at the jail but found only
Sergeant Alsop asleep at his high desk. Peter didn't stay,
concerned that the one minute he wasn't watching the
street, George would escape him.

Now that he was past Chambers-street and the edge of

town, there were fewer structures. He dismounted and led Lemual Wilson's horse, who kept bobbing his head, pulling at the reins. "Want to be back at the Tontine, don't you? Can't say I blame you."

There were people about. Some headed in the direction of Grand and Mott. Bunker Hill. Of course, the bullring. Peter stopped short, and the mare's snout nudged his shoulder. The bullring would be the natural place for George to go. And a bad place for a lone Constable. Removing his five-pointed brass star, Peter slipped it into his coat pocket. He adjusted his hat to cover his brow.

Sure enough, the piebald was tethered out front.

Peter tied Wilson's chestnut well away from the piebald and waited. The drone of many voices came from the arena, but no shouting. He supposed nothing was going on in the ring yet. Trust Big Ned to squeeze the most from each event.

After a while Peter decided this wasn't the way to do it. Had he seen another Constable, he would have told him to find Jake or rush over to the jail on Chambers and bring help. Something. But no Constable. He was alone in Big Ned's territory.

The thought of asking one of the patrons of the bullring or a passing citizen never entered his mind. In this neighborhood, that was like asking to have your throat cut.

Peter forced himself to stroll as he approached George's horse. "Steady, Tupper." He untied the animal and slapped its rump. When the piebald took off down Mott-street, he shouted, "Runaway horse!"

Peter kept backing away and shouting. "Runaway horse!"

Others took up the cry, part sincerely, part in drunken glee. "Runaway horse! Runaway horse!"

As he'd hoped, George came running. "My horse," George cried.

"What do I care for your fucking horse?" Charlie

Wright bellowed as he came after George. "We have work to do."

"My horse," George wailed, but he was afraid not to follow Charlie, who was going along Mott. "Maybe we'll catch up with him," he mumbled.

"Shut up."

"I was only—"

"Shut."

IT WAS JUST noon when the two men approached Number 39 Duane-street. Charlie stood back while George, acting on Charlie's terse instructions, went to the door of the gray house and thumped the brass horseshoe knocker. He stared at the curtains on the side window. Had they just moved? He looked around at Charlie. Charlie's gestures of promised mayhem were enough to terrify him forever.

After a short time the door was opened. The woman had a fair enough face, except for the scar. Her black hair hung long and loose about her shoulders as was the fashion of the day; but somehow, on this woman, the fashion seemed wanton. No matter, the tart was a mass of hanging flesh and George couldn't abide fat women. Damn. He was going to earn his pay.

"May I help you?" She had a Frog accent and was fanning herself with a red-and-black fan, though it wasn't anywhere near hot. She wore a tit-cut red dress. A sheer black silk stole was draped around her shoulders. A heavy moist scent flowed from her fleshy body.

"You are Simone Aubergine?"

The woman nodded, offering a sultry smile.

George responded with his finest smile. "I was told you don't object to callers of an afternoon."

She tilted her chin and slowly ran her fingers through her wavy hair. "And who told you this?"

"A friend."

"A friend of yours or a friend of mine?"

"I was hoping a friend to both of us."

"*Très charmant*. Well spoken, monsieur. And you are young and handsome. Please come in." Simone led him through the entry hall. His reflection in the mirrors on either side of the hall startled him. He was pale as death.

Simone Aubergine took him into a sitting room full of Frenchy furniture with thin legs. The fire was hearty, which gave him relief, for he was suddenly very cold. He sat on the edge of one of the sofas. Pink satin, hung with fringe. The ugly green-red-and-yellow floral needlepoint rug in front of the sofa looked like so much vomit.

"May I offer you . . . something?" She ran her tongue slowly around her full, rouged lips.

"Just yourself."

In one move she folded the fan and rapped him on the wrist with it. "Naughty boy." She caressed his cheek. "I won't be long at all. I must say good-bye to another friend, then I will hurry back to you, my *étalon*."

She left him with an impression of soft pudding and heady perfume. He listened as she walked through the entry hall out of his sight. By the time he got up to look, she had let her other guest out.

He was on the couch again when she returned to the sitting room. Without a word she took his hand and led him to the room in the back of the house.

Gold silk covered the bed smoothly. Simone pointed to the sidetable. When he didn't move, she tapped the table with her fan.

His hand shook as he dropped a paper dollar on the table.

"*Là*, you are generous. I shall make you very happy." She folded back the coverlet and lay back on the bed, lifting her red skirts, spreading her legs. She wore nothing at all underneath. "Come, come, darling, I don't have all day. Others will be visiting soon."

Her shuddering thighs and white belly repulsed George, but he'd paid his dollar—Charlie's dollar—and would get full value. It did occur to him, as he climbed the mountain of meat, that she wouldn't object when he took it back.

Just as his nature was about to be satisfied, he put his hands about her neck and squeezed. This quickened his pleasure, but she was so fat he couldn't strangle her.

"No, darling," she whispered, sweetly at first. But when he persisted, her face grew red, and fearful understanding flashed in her dark eyes. She fought at his hands furiously; he heard a snap. The bitch had rebroken his little finger. He howled and smashed her fat face.

The whore screamed. "Murderer! Murderer!" Pushing him off, she went bellowing down the hall, holding her skirts high above her head. "Murderer!"

George pulled up his trousers and gave chase, his mind reeling with all the terrible things Charlie would do to him for letting it go wrong. His whole hand throbbed. The whore was at the door, opening it. Once she got outside, all would be lost.

"Help me!" Simone shrieked to the man just outside the door. "He's murdering me."

"Not doing too good a job of it, is he?" said Charlie Wright (who-could-do-no-wrong).

He grinned as he plunged his knife into Simone Aubergine, just beneath her billowing breast.

Pocket Ledgers

COLLINS & PERKINS, No. 189 Pearl-street, have just
completed an assortment of Pocket Ledgers, the utility of
which to all merchants is too apparent to need illustration.

NEW-YORK SPECTATOR
FEBRUARY 1808

42

8 FEBRUARY. MONDAY. AFTERNOON.

The narrow alley wound its meandering way from Jay-
street to the yard in the back of the house in Duane-street.

Here, Peter had followed George and Charlie. George
had gone inside. Charlie waited at the front of the house.

Few except frequent visitors knew this alley existed.
Having once been a frequent visitor, first for Tedious
Brown, then for himself, Peter well knew the alley, and the
yard, and the house, and the woman. He also knew that
the small green cart and the brown donkey tied up outside
the back door belonged to Simone.

He'd been cautious to the extreme, worried all the time
that George might hurt Simone, that Charlie might choose
to investigate the back of the house and thus surprise him.
But Simone's terrified scream blew his caution away.

Peter burst through the back door and ran down the hall. The door to the street was wide open. Blood pooled dark and wet along the doorway and on the dirt walk. They had killed Simone, damn them. George, who'd always been a bully and something of a coward, had become a murderer, at least twice over.

Peter looked about. The street was empty.

Where had they gone?

Peter returned to the sitting room. Nothing. No one. Nothing. The scent of her pervaded the chamber. Breathing it made him sad. She had been a friend to him when he'd needed one. And now they had murdered her. But where were they?

He was about to return to the front door when he noticed that the sitting room floor was bare. Simone's fancy needlepoint rug was no longer in its usual spot in front of the pink sofa. She was quite fond of that rug. A remembrance of Paris, or so she had told him. He did not think she'd ever been to Paris. Montreal was more likely, or perhaps New Orleans.

He went back out the front door. Still no one to be seen. Except, over toward Thomas-street, some boys, rolling and swinging barrel hoops, were splashing in mud. Their voices carried over the quiet street.

Peter stood in the bright winter sun and listened. Wheels. And hoofs. He swore he could hear George whining. As quietly as he could, he went back into the house and along the hall to the back door, arriving in time to see George and Charlie carrying Simone's rolled-up rug. From its bulk, he felt certain Simone was inside it. They had obviously gone back along the alley while he was running through the hall from back door to front.

It took all of Peter's self-control not to cry out. Simone was dead, and that was it. His job now was to follow George and Charlie to see if they could lead him to anyone else. That was Jake's way. And now it must be his.

Indeed, George was complaining about Simone's

weight. Peter knew that Simone would have appreciated the irony.

Damn. The two villains had discovered Simone's cart and donkey. They dropped the rug and its contents into the cart and drove off. Peter stayed right behind them.

The street population of this squalid area was made up of homeless, out-of-work sailors, drunks, and urchins who holed up in empty buildings or built their nests in empty barrels. None paid attention to the cart and its two passengers.

The vehicle didn't go far. Just to West-street and the edge of the Hudson. George and Charlie dumped the rolled carpet on the dock. George lifted his foot to kick the roll into the river, as Charlie backhanded him across the face. A surprised George fell flat on his arse on the wooden dock.

"Idiot. That rug's worth money!" Charlie raged.

A street dweller, sleeping not ten feet away, grumbled in his dreams. Others clustered on the dock, but they posed no threat to George and Charlie. And likewise, they offered no help for Peter.

George unrolled the rug. Simone was inside.

Peter was unable to look away.

"Now," ordered Charlie.

Without standing, George rolled Simone into the water.

She made a tremendous splash and disappeared.

Charlie stood over George until he rolled up the rug.

"Let's go," said Charlie, throwing the bloody rug into the cart.

George scrambled to his feet.

"Let's go," said Charlie. This time he was talking to the donkey. But the animal would not move.

After more shouted commands and a vicious kick, Charlie abandoned the cart. He grabbed the rug angrily and threw it over his shoulder. He started walking north. Docile, George followed, nursing his aching finger.

Peter waited till they were a block away, then began to

trail them. Jake had taught him that the way to catch criminals was to stalk other criminals. Only Jake called them rats. Peter looked into the water and whispered a prayer. At that instant Simone rose to the surface, her arms thrashing. Good God, she was alive! Peter pulled off his boots, threw down his greatcoat, and dove into the cold waters of the Hudson.

A street dweller awoke, saw Peter going in, and cried, "Man overboard!" Then he drifted, snoring, back to sleep.

But some of his companions woke at the cry, and tottered to their feet to see what his call was about. They proved more helpful than Peter would have supposed. Without their aid and a pierside ladder, the young Constable would never have been able to haul Simone's heavy body out of the icy waters.

Peter's father had taught him well. He pushed the water out of Simone as she lay on the pier like a beached whale. Horrible to say, each push brought blood spilling, too. She was gasping for breath and bleeding copiously from her chest.

At the sight of blood, the street dwellers ran off.

"They've murdered me," Simone gurgled.

"Not yet." Peter pulled off his sopping jacket and tore off his shirt. The shirt he used to staunch her wound, then he put his greatcoat over her shoulders. He fairly dragged her onto the cart. His father would know what to do, but Rutgers Hill was too far. The best chance was the City Jail. Sergeant Alsop, for all his lethargy, had to know the whereabouts of the nearest physician.

TO LET—a lower front Office on Wall-st, the best stand in the city for a Notary, now occupied by Mr. George Ludlow.

NEW-YORK HERALD
FEBRUARY 1808

43

8 FEBRUARY. MONDAY. AFTERNOON.

"Your pardon, madam. I apologise for disturbing you, but there's no help for it." Jake Hays was bareheaded, having turned both his hat and stick over to Abigail Willard's butler.

"Mr. Hays." Abigail studied the High Constable. He seemed uneasy, yet his voice was undeniably commanding and his presence was powerful. "Please be seated, sir. Will you take tea?"

"No, thank you, ma'am." Hays sat almost awkwardly.

What had George done this time? Enough to bring the High Constable himself. Abigail steeled herself and waited for the law officer to speak. He was all head. His short, stocky body seemed uncomfortable confined to a chair, seemed to want movement. "It's your son, George," Hays began.

"Oh?" It was as she'd feared. What now?

"Is he here?" Hays's penetrating eyes met hers.

Suddenly Abigail knew the reason for this visit was not the customary peccadillo. She could not breathe. Slowly, carefully, she spoke. She could hardly make the words come out. "What has happened?" Hays didn't respond. His dark eyes were fixed on her. Abigail's hands began to tremble; she clasped them in her lap. "No, he's not here."

"Was he here yesterday?"

"No." Around her, but at a distance, such a far distance, she could hear the activity in her home. A delivery at the back door, the creak of the floor above as the housemaid went about her chores, even the bells of the ragpickers outside on the street. Tears came to her eyes. "Mr. Hays, you must tell me."

"Mrs. Willard, this is not what I'd choose to say to the mother of her son. I think perhaps some tea . . ."

Abigail pulled the embroidered band three times, signaling for tea. They waited.

"Mr. Hays."

The High Constable was aware that Abigail Willard lived alone with George, her youngest child, and that her other children were married, with their own children. But under his gruff exterior Jake Hays was a true Christian, a kindhearted man. He understood the feelings of a parent for a child. Even for a child that had done a murder. "Mrs. Willard, do you have someone, a relative, who can stay with you?"

"For heaven's sake, Mr. Hays—Is George dead?"

"No, ma'am, he is not."

Abigail breathed a sigh of relief. Whatever it was she could deal with. So long as he was not dead.

Nancy arrived with the tea tray. At Abigail's nod, she left immediately. Hays and Abigail sat in silence as Abigail went through the ritual of serving. She handed him his teacup.

He set it down on the table beside his chair.

After Abigail had poured her own tea and taken her

first sip, she, too, set her cup down. "I am ready for what you have to tell me, Mr. Hays." She pressed her lips together firmly.

"I'm sorry to have to tell you this, Mrs. Willard . . ."

Oh, my God, she thought, *the awful man lied. George is dead.*

"Your son, George Willard, has killed a man."

Abigail breathed a gasping breath. A duel. Of course. One would think after the Burr and Hamilton disgrace in '04, these young men would realize that society frowned upon their ridiculous masculine posturing and that the practice of dueling was no longer in fashion. . . . "Was it a duel? A matter of honor?"

A matter of dishonor, Jake thought, but did not say. "I'm afraid not. He killed one of my Constables and ran off."

Abigail's sharp loss of color brought him to his feet. The woman looked as if she would swoon. But she shook her head and said firmly, "Sir, my son would never do such a thing."

"I have the word of Constable Peter Tonneman, who has gone in pursuit of him."

She seemed to have heard only what she wanted to hear. "Peter? Good. Peter will take care of George. They are friends. Have been since childhood. They've always taken care of one another. That's what friends are for, after all."

"I must bid you good day, Mrs. Willard. Please get word to your son to surrender himself to me." Hays, sympathetic but stern, took his leave.

Outside, he told Noah, "She hasn't seen him."

"Mothers lie for their sons."

Jake shook his head. "I believe she's being truthful."

"Did you ask to search the house?"

"He's not there."

"What will you do now?"

"Wait for young Tonneman to do his job. In the meantime, Gutschenritter and Dick will keep a watch on the house. Willard might be fool enough to return."

WITHIN THE HOUSE, Abigail dried her tears and wrote a note. She folded it and sealed it with her husband's wax and ring, then pulled the band twice for Oliver.

When the butler arrived, she told him, "I must be informed immediately should my son return. In the meantime, see that"—she wrote the name on the sealed note with a flourish—"this is delivered directly to Mr. Jamison at Richmond Hill."

Abigail Willard was determined that no one would take her son from her for any reason.

JAKE WAITED OUTSIDE the Willard house. Having tied his horse to an elm tree, Constable Gutschenritter was standing on the corner pretending to be unobtrusive. He'd have to lose half his body weight to be that. Jake went over and over in his mind his conversation with Mrs. Willard. Most telling for the High Constable was what she'd said about her son and Peter Tonneman. "*Peter? Good. Peter will take care of George. They are friends. Have been since childhood. They've always taken care of each other. That's what friends are for, after all.*"

Jake was still worrying about that when Abigail Willard's footman came from the stable, mounted a horse, and rode off. The High Constable signaled Gutschenritter, who mounted his horse and followed.

44

8 FEBRUARY. MONDAY. AFTERNOON.

In the City Jail, Alsop was still snoozing at his high desk.
Jake and Noah sat at a table, waiting. The cells currently
held three prisoners. Garrit Ellis was not one of those prisoners, even though Jake could have brought Pockets before
a magistrate for his attempted robbery in Ned's tavern.

Jake had seen fit to let the cutpocket go free this time, as a reward for information supplied. Knowing Pockets and his sticky fingers, Jake could depend on him to be back.

The morning had been busy. After Peter had ridden off after George, and Jake had called on Abigail Willard, there was nothing for it but to go about normal rounds.

While Ward Constable Thomas Dick kept watch at the Willard house, Gutschenritter had followed the footman to Maurice Jamison's house, where something was delivered. Gutschenritter's best thought was that it was a letter. But then Gutschenritter's best thoughts were not worth much. All in all, Jake had not been comfortable with himself or this part of the day's business.

Noah filled their mugs with coffee, and Jake topped the steaming stuff with brandy from the bottle sitting between them on the table.

He drank.

Noah drank.

Jake took his leather case from his inside pocket, selected two cheroots, gave one to Noah, and lit both from the candle on the table. The only other light was a lantern on the sergeant's high desk. They each drew in the first breath of smoke and savored it.

"This the batch you soaked in brandy?" asked Noah, after a moment.

Jake nodded. "Like the taste?"

"It's all right."

"Let's sum up," said Jake, spitting tobacco.

"What's the need? No matter how you look at it, Ned Winship is your man. His threats against Quintin Brock tell you that. He's got this City in his pocket. Extorting money. Bribing people."

Jake made a growling noise and nodded grimly. "Right. Winship killed Quintin. Or had him killed. Same difference."

"And he killed Brown or had Charlie Wright kill him.

Either for what was in the box or over that Aubergine woman."

Jake pondered this. "You reckon Ned's her other lover?"

"What do you mean, other? The woman has five hundred lovers. It's her trade."

"I mean *particular* lover."

"If he was particular, he wouldn't lay with a whore."

Jake raised his black thicket eyebrows and sipped his coffee. "Charlie could be her lover."

Noah shook his head. "That man has no love in him. Not even carnal. He's an animal. Worse. He's a sharp stick you kill someone with."

At that moment the door to the City Jail slammed open. Standing before them was Peter Tonneman. His face and clothes dripped blood and water. He staggered under the limp weight of Simone Aubergine.

BY order of the Honorable Maturin Livingston, Esquire, Recorder of the City of New-York—Notice is hereby given to all creditors of Peter Brannon, of the City of New-York, an Insolvent Debtor, that they show cause, if any they have, before the said recorder, at his Office, situate in Liberty-street, in the said City of New-York, on the eighth day of March next, at one o'clock in the afternoon of the said day, why an assignment of the said Insolvent's estate should not be made, and he discharged, according to the directions of an act, entitled, "An Act for giving relief in cases of Insolvency," passed the 3d of April, 1801. Dated February 22, 1808.

LINDSEY & ANDERSON, Attornies

NEW-YORK EVENING POST
FEBRUARY 1808

45

8–9 FEBRUARY. MONDAY NIGHT TO EARLY TUESDAY MORNING.

The brightness blinded him. Everything seemed familiar and yet not so. Lanterns burned in front of every building. He knew that the young, efficient, courteous Night Watch was unfailingly reporting any lights out. Dark lamps were relit almost immediately.

The sounds of his horse's hooves on the cobblestones resounded in John Tonneman's ears. He appeared to be in Crown-street. But Crown-street wasn't any more. It had existed long ago in his youth, when the British ruled New-York. Tonneman found himself in front of a richly appointed brick building, flanked by two radiantly shimmering carriage lamps.

The balustraded tile roof of the three-storied house was also brightly lit. The dazzling illumination displayed a wide promenade with an unobstructed view of the North and East Rivers and New-York Bay at the foot of the island. He had been here before. It was as if he were outside himself, watching his younger self.

The horseman beside Tonneman said something in a low voice; Tonneman couldn't make out what. Peering into the brightness, he couldn't make out who the man was either. They dismounted. A royal groom took their reins. Tonneman and his shadowy companion were obviously expected.

They entered a great hall. Ahead was a splendid, sweeping staircase with mahogany rails and banisters. A bewigged no-faced butler in white satin breeches, jacket to match and a ruffled stock, led them from the spacious center hall to a chamber on the left.

Here, more light spilled from the elegant brass chandeliers and a large marble-mantled fireplace. A fire blazed behind the fire screen. When the butler opened the double doors, flames flickered in the large chamber. They threw an ominous cast against the shimmering gold damask curtains, against colorful silk and taffeta low-cut dinner dresses, against very white, very delectably rounded, very European bosoms, against the velvet and satin and silk of the gentlemen, against strange, malevolent faces, all looking at him expectantly. Again, Tonneman could not make out their features, yet he had the sense he had been here before.

The butler announced them in a deep voice. Once more, Tonneman could not make out the words.

He and his companion were greeted by a sturdy, commanding man. Lips moved, but there was no sound except for the clink of the glasses, the whine and whistle of the wind, and the crack of the fire in the yawning grate.

A footman offered a tray. Hands reached out for glasses.

Beneath their feet the carpets were French, the furniture substantial English Chippendale. Patterned paper of French design covered the walls, depicting scenes of gay ladies and gentlemen in sylvan gardens, but the walls billowed as if there were no substance to them. Tonneman could make out bits of silver and porcelain, but he could not see faces.

A woman dressed all in blue came to him. Her features, too, he could not see. But her eyes were blue, he knew that. As blue as cornflowers. He felt a great sadness, as in the death of a loved one.

His companion was talking to another woman. Tonneman could not make the woman out, but about her glowing face was a nimbus of red hair. Below, large white moons of breasts. Diamonds dangled from her earlobes and sparkled on her fingers.

Next to her, a younger woman in yellow waved her hands all about as if signaling for help. She, too, had substantial breasts. Huge pink pearls hung from her earlobes and about her plump neck.

Her face, like all the others, was a ball of white light. Still, within the light he could see her mouth open. And when it did he heard the wind howl. He couldn't hear any words but he knew she was saying, "I'm going to die. Help me."

His companion's image shivered; the glass of sherry he held trembled. Suddenly the sherry glass shattered in his hand, spilling blood, and more blood.

"Jamie!" Tonneman cried.

Blood dripped on him. Cold blood.

He awoke alone in his bed, wet. He could hear the rain battering the side of the house. In the pale light of morning and the flicker of the fire he could see that above him the ceiling had soaked through and rain dripped down on him. If it was that bad here on the second floor, he'd hate to see what it was like up on the third. He should have replaced those shingles when Mariana asked him to.

He rose from his bed, shaken by his dream. Mariana was not there, but that was not unusual. He would have liked to talk with her about the dream, but they had argued late into the night until she had pulled the bedclothes over her head and turned her back on him.

Jamie? Did he really believe Jamie could have been Emma Greenaway's unknown lover all those many years ago? No, of course not. Yes. But why? Tonneman smiled ruefully. Because she was a woman. It was so obvious. Jamie, being Jamie and thinking with what was between his legs, had unknowingly seduced the child before he met her mother, Grace. He had thought Emma a servant girl.

Jamie would have seen at once that Emma stood in the way of fabulous wealth. He would not be able to marry Grace if Emma exposed him. The girl had to go. Suddenly, for John Tonneman his treasured friendship with Jamie had turned to ashes.

Best he not think of Jamie for the while. He dressed for traveling. He opened the window and threw back the shutters. The rain had stopped and the sun was breaking through the clouds. The leak in the roof could wait another day or so.

While the rest of the house slept, Tonneman crept down to the quiet kitchen only to find Micah fussing with a packet of food while a boy in a cap stoked the kitchen fire.

> *Cockroaches*—In a large building, with various
> apartments, furnished for different purposes, containing
> ample means of subsistence, but not crowded with
> inhabitants, and in the proper climate, lift up a carpet or
> other covering which has served to conceal *Cockroaches!*
> As the covering is gradually raised from their backs,
> observe them with attention! Look at their heads and legs
> —how they work to hurry themselves out of sight!

NEW-YORK EVENING POST
FEBRUARY 1808

46

9 FEBRUARY. TUESDAY. EARLY MORNING.

Tonneman rubbed his eyes. The boy turned. Mariana.
Tonneman laughed out loud. So hard he had to sit down.
Tears streamed from his eyes.

"Oh, really, John Tonneman, just what is so funny?"
His wife stood before him, hands on hips, outrage issuing
from her like steam from a kettle.

Still laughing, he caught her arms. "You are. *We* are."

She looked doubtful, but didn't struggle to escape.

Micah giggled. Then quickly placed hand to mouth,
waiting for her mistress's rebuke. It never came.

"The route will be muddy," Tonneman said, "perhaps even impassable."

"Nevertheless, I will go."

He nodded. "We will go. The children will marry soon. It will be just you and me again. Did you see young De Groat with Gretel?"

"Yes. He seems a nice young man. But he's not one of us."

"Remember, I was not one of us. No matter. If it should come to pass we will not do what Jacob Hays's relations did to his young cousin. Your father—"

"Blessed be his name," Mariana whispered.

"—did not stand in our way."

Micah set coffee and bowls of oatmeal down on the work table, and Tonneman released his wife.

"Lee would like to be a physician," Mariana said.

"I know. A pity she cannot."

"There were women physicians in the Bible."

"We don't live in the Bible. We live in the world."

"Times are changing, John."

"True." He smiled at her. "There may even come a time when women will grow beards and wear trousers."

She sat opposite him. "I don't think your daughter's future is a joke."

They ate in silence until Tonneman set his spoon down. "George Willard murdered a man yesterday. They are out looking for him." He hadn't known how to tell her, so he just said it.

"Dear God. Who?" Mariana thought: *Poor Abigail.* Then: *Imagine that, I'm feeling sympathy for Abigail Willard.*

"That young man who came here with Peter and Jake Hays. You fed them breakfast."

"Not that young Constable?"

Tonneman nodded. "Duffy."

"Oh, John, what if it had been Peter?" She clutched his hand.

Wisely, cravenly, John Tonneman didn't mention that

their son had gone in pursuit of George. "You're not to worry about Peter. He's a man now. He will make the right choices. He seems to have taken to his new vocation. It is in his blood, as medicine is in mine."

"But John—"

"True, young Duffy's death has upset him, but that's only natural. Perhaps it has even put an additional measure of iron in him. I think Old Hays believes in him, too."

Mariana shook her head. "It's dangerous work now that the City has become so crowded, but as long as there is no more talk that he killed Mr. Brown, and I know it is what he wants, I'm content." Her brow wrinkled. "John? Under what circumstances did George kill Constable Duffy? No. Don't tell me. I have a more urgent question. Since George Willard was capable of killing Constable Duffy, do you think he was capable of killing Mr. Brown?" Without waiting for his answer she sighed and pushed her empty bowl aside. "Let's have a look at our summer home." She offered him her hand.

THE SUN HAD risen by the time they set out for the Village of Greenwich, Tonneman on Socrates and Mariana riding Peter's mare, Ophelia.

There was no wind to speak of. Raindrops glinted on the cobblestones and brick sidewalks. Sunlight, unseasonable warmth, and mud marked their journey.

Broadway, a wide and gracious avenue where it began at the Battery, became a country road after the stone which marked two miles to the north. They came to the stone bridge that spanned the ditch through Lispenard's salt meadow.

Dozens of blackbirds perched on the canal bridge. These feathered guardians scattered and complained angrily as Tonneman and Mariana crossed. A falcon rose from a treetop, shrieked at them, then soared into the sky.

The sweetness of the day was marred by Tonneman's

memory of his dream and troubling thoughts of Abigail. He should have gone to her, not played the coward and run off with Mariana to the country.

The stench of the glue factory the other side of Richmond Hill brought him back. Mariana had put a handkerchief to her nose. Tonneman looked at her. She was so lovely riding beside him. He wanted to tell her about his dream, but he couldn't.

"Is something else troubling you, John?"

He sighed. "You will be angry. . . ."

She stared at him. *He is going to tell me about Abigail Willard,* she thought. Urging her horse with her knees, she rode on ahead, turned, and waited for him to catch up. "Tell me."

"You have never cared for Jamie, have you?"

Jamie, she thought. *Jamie, not Abigail.* She was happy again. "No. Jamie thinks only of himself, only what is good for Jamie. He would trample you and all of us to get what he wants. It has always been so, John, but you have resisted seeing it."

He was pondering that when they caught sight of the working chimneys of Richmond Hill.

Except for the lazy swirls of smoke, there was no sign of life. Without comment they passed Jamie's sumptuous house. Mariana seemed quite content not to talk further about Jamie. Tonneman was distracted, recalling his dream in every chilling detail.

"I fear Jamie may have killed Emma Greenaway. And perhaps because Gretel saw them together, Gretel, too."

"Oh, John." She was silent for a moment, then, "Hickey. Remember? Hickey said, 'Which one was Gretel?'"

Tears ran down Tonneman's cheeks unheeded.

His grief touched Mariana. "My dear, it all happened so long ago."

"I know, but I must make this right."

"You are a good man."

He smiled at her, his face still wet with tears. "If it were not for the surrounding odor, I would have us stop here—"

"I have another suggestion." Mariana's eyes gleamed. "We could have a gallop. Are you game, my lad?"

His eyes caught her gleam. "With you, lass, anything."

They fair flew past the squat stone building with its two massive chimneys puking out greenish greasy smoke.

West of the big stone building was the knacker's house. Here the swine were slaughtered. The sound of frightened squealing drifted to the two riders.

The several workers outside the stone structure, their faces masked in dirty dimity, moved slowly. Their horses, drawing wagons, moved just as slowly.

Soon enough the terrible smell abated, and the Tonnemans slowed to a trot.

"That was—" he said, breathing heavily.

"—wonderful," she concluded, breathing just as heavily.

As his respiration returned, he was delighted to note that he didn't feel the familiar pain across his chest. There was life in him yet. He looked over at his wife. How he loved her.

They easily found the trail to the Village of Greenwich Isaac De Groat had described. The sun cast its warmth down on them as they passed through open fields. In the summer Tonneman knew these fields would be high with grass. Now and then they came upon partially fenced lots of unplowed land, but no dwellings. It seemed for John and Mariana that they were alone in this rustic world.

The path diverged eastward just south of the Manetta Water. Here they were surprised to come upon a tiny village. The streets were identified either by signs nailed to trees or painted boulders on the side of the road.

Three homes stood in Herring-street, set off by neat low fences.

Soon they found Christopher-street, a tree-marked lane

on which were a scattering of two-story frame houses, fenced lots, barns, and buildings.

They stopped to let a slight Negro boy and a yellow hound pass with a herd of sheep. Mariana swung off Ophelia. The shepherd, recognizing her for a woman, eyed her warily.

"The Onderdonk house?" Tonneman asked, smiling at the boy's confusion.

"End of the lane, but no one's there. Mr. Onderdonk died."

"I'm the new owner. John Tonneman, Doctor of Physick and Surgery."

"I'll tell Ma. She'll be right happy." The boy grinned and tipped his hide hat to them, then herded his flock across the dirt road. The dog, bringing up the rear, nipped at a straggling lamb's tail.

As Mariana ran ahead, Tonneman dismounted. He was amazed at the change in his wife. She was so full of joy. Hope, even.

Mariana opened the gate of the picket fence at the corner house. While both the fence and house begged for a coat of paint, the brick house with its green shutters still had most of the shingles on the roof. It looked quite sturdy.

The winter remnants of a garden and several large shade trees, now bare-branched, surrounded the dwelling. Tonneman tied their mounts to the post outside the gate. He found the key where De Groat had said it would be, in the small clay urn at the end of the garden path.

But Mariana had already gone inside. Evidently the door had been left unlatched. Tonneman could hear his wife's exclamations of pleasure as he followed her.

He couldn't have been more pleased. It was a large house, even larger inside than it appeared from the outside. The furnishings were spare, but utilitarian. In the sitting room were fine built-in bookcases containing leather-bound volumes, and a stunning corner cabinet of pale yellow with a shell carving at the top. Tonneman had heard that Onderdonk had been a fine cabinetmaker, and from the condition of his home, this was true.

The beams squeaked overhead and he could hear Mariana scampering up the stairs. "Where are you?" Tonneman called, standing in the huge kitchen. Its great hearth and brick oven were considerably newer than the one at Rutgers Hill. Tonneman walked to the center hall. Here a beautifully carved and posted staircase led to the second floor.

He found his wife in a large front bedroom. She had opened the shutters, and the sunlight streamed into the chamber from four good-sized windows.

A canopied bed was covered with a colorful bed rug. Mariana was sitting on the bed, her face infused with color, radiant from the sunlight. The room was surprisingly warm and cozy.

He sat beside her and put his arm around her. "Welcome home." His kiss had a certain urgency to it; she met him more than halfway.

THEY DINED ON the dried fruit, bread, and water they'd toted in their saddlebags. And shortly thereafter, they retraced their journey to the City.

"There's no surgery," Mariana said, as they rode along.

He rubbed his chin. "Perhaps it's time for me to give up my practice," he said, ignoring the fact that over the last few years his practice had dwindled to almost nothing. "I'd like to do some writing. As I seem to have developed my father's palsy, I might have need of an amanuensis, someone with a fine clear hand." He grinned at her, remembering how she had helped his father by writing up his cases.

Mariana looked at him suspiciously. Was he making fun of her? "And what will you write?"

John Tonneman thought for a moment. Up until now he had not considered retiring. Or writing, for that matter. He slowed Socrates to a walk. "I thought perhaps a family

history . . . beginning with my ancestor Pieter Tonneman."

They had passed the glue factory again and were nearing Richmond Hill when a horseman in a hurry crowded
them to the side of the road, spattering them with mud.

"Where the hell are you running to, you stupid bastard?" Tonneman called after the rider, who seemed to be
headed for Jamie's house. He watched the man with narrowed eyes as he and Mariana brushed the thick mud from
their clothes.

"What were you saying, John? A family history?"

Tonneman nodded, perplexed. The rider was someone
he recognized. Someone he had never expected to see again
in these United States.

Aaron Burr.

47

9 FEBRUARY. TUESDAY. MORNING.

The rain that hit during the night was over as quickly as it came.

Alsop sat at his high desk, rubbing his eyes, very troubled. While he was catching a quick nap, he'd missed all the excitement. He didn't know what was going on.

He knew that young Peter Tonneman was in one of the cells with that fat whore Simone. The day before he'd helped Peter bring her in, soaking wet and bloody. With much protestation, One-eyed Jerry had been convinced to give up his pallet and had to be content with a corner of the entry room where Alsop sat. Now, One-eyed Jerry's snores were keeping Alsop from dozing off again. Not to mention Bosco and Higgins, two of the most vexing miscreants he'd ever had the misfortune to house. They were two little scraggy thieves who barely equaled one man and had to work together to survive. They'd been fine until that bitch arrived. Now they were all noise, singing their stupid song, and only cell-banging and threats would make the wretched pair desist. Once the High Constable was out of here, Alsop would show them what for. At least they were sleeping now.

No sooner had that thought passed through Alsop's mind when the two pissants started their singing again.

"One hundred different whores on the floor, one hundred different whores. If another whore should crawl through the door, how many different whores on the floor? One hund—"

"Quiet," Alsop roared, running back to the cells, shaking his club. But the fucking innocent pissants were pretending to be asleep. "When the Old Man goes, your arses are mine," Alsop muttered. He trudged back to his high desk and closed his eyes, hoping for another bit of rest.

Old Hays's nigger, Noah, was on errands, taking word to Mrs. Hays that all was well with her husband, and to Mrs. Tonneman that all was well with her son, the fucking Special Constable. Old Hays and his ideas. Alsop glanced at noisy One-eyed Jerry with some annoyance. At least the pissants were quiet. Alsop scratched his lean belly and went off to sleep again.

JAKE WAS AT the door saying good-bye to Doctor Heller.

"She's a lucky woman. So much material and so many layers of fat. All that knife did was cut a bit of fat before it hit a rib. A skinny woman would be dead. But she needs rest. Wouldn't want the wound to fester."

"Thank you, Doctor."

Although the same age as Jake, Heller seemed younger. The physician was one of the graduate surgeons of Columbia College, which was evidence that no longer did American-educated physicians feel they had to go to London for further training. "Anytime. But try to keep it from the middle of the night."

"If you send me your bill, I'll see it gets taken care of right away." Jake offered one of his thin-lipped smiles, then watched Heller go out into the muddy streets. He closed the front door and gave Alsop a hard look. Then he went back to the cells and joined young Tonneman and Simone.

After all she'd been through, the whore's voice was remarkably strong. She was gushing at Peter. "You're a splendid, splendid boy."

"So you've said."

Simone lay on the pallet, an immense mound under another immense mound of blankets. Her black hair was wrapped in a towel turban and she looked like a plump Barbary lord. She was holding Peter's hand when she spied Jake Hays. "Ah, Jake. You are splendid, too."

Jake nodded. He had little use for flattery, or flatterers. He motioned to the boy. "Peter."

Jake stepped into the hallway and Peter joined him. "Let's review last night. You saw George Willard and Charles Wright throw this woman into the Hudson yesterday sometime after noon. Subsequent examination and her testimony led you to discover that she'd been stabbed under the left breast."

"Yes, sir. I know you taught me to follow one rat to find the other rats and that was important, but I thought saving a life is important, too."

Jake nodded.

"And," Peter went on sheepishly, "I needed Simone. She's my alibi. Between the time I left Tedious after our fight, and the time I found Charity, I was with Simone."

"You did the right thing. Let's go talk to her." Back in the cell, Jake said to Simone, "Now I'm ready to listen to your story."

"I have seen the light," said the injured prostitute with great sincerity. "I realize my protector doesn't love me any more."

"I would say," Jake said wryly, "that he loves you a great deal less."

There was a moment of blank silence. "Ah," ventured Simone, fluttering her fingers at him. "A joke."

"Yes," Jake admitted.

"Your protector?" Peter prompted.

Jake beamed, as much as a man like Jacob Hays ever beamed. Good boy, he thought, but didn't say. He more than approved of his new Constable's participation. The lad was growing into the job by leaps and bounds.

Simone hesitated. "It will be my death. . . ."

"It already has been," Jake told the woman. "You are Lazarus, reborn. If it had not been for this boy . . ." He paused.

Simone gave Jake a keen look, then moved her gaze to Peter. She nodded. "He loved me so much he wanted me dead."

"Who?" Jake asked, knowing full well.

"Butcher Ned."

Jake nodded. "A dangerous man."

"Don't I know it," Simone said with no humor. "Why do you think they call him Butcher? Not for the beefsteaks and chops of pork he cuts and sells. No. For the dead men in the Collect and two rivers." Once started, Simone could not stop. Between tears and oaths of revenge the whore told them that she'd been Thaddeus Brown's sweetheart. She had met Peter when he delivered little presents from Brown to her, and they had become friends.

"Only friends," she repeated, her fat cheeks dimpling, staring at Jake, daring him to say otherwise.

"Why do you think Ned wanted you dead?"

"He didn't like me being with other men."

"But you're a prostitute."

She shrugged. "Ned was jealous of Thaddeus. He was jealous of young Peter, here. But there was no reason. Thaddeus was just a passing interest. He would have tired of me or gotten religion again. Peter and I are just good friends."

"Is it possible Ned thinks you know too much about his business?"

"Why should he? I never pay attention to such things. No! It is the grand passion," she proclaimed proudly. "Ned wants me dead so no other man can have me."

Jake closed his eyes for a moment. Then he said, "Tell me about that evening when young Tonneman here had the fight with Thaddeus Brown."

Simone sighed. "Someone told Thaddeus about Big Ned, and Thaddeus was angry and wanted me to return certain gifts. . . . I came to see Thaddeus that night. His nose was bleeding. That was all. He chased me away, calling me all sorts of rude names. When I returned to Duane-street, I found Peter asleep on the sofa in my parlor, the sitting room. You know, my lovely pink sofa . . ."

"Yes," said Jake. "I know. Go on."

"I remember that night quite clearly because of the big snow. Peter stayed with me through the night. He rode off into the storm before dawn."

"That was the day I found Charity in New Jersey."

Jake put his finger to his lips. He liked that the boy didn't say "rescued." Humility was a good Christian virtue and Jake admired it. "Go on, Simone."

"I cannot swear that Ned killed Brown." Her cheeks dimpled. "But he *was* jealous of him."

"Go on, Simone."

"For me, Ned is jealous of everyone, I've told you."

"Very difficult not to be, considering your line of work."

Her cheeks dimpled again, but this time she made no comment.

"Surely a man like Thaddeus, a Quaker, would be no threat to Butcher Ned, when vying for your . . . affections."

Peter, listening carefully, pondered where Jake was taking this interrogation.

"But you don't understand," Simone protested. "Until

this horrible misunderstanding, I was Ned's one true love and he mine."

"And you were the only reason Ned and Brown were enemies?"

"Oh," she said airily, "they had some silly argument between them about Ned's construction business. Thaddeus intended to tell someone something, I don't know who, if Ned didn't pay him a great deal of money."

"Tell someone what?" Jake's voice was calm, almost soothing.

"Something about money and building the new City Hall and the canal. But I don't know anything about that. I never paid much attention to those things."

"Is that all?"

"What do you mean?"

"Who else besides Ned was involved with the construction business and the money?"

"You mean like Charlie?"

"Yes. Who else? Did Ned have any partners?"

"Oh, no. Ned never has partners." Again she spoke with a strong element of pride. It was as if she'd never been knifed and half-drowned. "He's the boss."

Jake rubbed his nose. "I wonder," he said.

48

9–10 FEBRUARY. TUESDAY TO WEDNESDAY.
AFTERNOON INTO THE NIGHT AND THE FOLLOWING
MORNING.

Peter left the City Jail in early afternoon, ordered by the
High Constable to go home, get some sleep, and meet back
at the jailhouse the next morning. Noah would take care of
returning Lemual Wilson's horse.

As he neared the only home he'd ever known, the
house on Rutgers Hill appeared flimsy, worn through like a
threadbare shirt. Tiles were missing from the roof, and the
old rooster weathervane was bent, a piece of its copper tail
missing.

If Charity consented to be his wife, he would need his

own home for her and the child. The children. Peter resolved then and there, as he came around the house to the surgery, that he would not demand that his sons follow him in his chosen profession.

Peter felt good about himself. He was sure he and the other Constables would capture George and Ned and Charlie, too, and that the murders of Thaddeus Brown and Quintin Brock would be solved. And he knew it was because he'd been good at his job.

He also knew that he was going to be happy with Charity and that she would bear him many sons. This was a new century, by God, and with His help Peter would live to see past its halfway point.

The surgery had a sign on the door. Peter recognized his father's wavering handwriting. *Surgery closed today.* He smiled. Of late the surgery had been closed most every day. His father's practice had become a fiction.

He opened the door and entered. Spotless as always. But no sign of the old man. Peter came through the house to the kitchen. Micah snoozed over a basket of mending. A tray of biscuits sat cooling on the table. He took three biscuits and left his bloodstained greatcoat, jacket, and shirt on the chair next to Micah. She never stirred. Where were his mother and father?

Upstairs, his parents' bedroom showed signs of a leak. Monday night's rain. Micah had cleaned up well, but the third floor had to be chaos. He chose not to go up and look.

His room was neat as a pin, the bedclothes laid back. He dropped the rest of his clothes on the floor and crawled into his nice clean bed.

The pity was he could not give himself over to sleep. His eyes burned in their sockets. His mind kept going back over the conversation between Simone and Jake. His head buzzed with Jake's oddly simple questions. And with Simone's answers. Each time she answered a repeated question her reply changed, a little frill here, a little flourish there, until her response was all embellishment.

Who else besides Ned was involved in the construction business?

Big Ned supposedly built things . . . like the new City Hall. He was very much involved in the labor of draining the Collect and filling it in and building Canal-street. That was the concern of the Collect Company. That was also the concern of the Commissioner of Streets.

At last Peter fell into an uneasy sleep. He woke only when he heard movement in the house. He washed up and dressed in fresh clothes. His sisters' voices drifted up from below, then his mother's.

He went down to his father's study and stood at the open door. John Tonneman sat at his desk, a bottle of brandy and a glass in front of him. The fire was out. The lamp on the desk was the only light in the room. Its illumination showed Peter that his father was not just "the old man," as he usually thought of him, but truly an old man.

His father picked up the glass of burnt gold liquid and sipped appreciatively. He smiled.

"Sir?"

"Peter, son, come in, sit down."

Peter was stunned by the warmth of the greeting. Was his father addled?

John Tonneman scrutinized his tall son from head to toe. "You look fine to me."

"Why shouldn't I?" Peter sat opposite his father. What was on the old man's mind? Another argument? Another sermon about being a physician?

"Your mother and I went up to Greenwich Village. When we came back, we found a message from Hays saying that you were with him on Constabulary matters."

"Yes, sir."

Although he was transformed by his day in the Village of Greenwich with Mariana, Tonneman was in torment over George Willard's behavior. Abigail's boy couldn't be a murderer; there had to be an explanation. What was happening to his world? The new century was in the beginning of its eighth year, and he was quite overwhelmed by recent events. "Is George indeed a murderer?"

"Yes, sir. I witnessed it with my own eyes. He killed Duffy in cold blood as surely as if he had used a gun or a knife. I caught up with him at the bullring at Bunker Hill." Peter stood and began to pace the small chamber, unknowingly imitating his father's habit.

"Bunker Hill." John Tonneman shook his head. "Ned Winship's domain. I could never understand how Jamie could do business with him." He poured another taste of brandy. "Is George in custody?"

"No, sir. More happened which is too complicated to go into."

John Tonneman drank what was in his glass all at once and poured still another. "Your godfather would disagree, but it's common knowledge that Butcher Ned is a scourge on this City."

"I followed George and Charlie Wright to a house in Duane-street."

"The French whore's house?"

Peter felt his face go red. "You know of her?"

The physician felt his face go red as well. "She has much celebrity in this town. And I am a physician. What is her name?"

"Simone Aubergine." This time the old man had really surprised him. Peter knew he should get on with it, but he couldn't let this go. "How do you know her?"

John Tonneman laughed at the shock on his son's face. "Boy, I wasn't born yesterday." He waved his hand, started to pour another drink, and did not.

"They stabbed her and threw her into the Hudson. Left her for dead. I pulled her out. She's at the jail. A Doctor Heller treated her. She'll be all right."

Tonneman nodded his head vigorously. "I know Lawrence Heller. Matter of fact, I taught him anatomy. Good man. Lots of new ideas." He was proud of Heller. And he was proud of his son.

"I had to let George get away, otherwise Simone would have drowned."

"It was the proper choice. Simone? You know the woman personally?"

"Sir, I was with her when Brown was being murdered."

A longish pause passed between them. "I doubted you, son, but I never truly believed that you killed Brown and stole the cash box."

"Would you have believed George Willard a murderer?"

The old physician thought for a moment. "Abigail's son, never. Richard Willard's son, perhaps. Poor Abigail. She will take this very badly. George is the light of her life."

"He might get away, but . . ."

"Even if he does, it's a terrible thing to have to live with. I can be of some comfort, but what will help is that she has Jamie to lean on."

"Who can lean on Jamie?" The question came from Mariana, who stood in the doorway. The fire in her eyes was one her husband hadn't seen in years.

"Abigail. What I told you about George."

"It's very sad, but I've never liked the Willards and I won't pretend to now that they have troubles. Peter, I asked your father, and now I'll ask you: Is it possible that George killed Thaddeus Brown?"

Peter had never seen his mother, or any other woman, for that matter, in trousers before. He was trying not to stare. "Perhaps, Mother."

She said, "Whatever did you do to your clothes? They're a complete ruin."

"It's a long story, Mother."

"Tell me at supper," she said, heading back to her kitchen. "It's on the table. Don't let it get cold."

"One moment, Papa," Peter said, as the old physician rose to follow his wife. "Did you say Jamie is in business with Butcher Ned?"

"Did I? I don't know. Jamie put together a syndicate

and has been speculating in land for some years. He kept asking me to go into it with him, but—" Tonneman shrugged. "I'm not a gambler, son."

"Land? Do you mean land around the Collect?"

"Among other places. Jamie's done well for himself. . . ." Tonneman's voice trailed off. He'd suddenly remembered what Quintin had said. Why had he never put it together before?

I T   W A S   J U S T   before dawn that Peter let himself quietly out of the house. The whale oil street lamps gave off thin light. It had turned colder. He wrapped his cloak around him and walked briskly to the jailhouse.

One-eyed Jerry was stretched out in the doorway, snoring. Another Constable slept in Alsop's place at the high desk.

Stepping over One-eyed Jerry, Peter walked past the dozing Constable. He lifted the lantern from the table and went on back to the cells.

"Who is it?" Simone's voice came at him, sharp and somewhat fearful.

"Only I. Peter." He held the lantern up to his face.

"Thank God." She was sitting on the pallet. "They will come back for me. C'est vrai. I must leave this hellish place."

Peter shook his head. "You're safe here. They don't know you're not dead in the river. Jake will help you, but you'll have to tell the magistrate everything."

"They'll kill me." She lay back on the pallet, fretful and exhausted. "If I don't die from my wound."

"Simone." Peter knelt beside the pallet. "Did you ever hear Ned mention Maurice Jamison?"

"Jamison?" She frowned. "Jamison?" She shook her head.

"Jamie."

"Jamie," she repeated. She shook her head. Then all at

once her face dimpled. "Oh, *là*," she exclaimed. "I lie. I have heard that name. Once. Ned took me to look at land near the Stuyvesant Estate. He said one day it would be valuable. On the way back we stopped at a house in Richmond Hill. This was July last." She sighed. "New-York is worse than Paris in July. He made me wait in the carriage." With a wan smile, she continued, "I didn't like that. It was hot in the carriage. I got out and walked around.

"There was an open window. People were talking. Of course, I listened. In my line of work you never know what can be of use. I heard my Ned say, 'It's ours for a song, Jamie.'"

49

10 FEBRUARY. WEDNESDAY. MORNING.

The Willard household was up and about. At least the servants were. The walks were being swept vigorously by a young woman in a man's coat many sizes too large for her. As Tonneman tied Socrates to the rail, Betty descended from a cart and directed a boy to carry goods she'd bought at the Fly Market to the kitchen. "Move smartly now, Justin," she ordered.

"A good morning, Betty."

"Oh, Doctor Tonneman!" She clapped her hand over her mouth. "You startled me." The cook's words were all but lost in the bugle blast of the knife grinder as he turned onto Liberty, from Greenwich-street, pushing his cart.

Abigail Willard had risen early. For her, it had been a long sleepless night. George had not come home and there had been no response from Jamie. She was taking a second cup of tea in the small sitting room off her bedroom. Her head throbbed and she felt quite infirm.

Perhaps this was all her fault. George was her youngest. Had the Colonel lived, he would have taught the boy discipline. Oh, yes, she thought ruefully. With the leather strap and the back of his hand.

She had her writing case open and was, with half a heart, attending to correspondence and bills. But George and this terrible trouble kept creeping back into her thoughts.

Where was Jamie? She'd sent a message to him immediately after Jacob Hays had left. If it weren't for her brother-in-law acting the surrogate father to George . . .

How she had relied on Jamie over these last years for strength and counsel.

Considering the High Constable's accusation, it was no wonder George had not come home last night. But the boy seemed to need no excuse for such behavior. It was something he had done more and more frequently over the years.

Each time she'd expressed her concern to Jamie, and he had reassured her, telling her that George often spent those nights he failed to return home with him at Richmond Hill. Abigail prayed he was there now. And that Jake Hays would not find him. And that he had not done this horrible deed.

Abigail had hoped to make a match for George with a Livingston, or Schuyler, or Beekman daughter. But alas, she thought now, allowing herself a wry smile, that was never to be. Her son had turned his back on anything resembling a profession. He had squandered his inheritance. He had not behaved well in the City of New-York.

The boy would have to wait on Jamie's death to come into the Greenaway fortune. After this new terrible thing had blown over, perhaps she could make a match for him in Philadelphia. Or if that didn't succeed, in Baltimore.

At that moment Tonneman's card arrived, accompanied by the sound of his voice below. In spite of her pain and fears Abigail's face brightened. John Tonneman always had that effect on her. He had been her first love. If she had married him . . .

She waved at the housemaid, Sara, to get him. "John," she called, hurrying to her bedroom. "Come up." Only then did she see what he'd written in spidery script on the card: *It is urgent that I see you.*

In her bedchamber, she inspected her coiffure in her silver hand mirror. It was an unnecessary effort; every hair was in place. The face, however, was that of an aging lady. Still, she took pride in her complexion and eyes. Odd, how small, poignant moments of regret appeared always with John Tonneman, to disturb her complacency.

She had meant to be seated in her sitting room when she received him, but she was too slow or he was too fast. He was already there, standing in her doorway, his shoulders stooped as if burdened with the weight of the world. How could she have forgotten? His son Peter was suspected of murder, too.

And yet it was Peter who was pursuing George. Life had become too confusing.

Tonneman took her arm. "Abigail, I have something to tell you."

"I know. The High Constable was here to see me yesterday."

Inwardly Tonneman breathed a sigh of relief. He'd been a coward for not coming sooner and telling her.

"It can't be true," Abigail said calmly.

The old physician did not respond. He held her hand and helped her to her chair.

"I understand Peter has gone after him. That's good. A stranger would hurt my boy. Your son could not hurt his friend. He will look after George, won't he?"

"My son will do his duty."

"That's all we can ask." Her eyes seemed to be focused on a point beyond the wall of the sitting room.

"Forgive me for intruding on your sorrow—" Tonneman began.

But she pulled her hand away and offered him a tight smile. "I have quite forgotten my manners. Would you care for some coffee? Tea?"

He shook his head. "I need to ask you about Emma, Abigail. And Gretel."

"Emma? What in heaven's name does Emma have to do with your daughter?"

"No, no, Abigail." It was indecent to press her at such a time, but he had to know. "Gretel Huntzinger. We named our daughter for her. Gretel was my father's housekeeper. My housekeeper. We all thought Hickey murdered Gretel."

A shudder went through Abigail's body. Her hand was shaking as she patted her hair. "Of course. How could I ever forget? Times were so bewildering and terrifying then. Emma had run off. Richard . . . we were all so committed to the King and were packing to leave for Princeton—"

"Not all, Abigail. You and Richard. Grace. Jamie."

Abigail nodded, patting her hair still again. Her hand trembled even more. "Grace and Jamie planned to marry."

"Yes. Jamie and Grace." Tonneman was distracted by his thoughts. Was he betraying his oldest friend? Or had his oldest friend betrayed him all those many years ago? And since? Day after day, living the lie.

He shook his head. But that didn't banish the suspicions that raged there. Had he lost his senses? No. It was true. He had to press on. Perhaps she remembered better than he. "Abigail, do you recall your dinner party? I'd returned to New-York with Jamie. After my father died?"

Her eyes misted. "How could I forget, my dear? You were so young, so handsome and courageous. I quite fell in love with you all over again."

He paused to bathe in the glow of her statement. She had loved him. But he loved Mariana. Yet he could not deny he also loved Abigail, and in some strange sense always would.

"My dear Richard was so jealous. Of your youth. Our friendship."

Tonneman, besieged with memories, was losing his sense of mission. He paced the small chamber. "Do you remember the wine goblet shattering in Jamie's hand that night?"

Abigail closed her eyes. "Yes. You wrapped the wound with your handkerchief."

"What made the glass break?"

She peered at him with astonishment. "Because sometimes they do."

"Perhaps Jamie held it too tight."

"Why would he do that? As I recall, he was quite at ease, charming."

Tonneman was still pacing the small space, almost going in circles. "Yes, Jamie was always charming. More than I ever was."

Abigail clucked her tongue softly.

Tonneman had not stopped pacing or talking. "But if the glass broke because he held it too tight, it could mean Jamie was angry or upset about something." He shook his head. "Quite out of character for Jamie, showing his emotions like that."

"Yes. I didn't know him then. But you're quite correct."

"Something happened in those first moments we were in your home."

Color flooded Abigail's drawn face. She lowered her eyes and took a sip of cold tea.

"You and Richard. Jamie and I. Grace and Emma. The Apthorpes."

Abigail sent her mind back. "It was a nasty cut. Jamie's hand was deeply gashed. Emma turned quite ashen at the blood, poor child."

"Perhaps she was pale before the blood."

"I don't follow, John."

"Betty told me that Emma had a lover. A gentleman. Jamie was a dedicated rake."

Again a soft cluck from Abigail.

"No! Forgive me for saying this, Abigail. He had an eye for young serving wenches and tarts." The pain in her eyes made him pause. Then he spoke slowly, deliberately. "Betty said Emma went out on the streets unescorted, in Betty's clothing. What if Jamie met Emma, the servant . . ."

"Oh, John. I can scarcely believe—"

He stopped pacing and faced her. "Abigail, listen to me carefully. Jamie always wanted to sit well above the salt. Grace was an attractive and wealthy widow. She could provide him with the life he sought. But not if he'd already ruined Emma."

Abigail was speechless. "Oh, dear God, no, John. You must be mistaken."

It struck him at that moment how odd this was. They had forgotten about the present and George, and were once more involved with Emma and Gretel and the past. As if the past were more important than today. Well, perhaps it was. "Who told Richard that Emma had been seen with a gentleman on the coach to Philadelphia?"

"I don't remember. Discreet inquiries were made. Richard was quite concerned about scandal, as was Grace. I believe Jamie may have helped them. Grace was frantic."

A small, urgent thought forced itself on Tonneman. Sam Fraunces's serrated African swords. Jamie had admired the collection at Black Sam's tavern. So much so he'd mentioned it to Tonneman in the most glowing of terms. Tonneman remembered that clearly. And just as clearly, he remembered that Jamie had never taken to Gretel, nor she to him.

"John, you can't be serious about Jamie and Emma." Abigail's voice was growing shrill with emotion. "Jamie is a dear member of my family, and you are my dearest friend." She put a restraining hand on his arm. "Please," she pleaded. "For my sake. Let sleeping dogs lie."

He stared mutely down at the woman he'd once loved. Still did, somewhat. But how could he love Abigail? She represented the elite. Always had. Mariana never would have said, *let sleeping dogs lie.* She would have exploded with passion at the injustice. She would have insisted this must never be. Wrong must be made right.

And what about him? How could he be so righteous when he was completely ignoring Abigail's awful trouble with her son in order to solve a mystery that was over thirty years old? Should sleeping dogs be allowed to lie when they covered up treachery and murder?

Tonneman bowed politely to Abigail and left. He wondered if he would ever again return to the house on Liberty-street.

50

10 FEBRUARY. WEDNESDAY. EARLY AFTERNOON.

There was only one place left for John Tonneman to go. All roads had been leading there for a long time. He'd just been too blind, or stupid, to see it.

If he had been looking to Abigail for vindication or even collaboration in his deductions, he had certainly not found it. But he had validated his own thoughts simply by stating them. Jamie had been poor Emma's lover. Emma had disappeared. Jamie had wed Emma's mother and inherited all her fortune. Maybe it wasn't a proper deduction, but it was a fair guess that Jamie had killed Emma to get Grace's money. With the serrated sword. Which he had then used on Gretel, probably because she had somehow discovered his secret about Emma. Perhaps she had seen them together. And who was to say a fair guess wasn't a deduction? As a matter of fact, that's what it was.

Socrates was tired and showed it with every step. Tonneman knew how the gelding felt.

The mud from Liberty to Greenwich-street made the way almost impassable. At Greenwich he turned north, and felt the brisk wind blowing from the Hudson. Gun-metal clouds obscured sunlight.

So beset was he with his tortured thoughts that he didn't notice the carriage across the road until he was upon it. Its right rear wheel had come off in the thick mud. The coachman had enlisted the help of a ragged man to right the carriage. Tonneman recognized the ragged man as a seaman he'd treated recently for gum inflammation.

Two finely dressed women stood on the side of the road, shivering in the chill, coat collars high, their hands in muffs, their feet soaking in the sludge. Miserable and impatient, they awaited the repair of their coach. Uninhibited by the activity, three fat pigs rooted near the women's feet, getting in the way of the repair.

No one was hurt. It was none of his affair. Tonneman passed them by and proceeded on his way.

On Duane he turned inland. Hudson-street seemed fairly dry and passable. He went north on Hudson, a country road lined with apple orchards and grazing land. Small herds of cows wandered freely, sometimes across the road. Their soft mooing carried in the stillness that surrounded anyone venturing outside the City bounds at Chambers-street.

Crossing the bridge over the ditch, all Tonneman could think of was how he would confront his old friend Jamie.

The stink of the glue factory let him know he was almost to Jamie's before his eyes did. And then, he was there. Richmond Hill.

Dismounting, he brushed at his clothes, straightened his hat, and stood as tall as his old bones would allow. He tied Socrates to the side rail and went to the front door. When Stevens answered, Tonneman said, "Tell Mr. Jamison I'm here."

"He's engaged, sir." Stevens's face betrayed almost no emotion.

Yet Tonneman did not overlook a slight twitch in the butler's eyelid. Something was in the wind. "Tell him."

"But, sir—"

"Oh, hell and damnation." John Tonneman pushed past the astonished Stevens. He marched into the parlor, where amazement after amazement awaited him. The room was dazzling. Candles and lamps blazed everywhere, reflecting and counterreflecting from sundry mirrors. Tonneman shielded his eyes. Also in evidence on the furniture and the floor were many bottles which once had held or still held wine or spirits.

On the French marble table, one of Jamie's proudest possessions, was a box familiar to John Tonneman: the missing cash box of the Collect Company. Also on the table was a pistol case. It contained a pair of silver-mounted pistols.

Jamie was clumsily loading the first pistol. He set it back into the case and picked up the second pistol. He was in the middle of a story. He did not acknowledge Tonneman's presence.

". . . Frenchman and a Dutchman are in the Kingdom of the Apes. The Frenchman compliments the apes, tells them how intelligent and beautiful they are. They reward the Frenchman magnificently. Gold and diamonds. The Dutchman tells the apes the awful truth about them, that they are ugly, and is put to death. The Dutchman died an honorable death. But he died."

The four other men in the room, Jamie's nephew George Willard, the notorious Ned Winship, and the even more notorious Charlie Wright (who-could-do-no-wrong) did not laugh. They and Jamie all appeared to be very drunk. The fourth man was the greatest enigma of all: Aaron Burr.

Jamie looked to his four companions. "Don't you find that amusing?"

"Not very," Burr said. His voice was deep and resonant. "What's your point?"

"Simple. Money is better than honor any day. You ought to know that."

Burr scowled but made no reply.

Jamie wore a single-breasted wine-red jacket with a stand-up collar, a buff vest, and dark trousers.

Burr, too, wore a single-breasted wine-red jacket with a stand-up collar, a buff vest, and dark trousers. If he was drunk he did not look it.

"You might be twins," Tonneman said, not smiling. "Dye your hair brown, Jamie, and you'd look just like him."

"Not hardly," Burr sniffed.

"Sorry, sir—" Stevens was hovering, scattering anxious apologies.

"Go away, Stevens."

"Sir." Quickly, the butler withdrew.

The smell of the glue factory was strong today. Tonneman wondered absently if Jamie owned the factory. Why else put up with the stink?

"How wonderful to see you, John." Jamie seemed amused at the shock on Tonneman's face. "Do you know what I have here? Matched pistols. Made by Hawkins of London." He held one out to Tonneman, barrel pointed directly at the physician's chest. "See the delicate silver engraving of the unicorn and the lion. Such fine work. And they're precise weapons, too. Mr. Burr has just made me a present of them."

Aaron Burr frowned and tried to pretend he was still in Paris.

Nothing would stop Jamie. The alcohol he'd been drinking slurred his speech. "They were given to Mr. Burr by General Washington. And you know what else? One of these was the very pistol used to kill Hamilton on that fateful day in July four years ago."

"Jamison, you are a fool," Burr said evenly. "Put those pistols away, you drunken old man, before you hurt someone. I have not given them to you and they are not *the* pistols."

"So you say. Ah, the second pistol is now loaded. Aaron is going to help us enact the duel of that momentous day in Weehawken. He'll play himself and I shall play that fool Hamilton."

"Bah," Burr exploded. "I've had enough of this farce."

"With several differences," Jamie continued. He pointed the pistol at Burr and smiled. "Hamilton didn't fire."

"He fired first," Burr growled.

"I, of course, will fire. I won't die like Hamilton." Jamie bowed. The dueling pistol flashed silver in his hand. "I will walk my twelve paces. The weapons will be loaded and offered. But I'm ahead of myself—I already have my weapon. George, you know the drill. George?"

"Gentlemen, present," George said in a drunken mumble.

"Burr raises his weapon."

"No, damn it. Hamilton raised his first," Burr insisted.

"So you say. Have it your way." Jamie gave Tonneman a broad wink. "Hamilton fired first. A fine bit of workmanship, wouldn't you say, John?" Jamie caressed the pistol, then abruptly aimed the weapon at Tonneman. He pulled the trigger. The hammer fell harmlessly with a loud click.

"Ah me. I lied. The second pistol was not loaded. I *will* load it now."

Tonneman could feel his sweat dripping from him. His heart was pounding.

Ostentatiously, Jamie loaded the second pistol and laid it in the case with its mate. He then dipped into the cash box. Playfully, he began throwing the bills at his nephew and Butcher Ned and Charlie Wright. When he made a show of throwing the money at Burr, Burr glared at him.

Tonneman's heart was beating rapidly. He had walked into the lion's den, and the lion was drunk—with power. He had come to confront Jamie about the past, and the present had smacked him in the face. "So it was you?" Tonneman demanded hoarsely. Grief and anger choked him.

Jamie chuckled. "Of course." He took a long pull from a bottle of wine. He looked at the label. " '83. A good year in Paris, but not in New-York. Very tasty." He shoved the bottle in Tonneman's face. "Drink?"

"No."

"How about money?" Jamie asked, tossing some bills from the box into the air. Then he stuffed more of the bills into Tonneman's pockets.

"That money belongs to the Collect Company."

Jamie chuckled. "Money belongs to whoever has it, John. I've been trying to teach you that lesson for over thirty years. But you simply won't learn. Do you know why? Because you're simple."

George laughed uneasily.

"Your mother's worried about you," Tonneman told the young man.

"What's your business here?" Butcher Ned demanded.

"It's not with you," Tonneman said, "It's with him."

Big Ned wiped his mouth with the back of his hand and broke the neck of a bottle against the marble mantel. "I've a feeling it will be with me by and by."

This frightened Tonneman, but he didn't dare show it.

"I'm an old man. I've lived my life." His words were directed to Ned, but he meant them for Jamie's ears, too. He had to get his business with Jamie done at last. "Did you kill Brown?" he asked, honestly puzzled.

Jamie merely grinned at his old friend.

Fury boiled in Tonneman. "What for? The paltry contents of that box? You have more than that a thousand times over. And you were going to let Peter swing for it."

"One can always use a little more money," Jamie said softly. "But you're right, John. Thaddeus Brown did not die for the contents of this box. He died for the greed in his soul, the foul Broadbrim. He had the audacity to tell me that if I didn't pay him a thousand dollars, he would go to you and Jake Hays and tell you about the missing fifty thousand. The fucking impudence of that worm. I took the cash box as an afterthought."

"So you killed him?"

Jamie smirked. "I don't kill people anymore. I hire people to do that. The way I hire people to clean my boots and scoop the shit out of my stable. Ned here did the honors."

"You said you don't kill people anymore. Did you ever? Kill people?"

"I would have thought you'd have figured it out by now. The serrated sword and all that. But of course you haven't." Jamie sighed and looked around for his drink. "You were never as clever as I hoped you'd be, John."

"But you are clever?"

"Of course I am. I'm rich. I have men with me who will kill for a price. And I can pay that price, and far more. You are here alone, accusing me of every crime since the Crucifixion. Yes, I'm clever. And you, John, are a damned fool."

Tonneman stepped back as if struck. "You're right, Jamie. I am a fool. A fool for calling you friend. A fool for not realizing it was you who killed Emma."

"Bravo. No Socratic logic there, but in a pinch it will have to do. So. I killed Emma with the serrated sword. Ergo . . . ?"

Suddenly, Tonneman was weary to his soul. He'd had enough. "You killed Gretel Huntzinger."

"Exactly. How clever you've become with old age. I had to kill the old bitch because she saw me with the young bitch."

"But Gretel didn't know Emma."

Jamie shrugged.

John Tonneman didn't know whether he wanted to strangle his old comrade or fall to his knees and cry. He turned and walked toward the door.

"Ned," Jamie said.

"Charlie," Ned said.

English, French & Italian Tuition

MRS. DA PONTE *respectfully informs the public that*
she intends opening immediately, a regular permanent
Academy, in the Bowery, near the Manhattan Bank, for
the education of Young Ladies. Terms will be made known
by applying at No. 29 Partition-street.

NEW-YORK EVENING POST
FEBRUARY 1808

51

10 FEBRUARY. WEDNESDAY. EARLY AFTERNOON.

Simone woke very agitated. Someone was standing near
her bed. "Oh, dear God," she said, crossing herself. This
was not her bed. Then the pain made her remember. This
was a miserable pallet in the City Jail. The figure that had
frightened her materialized into Jake Hays.

Her wound throbbed painfully. She rested her hand
under her left breast to ease the pain and—as was her
nature—to play the coquette. "Good morning, Jake. Did
you sleep well in your own bed?"

"I did."

"I wish I could say the same. I would be so happy to be
home in my own bed."

"You could be dead at home, too," Jake answered. "Here, at least, Noah and I can keep watch on you."

"Poo—you and Noah are gone most of the time. All I have is grumpy old Sergeant Alsop. He sleeps his life away." She sighed. "My wound itches. Would you care to scratch it, Jake?"

Jacob Hays shook his head. "You must be suffering to the extreme to waste your breath trying to tempt an ardent Scots Presbyterian like me."

Simone studied him a moment. "Can't you be tempted?"

"Not by you."

"Ooh, that hurts." The crescent-shaped scar disappeared into the dimple on her left cheek. "My wound hurts, too. A bit of brandy would help. . . ."

"Later."

"If you give me brandy, I'll tell you all about Peter Tonneman."

Jake yearned for the day he would be rid of this woman. He was heartily sick of her antics. And where *was* young Tonneman? He should have been at the jailhouse by now. "What about Peter?"

"Well, perhaps not about Peter. Although . . . he has come and gone . . ."

Jake Hays had never struck a woman. Never. But he was sorely tempted to strike this one. "Come and gone? What did you tell him?"

Simone shrank back. She believed the High Constable wanted to hit her. Still, he didn't frighten her. She'd been Ned Winship's woman, and lived to talk about it. "I told Peter that Ned once took me to a house in Richmond Hill—"

"Noah!" Jake bellowed.

"—and that I'd heard him talking to a man named Jamie about buying land. Is that important?"

But by that time, Jake was out the door of the City Jail.

●　●　●

THE ALCOHOLIC MIST slowly cleared from George's brain. He plucked one of the dueling pistols from the case, ran his hand over the silver carving, and shot Charlie. The ball caught Charlie full in the back of his head and blew his face out. George was amazed. He'd never been that good a shot. He didn't even know why he'd done it. Except John Tonneman was a friend of his mother's.

Ned pulled a sharp butcher knife from his boot. He swatted George across the throat. The boy's jugular burst, spilling blood onto the expensive Persian rug Aaron Burr had bought years before when he was one of the most important men in America. Maurice Jamison had gloried in owning that rug. Jamie always thought that in owning Aaron Burr's house and possessions he'd be important, too. Now there was a stink at Richmond Hill that was much worse than that of the glue factory.

Old Tonneman turned in time to see George fall. Nobody could survive a wound like that. Tonneman knew he was next. He ran.

Jamie pulled a scornful face. "What a waste. All the years I put into that boy. The apple doesn't fall far from the tree. His father was just not good stock."

Aaron Burr moved to a window, quickly distancing himself from the carnage. Once he'd been a quick thinker. Well, he had to think quickly now.

Ned watched as George's blood soaked into the carpet. He wiped his blade on the boy's body, then started out the door after John Tonneman.

"Take the other pistol," Jamie suggested.

Ned cackled. "For that old man, all I need is this sticker."

Old man, Jamie thought, amused. So was he, but he was a wealthy old man.

JOHN TONNEMAN MOUNTED Socrates. But something, perhaps the scent of blood, made the animal crazy. Rearing with a sharp whinny, the horse threw Tonneman into the mud and galloped off. Tonneman lay stunned, breathless, then dragged himself to his feet.

Now Tonneman ran for his life. Mud sucked at his boots, threatening to pull him to the ground. He ran into the woods. There was less mud here, but roots and clawing branches, wet leaves and slippery mossy rocks kept tripping him up.

His heart thundered against his rib cage. He'd never felt so frightened, or so alive. He wasn't ready to die. Not now, when he had so much to live for.

NED THE BUTCHER didn't hurry. There was no need. He knew the old man would soon run himself out. And then he'd have him. Ned loved this part. The hunt. The anticipation. He wasn't called Ned the Butcher for nothing.

PETER RODE OPHELIA hard, almost cruelly. George Willard was at Richmond Hill. Peter had suspected as much earlier. Now he was certain. It was amazing what a little rest could do. How it cleared the mind. There was something personal in this ride. Their childhood friendship was a lie. Peter had never liked George. The son of a bitch had always been a bully.

NED PAUSED WHEN he heard the approaching horse. One lone rider. Whoever he was, he couldn't be too much trouble. It looked like Mr. Jamison was going to get two butcherings for the price of one.

JOHN TONNEMAN HAD run in a circle. Panting with exhaustion, he reeled out of the woods to find himself once more in front of Jamie's house, bathed in winter sunlight, for all the world to see. A perfect target. He took a ragged breath. If he could get back to the woods before anyone saw him . . . His heart felt as if it would burst. He had to stop. Rest. All he needed was a moment. He heard the clatter of hooves. The pain was sharp. Ned had caught up to him. Oh, God. Not now. Not yet.

NOAH DROVE COPPER at a breakneck pace. With a sloppy road, going too fast could mean an injured horse. A destroyed horse. And the two of them and the carriage broken in a muddy ditch.

In the carriage, Jacob Hays, the High Constable of the City of New-York, chewed an unlit cheroot and concentrated on Maurice Jamison.

PETER KNEW HE was driving his horse too hard; he trusted Ophelia to take care of them both. Before him was Richmond Hill. A falcon overhead circled, and like a guide flew directly to the house. It perched on Jamie's roof as if waiting for Peter.

Chill sunlight squeezed through the clouds.

God help him, there was someone lying in the road. Peter tugged sharply at Ophelia's reins and stopped inches short of trampling the sprawled body. He leaped from his mount and knew even before he turned the man over. "Papa!" He held the still body in his arms. "Don't die. You can't die, you foolish old man."

Old Tonneman stirred. Eyes closed, he murmured, "It's not respectful to call your father a foolish old man."

Relief made Peter crow with laughter. His father wasn't dead. "Are you all right? Where are you hurt?"

"Not hurt. Merely old. Winded. And," he patted his chest, "the clock is not ticking as well as it should."

"It's good to know you'll be around for a while. There's a wedding I want you to attend." He hugged his father.

"Gladly."

"Ain't this sweet?"

Ned advanced on them. He could have sneaked up and cut one throat after the other in a wink, but he thought it would be more fun to deal with the two of them at the same time. And what was life for if not for fun? And for taking. His knife glittered in the sun.

"RUN, PAPA, RUN!"

Peter dove for Ned's legs. Ned slashed and missed with the knife, but found flesh and bone with his left boot. There was a satisfying sound, like a branch breaking. Ned was sure he'd broken at least one of the little bastard's ribs. There he was, on his back. Waiting for the knife.

OLD TONNEMAN STRUCK with all his might. The rock missed Ned's head and glanced off his massive shoulder. The blow was feeble, but enough to make Ned drop his knife. Ned backhanded the old man into the mud. Then he seized Peter by the throat.

NOAH SAW THE three men scrambling in the mud in front of Jamie's house. He knew he had no other choice. He ran Copper right into them. Two men went down into the mud. Only one staggered up.

Old Tonneman inched forward and bent over the body. "His neck is broken," he croaked.

Copper, breathing heavily, emitting puffs of white steam, tossed his head and wheeled back from the corpse. Jake and Noah stepped out of the coach. Noah calmed Copper with strokes and soft whispers.

Jake glanced at Big Ned's body. Then he stepped over it. The cheroot moved back and forth between his teeth.

"Jamie's in there," Tonneman said, gesturing at the

house. "So is Charlie Wright. Charlie's dead. George Willard, too. Also dead. Jamie had Brown and Quintin killed."

Jake was studying Ned's broken body. "I thought as much."

"So did I," said Peter.

"And Emma Greenaway and Gretel Huntzinger," Tonneman continued. The old physician shook his head. "He killed them himself. But that was another time. And the two women have been long dead."

"I don't—" Jake began.

"The skull in the ground," said Tonneman. He shook his head again. "Never mind. It's history. The past. It's over. Buried. That's the way it should be."

"Come along, Constable," Jake ordered. "Time to go and arrest a murderer."

"Wait!" Tonneman called. "There's someone else inside with Jamie."

"Who?" Jake demanded.

"You're not going to believe this—Aaron Burr."

The High Constable was so surprised he bit his cheroot in half and nicked his tongue.

JAKE HAMMERED THE front door with his stick. It opened.

"Sir?" Stevens inquired cautiously.

Jake marched right in, followed by Peter. Noah, who rarely went inside, followed too. He didn't want to miss this one.

Jake stepped around the first body.

John Tonneman could tell it was Charlie Wright in spite of the bloody mass of his head. The other body, of course, was that of young George Willard. Tonneman felt sick to his soul. Poor Abigail.

"Maurice Arthur Jamison." Jake's eyes swept the carnage with distaste. "I arrest you for conspiracy in the murders of Thaddeus Brown and Quintin Brock. What good will your money do you now? It's the rope for sure."

Jamie inspected his image in the shimmering mirror, tucked back a stray strand of hair, and straightened his cravat. Raising his glass to Tonneman, to Jake Hays, he drank, then tossed the glass into the hearth. It shattered with a hissing, tinkling crash.

He smiled. His fingers caressed the second pistol. "For Maurice Jamison, the gun that killed Alexander Hamilton will do." He raised the barrel of the dueling pistol to his lips. "So! I'm going to die as he died after all." Jamie put the barrel of the gun into his mouth and pulled the trigger.

BURR STEPPED GINGERLY around the bodies, the blood, and the fecal matter. He examined the weapon near Jamie's hand. "Not this gun. It was the other, Jamie. You were always such an ass, you annoying man."

All was silence.

John Tonneman stared down at the shattered body of his old friend. "Ah, Jamie, not even the divine scent of Caswell-Massey Number 6 can hide your vile odor now."

Aaron Burr turned his attention to Jake Hays. "It's good to see you again, High Constable."

Jake bowed courteously. "Sir . . ."

"How are your lovely wife and children?"

"Very well, sir."

"And my young namesake?"

"Thriving, sir."

"Well, then, Providence has been good to you, Jacob."

"Sir, I owe you my lifework. I am beholden to you. But I am sworn to preserve the law."

"Constable, your reputation has traveled even to France."

"There is, however, a great deal to do here. If while my back was turned, you were to disappear, what could I do? And who would believe me if I claimed you were here in the first place?" So saying, Jacob Hays, High Constable of the City of New-York, turned his back on the man for whom he'd named his son.

Aaron Burr sniffed the foul air, looked despairingly at the Persian rug and the beautiful pair of dueling pistols that had set his life on its ruinous path, and . . . smiled. It was too ridiculous not to.

"O grab me," Burr said, and hurried out the back door.

• ———————————— •

• ———————————— •

52

10 FEBRUARY. WEDNESDAY. JUST AFTER TWILIGHT.

Two Watch Men were lighting the lamps along Broad-way. Tonneman was suddenly anxious to be home. He nudged the ambling Socrates, who'd been waiting for him when he left the house in Richmond Hill. The animal snorted and moved his massive head up and down in an equine nod, flaring his nostrils.

Tonneman was riding along John-street, nearing home, when a runaway horse, dragging behind it a cart which had lost its right wheel, galloped past him in the other direction

heading toward Broadway. If the driver was in it, Tonneman couldn't tell. But before he could think more about
the runaway, the fire bells began.

It was a chilling sound, made all the more frightening
by the unmistakable smell of a large fire and the pall of
silence that always followed the first alert.

Then the shouting began. The volunteer fire brigade,
made up of many private citizens, came running; others on
the docks harvested water from the East River into the
water wagon.

A cold terror clutched Tonneman's heart as he saw the
direction in which the fire brigade was headed. Rutgers
Hill. Now he kicked Socrates to move faster. The horse
whinnied, clearly as unnerved as Tonneman himself.
Smoke filled the air. It streaked the darkening sky.

As he approached his home, cinders fell on Tonneman
like hot hailstones, singeing his clothes, burning his skin.
He stopped, dismounted, and hastily tied Socrates to the
Bernhardts' rail. It was a loose tie. Should things go bad he
would not like his horse to suffer death by fire.

A crowd of women and children had gathered in front
of the Bernhardt house; the women stood guard with buckets of water, the children with cloth bags for whatever
could be saved from the fire, and wet rags to slap out errant
cinders. Alarm bells clanged.

As in Tonneman's youth, New-Yorkers were still required to keep leather buckets and cloth bags hanging in
the halls of their houses. The law said that if fire broke out,
citizens were to hurry with water in their buckets and cloth
bags at the ready to help save the property of the victims.

"Doctor, thank God you're here!" Mrs. Bernhardt
shrieked over the clanging of the fire bells.

The glow of the blaze that was flowering out of Tonneman's house lit up the hill.

"My wife? My girls?" he cried.

"We haven't seen them. Perhaps—"

Tonneman didn't wait to hear the rest.

Sweat poured from his soot-streaked face. He recognized no one, yet the street and environs teemed with people. Luckily these fire wagons were speeded by horse power and were not the man-pulled relics of his youth. And with the unseasonable thaw, the water wouldn't freeze. Perhaps . . .

He had quite forgotten he was not young Doctor Tonneman until he felt the familiar warning pain grip his chest. He slowed his pace and tried desperately to breathe the smoke-clogged air. Impotently, he watched as the kitchen of his family home was engulfed in flames. Smoldering embers landed about him, mocking him. Men shouted and ran back and forth.

The firemen trained their two hoses on the roof. The flames roared when the water hit them. Tonneman kept searching for his family. Smoke stung his nostrils and throat. His eyes streamed. He called, "Mariana!" again and again.

"Papa!"

Leah, her face black with soot, was almost unrecognizable. She was across the road, safe. He went to her as fast as he could. His heart was pounding in joy and fear. Where was Gretel? Where was Mariana?

Now the area was nearly light as day, bright from the bobbing lanterns and the leaping, greedy fire. As he approached his youngest, he could see Leah gently rubbing Micah's arm. In spite of breathing in smoke, his nose told him before his poor eyes that Leah was rubbing rendered chicken fat into a burn on the servant girl's arm. Micah was crying.

"Hold still, Micah," Leah said, sternly. His little physician, Tonneman thought. The two girls were sitting on a pair of the kitchen chairs, as if they were still sitting in their own kitchen.

Tonneman inspected Micah's arm. "Where's your mother?" he asked his daughter. "Where's Gretel?"

"Mama's—"

"I didn't mean to," Micah blubbered. The girl had lost most of her hair and her lashes and brows. The burn on her arm was not serious, but her face had blistered badly.

"Leah, Socrates is tied in front of Bernhardt's," Tonneman said. "Get my bag. She needs chickweed salve on her face, then her arm."

His daughter narrowed her eyes. She wiped her greasy hands on her charred skirt. "Did I do wrong?"

"No, you did absolutely right. But now we have to do better. Your mother? Tell me."

"We weren't in the house when the fire started," Leah told him.

Tonneman let out breath he didn't know he was holding. The pain in his chest eased. "Now hurry."

As his daughter ran to do as she was bid, Tonneman turned round and round, scanning the crowd. The burns should be bathed in cold tea first, but one did what one could. Belatedly, he remembered Micah's words. "Mean what?" he asked abstractedly, eyes searching, as he wrapped the sobbing girl in the filthy gray blanket that he found at her feet. "Where's Mrs. Tonneman? Where's Gretel? Are they safe?"

Before the girl could answer there was a yell from the crowd as a wind of flame leapt from Tonneman's house to the barn. But the volunteers held off the new threat. The barn would be saved. For the nonce.

A glance north eased Tonneman's mind. His daughter Gretel was standing only twenty feet away with the lawyer, Isaac De Groat. Young Isaac had his arm around Gretel very protectively.

Tonneman was now worried about Leah. She had disappeared into the crowd and the smoke. But as his worry grew, she was at his side. "Here, Papa." She handed him his black bag.

"Good." He delved into the bag. "Where's your mother? Is she safe?"

"Oh, yes, Papa, we're all fine."

He was delighted. But first things first. He applied the chickweed salve to Micah's face and arm. Once he had attended his patient, he turned to his youngest child, his arms extended.

She ran to him.

He lifted Leah and swung her in the air, unmindful of his creaking bones and the ache in his chest. She laughed, her teeth white as snow in her grimy face. But her laughter lasted only a moment.

The flames reached the roof of their house and broke through, devouring the old rooster weathervane in their search for escape.

Tonneman set his daughter down. Together they watched in silence as the blaze spread slowly, almost thoughtfully, through the rest of the house.

Tonneman sighed. "Watch over Micah, Lee," he said, and moved on. *Mariana,* he thought, *where are you?* He walked toward his older daughter, calling, "Where's your mother?"

Isaac De Groat led Gretel to Tonneman.

"What?" the girl cried over the din of people and flames and water.

"Your mother," Tonneman replied as his daughter reached him.

"I don't know," she answered, kissing him, but not as his little girl; she was a young lady now.

"Have you seen her?"

"Yes, of course."

"She was here a minute ago," Isaac offered.

"Thank God," said Tonneman, the sweat pouring from him.

"She said something about a box," Gretel said.

"Stay here with your sister." Tonneman had a terrifying picture of Mariana running back into the burning house. For what? He threaded his way around bucket men and hoses. Anxiety wrenched him.

He suddenly knew what box his wife sought. The box

filled with mementos of his Dutch ancestor, Pieter Tonneman, and Pieter's wife Racqel.

Where the devil was she?

"Mariana!" he cried. "Mariana . . ." He couldn't imagine his life without her. He started to call her name again when he heard a gasp that carried over the crowd. The band of pain around his heart tightened.

Two of the fire brigade were carrying the remains of a human body from the devastated house. The air was bitter with the smell of burnt flesh.

"Where's the cart?"

"I'll be damned if I know."

"Who is it?"

The men stood about arguing the whereabouts of the cart. Tonneman knew—he'd seen the horse dragging it toward Broadway—but wasn't of a mind to tell them. He closed his eyes, swayed, leaned on his gate, which was, miraculously, still whole, and prayed to the God of Abraham and to Jesus Christ, with whom he had a slight acquaintanceship, having been raised in the Dutch Reformed Church.

"It's Will Griswold!" a voice cried. "Wretched sod. Burnt to a crisp." The chill in the air deepened.

"Tonneman."

Tonneman opened his eyes. He found himself looking at Thomas Floy, a stubby, powerful man, with thick sooty forearms showing from the rolled-up sleeves of his scorched jacket. Floy was Captain of the fire volunteers, and owner of the smithery in Pearl-street. "What?"

"He delivered for his father."

Tonneman stared.

"Jonathan Griswold." Floy's face was grimed with soot and ash. He dropped his voice to a whisper. "He's selling O Grab Me cider this week."

Tonneman nodded. He remembered Micah had said something about a barrel of cider. "Yes."

"Your kitchen girl was showing him your quick matches."

"Oh, my God. The Instantaneous Light Box."

"That's it." Floy shook his head. "Pitiable bastard set himself and the whole place on fire."

"That poor boy. Have you seen my wife?"

"She was outside with your girls when it started. Your wife's a true heroine. A bona fide Ethan Allen in skirts. Ran inside and got your kitchen girl out. Then like a fool tried to go back in. Pardon me."

Tonneman waved his hand, unable to speak.

"But we wouldn't let her." Floy continued, wiping his face and succeeding only in griming it further.

"My wife—"

"She's around somewhere. Maybe with one of your neighbors."

"Is it over then?" Where the devil was Mariana?

"It's over. Everything is fairly soaked. Nothing much left. Sorry for your trouble."

"No matter. It was an old house."

Slowly, reluctant to leave the site of so much excitement, citizens and the fire brigade moved off. Tonneman walked back across the road to his daughters and Isaac and Micah. Leah was holding a large, tarnished silver box.

"Where's your mother?" he asked, eyeing the silver box.

"Didn't you see her, Papa?" Gretel asked. "She was just here. She said the box was all we needed to start over."

Tonneman smiled wearily. "She would," he told his puzzled daughters.

"I'll find her, Papa." Leah ran across the street, now a sea of mud and charred wood. "Mama!" She disappeared around the side of the ruined house.

Tonneman trailed after her. His surgery seemed still intact, standing alone, and the barn was barely scorched. He wondered what it would cost to rebuild. He could hear Leah calling him. He followed her voice.

"Oh, Papa—"

"What?"

Leah was smiling and looking up at a spot above her head. "You're not going to believe this."

"What?"

"In that oak tree. Mama's up there."

The girl pointed to the tree that faced her parents' bedroom. The old oak tree John Tonneman had climbed as a boy, and used for shade when he sat alone thinking, or reading, and later with Abigail. Most of all, it was his Mariana tree. Where he'd first met her, thirty-two years before. "Oh," said Tonneman.

A worried frown crossed Leah's sooty face. "Mama's never done anything like this before."

Tonneman threw back his head and laughed. All at once he understood everything. "Yes, yes, she has. Go back to your sister."

The tree was bare, its branches shining in the moonlight. On a branch rubbing against the house, near where their bedchamber window had been, he saw the slender silhouette of a figure. Tonneman approached the tree.

"Are you going to stay in that tree all night?" he called.

"Not if I have a reason to come down," was the response.

He sighed, wishing for the words of a poet. Alas, he had none. "Am I reason enough?"

Silence.

"I said, am I—?"

"I heard you, old man. I'm thinking it over."

"Damn you, old woman, come down. I need you."

Mariana slid down into his arms.

● ▬▬▬▬▬▬ ●

*The Common Council was informed "the Labourers
employed in taking Mud out of the Collect have, in the
course of the last week, been totally discharged." The
expenses for three weeks work amounted to $576.55
besides the daily rations issued at the almshouse. On the
same day John Meghan was given $500 to pay Car-men
employed at the Collect.*

NEW-YORK EVENING POST
FEBRUARY 1808

● ▬▬▬▬▬▬ ●

Epilogue

22 FEBRUARY. MONDAY. MORNING.

Jacob Hays, High Constable of the City of New-York,
stood on the steps of City Hall looking over the gathering
crowd. His sharp eyes missed nothing. His right hand, big as
a ham, clutched his thick staff. Its gold knob gleamed in the
sunlight. With his squat body and the tall beaver hat on his
oversized head, he was, as usual, an imposing figure.

The sky was an azure field scattered with downy clouds.
The midwinter day was unexpectedly soft. Swarms of eager
citizens spilled from all directions into Wall-street.

Many had been there for hours. They'd been diverted
during their long wait by Kasper, the clown with the long
white hands and feet, who kept falling down.

Kasper had started the day perched atop the gallows in the square. Scampering down like a monkey, he stopped midway, pulled a red umbrella from under his bright red coat, and opened it. Then he jumped. Much to the people's surprise and delight, he floated to the ground unscathed. It was silly stuff, but it was Kasper's job to amuse the populace, preparing them for the serious words to come.

The gentle breeze belied the season. Jacob Hays relinquished one of his thin smiles. One might say there was a decided smell of optimism hanging in the air, too. Jake liked the phrase. He planned to enter it into his journal that night.

After a brief hiatus due to the vagaries of New-York politics and government, the Anti-Federalists were now back in power in New-York. Today De Witt Clinton was officially reclaiming the office of Mayor.

Hays's eagle eye found Peter Tonneman standing with Jake's niece, Charity, John and Mariana Tonneman, and their pretty daughters. The lawyer Isaac De Groat and the Goldsmiths stood at their side. Young Tonneman had Charity's hand clasped firmly in his. Old Tonneman was beaming.

Other City dignitaries joined the High Constable on the City Hall steps. On this beautiful, prematurely warm day Hays was not alone in his customary habit of wearing neither coat nor cloak.

The crowd was a bright spectacle, even with the random spots of somber Quaker browns, grays, and blacks. Their broad-brimmed, low-crowned hats mixed with caps, a scattering of old-fashioned bicornes, and the abundant high-crowned beavers.

Hays peered into the mass of people. His sharp eyes narrowed. "Hold my staff," he said to Luke Finn, thrusting the stick into the magistrate's hands, and slipping into the herd like a diligent sheep dog with his sheep.

In a moment he was on Gray Moe Daly. Wool cap or no, Jake's keen eyes had picked out Gray Moe's gray skin and hair. Moe might have covered his head, but for Jake there was no missing that skin and those brows. Besides, the day was too warm for a wool cap. Especially pulled that tight.

He seized the pickpocket. There was a purse in Moe's hand and four more in his coat. Jake displayed his catch to Magistrate Finn, then turned the miscreant over to Constable Gurdon Packer. Packer would see that Daly got to the City Jail. This time, with Magistrate Finn as a prime witness at his trial, Gray Moe would have a long stay in Bridewell.

Jake rejoined the other notables on the City Hall steps just as the once-again Mayor, De Witt Clinton, brought his victory oratory to a conclusion. The handsome Clinton placed his right hand on his breast, lifted his well-shaped head as if to catch both the sunlight and the adulation of the people on his face, and cleared his throat.

The crowd pushed in closer to hear the great man's final words.

Clinton whipped his right hand from his breast out to his audience. "One day within this century," he declaimed, "New-York will be built up densely from the Battery to the northern tip of the island."

The crowd held a shocked silence. Had they placed a lunatic in office? Then a hiss came. It was picked up and carried by the throng.

A Quaker fellow standing at the foot of the City Hall steps tugged at Jake's trouser leg. "Don't thee think friend Clinton has a bee in his bonnet?"

The High Constable smiled politely, but he didn't think so. No, he didn't think so at all.

A Footnote

We have learned when it comes to history that there are often twenty answers to every question, nineteen of them incorrect and the twentieth doubtful. Historians and old mapmakers constantly contradict each other.

Take Broadway, for instance. We thought we finally had it. In 1664, it was the Broad Way. By 1775, it had become Broadway. That was resolved. So we thought—until we saw a 1799 report that called the thoroughfare the Broadway Road and an 1807 map that labeled it Broad-Way, and an 1830's document that referred to it as the Broad Way yet again.

The Broad Way, Broad Way, Broad-Way, Broadway Street, Broadway, and the Broadway Road. We settled for Broadway from 1807 on.

Jacob (Jake) Hays was the first High Constable of the City of New-York. He was also the last. Hays was born in Bedford, New York, in 1772, to descendents of the first Jewish settlers in New Amsterdam. Today, there is both a Protestant and a Jewish branch of the Hays family.

Most everything about Old Hays, as we have described him, is historically accurate, except of course, as it relates to the Tonneman family.

According to some, Hays invented the art of criminal investigation. Among his innovations was following a suspect to determine where he lived or drank or had friends. Hays is also credited with inventing the third degree, exhaustive questioning, even physical violence, by the police in order to get a confession. The yellow wool to cordon off the scene of Hays's investigation into the corpse at the Collect was our own conceit. Jake was smart enough to have invented the Crime Scene. Perhaps he really did.

Until 1844, the Constabulary stayed as we have described it. That year, the New-York Police Department came into being and the title of High Constable was eliminated. But Jake Hays was so honored by his fellow citizens that he kept the title High Constable till his death in 1850, at the age of 78.

Lorenzo da Ponte, who was Mozart's libretto writer, did not present an opera at the Park Theatre or elsewhere in New-York in 1808. Not till 1833 did da Ponte open the Italian Opera House on Church and Leonard-streets. It failed. Da Ponte and Clement Moore (who was to write *A Visit from St. Nicholas* in 1823) became good friends after a chance meeting in a bookstore. It was through Moore, a professor of Oriental and Greek literature at the General Theological Seminary in New-York, that da Ponte became a teacher of Italian at Columbia.

The City Fathers were still fussing with the business of the Collect and its aftermath in 1834. Called Kalchhook or Shellpoint by the Dutch, and Fresh Water Pond and finally the Collect (from Kalchhook) by the English when it was a pristine freshwater pond, the Collect provided New-York with fresh water for only a short time before pollution fouled it.

The notorious canal through which the Collect was drained became Manhattan's Canal Street. The Collect Company, of course, is fiction, but the Manhattan Company is fact. The Bank it fostered was eventually absorbed and became the Chase Manhattan Bank.

Aaron Burr was twenty years old in 1776. After distinctive service during the Revolutionary War, he became the U.S. Senator from New-York State (1791–1797) and was one of the powers behind the influential Tammany Society political machine, which he helped establish. Burr was also one of the founders of the Manhattan Company and, through that, of the Manhattan Bank.

Burr tied with Thomas Jefferson in electoral votes during the 1800 election but had to settle for being Jefferson's vice president (1801–1805) when the hotly contested election was subsequently decided by Congress.

The long feud between Burr and Alexander Hamilton, the chief author of the *Federalist Papers*, led to a duel in 1804, in Weehawken, New Jersey. Hamilton was killed and Burr's political career was destroyed. In 1807, after his alleged involvement in a conspiracy against the United States, Burr was tried for treason. He was acquitted and went off to live in exile in France.

He finally obtained a passport in 1812, and returned to New-York, where he resumed his law practice, and prospered.

Historically, Aaron Burr was not in the United States in 1808. Despite all his faults, we believe that Aaron Burr loved the United States.

So he was not in New-York in 1808.

Or was he?

Foley Square now stands where the Collect once flowed, fed by many underground streams.

David Hosack's Elgin Gardens was a stretch of roughly twenty acres, five or six miles to the north of the City, which Hosack developed in 1801. There he raised a renowned collection of medicinal plants and cultivated foreign and American flora. Rockefeller Center now stands on the site of the Elgin Gardens.

The notices and/or advertisements which preface each chapter actually ran in the various New-York newspapers of the day. We collected them, some from original copies and some from microfilm, in the Library of the New-York Historical Society. The spelling and punctuation are true. Noah Webster's *An American Dictionary of the English Language* would not be published until 1828; therefore, uniform standards of spelling had not yet taken hold.

During De Witt Clinton's mayoralty, the New-York Historical Society was founded. The first location of the Historical Society was a rent-free room in the old City Hall on Wall-street.

The new City Hall on Broadway and Chambers-street, which was under construction in 1808, was eventually completed in 1812. It is the one we still use. In 1808, Chambers-street marked the outer edge of the City. According to a guidebook of the day, the building was "the handsomest structure in the United States, perhaps of its size, in the world." Built of white marble in the detailed manner of the French Renaissance, the Hall was something new to a City otherwise consisting largely of Georgian structures of red brick and wood.

However, the marble was limited to the southern, eastern, and western walls. Because the building stood at the outskirts of town and the north side looked out on only woods, the north wall was faced in ordinary brownstone. This was an eminently practical decision, considering few besides visionaries like De Witt Clinton expected the City to grow beyond Chambers-street.

The Quaker's comment about Clinton's prediction of the expansion of New-York with which we conclude this novel is recorded as fact.

In 1791, Vermont was the fourteenth state admitted to the Union. Kentucky, number fifteen, followed in 1792. After much bickering about how expensive it would be for ships to keep changing flags, a law was passed in 1794 calling for the official American flag to contain fifteen stars and fifteen stripes. The law went into effect in 1795. This flag of fifteen stars and stripes was flying over Fort McHenry at the entrance to Baltimore Harbor in Maryland, during the fort's bombardment by the British in 1814. It was this flag about which Francis Scott Key wrote *The Star-Spangled Banner*.

The law was changed in 1818. It now called for thirteen red and white horizontal stripes to represent the thirteen original Colonies, and for stars to be added for each new state.

When the Yellow Fever epidemic hit the City in 1798, the Bank of New-York bought land and moved its offices from Wall-street to the Village of Greenwich, where its wealthy patrons had moved to escape the Fever. The move proved to be fortunate. The City was hit again with "the Fever" in 1799, 1803, 1805, and 1821. Other banks joined the Bank of New-York along the same road. Eventually this thoroughfare in the Village of Greenwich was named Bank-street.

About the Embargo: President Thomas Jefferson declared it in December of 1807, because of the British violation of the rights of American ships and seamen. The Embargo banned all international trade to and from American ports.

Prior to Embargo (O Grab Me), American ports flourished. American seamen were highly paid compared to their English counterparts. As a consequence, British sailors often deserted when they put into American ports. The British, finding themselves shorthanded, began to kidnap American citizens to man their ships. The Embargo was extremely unpopular in the port cities, and smuggling was rampant.

By 1809, New-York was suffering greatly from the effects of the Embargo. With no shipping and no revenue, the City was devastated. People had no money; the Coffee-

Houses had few customers. The debtors' prison was filling up. On March 1, 1809, Jefferson signed the Nonintercourse Act, repealing the Embargo and reopening trade with all foreign countries except for France and Britain. James Madison, who succeeded Jefferson three days later, had his own go-rounds with Britain over the Embargo.

All this was prologue to the War of 1812.

M.M.
A.M.
New York City

About the Author

MAAN MEYERS is the pseydonym for husband-and-wife writing team Annette and Martin Meyers. Annette Meyers is the author of five Smith and Wetzon mysteries including, most recently, *Murder: The Musical*. Her next mystery will be *These Bones Were Made for Dancin'*. Martin is the author of five books in the Patrick Hardy series. *The High Constable* is the third in their jointly written historical mystery series featuring the Tonneman family of New-York. They live in New York City and have just concluded the fourth, *The Dutchman's Dilemma*.

If you enjoyed Maan Meyer's THE HIGH
CONSTABLE, you will
want to read all the books in this unique
series of American history mysteries!

The following is a special advance excerpt from
THE DUTCHMAN'S DILEMMA, which sweeps
the Tonnemans back to the year 1675, when
Manhattan Island has come under British rule
and New-York is a thriving city of some three
thousand souls. . . .

THE DUTCHMAN'S
DILEMMA
by
MAAN MEYERS

Look for THE DUTCHMAN'S DILEMMA at
your local bookstore
in hardcover from Bantam Books in July 1995!

The pearl-pale moon-glow found the blade. Holding the knife so tightly his knuckles blanched, the Searcher felt the painful glint and shielded his eyes from the gnarled face in the moon that seemed to mock him. When the moon hid behind dark clouds, the pain dissolved.

But the Searcher would have the last laugh before dawn. Even without the moon the way was clear. Darkness was the dearest of friends.

Wild gusts of wind caught the Searcher's cloak, billowed it aft like a miniature sail, revealing his fine red coat.

A fragmented voice rode the wind. The sound was too distant for the words to be clear, but the Searcher knew it was the cry of the Rattle Watch, calling five and all well. The Rattle men were the Night Watchmen of New-York, that once was New Orange, that once was New Amsterdam, and always was Sodom.

The Night Watch's cry skimmed over the sleeping village, followed by others, responding, all a garble, just noise in the March wind.

"Sinners," the Searcher muttered. Soon enough, they would know the damnation of hellfire.

The night was pungent with game and dung. The knife in the Searcher's hand quivered for a moment, then the feral blade took on its own life, slashing the air. A large buck paused on a hillock, his antlers rising like the Tree of Life. Sniffing the air, the buck turned, its hackles risen, then disappeared into the brush.

Shadowed, hulking against the sky, the windmills offered little guidance, but the Searcher needed none. The moon returned in time to light his way.

From behind the closed shutters of Arian Cornelisen's Breadloaf Tavern came a faint glimmer. Since midnight it had been the Sabbath. Cornelisen was tapping beer after hours on the Lord's Day. The Searcher vowed the tavern keeper would pay dearly for this transgression.

The way was clear. No dawdling now. God's work to do.

Or the Devil's, if need be.

Trees bowed against the fury of the gust gale that sprang out of nowhere and roared up the Bowery Road. God and the Devil were angry indeed. The Searcher felt the glow of satisfaction. His mission was blessed this night. Or damned.

Ahead the City and the Water Gate. Both this and the Broad Way Gate were closed from sunset to sunrise these days, from six to six.

Slipping off the road and into the woods, the Searcher crouched on the cold ground. Carefully, quietly, he moved aside some shrubs. The Water Gate sentinel sat on his haunches, leaning against the massive iron-clamped door that led to the east side of the City, head lolling, punctuating the uneasy air with snorting snores. The guard's partisan and wheel lock were leaning against the large door too.

The Searcher kissed his blade, then raised it to the moon.

OTTO WERSTEN HELD the lamp still. No help for it; the lantern flame flickered in the wind and went out. He should have been grateful for the moon, but Otto hated nights like this, bright nights of the full moon, which his ma called the Devil's own, when the ghosts of the dead and the witches walked. He was grateful that this night was near over. Excepting that he needed some light to find his way, he preferred the comfort of the dark. He had developed a keen eye for dark-seeing, better than his mates. They called him Cat-Eye.

As always, Otto had come on duty at ten o'clock with his lantern, badge, wood rattle, and staff, and now he was ready for his bed. He set the lamp down and reached for the flask in the pouch hanging under his arm. In so doing he knocked his rattle from his wide leather belt. Muttering, he knelt and ran his hand over the ground. The cold cut sharply even through his wool mittens. There. Careful not to make a sound—that was all he needed, to alert the rest of the Watch when he was about to take a drink —he shoved the rattle back in its place at his waist. He took a long draught of brandy, hand holding his rabbit skin hat, head tilted way back. So good. He wiped his lips with the sleeve of his threadbare gray duffel coat. The brandy brought a burning pleasure to his gut. What with dawn barely an hour away, and not wanting to take off his mittens, Otto didn't trouble to relight the lantern.

THE SEARCHER'S KNIFE stabbed the ground and dug at the earth. Standing, he threw clods of earth at the gate just left of the sleeping guard's head.

The sentinel swore and leaped to his feet, knocking over both his weapons. He scrambled for them, coming up with the spear first. "Who goes?" he cried.

The Searcher mewed like a cat.

The sentinel, his partisan pike pointing the way, came into the woods. "Here, kit, here, kit."

The Searcher mewed again and led the guard deeper into the woods. Then, with a shake of his head at the man's witless behavior, the Searcher circled round the guard and entered the sleeping City. All save one were oblivious of his coming.

SHUDDERING, OTTO CAT-EYE WERSTEN said a quick prayer, for he was a good Christian. He took one more swig of the flask, then packed it away. This night had been long. Longer than most, it seemed to him. He wrapped his thick Scots wool scarf once about his throat and pulled the flaps of his hat over his ears.

Otto's route took him down the Broad Way. He held his half-hour glass up to the cursed moon's light. The sand was almost all out of the top. Otto cleared his throat. He called:

"Half five the morning and all is well!"

Hard on his call, from over by the East River, Jan Kopper's call came to him on the wind, matching his. But Kopper's call was drawn out and with a richer tone. Always trying to go him one better, Jan was.

As he approached Stuyvesant's old home, the Great House, now called Whitehall by the beefeaters, Otto came to a trembling halt.

A horrible sound, a sound such as could come only from one of Satan's damned, overwhelmed Otto. The shriek enfeebled his body and dizzied his brain. He cocked his head and held his staff at the ready. Where had the hideous noise come from?

The Great House was the residence of Governor Edmund Andros's First Councillor, Nicasius De Sille. The Governor rarely came to Manhattan, happy to stay put in his regal mansion on Governor's Island in the Bay.

Apart from the Great House down a side path separated by a stand of dogwood trees and a high gate was a new structure, the First Councillor's carriage house.

Otto ran along the stone path, clutching his staff. The gate was open wide. Cautiously, Otto approached the carriage house. The awful shrieking inside the building had ceased as abruptly as it had begun; he heard the terrified stamping and neighing of horses gone mad. Someone or something was hammering against the carriage house doors. Otto shuddered again. God grant that it wasn't an evil spirit. Or maybe even the Devil himself.

In spite of his dread, Otto held his staff ready and dug his two feet firmly to the ground. As he reached out to open one of the large doors, both doors burst open. Something wet and hot splashed Otto's face. He was hurled to the ground as a crazed beast went galloping by.

THE FORT OF NEW-YORK, James-Fort, was less than a quarter mile from Whitehall Street. Within the old Fort stood the Chapel. Built in 1642 and known as the Stone Church, it was the first house of worship in New Amsterdam. Then, it was dedicated to Dutch Reformed Christian worship. Now the prayers of the Church of England were said here.

Shadows leaped across the stone walls of the Chapel. The Reverend Charles Gordon held his lamp high as he made his way from the rectory to the pulpit. This was his time, the moments before dawn on a Sunday, when he enjoyed a personal communion with God in preparation for services.

But this Lord's Day was not beginning well at all. The preacher drew closer, his lamp before him. On the lectern, in the middle of the open prayer book, as if a page mark, lay a bloody horror. "Dear God, preserve us," the Reverend Gordon gasped.

A ROOSTER CROWED. Otto's cat-eyes were fouled with something that blotted out the dawning sun. Mud? He drew his hand over them. Before he saw it on his mitten he knew; the smell of fresh blood gagged him even as he lay on the cold stone walk, half unconscious. He was soaked in it. Demented screams rent the air. Otto staggered to his feet. Was this blood his? He ran his hands over his body; no wound, no pain. The horse that knocked him down had doused him in blood. He rushed for the carriage house, whose doors now stood open, and ran into Richard Smythe, the stableman. Inside, horses screamed.

"What?" Smythe yelled.

Otto shook his head, spattering Smythe with blood. Mute with terror, he pointed with his staff toward the blood stench and the cries of the horses. Drawing the rattle from his belt, he whirled it vigorously to summon help for whatever abomination lay beyond the open doors.

Inside, two crazed four-footers were screaming and kicking holes out of their stalls in desperate attempts to get away from the death smell. Otto and Smythe had heavy going, their boots slurred through gross-mire. The early morning light blazed through the open doors and exposed the horror within. "Jesus Christ in Heaven," Smythe cried.

"Amen," Otto cried.

Smythe's hands took such a fit of trembling

that Otto pushed him back. The Watch Man stepped inside the carriage house. The Governor's majestic black stallion, a gift from King Charles himself, lay slaughtered, its butchered entrails spilling onto the straw.

MYSTERY—HISTORY—AND MURDER:
WHAT MORE COULD ANY READER
WANT?

DON'T MISS ANY OF
MAAN MEYERS' AMERICAN HISTORY
MYSTERIES.
ENTER THE UNIQUE WORLD OF
THE TONNEMAN FAMILY
AND DISCOVER WHY READERS LOVE
THESE
VERY SPECIAL MYSTERIES!

THE DUTCHMAN

by Maan Meyers

NEW AMSTERDAM IN 1664—Pearl Street is paved with oyster shells, and hogs roam the Broad Way undeterred by teeming throngs of hearty Dutch settlers, soldiers, sailors, freed African laborers, half-naked Indians, Jewish traders. Into Manhattan Harbor sail British warships demanding surrender, while an army of Englishmen are poised to invade from Breukelen just across the water.

PIETER TONNEMAN, the Dutch Schout (sheriff) has been drinking heavily to dull the pain of his wife's death. Now he must pull himself together to cope with proliferating crises. He has to persuade his cantankerous Calvinist boss, the notoriously stubborn Pieter Stuyvesant, that the Dutch citizens are more interested in their beer and their businesses than in fighting the British invaders.

THEN THERE'S THE RECENT chain of strange events, starting with the apparent suicide of a popular tavern owner and good friend of the Schout, followed by a mysterious fire, a corpse that disappears only to turn up again in a most unlikely place, and a violent death that points a suspicious finger in a startling direction.

AND—AS IF an impending invasion and a bizarre crime wave were not enough—Pieter Tonneman must confront the tantalizing Racqel Mendoza, an exotic Jewish beauty who is not quite officially a widow. Is Racqel the cure for the Schout's loneliness—or part of a ruthless spy ring responsible for the rash of murders?

"A GRAND MELODRAMA OF EARLY AMERICA THAT EVOKES THE SETTING OF OLD NEW AMSTERDAM AT ITS MOST INTRIGUING."
—*The Denver Post*

"FANS OF HISTORICAL MYSTERIES SHOULD RELISH THIS CAPTIVATING NOVEL."
—*The Sun,* Baltimore

THE KINGSBRIDGE PLOT

by Maan Meyers

THE YEAR IS 1775, a full century after THE DUTCHMAN, and Sheriff Pieter Tonneman's descendants are well established in the now-thriving metropolis of New-York.

HISTORY IS being made in the political turmoil of colonial America, but in New-York, murder becomes the focus of everyone's attention when a savagely decapitated body is discovered.

AFTER A LONG absence, John Tonneman returns from medical studies in London to his native city, now torn between Tories and Patriots as the colonies race headlong into armed rebellion.

RESOLVED TO steer clear of politics, the earnest young physician finds himself drawn into the violence by his growing feelings for an adventurous young woman from the Sephardic Jewish community.

A SECOND, HORRIFYING murder reveals that there is a killer on the loose with a taste for redheaded women.

HUNTING THE mad killer, John Tonneman makes a connection between the dead woman and a plot to assassinate General George Washington.

AND THEN another woman is murdered and the General barely escapes with his life as John Tonneman pursues a killer and uncovers a conspiracy through the jumbled rush of events that culminate in the momentous July of 1776!

BANTAM MYSTERY COLLECTION

____56498-6 **JEMIMA SHORE AT THE SUNNY GRAVE** • • • • • • • $4.99
       AND OTHER STORIES Fraser

____28686-2 **MUM'S THE WORD** Cannell • • • • • • • • • • • • • $4.99

____29195-5 **THE THIN WOMAN** Cannell • • • • • • • • • • • • $4.99

____28753-2 **WISH YOU WERE HERE** Brown • • • • • • • • • • $5.50

____29886-0 **BLOODLINES** Conant • • • • • • • • • • • • • • • • $4.99

____29484-9 **RUFFLY SPEAKING** Conant • • • • • • • • • • • • $4.99

____29684-1 **FEMMES FATAL** Cannell • • • • • • • • • • • • • $4.99

____56936-8 **BLEEDING HEARTS** Haddam • • • • • • • • • • • $4.99

____56532-X **MORTAL MEMORY** Cook • • • • • • • • • • • • • • $5.99

____56020-4 **THE LESSON OF HER DEATH** Deaver • • • • • • • $5.99

____56239-8 **REST IN PIECES** Brown • • • • • • • • • • • • • $5.50

____29544-6 **THE CAVALIER CASE** Fraser • • • • • • • • • • • $4.99

____56275-4 **SOUTHERN GHOST** Hart • • • • • • • • • • • • • $4.99

____56272-X **ONE LAST KISS** Kelman • • • • • • • • • • • • • $5.99

____56607-5 **DEAD MAN'S ISLAND** Hart • • • • • • • • • • • • $4.99

____56604-0 **MISSING JOSEPH** George • • • • • • • • • • • • • $5.99

____56173-1 **CABAL** Dibdin • • • • • • • • • • • • • • • • • • • $4.99

____56954-6 **FAMILY STALKER** Katz • • • • • • • • • • • • • • $4.99

____56874-4 **THE MISSING CHAPTER** Goldsborough • • • • • • • $4.99

____29441-5 **SORROWHEART** Lorens • • • • • • • • • • • • • • $4.99

- -

Ask for these books at your local bookstore or use this page to order.

Please send me the books I have checked above. I am enclosing $____ (add $2.50 to cover postage and handling). Send check or money order, no cash or C.O.D.'s, please.

Name _____

Address _____

City/State/Zip _____

Send order to: Bantam Books, Dept. MC, 2451 S. Wolf Rd., Des Plaines, IL 60018
Allow four to six weeks for delivery.

Prices and availability subject to change without notice.   MC 2/95